CAN WE SKIP TO THE GOOD PART?

MELISSA BRAYDEN

Edited by Lynda Sandoval and Avery Brooks

Cover design by Ink and Laurel

First Edition: 2025

ISBN (ebook): 979-8-9928823-1-5

ISBN (print): 979-8-9928823-0-8

Published by Brayden StoryWorks

For everyone who believes love stories matter
—yours most of all.

Prologue

It was one of those moments when Ella Baker felt like she was watching a movie but wasn't at all. She stared at the talking heads on the Zoom screen, shocked at what she seemed to be hearing. She paused, waiting for the actual words. The ones that would make it definitive.

"So, with all of that being said, it's with a heavy heart that I tell you that your position at Cornerstone Ideas has been eliminated."

Eliminated. That meant fired. Canned. Ella blinked, playing back the words from Jim, the HR guy who often left the microwave door open in the break room. But she still didn't quite believe their meaning. Maybe because her Friday morning working from home had played out like any other until an unexpected meeting had shown up on her calendar for late morning. She'd been happily working, flipping between projects for multiple clients while sipping her second cup of mildly sweetened coffee. This new development was an unthinkable record scratch.

"Are you sure?" she asked. The question was legitimate. Her graphic designs had been a selling point for the company in so many of their advertising pitches. Ella's work spoke for itself. At least, she thought it did. The problem? She'd never been the loudest designer in the room or the one who demanded her name be all over everything. Perhaps the higher-ups were unaware of her connection to their most successful campaigns.

Jim nodded. "We are sure. Yes."

"Hang on." Ella swallowed and found her voice. "I thought you said in your announcement last week that you'd concluded the layoffs. I don't understand." She was positive the email they'd blasted to the company had reassured the remaining employees that they were safe. She'd done a little chair dance, grateful to have survived but not exactly shocked.

Jim from HR watched her patiently from his side of the Zoom screen. Her manager, Marlene, shifted uncomfortably inside her separate square. Ella squinted inside her own. They were the dysfunctional Brady Bunch.

"That's true. We should have met with you last week. It was an oversight on our part," Marlene said.

They'd forgotten about her. Like bland wallpaper that faded into the background. Like Kevin from *Home Alone*. They'd passed right over her existence. "Seriously? You forgot to lay me off?"

Marlene had the decency to wince. "Things were a little chaotic last week, and you were lost in the shuffle."

"Right. Well, I don't suppose pointing out all I've done for the team will matter much." Her heart thudded. Ella had honestly wondered if this meeting might have been about a promotion, making her feel naive and stupid. What was she supposed to do now exactly? She had rent for this month and next, but then that was it. Maybe her landlord would forget she existed, too.

"We value all of your contributions," Jim glanced down at the form in front of him, "Ella."

"Jim, did you just forget my name?"

"No. Of course not," Jim said, scratching the back of his head.

"I think you totally did." Ella balked. "I've worked down the hall from you for five years. I brought you pumpkin bread in a Christmas tree tin."

"It was excellent," he said. But his voice was too quiet to be believed.

"You're not a good liar."

Marlene shifted again, but said nothing. This was the woman, the head of the art department, who Ella had bailed out time and time again. She'd stayed up until all hours to make Marlene's ridiculous last-minute deadlines. It all seemed so fruitless now. Ella was a nameless, unemployed oversight with forgettable pumpkin bread.

"We want you to know that your work for the company was very much appreciated, and, unfortunately, we have to part ways," Jim said. This was a script if she'd ever heard one.

"Thank you, I guess? I'm not sure what to say." She sat back in her desk chair with a thud. "This feels like a speeding truck hit me when I wasn't looking. You didn't even buy me dinner, Marlene." She couldn't believe she'd said that last part out loud.

"It's entirely normal to feel that way," Jim said, employing his kind eyes, which she imagined they taught in HR school. His tie was so boring. Blue with thick gray stripes. Jim needed better ties, back to HR school for him. "And we'll leave you to peruse the exit package we've put together for you. Take a look and let us know if you have any questions. I'm always here. Oh!" Jim's beady eyes lit up. Perhaps he liked these kinds of meetings more than he let on. "And go ahead and save the file to your personal devices because after confirmed receipt, we'll be shutting off your email and access to Teams. Really, all of your access. To everything."

"And we'll need your badge," Marlene said, leaning in toward the camera.

"You got it, *Marlene and Jim*," Ella said, emphasizing the names that she hadn't forgotten. "I will save everything before I'm banished from the kingdom for all time." Then, she remembered her morning. "How are you gonna make that deadline on the Harrison Glee account?"

"Oh." Marlene's eyebrows shot to the sky. "Were you working on that one?"

"I'm the project leader."

Marlene frowned, perhaps just now understanding her misstep. Cue the panic. It was, after all, their biggest and most demanding account.

"I'm sure you'll figure it out," Ella said in a sympathetic voice similar to Jim's. She wasn't usually this snarky, but the blind side had her scrambling for decorum. After a few more scripted platitudes from Jim, Ella offered a half-hearted wave and exited the Zoom like a mouse lost in a maze. She had no idea what to do next because she hadn't expected any of this. She felt like an absolute loser, and now she was that plus unemployed. She'd call her parents, but they were in the middle of the Caribbean on their third international vacation of the year.

Her phone buzzed on the table next to her. She half expected it to be Marlene calling to say this had all been a hysterical practical joke and to please keep working on the Harrison Glee project. Instead, she saw it was Rachel, and thank God, because it made her feel instantly better, a testament to their bond.

"They forgot to fire me," Ella said instead of hello.

"Holy shit." A pause. "Does that mean you're not fired?" Rachel asked. "That's good, right?" Rachel had been her best friend since they'd laughingly bonded over chocolate fudge Pop-Tarts in the dining hall their sophomore year of college. Recognizing each other at a gay and lesbian mixer a week later had only sealed their friendship. College had been an enlightening time for both of them as they came into their own, embraced their sexualities, and supported each other along the way. However, they were undoubtedly different personality types. Ella was quieter and more thoughtful regarding the things that came out of her mouth. Rachel Lenoir was more impulsive. She lived unapologetically, rarely leaving a room full of people in the same condition she'd found them. Rachel, with her gorgeous auburn hair, was more fashionable, social, and had always been more popular. In their duo, she generally held the spotlight, and Ella was more than okay with that.

"No, I promise. I'm definitely fired, but they forgot to ax me in the chaos last week. Can you believe that? It's the worst way to be fired ever, as an afterthought. That means no one was tossing and turning with guilt the night before. No one even cared enough to notice the oversight. I was a ghost at that company and didn't even know it. Can you hear that I'm in shock? I fucking am."

"Why didn't you tell me you were let go?"

"I am, right now. It happened two seconds ago."

"Wow. Then my timing is amazing. I wonder if we have one of those psychic bonds, and I just knew to call you."

"We do. It's clear now." Ella buried her face in her hands before releasing it. "So now I'm an unemployed loser who's also, would you look at that? Not having the best hair day." She'd caught herself in the mirror, which was much harsher than Zoom. With a quick finger comb, she attempted to tame her currently mutinous blond hair on its journey halfway to her elbows. She needed a trim and maybe a few more defined layers. Honestly, the neglect was on her. She'd put way more effort into her digital illustrations than her appearance these days. Something that, now that she had time on her hands, maybe she'd remedy.

"Your hair will rebound, you gorgeous thing," Rachel said. "I promise."

"Not sure my ego will." She shook out her chaotic hair,

which miraculously helped. "I honestly believed I was great at that job, but now I'm realizing they likely didn't even know which designs were mine or Katrina's, the girl who plays more *Candy Crush* than my mom." Then an awful thought struck. "Am I delusional about *everything* in life, or just my role with that company? Tell me the truth so I can cry an appropriate amount."

"No, babe, you're absolutely not. Everyone I know has been worried about layoffs. The economy is a disaster. Companies are downsizing and taking shortcuts. AI is terrorizing us all like a guy with a chain saw." She took a breath. "This is what I know. You're a genius when it comes to that Apple pen thing you whip around your screen. I'm never wrong."

She imagined Rachel hooking a strand of auburn hair behind her ear with that confident little shake of her shoulders. Her green eyes were likely sparkling, and her energy was even. Nothing rattled her. Rachel dove headfirst into any situation and made a meal out of it. Ella, not feeling so sure, scrubbed her face. She needed to be more like Rachel and fast. "Thank you. I needed that."

"And, I have the best idea ever. Move here already and keep me company. Yes, I said it again. You've ignored me the eight other times I've made the suggestion, but maybe now the time is right. Move to charming little Everly Springs, Virginia. I miss your face, and Oklahoma will get the hell over it."

Ella laughed. "Just like that, huh?"

"Yes. Exactly. You're a free agent. Let's get the band back together again. You'll love it here. This town is cute enough to feel small, but DC-adjacent enough for cool cred. Best of both worlds."

"A small town look-alike but not. So, it has chain restaurants? Is that what you're saying?"

"We have a McDonald's on the corner, if that's your jam."

"Well, now you've gone and done it."

"I know your weaknesses."

There was something about the way Rachel voiced that sentence and added a definitive period at the end that told Ella she wasn't kidding. "I wish I could. I could use my chaos twin about now. Unfortunately, I can't just pick up and—"

"Can't you, though. Now? After two seconds ago. Don't answer. Reflect."

Ella blinked and did just that. Rachel had a possible point this time. "Well, maybe a move wouldn't be so crazy. Reinvention might be nice."

"You know what I think?"

"What?" Ella asked, still numb, still staring at the now blank Zoom meeting that had ended with her job and her ego murdered in front of her face. All that had been missing was the theme music from *Psycho*.

"We join forces, like the good old days back in school, and smash up this world together while eating a lot of amazing microwave popcorn. Emphasis on the popcorn."

Rachel was fantastic at packaging her thoughts and knew it. Ella loved that about her.

"I have the best ideas, and you're going to agree about this one once you're here. Say yes already."

It was honestly nice to hear her excited about something. Rachel had recently emerged from a breakup-induced depression that had clung to her for months. She'd done a lot of lying around the house in yoga pants, FaceTiming Ella while sighing between tears. It was almost as if someone had pressed pause on the cool and vibrant Rachel and replaced her with a shell of herself, who cycled through anger and sadness. For Ella, so many miles away and helpless, it had been hard to watch. Rachel's ex-girlfriend had done quite a number on her, and it was refreshing finally to hear some enthusiasm in her voice. Ella, also familiar with the grief associated with breakups, had done everything in her power to nurse her friend through it, including check-ins multiple times a day.

Now, it seemed Rachel was extending a hand to Ella. It was the definition of friendship. It was what they did for each other, and in this moment, she was infinitely grateful for Rachel's presence in her life.

Ella blinked and quirked her lips to the side as she ruminated. "It's tempting, Rach. It is. The microwave popcorn is a big selling point. I'm giving you bonus points for including it." With the ghost of Zoom still leering at her, she closed the tab on her browser with a decided click. It felt damn good, too.

"I swear." She could hear the clack-clack-clack of Rachel's heels on tile. She was walking somewhere at work, which, for Rachel, was Montclair's, a well-known department store. "Hot fucking popcorn would end wars if given the opportunity. Why do people celebrate things with steak and lobster when there's popcorn just sitting there? I'll never get it. We, alone, know the secret, Ella Bella."

Ella grinned. "Let them spend their money while we're awesome on the couch with a big, cheap bowl and comfy pants."

In actuality, the proposed plan was sounding better and better with each passing moment. Plus, Ella noticed she wasn't spiraling after losing her job the way she would have been without Rachel on the other end of the phone. The timing had been a gift. And without the job, there wasn't a lot tethering her to Tulsa when she thought about it. Her parents had recently retired from their twin careers as CPAs and spent much of their time traveling with their loud friends who ordered heaps of red wine, leaving Ella and her brother to keep up with them via their social media posts from various adventures. A photo of the six of them clinking glasses in Copenhagen! A similar photo of them cheersing in Munich! How about another shot of raised mugs in Florence? Sure, they'd invited her here and there, but she didn't exactly have the time off at thirty-four years old to spend weeks in Milan or Corfu. Not to mention, she'd stand out in those photos like a pop song on a playlist of golden oldies. She also had a feeling they'd only invited her out of obligation. The idea made her shift in her seat. She'd been an afterthought in that case, too.

"Seeing anyone special?" Rachel asked. "Because if not, I have a list of eligible women in this town, and even a few decent men, I could set you up with. Another check mark in the reasons to move column."

"Thank you for honoring my fluidity, madam," she said in her upper-crust speaking voice.

"It is my pleasure, other madam," Rachel said, matching the voice they'd used in the old days of Lunsford Hall, lying on the floor of Ella's room until 1 a.m., figuring out how they'd take over the world.

"But I think I'm good as is." Romance, regardless of who, was not at all on the forefront of her mind. Ella had purposefully steered clear of anything flirty or romantic for quite some time. It had been eleven months since Britney LeCroy had called off their engagement exactly six days before their wedding. They'd booked the cutest little chapel on the lake and had just turned in their final draft of the seating arrangement to the wedding planner. Ella had even finished writing her vows. But on a rainy morning in Ella's kitchen, Britney had explained with very definitive hand gestures that their interests were in such conflict that they'd never make it in the long run. The example she'd given when tossing their relationship in the trash? Britney liked bird-watching, and Ella enjoyed lazy mornings at coffee shops. She'd waited for more. There hadn't been any. Ella had stared in disbelief. Well, good God. With those kinds of differences, they couldn't possibly forge a successful future. They'd be insane to try, Britney had said. Ella could have argued that their unique qualities were what added texture to their relationship, which, in her opinion, had felt solid in every other sense. Well, until that stomach punch of a moment changed everything. Because the idea that Britney wasn't *all in* was enough for Ella to allow her own heart to break and walk away in favor of a life with someone who loved her for those lazy mornings. Her ego had sure taken a hit, though. And the new blind side this morning certainly didn't help her feel like a valued human in the grand scheme.

She blew out a breath. "Maybe I'm coming to Virginia."

"What's that you say?" Rachel asked. Ella could almost see her placing a victorious hand on her hip. Very few people said no to Rachel, and this was another example. Honestly, it felt like a life jacket when Ella was sputtering water. How could she not grab it?

"I said, let's do this!" she yelled into the phone to the sound of Rachel laughing and whooping. With a slow breath, Ella pulled herself out of the deep end and focused on the horizon. Life was what one made of it, right? Maybe this was just the opportunity she needed to turn the page and level the hell up and whatever other idioms she could come up with. "Tell the great state of Virginia that I'm on my way."

ONE

Hoopty-Do

When impulsively packing up your life and moving to a new town without much of a plan, it was imperative that absolutely fucking everything go wrong. Ella had tempted fate and was finding out. On hour six of her fourteen-hour drive, her sound system and radio had gone out entirely, which made sense. Her car was older than her very straight-looking high school prom photo and just as suspect. After that, the snarky GPS woman had sent her on a long mission down a lonely road that had finally concluded with a dead end and a literal suggestion that she needed to walk the rest of the way. What the hell? She'd named the woman Beatrix Navigatrix and decided they were at war. She was also confident that Beatrix had thoroughly enjoyed that little stunt. Oh! And she was woefully out of snacks with three hours left to go on her drive. Horrific. Snacks were the backbone of any road trip. Ella swallowed her frustration and pressed on, excited for the shiny new life waiting for her in Everly Springs, just a hop, skip, and a jump from the big city where so very much happened. She liked the idea of a quieter existence with the flashy prestige of all those monuments just an hour's drive away. Maybe she'd even work on building her Instagram presence, learn more about pop culture, or take up pickleball. Isn't that what trendy people did? She sighed and faced her reality. "Nope. Not sure I'm capable of trendy." Either way. This move was about reinvention, and she was more than eager to give that a shot.

Two hours into her journey, the song descended upon her. The jingle of her youth, the anthem of all third graders in Mrs. Levitz's homeroom class. She began to sing it for the seventh or eighth time. "Oatmeal Hoopties to start your day. Ohhh, ohhh, ohhh. With Oatmeal Hoopties, things will go your way. Ohhh, ohhh, ohhh." She briefly closed her eyes. What in the name of Hoda Kotb was wrong with her? The big box cereal companies had claimed victory over her brain and weren't releasing it. It had come to this: a dark road in the middle of the night as she belted out the subpar lyrics to jingles meant to make her crave sugary carbs in the morning, and dammit, it was working. Give her these Hoopties! What she would pay right now for a convenience store to appear on the horizon under a spotlight from God with a busting-at-the-seams cereal aisle.

"Oatmeal Hoopties to start your day! Dammit, no. Uh-uh. Stop that immediately." She hit the steering wheel in stern admonishment, but then relented, allowing herself to sing a quieter, more dignified version. She eyed her navigation screen. Beatrix was probably enjoying this battle. But not long after, Ella's luck changed. In the distance, she saw a billboard for a Stop and Grin ahead, and exited in time. The lights of the gas station were a glorious beacon from heaven. Five minutes later, she happily strolled out of the automatic sliding doors with an individual cereal serving and a small carton of milk. Sitting on the hood of her red Mini Countryman in her comfy royal-blue coat, she consumed the wonderful cereal as the only other customer (possibly for hours) passed her on the way to his car.

"That's how you live life," he called cheerfully.

She wasn't so sure of that, but had hope. "I'm working on it, Sir-with-the-Ballcap." He tipped it and slid into his beat-up Chevy.

Alone in that parking lot, Ella took a moment, setting the cereal aside, to take stock. She was actually doing this brave thing. When Rachel had called within five minutes of Ella losing the absolute best job she'd ever had, it felt like an important sign blinking at her through the darkness like this very convenience store. Now, here she was, on her way, sponsored by Oatmeal Hoopties, and owning it. She couldn't help but smile alone beneath the stars, knowing this was a bold new chapter in her life. She could feel the weight prickling her skin and warming her cheeks. She was proud of herself, of the bravery she'd shown and the initiative she'd harnessed.

The rest of her journey was quieter, more introspective as she sorted through her plans. She'd need a job, obviously. Then, friends, a favorite grocery store, and a cute coffee shop where they might learn her order—that'd be new. Eventually, she'd need a place of her own, though Rachel had been kind enough to offer up her second bedroom until Ella was on her feet financially.

It's okay to be scared. It's okay to be scared.

The mantra had been in her back pocket ever since she'd decided to pack up and move, and she needed it on the last leg of the trip more than ever. Ella placed a hand over her rapidly beating heart and grinned. Everything was going to be okay.

EVERLY SPRINGS WAS quiet when she pulled into town. The streets were hushed, lit by the occasional amber glow of a streetlight casting long shadows on sidewalks lined with tidy, older homes. As she drove on, dipping her head and peering out the upper portion of her windshield, Ella caught sight of a few recognizable signs—Dunkin', Chipotle, a CVS that kept its lights on all night. They hinted at suburban convenience, while a darkened diner and a bookstore with a hand-lettered window display offered a mom-and-pop charm. It was the kind of place that slowed down after dark but didn't feel forgotten. Not quite rural, not quite suburban. Everly Springs felt like the edge of something. She couldn't wait to get to know it better.

When she parked her Mini in front of the one-story white house with the red door, she made a point to memorize the moment as a culmination. Her shoulders ached, and her eyes were bleary from staring at a dark road, but she smiled as she knocked and waited with eager anticipation.

"Finally. Get in here immediately," Rachel said, seconds after swinging the door open. She wore sea-green sweats that looked soft, almost furry to the touch. The legs swayed out with a bell-bottom cut. "I have beer and wine, and I missed your stupid face."

She fell into Rachel's open arms. "Bless you. I think I've earned it. No radio. So much cereal singing."

"What?"

"Thank God it's no longer important. Accept me into your world?"

"Yeah, weirdo." She flashed a picture-perfect smile. "Without delay."

She took a last glance up at the white house before being pulled through the threshold. The rest of the exterior was probably adorable, and if it hadn't been well after midnight, Ella would have devoted the proper amount of time to absorbing every detail. In the dark, with only a porchlight to illuminate the exterior, she was filling in the blanks.

"Welcome to Chez Rachel. What's mine is yours, and I almost mean that." Rachel tossed in a wink. She wasn't exactly kidding, either. Rach said what she thought and didn't apologize. Ella found it refreshing in so many ways. Intimidating in others. As close as they were, it had been a few years since they'd inhabited the same space for long. Back in their OU days, they'd lived together for their last year of school in an apartment a block from campus. But in all honesty, it was probably more stressful on their friendship than not, which was all the more reason for Ella to be proactive about finding her own space in the coming weeks.

"You're gonna die for this living room. I splurged and had it designed by Carter Lunsford. Behold." With a sweeping gesture, Rachel presented the space, which was breathtaking. Whoever Carter was, they knew their stuff.

An L-shaped white sectional that would seat five was nestled on the back wall and extended into the center of the room. Sage curtains with the softest cream accents swooped from the many perfectly square windows. What looked to be floating shelves appeared on nearly every open wall space, housing vases, clocks, and framed photos, one of which featured her and Rachel from the day they graduated eleven years ago. What tiny babies they'd been, so unknowing about the world in front of them. Careers, heartbreak, and mortgages marched toward them as they toasted the big, bright future. "Rach, this place is seriously gorgeous."

"Doesn't it feel spacious in here? All Carter. He worked his magic and charged me like I was a Real Housewife. Well worth it." She tossed a manicured hand to the side as she strolled through the room. "When you find a place, I'll give you his Instagram. You'll love what he can do with a throw rug."

"I will," she said, realizing she'd likely never afford this Carter. "I'm just sure of it."

"Fuck it," Rachel said, selecting a bottle of wine from the six-bottle rack on the kitchen counter. "I'm opening the good stuff. My best friend is here and deserves to be spoiled after her dusty drive."

"That's true. I've battled dust and won."

Rachel poured with a flourish, raising the bottle at the

final moment to show off a little. Ella resisted the urge to applaud, reminding herself that she'd be doing that a lot if she got started. Instead, she turned to her friend. "It's really good to see you."

They smiled at each other for a moment. Finally, Rachel covered Ella's hand, her expression one of quiet sincerity. "This was a good move, E. There's so much going on here. The tech scene is bustling and hiring all the time. You want to work for a politician? We have thousands just up the interstate looking for all kinds of digital artists. Want a girlfriend? I can definitely place you right in the middle of the whole scene."

"Let's slow our roll on that last part. At least until I figure my life out."

Rachel touched her oval-shaped wineglass to Ella's. "You and me both. After Max and all her bullshit, I don't know that I want back in that ring ever again."

"Cheers to that." She tipped the glass to her lips and let the bold, smooth flavors wash over her taste buds. Raspberries, earthiness, and a hint of spice. "This is good stuff."

"Told ya." Rachel led the way to the couch and sat back in total lounge mode, glass and wrist dangling. That's when Ella realized that her outfit was a near match for the drapes. She'd designed herself right into her own color scheme, which was so quintessential Rachel Lenoir that she almost had to laugh. Ella could never master that kind of coordination for … anything. Call it the artist in her, but she flew by the seat of her pants, a happily creative mess winging it most of the time.

"So, how have you been since the nightmare that was Max?" Ella asked. "Still going through it? I haven't laid eyes on you since you were in Tulsa a couple of weeks before the breakup."

"Sad, pissed off, and sad again. I'm sure you can identify." Ella's own breakup occurred a good six months before Rachel's, but she remembered every awful stage. "She got most of the friends when we split. At least the good ones. Fuck her."

"Fuck her. We hate her all the more." Ella did, too. Because that was how friendship worked. You showed up for each other, and loyalty was everything. Max, after playing the role of a loving girlfriend, had up and ghosted Rachel after their four-month relationship. Though Ella had never met Max in person, it was clear from the stories Rachel had passed along that she was a shady, self-involved player. No one deserved that.

"She's probably on woman number five by now," Rachel said with a disgusted shake of her head. Her green eyes narrowed. "I feel like four was a brief interlude, probably motivated by boredom. That's how she is. Maybe even just to taunt me." She sighed, her gaze falling to the fabric of the couch as if the thought just stole the wind from her sails.

"So, you've seen her out with these women?" Ella asked.

"Glimpses on Insta. Plus, I hear things and can fill in the blanks."

Ella couldn't imagine dealing with that kind of pointed animosity. If Britney had thrown jabs at her post-breakup, the healing would have been exponentially harder. "I'm so sorry she targets you like that, Rach. I'm just relieved she showed her true colors before you were any further in."

"I'm glad you didn't marry Britney, too." Rachel sipped her wine. "We're like the breakup twins, and, honestly, that helps."

"Now, if only you'd lose your job, we could be the *unemployed* breakup twins." Without prompting, they both raised their glasses high in the air.

"To life and the way it continues to throw us into oncoming traffic," Rachel said with mock joy.

"I heard that."

"You hungry?"

"Maybe." Ella looked behind her. "Do you have Oatmeal Hoopties?"

Rachel smiled, pride radiating. "It's like I knew you were coming or something."

Ella exhaled and sat up a little taller. This was why they were close. No one knew her like Rachel did. And in that moment, Ella knew without a doubt that she was right where she was supposed to be. "Hey," she said to her louder, cooler friend, someone she could probably learn a lot from.

"What?" Rachel asked as she rounded the couch to the kitchen for a bowl of sugary cereal that would be Ella's second helping today.

She shrugged. "I love you. You know that?"

Rachel placed her palms flat on the perfectly white speckled granite. "I love you, too, E." A pause. "And thank fucking God you're finally here!" she yelled and hit the countertop. She had an aversion to excessive sentimentality, and that was okay. "All right. Mushy part of the evening is over. Let's eat, veg, and then sleep late, because it's the wonderful weekend."

"You and me," Ella said, moving two fingers from her eyes to Rachel's. "Like this."

"Always, you nerd." She handed Ella her bowl.

"Love you."

"Stop saying that."

"I can't help it," Ella said. "I feel like gushing."

Rachel popped a bite of popcorn and smiled. "Fine. Love you more." She blew Ella a kiss and they dug in, allowing the evening to fall off of them. Ella leaned back into the cushions, the soft glow of the TV dancing across the room. Her shoulders dropped for what felt like the first time in weeks. This—this easy rhythm, this quiet understanding was exactly what she'd needed. There was a lot to look forward to, and Ella couldn't wait to get started. Her new life was here, simply waiting for her to dive in.

Max Wyler was not about to let the fatigue that infused every part of her body get in the way of the workout she'd desperately craved all day. Forfeit wasn't in her DNA. She couldn't have foreseen that the mediation between her new clients would become as complicated as it had that afternoon. Divorces were never easy, but when one of the parties, the asshole husband in this case, was condescending and manipulating the couple's assets, it made her job all the more difficult.

She started with a two-mile run on the treadmill, allowing the slight pull of her muscles to distract her from the mental stress she still carried from the late-afternoon session. She'd always been levelheaded and capable of zeroing in on the big picture, which is why her transition from family law attorney to divorce mediator had been such a natural one. Days like today, though, had her reaching for a release. Sex, exercise, or food usually did the trick. Today, she'd chosen the least complicated path. She kicked her own ass in a rotation of cardio and strength training, finishing with fifteen minutes of self-directed yoga to return to a more peaceful stasis.

By the time she rolled her mat and wiped down her equipment, the tension in her shoulders had finally started to loosen. She gave herself a moment, then made her way to the locker room, where the real reward waited.

She paid extra for her gym membership for perks like private, spacious showers, soft lighting in the locker room, a hydrotherapy pool, and fancy toiletries for the taking. She wasn't rich herself, but her clients certainly were, and that allowed her to live a comfortable existence, albeit with a few splurges here and there.

"Maxine Wyler, where exactly have you been?" Amanda Jimenez leaned her back against the counter, where Max was brushing out her now-wet, dark hair. Amanda had chosen to wear only a towel for their conversation, which was so very

Amanda-like. Not that Max minded the view. Amanda was blessed in the boob department and flaunted the gift generously. She liked to flirt, but always respected Max's boundaries, which made their friendship easy.

Max offered a brief wince. "Thirteen-hour days have a way of cancelling my gym plans."

"That, yes. But I haven't seen you out either. And I've looked. I've missed you holding those smoky drinks you like." She added a sexy pout, and if Max wasn't mistaken, she'd also just shoved her breasts about a foot higher than they'd been even a mere moment ago.

"Oh, the smoked old-fashioned at Dexter's Pub. I miss them, too. What's new out there?" It was Max's way of checking in on the nightly scene she'd been out of for the past couple of months. This city had relatively decent bar options for queer women, with about three locations where people tended to gather. But the community was circular in nature, which made Max grow wary. Everyone seemed to know everyone, which made dating kind of like threading a needle. You had to be delicate in who you flirted with or took home for the night, because it was, in all likelihood, going to upset somebody else. She'd been spending more time in DC these days for that very reason. After her last relationship, which had been tumultuous to say the least, casual definitely felt like the way to go. Less drama. Love seemed like a mythical concept these days, and that stance was only reinforced by the dissolving relationships she handled daily at the office.

"What's new? Let's see ..." Amanda paused. "Teresa Rowe is engaged. Ivy just graduated from bartending school. Melinda is done with sex until politics turns around."

"Lies."

"Right? Surely, there's something else she can do to fight back. Can you imagine never taking your clothes off and pressing your body to another woman's again?"

"Excuse me," an older woman said, reaching between them for a sample bottle of moisturizer.

"You're going to love that," Amanda told her in a soothing voice. "Your skin will never feel so soft. Use it generously."

"Oh, I will. And now I'll leave you two to your naked pressing."

Max had to smile. "Sorry about that," she said after the woman.

"No need. I was frisky once or twice. Still am on occasion." She touched her hairdo, held up her moisturizer, and slowly sashayed her way back to her locker.

Max decided to be just like that woman one day, not easily offended and dancing her way from one spot to the next. Until then, she had about eighteen things on her to-do list, which started with surviving her grandmother's visit to the States, scheduled for less than twenty-four hours from now. She came from a Filipino family on her mother's side, steeped in conservative values that didn't always line up with her own trajectory. That meant she would bite her tongue and keep the peace until the family dinner she was scheduled to attend was in her rearview.

"What unhappy thought just ruined your serenity?" Amanda asked. "Your whole demeanor changed. I hate it."

"Do you have a good relationship with your parents?" Max asked, squinting at Amanda through the mirror. They'd known each other for years. Amanda was a handful, but a familiar one. Max could be herself.

"No. My father split when I was seven, and my mother and I are the same person, so you can imagine how that goes." She slid a strand of short brown hair behind her ear. It was just long enough to fit. "Why? Are yours awesome? You seem well-adjusted and emotionally available."

Max laughed. "If I do, it probably wasn't nurture."

"Ouch. What's going on there?"

"Just a family dinner. No big deal, except expectations for

perfection will be high. That was always the case in my house. No screwups. Ever."

"Oh. Want some company?"

"I do, actually. But I'm afraid I don't have choosing rights. My mother would probably die if I brought a woman to my grandmother's dinner." She added a depressed laugh. "I've been out for years, but she likes to live in delusion that it's all just a passing phase."

"See, I've met you, and it's not." Amanda adjusted her towel, as if she had abandoned the seduction for the moment. It'd be back. It always was with Amanda. They were friends who'd shared a night once upon a long time ago, but Max couldn't imagine more. They weren't a match.

"Thanks for getting that." Max leaned close to the mirror and fluffed her hair, now mostly dry from the shower.

"I'm going to need your ab routine," Amanda said. "Yours are popping today."

"Don't get too excited. They always look their best in the hour after my workout, and then I watch them slowly fade into oblivion again."

"You downplay everything, you know that? Own the stellar abs. Take the compliment, at least temporarily."

"Fine. Thank you," she said, pointedly. "I'm a queen, and this is my fleeting reign. By lunchtime, the throne will be empty and the kingdom ruled once again by carbs."

"See? Much better." Amanda shifted her weight. "Please tell me you're not taking a male date."

"No. Never. But she'd love that." It was true her mom was excessively concerned about Max bringing a woman to dinner and had flat out asked her to bring a man, likely any man she could find.

"It doesn't have to be someone you're in love with," her mom had said. "Make him cute and successful. We'll spend an evening together and call it a day." She'd added a laugh to soften the sentiment. In the end, masquerading wasn't something Max would ever do. She'd attend the dinner alone and answer absolutely every question about herself truthfully, feeling uptight and counting the moments until the party was over. Why? Because it seemed to be built within her to keep her mother happy.

She wasn't seeing anyone right now, and if she ever was again, maybe she'd handle the situation differently. It wasn't even about her mother's own values. Her mom was a champion of the LGBTQ community and their quest for equal rights. Unfortunately, appearances mattered most to Dr. Mayumi Wyler. Optics toppled everything. When her mother had married Max's very white father, the decision seemed to have fulfilled the quota for family scandal, leaving no room for Max to be a happy lesbian in their shocked midst. At least, that's what her mother chose to believe. Max, being a no-drama individual, chose not to force the issue. Yet.

Amanda turned to her. "Well, just know that if you want to vent, or grab a drink, or any other kind of stress release you can come up with," she took a healthy pause to let that last part settle, "I'm your girl."

"Thanks, Amanda. I appreciate that more than you know." Taking her up on that very overt offer wouldn't be the worst thing in the world. Those no-strings-attached hookups used to be her favorite. Was she aging out of them at thirty-five? She wanted more than just a quick night with someone these days. Life had to come with a larger meaning, right? At the same time, she had little interest in love and the idea of "always and forever until the end of time." Nope. Everything had an expiration date. Even perfectly chilled champagne loses its sparkle eventually. "Maybe we could grab lunch some-time soon? Catch up."

Amanda smiled. "I'd love to, Wyler, and I'm holding you to it." She offered Max a gentle shoulder bump and headed for the lockers, likely to retrieve her wayward clothes. As if summoned by the mere mention of emotional complexity, Max's phone vibrated. Her mother.

"Hey," she said after sliding onto the call. "Just finished at the gym."

Her mother sighed. "It's late, Maxine. You shouldn't be at the gym alone, a woman. It's not safe."

"They have security guards, cameras everywhere, and the parking lot is fully lit." She dropped her brush into her bag and reached for her clean shirt. "Plus, I still have the pepper spray you gave me for Christmas. Haven't even had to break into the bulk pack of replacements."

"You have to make better choices."

"I will. Starting first thing tomorrow." She offered a grin as if her mom could see it. Anything to keep things light on what was a stressful week for them. The conditions were perfect for a full-on argument she wanted desperately to avoid. Those never went well, and Max always lost. With her mom as primary caregiver and her dad as the cheerleader way in the background, her childhood hadn't always been easy. She'd learned how to sidestep potential land mines, and this week was full of them. Maybe that peacekeeper quality was the reason she'd gravitated so readily toward mediation. She knew how to avoid an argument, and now she was getting paid to help others do the same.

"The reason I'm calling," her mother said, "is that I need you to pick up your Lola from the airport at 2 p.m. tomorrow. Do not be late. She's incredibly nervous about this trip. Do you understand?"

"Of course." She'd have to move some things around, but this was her grandmother, so she'd figure it out.

"But before that, please swing by the little grocery store on Burrow and MacMillan and grab several bags of ice and bring them to the house. You probably already want to be dressed by then."

Max paused. The dinner was scheduled for seven, and she

knew she would also be expected to help with the final preparations. "Mom, I just want to remind you that it's still a workday for me. I have a variety of client meetings that have been scheduled for months. These people have rearranged their lives to both be available." Max's services were in high demand, and her mediation clients booked out far in advance. "Unfortunately, I can't cancel the day before."

"You can if you want to," she said without hesitation. "I have important patients, too. And when I need the time, they're rescheduled by Audrey. Or does it not matter to you that Lola is coming to town?" She said the final sentence as if she just couldn't believe that would be the case. She was a woman who knew how to drive home a point.

Max closed her eyes and paused. "Of course it matters to me. I'll talk to Sonya and see if we can move some things around."

"Thank you, Maxine. We're going to have a fun night."

She pulled in air because the chances of that were so slim. *Steady now.* "Yes, we are. Send me that flight information, and I'll see you tomorrow."

Max clicked off the call and stared down at her phone, stealing a moment to regroup, then picked it right back up again. "Sonya, hi. Don't murder me." Her assistant and friend never failed to answer her calls. Even after hours.

"Oh, no."

"Yeah. I need you to work your scheduling magic. Can you take my entire afternoon tomorrow and shove it into the morning? Move the Sandersons to next week. They're not urgent. That should help."

"They're going to be *thrilled*," Sonya said, extra precious with that last word.

"If they'd compromised a bit more in our first two sessions, we wouldn't even need this next one."

"Sure. They'll listen to reason. The Sandersons are so levelheaded." Dry delivery was Sonya's superpower and one of the reasons Max had met her salary demands years before. Her wit and organizational skills got her that first raise. The two of them had grown closer with each day they'd worked together, having developed a shorthand and communication style that was straightforward and humor-laced. That earned her a second. "I'll sprinkle legal fairy dust and make it happen."

"You're the best assistant in my whole office."

"Which is easy since I'm so lonely there." Sonya had been angling for Max to expand the business and hire other mediators, which was something she was honestly considering, given the demand.

"I'm bringing donuts in the morning, and they'll be your twelve new friends."

She could almost hear Sonya softening through the phone. "That would help with the Sanderson drama."

"Thought so. See you in the trenches."

"Over and out."

TWO

Read It and Weep

E verly Springs, Virginia, was much smaller than Ella had
envisioned. She'd spent the last two days getting to know
the small city that seemed to favor local businesses. The town
had a charm that snuck up on her, comprised of porch swings,
friendly hellos from strangers, and the kind of storefronts that
felt more personal than supremely polished.

On her third morning, with nowhere to be, she let her feet
lead her through the town's main drag until a familiar word in
loopy, hand-painted letters caught her eye. *Books*. A bookstore?
She paused immediately, her heart fluttering with happiness at
the find.

The storefront itself was narrow and sandwiched between
a boutique pet store and a barbershop that looked like it
hadn't changed in fifty years. The bookstore's large front
window displayed an arrangement of books propped on
wooden crates, framed by twinkle lights and a curtain of ivy
creeping down from the awning above. The paint on the door,
deep green with a brass handle, was chipped in a way that felt
earned rather than neglected. Above it all hung a hand-
painted sign with swooping white script: *Doug's Books*. Ella
already loved the store's vibe. It looked like the kind of place

that had been there forever, and that no one would dare suggest changing.

Intrigued, she pushed open the door and stepped into a store that looked like it had been designed by someone who loved books just a little too much. The interior followed up on that concept, delivering a small space crammed with more bookshelves than should have been legal.

In fact, was it? She scanned the overrun shelves, actually a little in love with the variety of covers all shoved together in haphazard rows like some eccentric wizard had arranged them. There was beauty in the chaos, the mismatched covers of all shapes and sizes lined up like soldiers beneath small signs that indicated mystery, science fiction, or romance.

"Can I help you find a particular story?"

Ella turned to see a thin, partially balding man, with glasses sliding down his nose, regarding her. He seemed incredibly bookish, which she appreciated. Very on-brand. Interestingly, he wore a white apron, as if he worked in a bakery. There were no pastries in sight, however. His phrasing of the question had also been unique. He hadn't asked to help her find a particular *book*. He'd said *story*.

"No, thank you. Just getting a feel for the store. You have so many books in here. Well done."

"Well, I am *Doug*," he said, pointing at the sign on the wall as if it should explain everything. "I like books." A pause. "That's why I've named the store Doug's Books."

"Right. And that holds up." She nodded, and they stared at each other for a beat past comfortable.

"And we have coffee." Doug blinked but didn't move a muscle. "Yonder."

"Yonder?" People apparently said that in Everly Springs. She'd make note.

"Yes. That's what I said."

"That's fantastic, and probably why you're wearing the

apron. It's all coming together now." She added a laugh, imagining he'd join her. He did not.

"No." A pause. "I own the store, so I wear the apron. But only when I'm working. That's probably assumed."

Again, sensible. She couldn't argue. "Well, I'm Ella. New to town, and since I'm here, I'd like to give you my card, just in case you'd ever like to do any advertising or event planning that might require a graphic artist. That's what I do. Graphic art."

His eyes lit up for the first time since she'd entered the shop. "Yes! I host book signings and could use help with the flyers. I hate flyers so much. Do you do flyers, by chance?" He took a dedicated step forward.

"At this juncture in my life, Doug, I will do anything for a dollar."

He leaned in. "Oh, don't say that to too many people."

She laughed at the horrified expression on his face and knew, without a doubt, that she was going to need a lot more Doug in her life. "Good call. I'll refrain."

Then all of a sudden, he straightened as if a fantastic idea had just arrived with a suitcase. "And you really should pin one of those cards to the bulletin board on the back wall, above the little coffee nook. Serve yourself, by the way, and put a dollar in the jar. We're on the honor system around here."

"Oh, will do, Doug." She liked using his name.

"That bulletin board gets more play than my Aunt Millie in her good years." He stood there, wide-eyed and stone-faced, waiting for the comment to settle.

"Well ... good for Aunt Millie. That's my first thought." Ella raised a brow and nodded. "I'll have to check out this bulletin board with that kind of endorsement." Doug nodded and left her space to wander. She made a point to take her time, enjoying every detail of the unique shop. The inter-twining aisles had no rhyme, reason, or organization to their arrangement, further bolstering the child-lost-in-a-mysterious-forest feel. Finally, she made her way to the small coffee nook, poured some of the suspicious dark brew into the uneventful paper cup, and took a sip. Her eyes closed. It was not only well brewed, it felt like a warm embrace from a long-lost coffee relative. "Doug!" she called. "This coffee is amazing. You are to be commended by the coffee officials. I don't know any, but maybe some will find their way in."

"I know." Doug's voice floated quietly back to her over the shelves between them.

Realizing that was all she was going to get, Ella carried her favorite new cup of coffee over to the bulletin board to pin up her card. The brown corkboard on the back wall was already crowded with ads, flyers, and notes of all sizes and colors. Most of them overlapped in chaos reminiscent of the store itself. Some of the posts advertised for roommates, while others sold items like a "used bike that's seen damned better days."

"Same," she mumbled to the flyer. Next to it hung a blue index card with the words *Read It and Weep Book Club*. She smiled, moved past it, but found her gaze backtracking to the words scrawled in thick black Sharpie. *Interesting*. She'd always wanted to belong to a book club, but had never really stumbled upon the opportunity. She loved to read, but it had gotten away from her in the last few years. Then there was the fact that she'd never really read with anyone before, not even a buddy. Certainly not strangers. But wasn't she reinventing herself and turning over a new leaf? If this wasn't the time to try something different, then when was? She studied the details on the card. It seemed the club met on Tuesday nights and asked new members to send a message to the number on the card for the current week's book selection. She snapped a photo and decided to let the idea linger in her brain for a bit, see how she felt.

"Hey, do you know much about the Read It and Weep

Book Club?" she asked Doug as she passed the checkout counter on the way out.

"I do. Feisty women who have lots of opinions. They call themselves the Weepers. I don't mess with 'em."

"My kind of people."

"If you want to join 'em, this is what they're reading this week." He pointed at the small pyramid of books on top of the counter. "You'd think they'd meet monthly, but no, they tear through books like raccoons to a bag of trash. They gotta have their romance, too. Did I mention all the books are romance?" He scoffed as if personally offended by their inability to branch out. "There are lots of genres to explore, but Stevie just refuses to budge."

Ella considered herself a reasonably fast reader, and it wasn't like she had too much going on. Why not? She returned to the counter and checked out the selection of the month. "Romance," she murmured. It had been a while since she'd read one of those.

"Parker Bristow is a bestseller," Doug said, ambling behind the counter. "She brings all the girls to the yard." A pause. "I should know. I'm the yard."

"Does she?" Ella flipped the book over and paused at the two women looking rather in love on the cover. "Oh. It's women. Like actually." She didn't know how delicate she needed to be with ole Doug.

"Ah, yep. Bristow's veered into the sapphic lane these days. So have the Weepers. That's what they call it. Sapphic."

She met his gaze and he met hers, unwavering. "You're very astute, Doug."

"I know."

Ella wanted more information, her interest significantly piqued. She knew one thing for sure, book club or not, she was taking a copy of this book with her and exploring a romance that might speak to her more than she was used to.

She handed over her credit card and waited as Doug rang her up.

"I will definitely be back," she told him with a smile. The coffee alone would haul her in.

"You will," he said, handing her the book in a cute little blue bag with millions of books all over it. This place had a definite point of view, and it involved there being lots of books in the world. Doug was running with the theme and not looking back. "And I'll be using your services sooner rather than later for flyers. Flyers can kiss my ass," he said to no one in particular. She wondered about their sordid history.

"So, I have a new client?" she asked, standing a little taller. This had been such a worthwhile stop. Her excitement rose and swarmed.

"Ah. Yep. You do. Provided you're any good."

"Well, I am."

"I'll call soon so we can do the planning properly."

"Looking forward to it. Have a great day, Doug."

But he was already off and puttering again, headed down one of those curvy aisles. "Enjoy your Bristow," he said without looking back.

"Planning on it," she called sunnily, pleased with her afternoon, pleased with the store, and thinking she might be the newest member of this town's feisty gay book club.

Max checked the time on her desk clock as she slid out of her stupid heels and into the short boots that allowed her to sigh happily as she sank into wonder and comfort. Boots had so much more to offer the world than heels. So much more agreeable. So much closer to the ground. What had she ever done without these boots on her feet? She glared at her discarded pumps and shook her head. "Angry, angry shoes."

"Are you shaming your work heels again?" Sonya asked.

Her curly red hair was untamed and awesome today. Max was well aware that Sonya's hair inspired her mood, which meant Sonya was on fire and flitting from one task to the next without the hair binding. Free hair was honestly when she did her best work. "They're just shoes."

"Little bitch ones," Max muttered. "And hold all my calls, please. I'm hanging up my hat for the day and taking a bottle of cheap wine to my smutty book club." She'd joined on a whim a year ago when her friend, Ariana, who was the ex-girl-friend of a friend of Max's (who then began dating Ariana's other ex, who dated everyone in town), had invited her after they'd chatted about books at a party.

Sonya nodded, hands on hips. "Love that for you. Smut is good for the soul. And the cooch."

"Sonya." Max went still, mid-hair-fluff. "Really?"

She didn't pause. "Smut in hard copy is even better."

"I will give you that. I like being able to read a sexy sentence twice if I so choose." She grinned. "And I do."

"There you go. You need a night to get good and tipsy while you pretend to discuss the sexual escapades of fictional characters."

"I'm telling you, you should read one of these things," Max said, organizing her desk for the next day's agenda. "While they're fun places to get lost, I also think they set completely ridiculous expectations about falling in love." She laughed sardonically, because love had wholly eluded her. "Can you tell I speak from experience?"

"You don't have to remind me. Your last girlfriend was more into herself and her outfit than any other person on the planet. That was probably enough to keep you on the love bench for a while." She came further into the office, clearly on a mission. Her eyes softened. "Just don't stay there too long, or who will you ask what the two of you should do for dinner every night for the rest of your goddamn life? Huh? Who?"

"I don't know, but you make it sound so appealing." Max

softened a little, remembering how Sonya had been her sounding board at the end of that relationship. Well, if you could even fully call it that. The whole thing between her and Rachel had been surface-level and short-lived. But even with that in mind, it had taken Max a little while to recover from the disappointment. It also made her wary of the work-to-reward ratio that always came with romantic relationships. Who had the energy, honestly? She had enough on her plate and believed now that love, in all of its revelry, was overrated at best and a publicly hyped farce at worst. Didn't mean she minded the books. The spicy scenes were actually a lot of fun. "Another reminder why romance should be left between the pages."

"Aw, Max. I never imagined you to be a full-on cynic. But look at ya." Sonya placed her hands on her hips and grinned. "I'm worried I've rubbed off on you, but I'm also a little proud."

"I have a feeling my working with couples on their way to Splitsville all day might have contributed, but we'll give you partial credit, too." She offered a wink and went back to packing her attaché.

"Does your unfortunate mood have anything to do with your grandmother's dinner last night?"

She went still. "Oh, are my battle scars showing?" Max shrugged and zipped the brown leather bag, a five-hundred-dollar splurge she didn't regret. Sometimes, looking the part of a successful attorney and businesswoman helped her feel more like one. "It was probably the most painful three hours of my adult life."

Sonya winced and leaned against the doorframe, the stance she adopted when they were getting into something. "I was hesitant to bring it up, but you've been quieter than normal today. That bad? Really?"

"Oh, yeah."

When Max had arrived at their family home with her

nervous grandmother, her mom had immediately rushed to them, already dressed in her tailored burgundy dress and heels, hair perfect. She'd greeted her mother and turned in frustration to Max.

"You should have been here sooner. She's tired. I can tell."

"I'm sorry, Mom. We came as soon as we retrieved Lola's bag."

"Well, she needs to sit and have some tea." She leaned in and dropped her voice. "And I could have used your help, you know."

"Of course, but I thought this was how I was supposed to be helping." It didn't matter. Her mother was already ushering Lola into the living room, leaving Max in the entryway feeling like she'd somehow failed. Alone, Max laughed low and to herself. She hauled in a deep breath and geared up for so much more. When her mother was stressed, she tended to focus more on Max and her perceived shortcomings. The fact that Max had become a lawyer instead of a doctor. The fact that she didn't attend church. Her sexuality, which also came with her mom jokingly asking when Max was going to marry that "cute male attorney" down the hall from her office. But it was high-stress events like this dinner when Max knew the passive-aggressive claws would really slide out, making her wish for a sibling to divvy up the attention. Her father, smart and aloof man that he was, would pull a disappearing act at the most opportune moments, leaving Max to juggle her mother's sharp demands like knives at the circus.

"Why couldn't you have at least brought a date along for Lola to meet?" her mother had whispered in her ear shortly after they'd finished the salad.

"But I'm not dating anyone."

"And why is that?" Her mother lifted her hair and let it fall. She studied her work intently, then adjusted one strand at a time as if Max had arrived a rumpled mess. "You're beautiful and successful, and I want her to see that."

"Thank you, Mom."

"Don't thank me. Make me proud. I want to be a Lola someday, too. That's all."

"I should probably get a wife first," Max said with a small smile. She would pay for that and knew it. As if on cue, her mother sighed loudly and stalked away. "You are too stubborn for words."

While conservative in many ways, Dr. Mayumi Wyler was supportive of every gay person on the planet except one. Yes, most were welcome to choose their own happiness, it seemed, except for her daughter. She'd planned Max's life out to the most mundane detail before her fifth birthday, and was personally offended when it seemed Max had plans of her own. She was supposed to be a doctor, but wasn't. She was supposed to be married with two children by now, but missed that mark, too. The list went on and on, which might be why she found herself constantly trying to make up for the perceived shortcomings. A therapist had once called her classic, and she'd declined to go back.

Orienting herself back to the moment, Max turned to Sonya. "Now that I'm a safe distance away, I can catch my breath and tell you that my mother is an unhappy person unless she has control of the world, and I don't want to be like her." She blew out a slow breath. Hearing the words out loud had a sobering effect. "And I'm simply choosing not to be."

"Hear, hear."

"So, I'm going to my weekly book club gathering, and I'm going to drink red wine, eat cubes of cheese, and escape."

"If I didn't have Jerry at home, who wants to go out tonight for steak and onions, I'd hop in the car with you. Jerry never remembers to haul me in by my waist and kiss my neck like those romance covers, though."

"I don't think you're alone in that. Hence, the word escape." She tidied her desk. "As for tagging along, you're welcome at Read It and Weep anytime. They're a pretty eclectic group. Eighty percent queer, though. And preoccupied with the steamy scenes most of the time." Max reflected on last week's discussion. "A lot of emphasis on female lips clinging to other female lips."

"I better clutch my pearls then," Sonya deadpanned. Not much ruffled her feathers, which was one of the reasons they got along so well. "And learn to finish a book."

Max smiled. Sonya had a way of pulling those out of her. "You nailed it, Sone. See you tomorrow."

"I will count the suspenseful seconds." As Max passed by, Sonya kissed the shoulder of her jacket with a loud smack. "Hey. Look at me," she said with a voice tight with sincerity.

Max paused and met her gaze. "Yeah?"

"Love you or something."

She felt her muscles relax and warmth sprout in her chest. "Love you back." That simple exchange was enough to lift Max right out of her post-birthday party hangover. Kindness mattered, and Sonya had her back. Hell, she had Sonya's right back and would take a bullet for that woman in an instant.

"Now, go get your sexy girl-on-girl action."

"On the page."

"Whatever."

Max walked backward through the small six-person waiting area outside her office. "It's a good one tonight. They get it on three and a half times."

"How do you account for half a time?"

Max paused, stared, and waited.

"Ohhhh."

"And there it is."

THREE

Porchlight Chemistry

E lla wasn't sure why she was nervous climbing the stairs of the cute little one-story, beige and blue house that had maybe seen better days. It could have used a new coat of paint, and the second of the three stairs leading up to the porch was a little wobbly, but the house came with warm and homey vibes. The sheer volume of colorful pillows piled onto the wooden porch swing out front suggested the owner loved this place and valued soft, comfortable spots. A miniature garden spread to the right, with a happy little gnome kicking his heels in the air.

"And a good day to you, too, sir," she told him quietly, a manifestation of her nerves. She closed her eyes and hoped to God no one inside heard that.

She turned back to the house, ascended the remaining steps, and knocked on the smoky-blue door, all the while remembering to stay cool and breathe like a human. At her side, she clutched her copy of the book Doug sold her, notes on the reading, and a bottle of twelve-dollar Merlot that she probably couldn't afford.

The door swung open, and a glamorous woman with shoulder-length blond hair, likely from a bottle, looked back at

Ella with a smile. She was older than Ella, maybe in her mid-fifties. But there was nothing motherly about her. If she'd been her teacher, Ella would have had a crush. She wore jeans with noticeably frayed hems and stood barefoot, a tattoo of a turtle showing on her big toe. She grinned with a warmth Ella hadn't been prepared for. "Well, hi. Are you Ella?" She reached out and placed her hand over Ella's.

"I am. Stevie?"

"The one and only, other than Nicks. No one can top her, so I don't try." She tossed open an arm and gestured behind her. "Come in and get comfortable. The couch, the floor. Hell, if you can climb the wall and sit on the ceiling, we won't discourage you because you're new and have wine." The words sounded more like a celebration. "Welcome to Weepers. Follow me." She accepted the bottle and led Ella down a short hallway, past what looked to be a small room with shelves lined with books. Stevie had her own mini-library, complete with an oversized, white, comfy chair. Nice. Ella already liked the feel of this place.

"And here are the rest of our club members," Stevie said. "They get here early to eat and gab." Only the members were in the midst of what seemed to be a boisterous conversation and took no notice of Ella's arrival.

"I don't care if the meet-cute is on page two or ten, but it needs to be early enough in the book that I'm not starved for character connection," a young brunette said from her spot on the couch to the left, feet tucked beneath her. She looked very much at home. Pretty with her long hair pulled partially back and noticeable dimples.

"That's Ariana," Stevie called from the adjacent kitchen. A square, open window separated the two rooms.

"Hi," Ariana said with a cheerful wave. "Stevie said we were getting a newbie tonight. Come in. Come in. I promise we're friendly." She went right back to her conversation with the young blond woman across from her, her hair pulled halfway up, with wisps escaping. They both seemed to be in their twenties.

"Meet-cutes shouldn't be rooted in rules," the blond said in a calmer voice, offering Ella a wave in the exact moment she was making her point. "If the author wants a cute later, I'm flexible."

"Morgan!" Stevie shouted and pointed through the window at the blond. Aha, she was introducing them as they came up via shout. Ella nodded her understanding. *Morgan, it was.*

The living room was more spacious than it looked from the outside. Cozy without feeling cramped. Two plush couches faced each other across a weathered coffee table that reminded Ella of a tree stump. A pair of oversized armchairs angled inward at the corners, as if they were leaning in to listen. The whole setup invited conversation, the kind that lingered. Ella could easily picture a lively book debate happening here, with members going back and forth, wineglasses in hand. Maybe Stevie had arranged it with book club nights in mind. Intimate, intentional, a little magical. Ella loved everything about it.

"And that over there is Olive!" Stevie called. A woman on the couch next to Morgan nodded, but didn't speak. Her hair was dark, and in a past-her-shoulder French braid. She seemed more reserved than the other two, sitting upright with her legs crossed. She offered a conservative smile.

"Hi," Ella said, raising a hand. "I'm new."

"Nice to meet you," Olive replied, leaving it there. She appeared more shy than unfriendly.

"Sorry for babbling over your entrance," Ariana said, turning to Ella fully. She was the bubbly one, Ella decided. "We fall into this room and just get going. It's like a light switch. Or Pavlov's dog."

"Runaway trains," Morgan said. She had a kind smile and a gentle demeanor.

"No. I encourage the debate," Ella said. "I'm not exactly clear on the term meet-cute, though."

Morgan and Ariana exchanged a look. Even Olive raised her eyebrows.

"We love a newcomer," Stevie hollered through the window, which kinda reminded Ella of a restaurant's pickup window. "Who wants this one?"

"Oh, me!" Ariana said, without missing a beat. "A meet-cute is this completely unexpected, sometimes awkward, sometimes awesome first meeting between the two main characters in a romance. It kicks everything off."

Morgan nodded enthusiastically. "It's honestly one of my favorite parts of the story. Their first glimmer. They might bump into each other at a coffee shop and spill things all over each other. I love a good spill."

"Ah, I see," Ella said. "I don't think I realized there was a name for that kind of thing."

"I like the moment, too," Olive said. "Sometimes there's an argument. What if there were only one cup of coffee left? Shouting can be sexy."

"Or they both wanted to buy the same lamp at the rummage sale?" Morgan asked with a smolder.

"Oh, lamp wars are the best!" Ariana said, sitting up taller. "Two women wrestling over a lamp is the stuff of my fantasies."

Olive frowned. "I've never read wrestling in a meet-cute."

"And isn't it about time?" Ariana asked. She returned to Ella. "Whatever happens in the meet-cute, the reader wants to see the characters interact more in the future."

Ella held up her copy. "There's no wrestling, but I like how this book's meet-cute is a little fiery."

"Oh, maybe we should wait for Em before diving into this week's talk," Olive said, her brows pulled in.

"Wait no more. I'm here."

At the sound of the new voice, something sharp and electric zipped down Ella's spine, an involuntary reaction, as if her body had registered something significant before her brain caught up. She turned toward the door.

The missing member of the club had apparently let herself in. Ella's breath caught. The woman was stunning. Not in a loud or obvious way, but in a manner that made Ella momentarily forget what she'd been saying. Dark, dark hair with a subtle curl. Eyes that seemed to take in everything at once. Confidence, but not arrogance. Ella straightened, like her spine had suddenly remembered its job.

"That's Em," Stevie yelled.

"True." The woman smiled, and her voice, low and smooth, settled under Ella's skin like warm honey. "Joining us?"

"Yes, I am." Ella heard herself speak before she knew what she was saying. Heat bloomed just below her collarbone. Not the time to be super gay and drooling, but, apparently, that was the plan.

"Yes, I am," she repeated, and winced inwardly at the echo. What was that? Her voice sounded weird, a little too eager. "I'm Ella. Nice to meet you, Em."

Stevie brought in a tray overflowing with cheese, crackers, popcorn, Hershey's Kisses, and grapes. "All the best snacks for wine." She hurried back into the kitchen and returned with two open bottles, including the one Ella brought. "The important stuff. Makes the conversation flow." She ran her hand through her beautiful hair and sat on the couch next to Olive, leaving the two chairs free for Em and Ella. That had an interesting ring to it. She settled in, now totally familiar with the term "meet-cute," and excited for this discussion. It also felt good to be diving into something new while out of the house, seeing people other than just Rachel.

Ella raised her hand halfway. "Can I start by saying thank you for having me? I've never been a part of a book club before."

"A cherry pop," Olive said quietly to a raised eyebrow from Morgan and a laugh from Stevie.

"I guess that's true," she added. "In fact, I've gotten away from reading. Hoping this might change that."

"We love that you're here," Ariana said. She seemed the most outgoing in the group and somewhat of a leader.

The others nodded.

"What did you think of *Life in the Fast Lane*?" Morgan asked, referencing the book, and moved until she sat cross-legged on the couch.

"I am shocked to report that I adored it. Especially with the racecar backdrop. It's not usually my thing, but I was hooked." She wasn't sure how personal she should get here. "Confession: I've never read a romance novel featuring two women. I thought Bristow nailed it."

Something about her comment prompted most everyone in the room to exchange a look with someone else. Em seemed to take the cue. "I don't know where you identify, but I should tell you that most of us fall somewhere along the queer alphabet."

"Except me," Stevie said. "I'm the boring straight woman in the room, but I simply adore the sapphic books anyway. The emotional connection is more prominently featured than in the straight ones I used to read."

"Speaking of your heterosexual lifestyle, where's Dominic tonight?" Ariana asked, looking toward a hallway that likely led to bedrooms.

"At the card house, like always. There's a poker tournament tonight. With any luck, maybe he'll bring home the five-hundred-dollar prize, which we can add to our cruise fund. Who wants more wine?" Olive extended her glass, and Stevie poured.

"I'm bisexual," Morgan said. "Or pansexual." A pause as she studied the wall. "I never know how to label myself. I like who I like. I wish that were one of the labels." She capped off the comment with a smile, and Ella couldn't help but smile, too.

"And we're just garden-variety lesbians," Ariana said, gesturing between herself and Em. She shrugged. "Just thought you should know who you're sharing the space with since the book is sapphic and all." She watched Ella cautiously as if waiting to see if she'd storm out of the room, maybe scream in horror, and slam the door.

Then it dawned on her. They didn't want her to dive in headfirst if she was some radical bigot, in for the shock of her life when she got to know the group better. And then it made her sadly wonder if that had happened before. "Oh, I'm sexually fluid." She winced. "I generally date whoever I'm attracted to as well." She nodded to Morgan. "I usually say bisexual." She nodded a few times. "But my former fiancée was a woman." She'd likely offered too many details, but felt strangely at home with this group and wanted them to know she was one of them.

Ariana's eyes widened, and her mouth turned up. "Well, pull up a chair, ma'am. You have stumbled into the right book club."

Excitement bubbled, and a comforting warmth hit and spread out. She felt like a puzzle piece that had just snapped into place. It was a unique sensation. "I'm getting the feeling I have."

"So you think Bristow nailed it?" Em said, putting them back on course. Something about her tone made it sound like she didn't entirely think so. Ah, book club discourse was in effect. Ella was in, her thoughts bursting to be shared.

"Well, I felt the emotional connection slowly built to the point that I wished they'd hurry up and fall in love already," Ariana said. "What about you?"

Em exhaled. "I think I was hesitant to buy in. She was going for the slow burn, and that's fine, but how many adorable, flirtatious scenes did we need to get the message?

Let's get to the external conflict. I was ready for the strife much sooner than we got it."

Morgan opened her mouth to speak, but Ella couldn't hold herself back, feeling the need to defend the scenes she loved. "But, I would argue that we have to fall in love with the couple, and seeing how they interact in everyday situations allows us that glimpse. It's not padding. I'd argue it's foundation. Otherwise, what are we rooting for?"

"I like her," Stevie said, pointing at Ella and then taking a gulp of wine. "Best new member we've had since Olive."

"Thank you," Ella said, smiling in solidarity at Olive, who also seemed to sit taller. She switched her focus to Morgan. "Sorry if I cut you off. I might be overly excited to be here."

Morgan laughed. "Not at all. I just wanted to share how much I enjoyed the little things the two mains noticed about each other." Only Ella had to play that sentence back because Em was pouring a glass of wine about two feet away, and she had a perfect view of the action. Her hands were captivating. She had long fingers and slender wrists, yet she moved with such confidence and owned every square inch she traversed. Ella snuck a glance at her profile, and didn't think it was fair for someone to appear so unaffectedly attractive. Em had thick, dark lashes and full lips that curved naturally upward. But her eyes captivated Ella the most, luminous and—whoops, she was supposed to be listening.

"Oh, those kinds of observations are wildly sexy," Ariana said.

Ella swallowed, panicking for a moment until she realized they were still caught up in book chat.

"You know what I found fascinating?" Olive said, gesturing with a cheese cube. "The secondary characters." She popped it and spoke around her subtle chew. "We never really went home with any of them or heard their internal thoughts, but the author offered us glimpses of their own parallel stories running behind the scenes. They had real lives.

I could tell!" Just then, her cell phone vibrated, and Olive took a moment to read the text. A smile came onto her lips, and pink blossomed on her cheeks. Ella wondered who had put it there. Maybe Olive had a saucy date later. A scandalous affair, perhaps? No one would suspect her.

"Yeah, but couldn't she have offered more than a glimpse, so that we felt like we knew them better?" Em asked, her brows pulling in. She'd voiced skepticism twice now. Not the softest one in the group, and that was okay.

"All right." Ariana studied her. "Something's up with you. You're dark and moody today, like a rain cloud just knocked you upside the head and you're pissed off about it."

"I would say that's fair. I hate those aggressive rain clouds." Em sighed and went serious. "Rough week is all." She touched her forehead briefly, which Ella recognized as a sign of vulnerability. She likely wasn't sure what to do with her hands when confronted with personal questions. Ella memorized that tidbit for reasons she wasn't sure about. She had a hunch, though. There was something about this woman that she found captivating.

"Want to talk about it?" Morgan asked softly. She did seem to have an empathetic quality that was easy to admire. Ella had a good feeling about all of these women, which was hard to come by these days. She predicted she'd be back to book club, if they'd have her.

"Uh, actually, I don't. I want to lose myself in one of these suckers," Em said, holding up *Life in the Fast Lane* with the two illustrated women making sexy eyes at each other on the cover, race car in the background. "And pretend life always ends with an HEA. I'm just having a hard time suspending disbelief these days. Too much real-world clutter."

"HEA," Ella mumbled, thumbing through the copy in her hands for a clue.

"Happily ever after," Stevie offered in a stage whisper. "You're too cute, sweet girl."

"That's code for new," Ariana said with a sideways grin. "And don't be afraid to ask whatever questions you have about romance shorthand."

Em nodded along. "We're super fans of the genre and are here for your every need."

Ella laughed and arched a brow. "Every one, huh?" Apparently, her wine just let words fly out of her mouth like a flock of canaries in the spring.

"See? I like her, too," Ariana said to the room. "I like you, Ella."

"Thank you. The feeling is mutual. It's sealed, and you're not gonna be able to get rid of me."

"The lovefest is palpable," Em said with an edgy glint. Ella also liked that edge. It made her skin tingle in all the right places.

Olive leaned in. "Let's talk about the way Zoe likes to tell Jolene how she tastes when they kiss ... and otherwise. Who else had a big reaction? I had to set the book down and revel." Her words were spicy, but her conservative delivery was reminiscent of a librarian, creating an intriguing dynamic.

"Oh, you're going for it," Stevie said, nodding. "The passion fruit soda reference for one. I needed to stand in front of my freezer."

"Same," Ella said. "It showed me that she was a detail-oriented woman. I liked that." She felt Em watching her as she spoke, and a shiver went down her spine. And when the room moved on with the conversation, Em didn't look away. What was she supposed to do with that? Instinctually, Ella turned and met her gaze, and something noteworthy, something unnameable, locked into place. For a moment, they stayed just like that, quietly watching each other as the volume in the room seemed to fall away until it was just them.

"Sorry. Was that too personal? Just smack me with a frying pan."

Ella froze. What had she missed? A frying pan?

"Um, Ella, you there?"

Someone was speaking to her. That's why it had gone quiet. They were waiting for her response.

She blinked and turned to the room filled with expectant stares. "I'm the one who's sorry. What was the question?"

More looks were exchanged, smiles suppressed. Had they caught her and Em having a staring contest? That's what it had been, hadn't it? Her skin was sensitive, and her mind felt like a merry-go-round, so it had to have been something. A moment. She liked the term.

Ariana straightened, attempting to smother a smile. "I just asked if there was a Mrs. Ella in your life? Or one in the running."

"Oh! No. I just moved to Everly Springs from Tulsa. Single. Unemployed. Ready to start over. I sound like such a cliché when I hear it out loud, but I'm definitely in transition."

"You're from Oklahoma!" Stevie exclaimed. She seemed intrigued. The news made everyone sit right the hell up. "I wondered why none of us had ever encountered you before."

"Oh, wow," Morgan said, placing a hand over her heart. "Right in the center of the country. You're like our own personal Dorothy. At last."

"Who knew you've been waiting for one?" Olive said.

"I get how it would seem that way," Ella said with a laugh. "Tulsa isn't as sleepy as it sounds, though. I promise. Like eighty million Starbucks."

Em smiled. "You'll bring a new perspective to our discussions. Very cool." They shared a soft smile before Ella focused on the wineglass in her hand, anything to ground her. They pressed on, turning over the intricacies of Parker Bristow's cleverly woven romance. The more they talked about the story, the more Ella felt herself pulled into the world. The other women in the group made her think about so many angles that she'd missed on her read, which energized her all the more. In fact, she planned to read the book a second time starting that very night. She'd always enjoyed romance novels, and the rediscovery of a lost love was honestly just what she needed.

"So, will we see you next week? We're trying an enemies-to-lovers," Olive said. She quickly rushed to explain the trope, remembering who she was dealing with.

"Sounds fiery."

"They're the best," Olive said with a ferocity Ella hadn't expected.

"Down, girl," Em said with a grin.

"Yes, I'll be back. I just need to swing by Doug's Books for the new read."

Stevie stepped in. "Sweetheart, I already gave him a list of our next five or six selections. You can scoop 'em up all at once. But don't get too far ahead or your feelings won't be fresh when we meet." Ella appreciated how important the discussion seemed to be to this particular group. Nothing like the clichéd book club reputation that had women skipping the reading part to drink wine and gossip. Not that she wouldn't enjoy that, too.

"Perfect," Ella said, more pleased with tonight than she would have expected.

As everyone began to pack their belongings and break off into side conversations, she surveyed the room. Empty wine-glasses littered the surfaces. The charcuterie board Stevie had made for them had been demolished, with only a stray sweet pickle, two cheese cubes, and a lonely slice of round salami remaining. A sure sign of a successful meeting. Both bottles of wine had been killed, and a third had been retrieved and opened, with about a glass remaining. The decibel level in the room had surely tripled since they'd kicked off the meeting, and six of them now talked over one another comfortably, all formality abandoned. Laughter had been a highlight of the night and continued freely. Ella's face hurt from smiling so much. She ruminated on one of her favorite moments.

"Stop it. I can't believe you thought her housekeeper was some kind of voyeur!" Ariana had yelled with tears of laughter glistening in her eyes. She waved her hands in front of her face as the rest of them fought the same battle. Stevie was doubled over. Em wiped her eyes. Ella struggled for air.

"What?" Morgan asked in defense, though she was laughing so hard her eyes had misted, too. "She kept watching their exchanges throughout the whole middle section. What was I supposed to think?"

"That she was bored and interested in their conversations!" Stevie called out, up on her knees now. "Not that she wanted to watch them get naked!"

Morgan brought her shoulders to her ears. "Listen, I thought Bristow was taking us somewhere new and upping her typical spice level."

"To housekeepers who are a little dirtier than the houses they service?" Em smiled and shook her head in amusement.

"Yes! Exactly that!" Morgan cried out. "I thought she was a dirty girl, and, to tell you the truth, I wasn't sure I minded."

Ella's stomach still hurt from the laughter, just imagining the prim housekeeper of the wealthy main character entering the sexual fray. Morgan was shaping up to be a treasure to protect. The group had been rowdy, but Em, who, for whatever reason, had stolen her focus, always maintained an element of control. She would describe her as quiet, but she wasn't that—more like intelligent and calm. The group seemed to both adore and look up to her. If Ariana was the most vocal member of the group, often steering the conversation as moderator, Em seemed to serve as their quieter leader. Intriguing. Ella could admit to wanting to know more.

There was always next week. She thanked Stevie, who kissed her cheek with a smack, said her goodbyes to the rest of the group, and headed out to the cute little porch in search of her Mini.

"Headed out?"

She turned, and there she was, sitting on the wooden porch swing, the blue-hued moonlight illuminating a portion of her face. Em. She suppressed the dreamy sigh that threatened to escape. "Didn't see you there."

"Forgot to turn the porchlight on. I was just taking a minute before heading home. The fresh air helps me regroup."

Ella wasn't sure what to say, but she didn't want their moment alone to end. If only her thoughts would settle. "Where's home?"

"I'm about four miles east, not far from what we would consider downtown. But for newcomers, it's that way," she said, pointing to her left.

"Very helpful. You'll find that I'm directionally challenged and self-aware enough to admit that." She rocked back on her heels. "Now you know."

Em smiled. "Then I should walk you to your car so you don't get lost along the way."

Ella went up on her tiptoes. "I won't say no."

As they covered the twenty-five feet, Ella couldn't help but admire the clear, crisp sky. Maybe it was the romance novels that had her noticing every picturesque detail. "It's nice out tonight."

"Want to take a stroll around the block? This street is basically a circle." Em shrugged. "Not quite ready to go home. I'll likely start working, and who wants that?"

"No one," Ella said, a hit of energy zapped her at the idea of walking with Em, just the two of them. She was about three inches taller than Ella was, and somehow that seemed to fit their ... everything. "Let's do it."

MAX WASN'T sure what made her ask Ella to take a walk, other than the obvious. She wanted a few more minutes with her. First of all, she was captivating. Pretty and blond, with eyes that latched onto anything she found intriguing, which tonight had been a lot. They were newly into September, which meant the days were chilly, but the evenings were cold. At least tonight there was no harsh wind to brace against and a nice bright sky to enjoy. It almost felt like the stars had joined them for their walk. "So, what's your story, Ella?"

Ella eased her hands into her pockets and glanced over at Max as they walked. "I was at a crossroads in my life, and a good friend suggested I move to where she lived here in Everly Springs. That's code for I lost my job and needed a clean slate."

Max nodded. "Completely understandable. I see a lot of that."

"At work? What do you do?" They followed the road as it curved to the right.

"I'm an attorney who specializes in mediation. Mainly for divorcing couples."

Ella's brows shot up. "Oh, so you really do see people looking for a new start."

"I'm the local expert," she said with a sardonic laugh.

"No wonder you're a romance skeptic."

"I'm not a skeptic when it comes to romance. I believe it's real. It's just not as monumental as those kinds of books would have us believe. Doesn't mean I don't enjoy pretending."

"Pretending! Listen to you. I just got here, and you're already trying to kill it for me."

Max laughed. This woman was beyond cute. She wanted to take her to bed and maybe protect her from the world for as long as possible. Did she go there, or just let things be what they were? "I would never want to do that. I like that we disagree. It will make our life together more interesting. Our grandchildren will enjoy the bickering as they eat pancakes in the kitchen."

Ella laughed loudly. "Wow. I'm coming up short after that one."

Max softened. "I'm kidding. You'll learn I like to tease."

"But ..."

"Yes?"

"Correct me if I'm wrong, but did we have a moment earlier tonight?"

"I think that's left to one's interpretation."

"Okay. What's yours?" Ella asked. She seemed nervous, which just made Max like her all the more.

"We definitely did."

"Oh."

Max couldn't tell if she was blushing because her cheeks were already pink from the cold. What she did notice, however, was that she was not wearing gloves and was rubbing her hands together.

Max stopped them beneath the streetlight. "Where are your gloves? Give me your hands."

"You don't have to do that," Ella said, but she placed her hands in Max's. Max was wearing her cashmere-lined leather gloves and used them to cover Ella's likely frozen fingers.

"I don't have to. No." She met Ella's gaze and lost herself in those blue eyes that were both beautiful and sincere. Max was a sucker for that very combo. A flutter arrived in her midsection, confirming the attraction. The two of them just stood like that, content in the silence underscored by the very distant buzz of the haloed streetlight.

"I wonder if the others are wondering what happened to us." Ella's voice was quieter now. Her gaze didn't move from Max's.

"They probably forgot all about us."

"Yeah."

She was hypnotized and in love with this moment. She would stand on this street corner with this captivating woman for hours if she could. How long had it been since someone truly snagged her attention in this short a period? And right after she'd denounced romance in front of Sonya and the book club. Almost as if fate was daring her.

"Let's get a drink sometime."

Ella blinked. "Yeah. Let's do that." The way her mouth formed the words sent a ripple through Max's midsection. She wasn't the type of woman who could let a moment like this pass unseized. It needed something, and she knew just what. Without waiting, she took one step in and caught Ella's mouth with hers. Satisfaction rained down in heaps when Ella kissed her back, slow and perfect. God, she could have luxuriated in those lips all day, lost herself on the street corner, and never regretted a second of it.

She pulled back ever so slightly and locked onto the blue eyes. "Had to." Her hand was still on Ella's chin.

"Do you always act on impulse?" she asked, looking up at Max, her breasts pressing against her white sweater, visible beneath her unzipped coat. Max had been aware of the perfect way it hugged her curves all night.

"No. That's the tricky thing about tonight. I seemed to have left my control back there. Or you absconded with it when you arrived."

"Absconded is a big word."

"If that impresses you, I have lots more words I can say." Max straightened fully and took a step back. She enjoyed their volleys. Ella was quick in addition to attractive.

"Let's not go using them all up," Ella said and passed her a grin.

"Yet, you mean."

Ella watched her as if trying to figure this all out. "Wow. You are very unexpected." She whispered with her eyes bright. Max loved the shade of blue, somewhere between slate and sky.

Max handed over her phone. "Give me your number so we can schedule that drink."

Ella typed and returned it. "If nothing else, I'll see you at next week's meeting."

"I don't want to wait. I want to hear all about Tulsa."

"Oh, you do, huh? *Tulsa* is riveting conversation material for you?"

Max nodded eagerly. "Hell yeah, it is. Oklahoma is on my list of must-get-to destinations. You can tell me all the ins and outs."

"Tornados."

Max raised a brow. "Mhmm. All about those."

"Ranching."

"Riveting."

Ella offered a sideways smile that Max liked very much. "Even got a little oil and gas to toss in."

"See?" She leaned in close. "Now, how can I resist drilling stories?"

"I had no idea you had such strong feelings on the topic. I guess you've found the right girl to get drinks with then," Ella said, holding her ground.

"My lucky night."

"It's also a *cold* night. Walk back with me?"

"What? Before we get into even more trouble?"

"Yes, Counselor." Ella didn't wait. But for just a minute, Max took a moment to watch after her and revel. Tonight had come out of nowhere, but she was feeling lighter than she had in months. She'd needed this little bit of fun. This release. And that kiss? She hadn't even begun to process how good it had been, like a fire had finally been lit. It felt so ridiculously gratifying after so long of feeling so … numb. And if they kissed that expertly, with chemistry zipping between them so palpably, what would they be like in bed? Max couldn't even go there right now, because torture was not on her list of favorite things. Plus, she savored the unravel so very much, and the club would serve as a nice way for them to get to know each other over time. They had a standing date every Tuesday already penciled in.

FOUR

Exes and Ohs

F riday had been a whole lot of nothing for an unemployed woman in a new town. Ella'd spent the afternoon cleaning the house, because it was the least she could do for Rachel, who allowed her to stay rent-free until she found a job or took on enough freelance work to contribute. She was working on that last part. However, the day had taken a sweet turn with a buzz from her phone. Ella had grinned at the screen moments after Em's text arrived. She'd dropped the vacuum straight onto the floor, abandoned in favor of her scorching new love life. At first, she just took a moment to celebrate the text before even reading the words, because had she dreamily relived that unexpected kiss over and over like her own private greatest hits station? Why, yes. Yes, she damn well had.

Fine. Time to read the words.

> Just making sure you hadn't forgotten about me. Also wanted to say hi.

Oh, and those were excellent words, too.

> Who is this?

Ella bit her lip, grinning.

> Surely not the kissing bandit of the Read It and Weep BC.

She'd hit send and then second-guessed her whole approach like an eighth grader. Had it been too much? Why was she suddenly so sure of herself in the flirtatious arena? But she'd noticed something on Tuesday. She was a different version of herself with Em, and she liked it. She'd felt the change as soon as the two of them began to interact. This woman had mysteriously reached in and snatched out this whole other confident Ella. Call it part of her new life, but she enjoyed the more foot-forward Ella.

> You're onto me. Very astute.

Ella relaxed and quit thinking.

> I've been called worse.

> What are you wearing? (Kidding)

> Since when do you kid?

After ten minutes of good old-fashioned flirting, they made a plan. Em had taken the lead.

> So, I'm getting together with friends at this little bar on Eighth and Highline tonight at 7. Join us? I'll buy you any drink you want.

She glanced at the clock on the microwave across the room. That was soon, which meant very little time to prepare, to pep talk herself in the mirror like the true underdog champion she longed to be. Suddenly, she was her old self again. Nerves swarmed. She had an idea.

Can I bring a friend?

The more the merrier.

When Rachel arrived home twenty minutes later, Ella was waiting with her most winsome smile. "I need you. Are you free tonight?"

"I could be persuaded. But work kicked my ass. The holiday decorations that were supposed to arrive last week aren't going to be here until next week, and that completely fucks the scheduled decorating days and leaves me with more overtime." She sighed dramatically.

"Aww, Sweetie. You sound like you need a night out." Ella framed her face with her hands, blinked slowly, and smiled like a guardian angel here to make her wish come true.

"You're way cuter than the stream of disagreeable customers we dealt with today." Rachel's job as assistant manager at Montclair's Department Store was apparently very stressful. It often took her a good hour to decompress once she arrived home. "Don't get me started on the sweaters I'm supposed to move. Those things are getting boxier every year, by the way. You've been warned."

"I'll steer clear."

She dropped her oversized tote on the kitchen counter with a thud. "So, what's tonight?"

"Do you remember me talking about Em from the book club?"

"I do. One of the most romantic moments of your life, you said." She pulled a face and shrugged. "How would I forget that?"

"Well, she's going to be at this little bar with some of her friends and has invited us over. Very casual, which is how we should approach this."

"Which bar?"

"McHenry's."

"I know it well. They make a blueberry mule that will change your life. Let me slip into something French kiss worthy. You're buying."

Ella relaxed into a grin, anticipation bubbling. "Only fair."

"I want to meet the woman who has you skipping through my kitchen," Rachel called from the walk to her room.

Tonight was going to be a good one. She could tell by the way everything had simply fallen into place just before she'd fully committed to a mundane night of chocolate-drizzled popcorn and a docuseries on the scary, bald cult leader. Those plans wouldn't have been awful. This was objectively better. She relaxed into the couch with a grin and then remembered that she would need to change, too. Joggers and a T-shirt with the Sprite logo weren't going to blend. "Dammit," she said, leaping up and rushing into her chambers, as she referred to her en suite at Rachel's house. She hurried to her closet on a mission and sifted through one wrong option after another. What from her wardrobe said *kiss me again* without screaming *I'd trade my morals for one night with you?* The line was a mysterious minx.

"I need help!" Ella yelled down the hall to Rachel's room. "This is a grade A fashion decision, and I'm a C+ student at best."

"Calm down," Rachel said, arriving in the doorway, hands up. She was already gorgeous and put together in a low-cut purple sweater, black miniskirt, tights, and booties. Damn that girl. Ella would kill to have that kind of ability, to disappear behind a door for five minutes and come out in an ensemble that was a definite win. "I'm here and you're going to be just fine," Rachel said with ease, strolling into the room. Another day at the office for her. She performed a flit-flit gesture, and

Ella took a step back from the closet to make way. Rachel assumed her spot and perused the offerings one hanger at a time until she selected a long-sleeved navy top with a scoop neck and paired it with her low-slung jeans. Ella wasn't even sure why she still owned those things.

"Oh, no. Those jeans are so uncomfortable."

"You look amazing in them," Rachel said with dead serious eye contact.

"Sold."

When they arrived at McHenry's, Ella was surprised to see that the little bar was not so little after all, and something with a decent beat played over the sound system, making her bop her head. Round wooden tables dotted the center of the floor, and a series of banquettes flanked the perimeter of the large square room.

"Shall we grab a drink or find your girl?" Rachel asked. A second later, she whirled around, putting her back to the room. "Fuck my life. My ex is here."

Ella widened her eyes, feeling guilty for putting Rachel in this situation. "Oh, God. I'm so sorry. Do you want to leave?"

"Hell no." Rachel waved her off. "She doesn't own this town. And she won't dictate where I will and will not go with her presence. Where's your girl?"

She scanned the room and saw Em approaching just over Rachel's shoulder. "She's coming over."

Rachel turned. "So's Max."

Confused, Ella attempted to brighten and sent Em a grin. She had her dark hair partially pulled back. "Hey, you."

"Hi," Em said. "You made it."

"Yes. And I want you to meet my best friend. This is Rachel Lenoir."

The smile dimmed noticeably on Em's face. She seemed more than confused. At the exact moment, Rachel turned and looked from Em to Ella in confusion. "What is happening here?" she asked in an icy tone, taking a step back.

Ella frowned, feeling a step behind. "I just wanted you two to meet."

"We know each other," Em said calmly with a sidecar of regret.

"She's my ex," Rachel stated.

Ella blinked, trying to catch up and failing like a second grader who hadn't studied for the spelling test. "What? How is that possible?" She touched her head. "I'm so lost right now."

Em took the lead. "Rachel and I dated for a few months."

Rachel folded her arms. "Not my best decision."

This was not going well. "But the bad ex was Maxine. Max." Em must have been someone from an earlier relationship.

"Exactly." Rachel extended an arm toward Em and then re-extended it for emphasis. "Meet Maxine Wyler."

"Not Em?"

Em slid her hands resolutely into her back pockets. "I usually go by Max. I thought you knew that. The book club calls me M for my first initial."

"How would I know that?!" Ella went still, and her blood ran cold. This was the worst possible kind of misunderstanding. But then the reality came flooding in. That meant that the woman who'd shared the best kiss of Ella's life was the very same Max who'd ghosted Rachel at the end of their relationship, who'd been self-involved and unsupportive in the midst, who'd checked out other women when they'd gone to restaurants together. This couldn't be reality, yet, it was.

"Okay, so I think we've cleared up that mystery," Rachel said with a clap of her hands. "I'm going to go." Rachel turned to her in question. "You?"

Ella met Max's gaze. Seeing her in this whole new light was jarring. Somehow, it didn't seem possible that the two women in her mind were one and the same. But her brain's slow uptake didn't matter in this moment. Her friend's heart did. There was no question at hand. She had Rachel's back and always would. She'd deal with her own feelings in good enough time. "Yeah, I'm coming with you."

If Max's eyes carried a hint of hurt, Ella refused to register it fully, not after how she'd treated Rachel.

"Ella," Max said quietly.

"No," she said unequivocally. "Just no."

Max straightened, and any trace of emotion fled from her face. Steely. That was the best word to describe her. And that was fine. In fact, it made this all much easier. "Got it. Have a good night. Rachel." She met Rachel's gaze evenly, but Rachel only glared.

They left McHenry's in a haze of shock and fumbled with what to do next, finally deciding to stop for a drink downtown just the two of them. "No point in letting our cute outfits go to waste, right?" Rach slid a strand of auburn hair behind her ear and sashayed through the parking lot, probably trying to take back the night.

"Definitely no point," Ella said, numb and grappling. She followed Rachel into Dirty Little Secret, the swanky little martini bar she frequented. Her head had begun to throb, but she set the pain aside, trying to do what she could to ease Rachel's night, after this mortifying blunder. She'd been kissing Rachel's ex and gushing about it to her while a guest in her home. Bad friend form.

"Ms. Rachel, right this way," the host said as soon as they arrived.

"Thank you, Peter. I need one of Marco's cucumber martinis with a double twist. We'll take two." She turned back to Ella. "Trust me."

"I do."

He led them through a blue and green room that seemed to glow until they arrived at a curvy high-top with see-through chairs. Ella would have to up her sophistication game if she planned to frequent places like this one. "I'm not cool enough to be here."

"Well, you're with me, so all is okay." Rachel smiled and tented her hands. "What a night, huh? I'm so sorry this happened to you. I know how excited you were about Max, but trust me when I say you're so much better off." She shuddered. "I would absolutely hate for you to go through what I did. Can you imagine her doing a number on both of us? She's not at all someone you can let your guard down with. Mark my words."

"No. And I should have realized so much sooner. I think I saw a photo on Insta, but you all were in a group, and people can look so different in person."

"So, what about book club? How are you going to be in that same space with her? You know, I wouldn't be surprised if she knew exactly who you were and showed you all of that attention to get back at me."

The idea hadn't occurred to Ella, and she deflated even further, her stomach gnawing itself into knots. "I guess it's possible."

"It's more than possible. I talked about you all the time, and Max is incredibly intelligent." Two cucumber martinis were placed in front of them. Ella resisted the urge to gulp hers. "Fantastic chance she knew exactly what she was doing. I'm just glad I went with you tonight."

The more Rachel talked, the more dejected Ella became. The year had been a tough one, and this was the first spark of connection she'd felt on the romance front in a long time. And if she'd been purposefully manipulated for her proximity to Rachel, then this whole thing was exponentially worse. Those old feelings of worthlessness that had clung to her after her engagement dissolved were creeping back in again. She felt silly for getting excited about Max and for thinking they had a legitimate connection right from the start.

She sipped the martini, and Rachel was right, it was good. "Well, I'm sorry I allowed this to happen. As for book club, um, maybe I bow out."

Rachel frowned. "But you were having such a good time."

She had been. She'd already finished next week's book about the two flight attendants who fell in love literally midair, and there were still a few days until the club's next meeting. Read It and Weep had been her bright spot and something she was genuinely looking forward to. "That's okay. I can find another hobby. Or maybe there's another book club in town. I'm sure there is." She couldn't imagine one where she fit in as well as she had with the Weepers.

Rachel sat back. "No way. I think you should still go. Max will do her Max thing, and you'll focus on the books."

"I could do that pretty easily," she said, and tapped the base of her glass. "I mean that's what we're there for anyway. The books are the main draw."

"Hold on. Did I ever tell you about the time we were at the movies and she left me there?"

Ella took a fortifying breath. "You absolutely didn't."

"And I had been wanting to see that movie for so long, you know how I am when something has me excited, and she just didn't care. That was part of our problem." She leaned in, her emotions escalating. "She thought everything in her life was more important than what I had going on in mine. No one is ever as smart, interesting, or as in control as she thinks herself to be."

The rest of their night was a lot like that. She cut herself off after one drink, but Rachel pressed on, regaling Ella with stories of how Max had been awful during their time together. With each passing detail, Ella found herself sinking lower in her chair until she finally looked around the mostly empty bar. "You think we should head home?"

Rachel pointed at her. "That's good looking out. If I have another one, I'll lose my whole morning tomorrow, and I have Pilates at nine. Get me to the weekend, already." She tossed in a laugh and slung her arm around Ella's shoulders as they walked to the car. "I am so glad you're here, E. You're an amazing best friend."

God, that helped. She smiled, and warmth enveloped her. Rachel's words helped pull her out of her doldrums. "I'm glad I'm here too and feel the same about you."

Rachel linked her arm through Ella's. "Let's make popcorn and veg on the couch until we fall asleep."

She rested her head on Rachel's shoulders as they walked, grateful and satisfied. It was easy to reach for more. Perhaps this was a valuable lesson to approach life at a slower pace. She'd look both ways before she crossed next time, and protect herself and those around her with more vigilance. "You have discovered the key to my true happiness. Speaking of keys, I'll drive."

As they pulled away from the bar, Ella watched through the windshield as the night blurred past. The ache inside her wasn't sharp. It was quieter than that. More like a hollow space she hadn't known existed until something had briefly filled it. Whatever spark she'd imagined with Max had been built on an illusion, and now that it was gone, she couldn't help but mourn it anyway. Not the woman, but the possibility. The connection she'd let herself believe in, even for a little while. And losing that? Somehow, it still hurt.

For someone who'd been valedictorian of both her graduating classes and the fastest ladder climber at her law firm before going into business for herself, a night like Friday should have been something that Max could bounce back from easier than she had.

She'd been grumpy all weekend, not understanding how the intelligent, kind, and funny woman she'd met at book club was tied to Rachel, who'd been one of the worst dating experiences of her life.

She'd decided to take it out on her workout, landing one hit after another on the boxing bag at the gym. A right hook. But why Rachel of all people? Why not someone else from her past? Anyone. Left cross. *Thud.* And the look on Ella's face when she saw Max in this whole new light. Right cross. *Thud.* She wasn't even given a moment to explain or defend herself —cross, hook, *thud.* After fifteen minutes, she grabbed the chain above the bag, steadied it, and stepped back, sweat running down her neck to her chest.

"I could watch you do that all day."

Max turned and found Amanda, a towel on her shoulder, grinning at her with a hand on her hip. "And I could lose myself in that for another hour."

"I certainly wouldn't want to be whoever you were imagining. Bad day?"

"Bad week."

"Tell me so I can watch the little droplets on your collarbone." Amanda was out in full force today, but Max knew she meant no harm.

"A woman I met, who seemed pretty great, turned out to be best friends with my ex."

"Ah. The community is so interwoven, it's criminal." She softened. "But you had something shiny and exciting and now—"

"Back to regularly scheduled programming. It's whatever." She began to towel off, and Amanda offered a pout. "Do you objectify everyone here?"

"God, no. Just those who look like you." She fluttered her lashes. "Plus, I know you well enough to show you my playful side. We're both adults who get the game. At least, I hope."

"Nah. We have a fun give-and-take." Amanda was right about them both being adults, and her words empowered Max. Dammit, she was an adult, and if Rachel, that nightmare of a person, wanted to keep her friends on her side of the yard, that was her call. Max would keep walking.

"Where'd you meet her? The woman who finally caught your eye. We all know it's not easy to do that."

"Book club."

Amanda laughed. "I thought you were serious for a moment."

"I am."

"Book club?" Amanda practically shouted. "Well, slap my ass and call me Nancy Pelosi. You're a reader, too?"

A couple of dudebros arrived to beat on a bag, so Max stepped out of the space and dropped her volume. "I love to read. And it was her first meeting. I kind of doubt she'll be back given what's happened since."

Amanda nodded thoughtfully. "Yeah, I would take that bet."

"You think she'll be back?"

Amanda stared at her. "I know she will be."

FIVE

Rivals and Revelations

The Uber dropped Max off twenty minutes early for book club, and for a second, she stayed frozen in the back seat, pulse tapping high in her throat. She hated how nervous she felt, how the air seemed thinner just thinking about walking through Stevie's door and seeing Ella again. She'd told herself it was better to be early than to walk into the group cold, but, really, she was hoping for a quiet moment to steady herself. Maybe Stevie would be in the kitchen, and they could chat—nothing deep, just something to anchor her. She wasn't ready to face Ella. Not yet. But being first gave her a chance to breathe.

As always, she let herself in and found Stevie doing Stevie. In other words, prepping gorgeous trays of food for the group and grooving to Celine Dion's greatest hits in her kitchen.

"What's up, M? You came to see me shaking my ass?"

"I came to help," Max said and offered a hip bump. "Put me to work."

"My lucky day. You can slice the salami," Stevie said. She handed Max the knife. "And here's the chub."

"Stevie." Max stared down at the whole salami in her hand, laughter bubbling. "Please tell me that this phallic tube of meat is not called a chub. Stop it. That can't be true. I won't survive this knowledge."

"It is," Stevie said and joined her. "Some butcher years back had a good ole time naming that one."

"Looks like a chub," Max said, using the voice of a gruff male butcher. The laughter took over, her eyes filling with tears. "Just gonna call it a chub."

"I'll take one chub!" Stevie said, asking as a customer.

"What's so funny?" They looked up to see Ella standing there, wine in hand, smile on her face. She looked to Stevie. "Last time you said just to come on in. I hope that's okay.'"

"Of course, sweetheart. Come in. Come in. I'll take that," she said, stealing the wine and beckoning Ella to join them in the kitchen.

"You're early," Max said, eyeing her, nerves firing. "And you came back."

"I realize that last part might be surprising," she said, meeting Max's gaze. "But I enjoyed the club and can focus on the group."

"Fair enough. Glad you did."

"Thanks. Me, too."

If there had been a literal ocean between them, their exchange couldn't have felt more distant.

Stevie had been taking in their conversation like a riveting tennis match, and finally jumped in. "Ella, how are you at slicing fruit?"

"Oh, it's what I was born for. How can I help?"

Stevie slid her a cutting board and a carton of strawberries, giving her a brief rundown of how she usually cuts them herself.

"Any reason you showed up ahead of schedule?" Max asked, keeping her eyes on her own project. Ella stood next to her, slicing. She smelled like orange blossoms and vanilla.

"I wanted to see if Stevie needed anything. You?"

They'd still not looked at each other. "Same." They cut

their respective contributions in silence until Max couldn't take it anymore. "Hey, Stevie. Is Dominic around?"

And just like that, Stevie, who stood at the sink, burst into tears. For a moment, Max didn't move. Stevie, the kind of person the word spitfire was made to describe, had never come close to crying in her presence. What in the world was happening, and more importantly, how should she handle it? She and Ella turned to each other in the same moment.

"Do you want to …?" Ella asked.

"Yep," Max said, setting down the knife. They moved to the sink at the same time, flanking Stevie on either side.

"Hey, what's going on?" Max asked, taking the lead. Ella placed a hand on Stevie's arm for support.

"Um, it's just, uh … Dominic and I are splitting up." She exhaled slowly having gotten the words out. "He's staying at his friend's place and will be back to get the rest of his stuff this weekend."

"Fuck. Stevie, I'm so sorry." Max couldn't believe it. Not that the two of them were tied at the hip or anything, but the environment seemed to be a pretty stable ship. "That fucker."

Stevie gulped in air and gripped the sink as if to say Jesus, give me strength. "No, no. It was me! This is all my fault."

"Oh," Max said, and exchanged another look with Ella, whose eyes were wide. She'd certainly been tossed in the deep end early. "Were you just not happy?"

"I think I'm …" She added a moving forward gesture, but her voice trailed off, leaving them guessing.

"Feeling like you need more?" Ella offered.

"No. Just maybe different … you know? A different kind of … thing."

Max nodded. "You feel like the newness has worn off after all these years?"

"No," Stevie said. "I'm not bored."

She decided to go there. "So what exactly are you?"

"Maybe ... gay." She scrunched up her face as if to brace for something scary.

Max's lips parted in shock, and when she looked at Ella, her eyes had tripled in size. After knowing Stevie for three years now, she hadn't seen this coming. Not even once.

"Oh," Ella said, settling back on her heels. "Well, that's not something to be ashamed of. If anything, understanding yourself a little better is a cause for celebration."

Stevie opened her eyes. "I'm not sure it feels that way."

"Maybe you're still getting used to the idea," Ella said. "I'm sure Dominic is, too."

"He's sad and surprised, but he says he gets it. Wants me to be happy. But, fuck, you all, I don't know what I'm supposed to do next. I feel like a dandelion swept up in a tornado."

Max placed her back against the counter and looked Stevie in the eye. "Once you're ready, and not a moment sooner, you dip your toe in. Simple." She lifted a shoulder like it was no big deal. "See if there are any women out there you'd like to date."

Stevie barked a laugh. "Can you imagine me asking someone out?" She hooked a thumb. "I've been married and settled for over thirty years. I don't know how to do that. I don't know how to flirt. And who buys dinner?"

"I can imagine that the situation is daunting for you. Please know that your feelings are entirely normal. You don't have to know any of these things," Ella said and covered Stevie's hand with her own. Her words were soft, coated in warmth and sincerity. It was a good reminder for Max to dial it down, too. Take a gentler approach to Stevie, who wasn't at her strongest. "You have such a fantastic support system in all of your friends." She smiled warmly. "And I'm one of them now, too. You have my number, and I expect you to use it."

That seemed to make Stevie feel better. "I just might take you up on that, and make you regret the offer."

"Trust me. Not possible."

Stevie grabbed a towel, dried her eyes, and exhaled slowly. "Now that my dramafest is on a brief hiatus, I think I'll go fluff my damn hair and pinch my cheeks before the others get here. Is my eye makeup ruined?"

"Not at all," Max said. "You're gorgeous." And she was.

Stevie paused and looked back before exiting the kitchen. Her features went soft. "Thank you both. I mean that."

"Anything for you, Stevie," Max said, knowing she'd been the backup at best. Score one for Ella and her smooth handling of the live grenade they'd just been lobbed.

"How did you do that?" Max asked quietly once they were alone. She returned to her station alongside Ella.

"Do what?" Ah. The chilly curtain had fallen firmly back in place. Ella had gone back to slicing and kept her eyes on her work. Apparently, their joining forces was only on Stevie's behalf.

"Know exactly the words she needed to hear. Can you pass me that tray?"

"I didn't. I just thought about what I would want someone to say to me." She handed over the tray, and their hands brushed against each other in the transfer. Max ignored the pricks of warmth that moved up her arm. "I can finish up in here." Ella turned, her hand on her hip.

Max held up both palms. "I think that's my cue." She crossed behind Ella on her way to the living room, hearing Morgan's voice drift in through the window that divided the two spaces. But she had a final thought. "You know, it's possible that all the things you seem to think about me aren't exactly who I am."

"If you say so."

Wow. The softness Ella'd reserved for Stevie was nowhere to be found in her frosty delivery to Max. Ella clearly didn't like her, and as much as she thought about all the things Rachel could have said about her to Ella, none of them would warrant this kind of ice out. "So it's going to be like that?" She sounded so juvenile, even she could hear that.

Ella shrugged, features still. "We're in a book club together. I don't have to like it, but I can certainly be cordial, and it seems you can be, too. What more is there to say?"

"Nothing," Max said, her own disdain emerging. Why had she liked this girl again? "I'll leave you the kitchen."

"Mhmm."

Max grabbed one of the wineglasses Stevie had set out as she passed. She wasn't driving tonight and planned to take advantage of it, sick of life's bullshit and ready to forget it all. Ella Whatever-Her-Last-Name-Was included.

"Hey, you," Morgan said from her traditional spot on the couch. The wine was already open, which was a good thing. Max helped herself to a splash of red. "How was your week?"

"Shit. And I don't use the term lightly."

"Oh, no." Sweet Morgan's face pulled into a frown. "Your mom?"

"I'm not sure she's speaking to me after I refused to play straight in front of my grandmother." She sighed, still feeling like she ruined the dinner, whether she'd been on the right side of the argument or not. Everyone should get to enjoy their one day of the year. She still had trouble forgetting the look on her mother's face when she'd told her extended family that she was a lesbian a few years back. Her splash of wine was gone. Another was called for.

"Do your parents like you?"

"Um, I think so," Morgan said with an apologetic cringe. She was showing her innocence again. "They're married and settled and more supportive than most of the parents I know. I mean, they make spaghetti every Thursday. Some people might say boring."

"I would never say that. Mine aren't awful by any means, but sometimes they make me feel like …"

"You disappoint them," she said quietly.

"Yes. That." Max tossed back the rest of her glass and then set it aside. Maybe she'd take a break.

"Sorry. Didn't mean to interrupt."

She turned back to see Ella standing a few feet behind her with a completed cheese and charcuterie tray worthy of a photo shoot.

"I hope Stevie won't mind me finishing up on her behalf."

"Where is she anyway?" Morgan asked, craning her neck to see down the hall.

"Me?" Ariana asked, appearing in the entryway. "Right here. And, surprise! I brought Olive. She was loitering out front, so I thought, why not?"

Olive, bless her, dropped her brows and reddened. "I was just walking up. No loitering."

Ariana loved to mess with her. She slung an arm around Olive's neck and grinned. "It was a joke, Olive. You make it too easy."

"I'm not a loiterer," Olive said quietly to Morgan as she slid onto the couch.

Morgan patted her knee. "I know this about you."

"Hi, there, everyone," Stevie said, appearing from the hall-way. "Brief announcement. I already told Ella and M, but let's just get it out there." Ariana and Morgan exchanged a look. Olive sat taller. "Dominic and I are going our separate ways."

"Stevie," Morgan said quietly. She was close enough to reach out and squeeze Stevie's hand. "I'm so sorry."

"He didn't cheat on me. We still like each other. It's probably just that I'm primarily interested in women."

"Oh," Ariana said, nodding.

"You saw this coming?" Max asked quietly, eyes still on Stevie.

"Hundred percent," Ariana said without moving her mouth. "Hey, we got you," she told Stevie.

"We don't have to make a big deal about it. I just thought you should know. You're my friends, and I love you."

"And we love you," Olive said. "Is there anyone … special?"

Stevie's eyes went wide. "No. I wouldn't know the first thing about women."

"Luckily, we do," Max tossed in with a wink. She felt Ella's eyes on her profile, but didn't spare her a glance. If she wanted to coexist, that's what they would do. "I'll be your wingwoman anytime."

Stevie, the most confident woman she'd ever encountered, actually blushed and waved her off. "Enough of my drama. Let's talk about this book. These two should be presidents of the Mile High Club."

"First of all, who here is a member?" Ariana asked.

To everyone's absolute shock, the only hand raised belonged to Morgan.

"I'm sorry, Madam School Teacher," Ariana said. "We're going to need that story."

Morgan shrugged. "It was a long flight, and my situationship at the time needed some assistance in the restroom. I merely obliged." She picked up her copy of the book and thumbed through it. "Now, let's get back to business. The flashbacks were my favorite."

And they were off. Dishing and dissecting. Throughout much of the back-and-forth, Max sipped her newly poured wine and tried to stay with the conversation and not think for a minute about the way Ella's blond hair brushed her shoulders, prompting her to flip it behind her back until it finally made its way to rest on her shoulder again the more she talked. The hair battle left her hot and bothered, and she hated it.

"I found myself pulled in every time they kissed," Ella said. "I don't care what was happening that might have pissed me off in the scenes leading up, but when those two grabbed each other and went for it? My heart went right along with them."

"Right, but on chapter," Max paged through her hard copy, "eighteen, I was rolling my eyes. They're at this huge impasse, and they pause their very intense argument because one can't stop lusting after the other one to the point that they have to kiss."

"It's fiery and awesome." Ella shrugged and turned to her. "I think it speaks to their level of chemistry. The heat cannot be contained."

Max snorted. Not her best moment. This was the wine egging her on. "It's unrealistic."

"Maybe that's why I like it," Ella said flatly, eyes flaring. "Isn't romance about escape?"

"Why does it have to be? I'd love to see a glimpse of the real-life love we all battle every day represented on these pages." She raised a shoulder and let it fall. "That's all."

She blinked. "I can't say I agree in the slightest."

"And that's not surprising."

That's when Max realized the room was watching their exchange intently, confusion hanging from all four faces. "It's good to disagree," Stevie said brightly, clearly attempting to reclaim the discussion and shift them into friendlier territory. "It celebrates our different perspectives."

Ella did the brush-off-the-shoulder thing, and Max resisted an eye roll. It was going to be a long night.

Oh, for fuck's sake. Ella's second book club meeting was proving to be way more complicated than her first. To kick them off, Stevie dropped the coming-out bombshell. And now, Max was on a very determined mission to undermine almost every word out of Ella's mouth. Meanwhile, she was waging a battle within herself to reconcile the various versions of Max in her mind. She needed to fixate on something other than Max Wyler, who'd spent the better part of the evening being awful.

"Why are you so awful tonight?" That was the sentence that leapt from Ella's lips the second they were alone following the more tumultuous book club meeting. The others had gathered up wineglasses and plates and were chatting away in the kitchen.

Max turned to her, incredulity bursting onto her features. She was all parted lips and dropped brows and caught Ella in a sideways stare. Say what you would, but she really had the best eyebrows, so expressive and perfect, bested only by those big brown eyes that were regarding her now with less than careful judgment. "I'm the awful one? Me? What did I do?"

"You challenged every opinion I offered tonight. You didn't do that with anyone else in the room."

"I provided a counterpoint, which is actually what a book club discussion is designed to include." She held out a steadying hand. "But I realize you're new. Maybe next time you won't be caught off guard by a little back-and-forth."

Oh, that comment got under her skin. She saw Max's lawyer side coming out. "See? That was patronizing and uncalled for, making me seem sensitive and unprepared."

The fire in Max's eyes weakened. "Sorry. I heard it, too, that time."

"You were lawyering me."

"A little."

They both exhaled at the same time, and if they had been on the same side, it would have been humorous.

Max's mouth pulled sideways. "Is it imperative that you dislike me automatically just because I wasn't a match with your friend?"

"You stomped on her heart."

"We ended months ago. Do you know how many people I've dated since? Zero. She was dating someone two weeks later, so it couldn't have been that broken."

That pulled Ella up short, and she wondered if it could be

true. Had Rachel moved on that quickly? "I'm sure if she did that, it was out of necessity. A rebound."

"Great. But why is that my fault?"

"You ghosted her."

"I absolutely did not." She squinted and regarded Ella with a question mark hanging over her.

"What in the world are we talking about over here?" Ariana asked, striding toward them with both hands in her back pockets. She'd pulled her brown hair into a ponytail earlier in the evening when the discussion had turned lively. "A continuation of the first kiss debate? You two had some strong opinions."

Ella decided that honesty was the best approach. "Max used to date my best friend."

"Say again." Ariana blinked widely. She swiveled to Max. "The only person you've dated in forever is ..."

"Rachel," Max said resolutely. "Remember her? They live together."

She swiveled back. "You live with Rachel?" Ariana asked, eyes even wider. "Sorry if it seemed like I shouted that. I wasn't expecting that information." She returned to Max. "The Rachel?" she mouthed as if Ella wasn't standing right there.

Max nodded wholeheartedly about six times.

"Yes. I'm currently staying with her until I find my own place." Ella felt the need to explain further. "Rach and I went to college together. She's my best friend."

"Well, that's great," Ariana said, but her eyes went flat. Fire flared in Ella's chest, and she resisted the urge to stand taller in defense of her friend. Apparently, the group had opinions. Probably Max's doing. They'd heard *her* version of the story, and probably not at all how Max had crushed Rachel's heart like a bug. Ella shoved aside the knowledge that she hadn't actually heard Max's story herself because that seemed beside the point. Rachel was someone she cared deeply about. She was a good egg, if a little caught up in her own trajectory. Just that morning, she'd monologued her list of grievances to Ella without so much as taking a breath. Her lawn care service dared to raise prices. Her blueberry bagel should be way more crunchy after a good toasting. Her assistant at work needed a hairstyling tutorial. Her car. The morning news anchor. Her friend, Stephanie. All without asking Ella a thing about her life or morning. An oversight, surely, but thinking of others was maybe one of Rachel's weaknesses.

"Well. What a small world!" Ariana said, regrouping with a burst of faux enthusiasm.

"It turned out to be, yes," Max said, with a matching grin and an exaggerated hand to her hip. "So tiny, one can hardly believe it!" The bite in her tone said a lot.

Ella turned to Max and could almost visualize the daggers flying from her own eyes. Ariana must have, too. She looked from Ella to Max and back again. "Oh. There's more to this story, isn't there?"

"You don't want to know," Max said, throwing back the last of her wine like she was shooting a whiskey.

"But maybe I do," Ariana said through a squint.

"A story for another day." That's when Ella caught Max sway and place a steadying hand on the back of the chair.

"If you say so," Ariana said with a curiously arched brow. "I'll let you two kids talk about whatever might require hashing out. Or therapy."

"Funny," Max said to Ariana's over-the-shoulder grin.

Once they were alone, Ella harnessed her inner adult. "I don't think we need therapy, but a touch of courtesy floating between us might make nights like this easier."

Max shrugged, eyeing Ella in a way that made her insides feel fizzy like champagne. She squirmed against the sensation because *what the hell?*

"We could shoot for that next week. See how it goes." She

turned and grabbed her bag, correcting her course and footing.

"Hey. I'm thinking you shouldn't drive."

Max straightened, showing off the three inches she had on Ella. "I agree with you. That's why I took an Uber here."

"You planned to drink too much?"

"You don't ever do that?"

She shrugged. "It just sort of happens to me organically."

"What can I say? I'm type A. I plan most of my choices."

Ella still felt off-balance and knew why. Even Max in an Uber when she wasn't fully herself still made Ella decidedly uncomfortable. What if something happened to her? It was a stranger's car after all. "Follow me, Type A. I'm giving you a ride."

"*Pftt.* No."

"Stop!" Ella huffed in frustration. "I don't want to argue. I've spent the whole night doing that. Just get in my car, tell me where you live, and we'll spend the whole ride staring at the road in silence."

"God, your sales pitch could use work."

"I'm about to save you twenty bucks and small talk with a stranger who may or may not smell like peppermint Fritos."

"Well, when you put it that way."

"Smart decision."

After a round of goodbyes, they shuffled grumpily and individually to Ella's Mini, which happened to be freezing. "It'll warm up in about five minutes. Seven tops."

Max nodded, and the small cloud of her breath disappeared in the frigid interior. She lifted her shoulders to her ears and tensed as Ella backed out.

"What are you doing over there?" Ella asked.

"Me? Just trying to stay warm."

"I think you're trying to crawl into your own ears." She glanced behind her. "Here." She located the blanket she kept in the back seat, in case she ever found herself in a natural disaster, and tossed it onto Max's lap.

"Thanks. If you give me your phone, I'll type in my address, and Waze can do the rest."

"Perfect." Ella handed over her phone and kept her eyes on the road as Max offered interim directions, like "Turn right at the stop sign" and "You'll want to be in the left lane."

Apparently, Max lived in a condo in a more urban portion of the city. The closest thing that Everly Springs had to a downtown district. That fit what she knew of her. Seemingly sophisticated and lawyer-like. Of course she lived in a high-rise. Of course.

"How long have you lived in your building?"

Max looked over at her, her brows raised. "So, we're not doing the silent ride thing?"

"No. We're not," Ella said. "Change of plans."

"Four years. When I left my firm and started my own business, I needed to simplify as much as possible. I didn't have time for yard work or home maintenance."

"You don't miss nature?"

"I know where to find it, Ella."

The sound of her name on Max's lips was not at all satisfying. Except it was. She squeezed the steering wheel, and pin pricks of heat said *hello, we're here now.* The drive to Max's place wasn't a long one, and when they pulled up to the tall, thin gray building, Ella exhaled. Relief swarmed. The drive was over, and she would soon be able to clear her head and regain her rational trajectory. Max was a disrupter, plain and simple.

"Thanks for the ride." Max eased a long leg out of the car and flicked Ella a look. "Did she tell you we dated for exactly twelve and a half weeks?"

Ella frowned. "I feel like it was more than that."

"You can feel all you want, Ella." Max sent her a smile that was probably meant to be knowing but just read as sexy.

"In fact, I encourage you to feel. But I'm quite capable of reading a calendar. Maybe I'll see you at book club next week." She didn't wait for a response and closed the passenger-side door with a thud.

Ella should have driven away, as any intelligent, well-adjusted woman would do. Instead, she sat there and watched Maxine Wyler walk to the double glass doors of her building, her hips swaying slightly back and forth as if she owned the world.

"Twelve weeks is still a long time," she told the empty car. "Super long." Her forehead fell to the steering wheel, and she clung to the one thing she knew for sure. She needed a bowl of Oatmeal Hoopties and fast.

SIX

Attacking Cupid

"The problem with that, Shawn, is that your days at the beach house align with all of the good holidays." Patricia Monteleone eyed her soon-to-be ex-husband across the conference table, which Max had paid way too much for when opening her office. The carvings on the corners made her feel like a badass, and she'd wanted to show off a little bit, play the part of successful mediator before she actually was one.

"Then what do you propose? I'm all ears." Shawn sat back in his chair, unflinching in the face of Patti's rising emotion. The more upset she became, the calmer he was. Max had a feeling it drove her up the wall.

"We split them up."

"No," he said, sitting up again.

"I think it's admirable of you both to want to share the beach house, but it might be in everyone's best interest if we make a clean break."

"Then it's mine," Patti said. "It's been in my family for years."

"That's a compelling argument. What can we offer Shawn in exchange?"

84

"Nothing, because I want the beach house," Shawn said, finger to the table. "She never even wanted to stay there. I had to drive that train. I fish. She hates it. Fuck this."

"Okay, let's take a step back."

Max's day was much like that. One stalemate after another. They were certainly making her earn her fee. After three sessions with three different couples, she was ready for a latte, a cocktail, or both. She grabbed the pesto turkey sandwich from Pete's Perfect Pita that Sonya had dropped off on her desk instead. After unwrapping the still-warm sandwich, she reached into her drawer for this week's romance novel, *Tried and True*, about a couple who fake date at a ski lodge to impress one of the main character's group of snobby friends. Twenty minutes into her reading and eating session, Sonya's voice yanked her back into reality.

"You spend way more of your lunch hour on those books lately. You need to get laid?"

"Yes." She highlighted a fascinating passage. "But it's more than that. Book club has me on my toes."

"Hmm. Why is that? I thought it was your escape?"

"There's this new member who has all of these opinions that I happen to disagree with."

Sonya laughed low. "And the attorney in you is ready to shoot them down point-by-point."

"Well ... yes. I suppose that's entirely accurate." She set the book face down on her desk, needing to say more. She felt the variety of emotions rise without permission. "This woman has a way of getting under my skin. She's completely falling for these stories and thinks these authors have romance all figured out."

"And you're the resident cynic?"

Her shoulders slumped, and understanding began to seep in. "I guess, which I didn't see coming, but here I am, attacking Cupid. These books compared to real life? C'mon."

The phone was ringing at Sonya's desk, but the amusement behind her eyes said she didn't want to walk away from this conversation. "I'm tickled. We need to get a drink soon."

"God, yes."

"Until then, please consider the option that your very prepared arguments for book club might be fueled by more than your desire to put Little Miss New Girl in her place."

"Stop bringing up good points. It's not what I pay you for."

She tossed her head back into the room like an exotic dancer of the mediation office. "Check again," she said in a throaty voice. Max threw her stress ball only to have Sonya catch it like a pro.

Two bites of her sandwich later, the intercom on her desk phone buzzed. She clicked on. "Yep?"

"Your mother is on two," Sonya said, returning to her professional demeanor. The duality was impressive. "Do you want me to tell her you're unavailable?" A pause. "Yes?" That last part was a friendly nudge. It was nice to have an assistant who had her back.

She wanted to take the nudge. Dodging additional stress sounded like a wise plan, but Max was programmed to jump when her mother asked her to, and self-awareness did nothing to stop it. "No, I have a minute." She clicked over to line two. "Hi, Mama. How's your day?"

"I just finished the crossword puzzle in today's *Times*."

She smiled. "Did you use ink this time?" It was practically rhetorical.

"Yes. I'm calling because you never got back to me about the networking group I mentioned. Jeanette swears that her son saw his business triple once he joined."

"Mom. My practice is doing great, remember? Better than okay." In fact, she had to refer several potential clients to a colleague when her schedule didn't allow her to handle them personally. She was considering hiring two additional attorneys in the coming months and expanding her practice.

Her mother knew all of this, but had some block when it came to acknowledging that Max had done anything favorable.

"Can it hurt to improve?" She plowed forward without pause. "There was a feature on him in *The Journal*. Did you see it?"

"I didn't see it. No." The implication was that there had not been a feature on Max or her practice.

"A feature is a big deal, Maxine. We could send something like that to Lola. She'd love it. I'll send the link to your email. Then maybe consider joining the group."

"Maybe." She had no such intention.

"I'll tell Jeanette you'll be at their next cocktail hour, and her boy can be on the lookout."

"Oh, let's not leap too far ahead."

The line went quiet. "Okay. You make whatever decisions work for you. I won't ever mention it again."

Mom guilt had arrived front and center. This woman was a pro. "Mom. I'll look into it, okay?"

"Thank you, my sweet girl. Come by for dinner on Thursday. I'm making chicken tinola." It sounded like an offer, but it wasn't. If Max didn't at least swing by and eat a couple of bites of that food while her mom tried to influence her life, and her dad checked out of the conversation via a football game, she'd hear about it for months.

"Yes, Thursday. See you then," she said quietly and clicked off line two. She sat back in her chair and shook her head. "Just another day in the life of Max Wyler," she said to no one.

"Told you not to take the call," Sonya said from out front. "Maybe listen to me once in a great while." The stress ball came flying back through the door just in time for Max to catch it at the last second. It was a metaphor. Her life lately had been anything but predictable. She picked up her book and went back to highlighting, planning to arrive prepared for the next meeting of the Weepers. Because Ella Baker certainly would.

~

BeLeaf Foods, two blocks from Rachel's place, was perhaps the swankiest grocery store Ella had ever set foot in. Had she realized how fancy it would be, she might have selected a store a little more … in line with her financial position. She strolled the aisles slowly, taking in towers of exotic vegetables without a single blemish. Prices advertised on wood-framed chalkboards. Warm lighting that made everything glow as if sanctioned by heaven itself. Yep, she was a little out of her food league right now. And what was one supposed to do when their bank account was slowly dwindling to nothing, but they still had to eat? Shop with a phone calculator in hand, that's what. Ella typed in the price of each item as she added it to her basket. She also winced as the number on the readout grew and grew, edging up to the maximum amount she'd allotted for the month. Ella stared at the price tag on the carton of grapes in her hands and balked. Nearly seven dollars? No, thank you. She sadly placed the package right back on the refrigerated shelf.

"Not the season for grapes?"

She turned to see Max leaning over the handle of her own cart. She wore a forest-green belted coat more suited for a runway than a grocery store and slid a strand of hair that had escaped her perfectly tousled ponytail behind her ear. Ella was now wildly aware of the rip in her jeans that had seemed casual and unaffected until this very moment. "The rip is intentional," she said, pointing to the exact spot on her knee.

Max glanced down, and the edge of her mouth pulled a touch, but she didn't give in to the smile. "Non sequitur."

Ella lifted a helpless and embarrassed shoulder. "How I roll."

"Is that a calculator? Very thorough shopping."

"I'm unemployed. I have to be." Her tone was flat, matching her afternoon.

Realization must have crept in. Max flicked a glance at the grapes and back to Ella. "What is it you do again?"

"I'm a graphic designer. Sometimes people forget to fire me."

"Not sure I follow," Max said, squinting.

Ella nodded. "And that is for the best." Why was she saying so much?

"Let me guess." Max placed an index finger on her cheek. "You design covers for romance novels."

Ella paused. "Very funny. No. I've done everything from corporate logos to print ads to social media campaigns, and most recently, app interfaces, which I can attest, are not the most inspiring."

"Well, that's a shame."

"But do you really think so?"

Max looked at her, lips parted in disbelief. "Why do you consistently question my intentions? I promise they're good. I just don't understand instant conviction. Don't I at least deserve a firsthand chance?"

Ella blinked, relenting. "It's not like I think you're *completely* awful."

Max straightened, one arm bracing against her cart. "Wow. Not helping."

"No, I didn't mean it like that." Ella pinched the bridge of her nose, fending off guilt. "I realize you're not a bad person. But I'm a loyal friend and I remember Rach crying on the phone over things you said or did and—"

Max held up a hand. In the flash of motion, Ella saw that her nails were done. Short and manicured with a mauve polish. They'd been a paler pink last week. "Like what? Just for learning purposes."

Ella snatched the first available memory. "Well, you left her at that birthday party with no way to get home."

Max frowned. She looked back and forth as if piecing together the meaning. "*Christine's* birthday? Is that what you're talking about? I did leave, but only because Rachel announced to the room that I wasn't paying enough attention to her because I greeted a former client. She then informed me she never wanted to see me again."

"I don't think that's—"

Max continued calmly. "She literally told me to leave in front of everyone, which was one of the more embarrassing moments of my life." Max frowned and shook her head, a new thought hitting. "And she drove us there. I was the one who had to call for a ride."

Ella paused, not sure what to do with that information. Rachel *was* prone to hyperbole. They stared at each other. "I heard it differently."

"I can tell," Max said quietly with a lacing of disappointment. "And that's okay. I'll let you shop."

"All right," Ella said, her brain foraging for understanding. It was clear that the details she'd just imparted had hurt Max's feelings, and when she balanced that with the sad version of Rachel, she wasn't sure which one deserved her sympathy. Feeling out of her depth with Max and depressed about her meager bank account, Ella finished her shopping and made her way to the front of the store.

One of the three cashiers with open lines waved her over immediately. "A woman left these here for you."

"Me?"

The young cashier nodded and handed her a bag. "Oh. Well, thank you," Ella said, accepting in confusion. She peeked inside and paused at the sight: a large carton of plump green grapes. She tried to swallow against the uncomfortable guilt. Max didn't owe her anything. Yet, even amid their uncomfortable conversation, she'd offered an olive branch.

"She bought me grapes," she murmured. What the hell was she supposed to do with that?

Ella paid for her remaining groceries with a shaky hand and an uncomfortable lump in her throat. She was thrown and floundering in more ways than one. She didn't have a grip on her place in this world or even her professional trajectory, but maybe the picture she'd constructed of Max wasn't entirely accurate. No one was all bad, right? She held the carton of grapes to her chest, humbly realizing that maybe she didn't have anything figured out. Anything at all.

SEVEN

The Pact

———————————

Something important was happening at Doug's Books. Ella peered through her windshield at the line that drifted from inside the shop, out the door, and down the sidewalk. She'd stopped by to pick up copies of the book club's next two selections and drop off a newly designed flyer for her services. Doug had made it clear that the corkboard was a free-for-all. She'd illustrated the page and brought it to life on her tablet, opting for a bookish and fun aesthetic rather than a corporate and symmetrical one. Maybe she'd tap into her creative juices a bit more and search out avenues that could ignite her passion for art once again. Even just making the flyer had made her feel more like herself than she had in, well, years. Corporate work paid the bills, but what if there was a way to do that with work she actually loved?

She excused her way around the line, made up of mostly women, until she found enough space to make her way up to the front desk.

"Got your books," Doug said over the top of his readers and reached beneath the counter, producing the two brightly colored romance novels with the cute little couples on the front.

"Thanks. What's going on today?"

"Alexandra Raymond is here for a signing. My sister, Polly, knows her mom, Ruth Anne, so I managed to secure a date on her schedule. Like getting tickets to the Eras tour."

"Oh, wow, Doug." She swiveled to him, hand on hip. "You're up on your pop culture."

"The Swifties are big readers. I have to know my clients. Plus, *Midnights* is an intellectually advanced album."

"You continue to surprise me, D-Man."

"Well, don't get a big head about it," he said with a sour look on his face. "And I don't like that nickname, either." The whole exchange was so very Doug that she gave herself a celebratory squeeze, as a throng of happy women snuck by her clutching books. She surveyed the buzzing scene, impressed at how many people they'd managed to squeeze into the store, including two women in business suits who seemed to be in charge of the line and the signing rules. Of course, the secret service of the publishing world. Ella was intrigued and a little jealous of the people in line.

"Maybe I should grab a book and have it signed." Honestly, her newfound love of romance novels had been her lifeline lately. Whenever her own life had her stressed, she picked up one of the book club selections and let herself drift into the land of happy people kissing. Doug reached behind the counter and produced a copy of the book on the poster. "A scientist and a barista fall in love. At least, that's what I'm told."

"Not a romance reader, Doug?"

"I read what I want to read." He waved her off, his grumpy cheeks colored pink. After he'd rung her up, Ella, once again, scooted past the impressive line to the community corkboard and tacked up her flyer.

"I love the colors you used here."

Ella turned to see a put-together woman peering over her shoulder at the flyer.

"Thank you. I'm a graphic designer looking to pick up a little work," she said, remembering to market herself. "If you have any projects, let me know. Tell all your friends." She offered a laugh to let the woman know she was half joking.

"Do you have a card? I'm always looking for new cover artists."

"Oh," Ella said, her ears perking up.

"And it looks like you illustrate," she said, taking in the details.

"I do. Yes. Let me just ..." She reached into her bag and shuffled through its chaos until she located her business card case. "Here we go." She handed the woman her card. "That's me. Ella Baker and all my info. I welcome commissioned work and have a portfolio online."

"Any cover work I can take a look at?"

"Um, book covers?" She'd never designed one of those in her life. "If you give me a few days, I'll get some samples up on the site." Ella's adrenaline was already firing. "So, do you work for Ms. Raymond?" Ella turned to the massive line.

"I am her. Alexandra. So, I guess you could say I work for myself. Nice to meet you," she grinned and consulted the card, "Ella. I'll check out your work and have my assistant reach out if it seems like we might be a good match."

"That would be wonderful. Yes. Please do."

"Have a nice afternoon."

"Have a nice signing." Ella watched in mystification as Alexandra took her spot in the signing chair and grinned at the woman clutching three of her novels like precious children.

And while it would have been nice to have her book signed, Ella couldn't imagine losing an hour in line when all she wanted to do in this world was seize the fire that had been lit beneath her and get to work on some sample covers.

"Gotta go," she called to Doug as she dashed off, waving

goodbye to him with her books. "I'll be in next week to talk about your social media."

"I don't have any," he called back.

"Exactly!"

When Ella arrived back at Rachel's place, she sat down in front of her laptop and didn't move for three hours, only giving in at that point for the restroom. By midnight that night, she had drafts for four different covers of varying themes, all romance. After a few hours of sleep, she went right back to work on them, in a groove and committed to perfecting each design.

Within the week, she'd had very little sleep, meals on the fly, but she'd done it. The drafts were now complete. She had four pre-made covers, a business concept, and a basic website ready to go. She could continue to enhance her aesthetic and commit to branding as she moved forward, but for now, she was on her feet and taking life by the throat. *Fire me, and I'll just build my own graphic design empire.* Pretty sure no one will forget about me then, she thought with a smile.

It had been a whirlwind, but Ella knew she was onto something here. Everything just felt *right* about this venture. Plus, all signs were pointing her in this very specific direction. Doug's Books. The book club. The encounter at Doug's Books. And the way she felt satisfied and fulfilled in this whole new way. She was onto something pretty cool and allowed herself the grace to acknowledge and celebrate that. Cover Crush Studios was born. She added the pre-made cover designs to her webpage, hit publish, and sat back in the desk chair Rachel had insisted she steal. "I barely ever work when I'm at home," she'd said, wheeling the white leather chair into Ella's room. "You're the one who goes hard on her iPad lately."

It had felt nice to be supported. "Well, I will certainly put it to good use." She sat in it and grinned at how ridiculously comfortable it was. "I'm now a graphic design princess. You're a gem, Rach."

Rachel tossed a strand of her hair and said, "You noticed," before heading for the door. "Now turn out some amazing covers. The public demands it."

"All right, all right, demanding public. Calm down." But the cheerleading only bolstered her, and she dove in with a grin.

So, the plan was, Ella would work up a social media campaign once she'd had a chance to rest and maybe eat a giant bowl of spaghetti and meatballs while watching *Sleepless in Seattle* because, apparently, she was a romantic now. Good for business, too.

AFTER A LATE CLIENT session at the office that had her brain swirling like a blender, Max pulled into Stevie's driveway for Read It and Weep later than she usually preferred. The sun was already down, and the temperatures were firmly on the side of frigid. She stood next to her car and pulled in a deep inhale, the cold burning her lungs and waking her up.

All the usual suspects were inside, judging by the car lineup. Ella's red Mini Countryman was second in the driveway. She paused to stare at it, giving herself a pep talk before going inside. It was best that she give Ella her space. After what she'd learned at the grocery store, it was likely Max's entire character had been handed to Ella on an unreliable platter. She could spend her life correcting it all, or move forward, focusing on the friends who actually liked her. Life was too short, after all.

Max let herself in to the sounds of laughter from the living room, and Ariana regaling the group with details of her latest setup. Just as she expected, she'd missed a good portion of the gossip that always seemed to happen before they got into the book talk.

"What have I missed?" she asked as she entered the room.

Morgan hopped in her seat like a kid with the answer. "Instead of a goodnight kiss, Ari's date asked her if she liked feet photos."

"Stop." Max laughed and stole a glance at Ella in her customary chair to the left of Max's empty one. "And what did you say?"

"I politely declined her offer to send some nude toe pics my way. I think she was hoping I'd offer the same." She met Max's gaze solemnly. "I'm afraid I let her down."

"Only you, Ari."

"I once had a guy massage my scalp in his car after dinner," Ella said. "We'd known each other for under two hours."

Stevie leaned forward. "Now, that doesn't sound half bad. There's a lot I'd do for a scalp massage." She added a bark of laughter, which made Max smile. "Ella, you seem sweet enough to attract some weirdos."

Ella scrunched one eye closed. "Is that code for pushover?"

"She's hardly that," Max said gently, taking a seat.

"Thank you," Ella said back quietly.

"Rough day at the office, M?" Olive asked with sympathetic eyes. "You look a little stressed."

"Not a single person offered to massage my scalp." She relaxed into a smile, attempting to let the day fall off of her. "Sorry," she said quietly to Ella, who nodded once.

"Speaking of not being a pushover, I have a bit of a career announcement to make," Ella said. She held up a hand. "It's minor, but I think I want to launch a new business and start designing these." She turned this week's cover around and pulled a nervous face.

"Ella, that's perfect," Ariana said with a wide grin. "You're gonna be the coolest member of the Weepers. You're legit going to be part of the romance industry."

"I want an autographed copy of your first book design," Morgan said, hand to heart.

"It's a great idea," Max said. "You have such a good handle on these books that I'm sure you'll come up with some amazing covers."

"Real talk." Ella hooked a thumb her way. "This is all very new, and Max was partly responsible for planting the first seed."

She sat taller and grinned, surprised to hear she'd been a part of this process. That's what attention from Ella Baker did —left you grinning like crazy. "I definitely can't take credit. I asked a question at a grocery store." But the kernel of having been a part of the process lodged, and her face felt hot.

"Well, it landed. Then I got to meet Alexandra Raymond at Doug's when she saw the flyer I'd designed and asked, guess what? If I did covers." She looked over at Max, incredulous. "The back-to-back mentions felt like a sign." She shook her head, grinning, looking adorable and excited. "I guess I've been really stressed about my career, and now that I have a project, even if it's small, I can breathe a little better." Max had zero right, but she wanted to remember the way Ella looked in this moment. Passionate Ella was a favorite. Excited was up there now, too. She was less of a fan of the judgmental slash angry version, but at the same time, Ella was never cruel. Her one regret was that Ella couldn't see her for who she truly was.

"I love when we do group updates. Stevie, what about you?" Ariana asked. "How's your journey into the lady pond going?"

"Ah, hell. It's just easier if I stay in my house and host my friends who talk about books." She reached for a celery stick, looking more vulnerable than Max had ever seen her.

"You take your time," Olive said, nudging her.

"Or don't and rip the fear off like a Band-Aid," Ariana said with a shrug. "There's always Sally Sue's."

Morgan sat upright like a child whose parents had just dangled Disneyland. "I'm with Ari. Sally Sue's would be fun." Her eyes went even wider. "Hey, we could all go."

Stevie raised an intrigued brow. "So, I'd just walk around and offer to buy some woman a drink." She covered her eyes. "I don't think I could ever do that. Wait. Maybe I could do that."

"You certainly could do that." Ella leaned in and regarded the group. "Is this a gay bar?"

"Exactly that," Morgan said. "Halfway between here and the city. It's part jungle cruise, part country and western. Sal couldn't decide on theming. There's line dancing and safari imagery." A lightbulb went off. "That's right. Everyone, Ella's new! We have to introduce her to Sally Sue's." She swiveled, excitement flying off her like sparks. "And Stevie, you can just tag along and get your bearings. Dip your toe into the sexy woman scene and maybe even flirt a little."

Max smiled, impressed by the expert manner in which Morgan had just taken the pressure off Stevie by making this about Ella. Knowing her big heart, the low-pressure delivery had been intentional. "A group event it is, in Ella's honor."

"Now, I need a new outfit," Ella said. "I don't have western wear or safari clothes. Except, I'm on a spending restriction until I sell some book covers, so you're stuck with the wardrobe I own."

Max shook her head sadly. "I don't know that we can take you with us under those conditions."

Ella sucked in air in offense.

"Ignore her. You're coming," Ariana said. "You, too," she told Stevie.

"Oh, fuck a duck," Stevie said. "I'll work on getting myself primed."

It became apparent an hour later that tonight's book club

chat would take a back seat to the group's own personal catch-up session. This brand of detour tended to happen every six weeks or so. There was something to be said for spending a couple of hours decompressing together. Max enjoyed those nights every bit as much as their more focused meetings. That's what made the book club so awesome—the group friendship and the bond that only seemed to grow the more time they spent together.

She was already on the way to her car, feeling so much lighter than when she'd arrived, when the sound of her name caught her attention.

"Max!" Ella yelled a second time and came bounding down the slightly sloped driveway. "Wait a sec."

The cold wind hit her face, making her shrug further into her coat. "What's up?"

"Gah!" She laughed as she approached. "Why in hell is it this cold? It's barely October."

"You're not in Tulsa anymore." She offered a slight smile.

"Never have I been more sure." She exhaled and relaxed her own grin. "I just wanted to thank you privately."

Max turned her face to the side and regarded Ella, whose own coat was thin at best. It made her want to take off her own and hand it over. "Thank me? For what? You need a bigger coat."

"I was just thinking that. I'll put it on the 'someday when I'm employed' list. For the grapes. You didn't have to do that, ya know."

She shrugged, trying to downplay. "You looked like someone who would give them a good home. Grapes deserve the best." Vulnerability wasn't in her comfort zone, and she'd do anything to wiggle away from it.

"Also, I owe you an apology." Why were Ella's blue eyes so luminous at night?

"Oh, I like that." Max straightened, waiting to hear what was next.

"I thought you might." Ella studied the treetops as Morgan and Ariana headed to their cars parked along the curb.

"It's too cold for any human! Also, don't look so serious over there," Ariana called.

"We're talking about foot photos, so we have to," Max called back.

"I will murder you in your sleep," Ariana returned.

"I will wait for you all night."

Max took a moment to enjoy the exchange and waited until they could recapture their privacy. Once the others were tucked away in their cars, she turned back to Ella, whose eyes once again made Max's bones go to liquid. She wasn't sure she would ever get used to their effect. She also wasn't sure she wanted to.

"Back to what I was saying. I probably rushed to judgment when I realized who you were."

Max nodded. "I get it. You were expressing your loyalty to Rachel. That meant slamming the door in my face on anything between us."

"That's a brutal piece of imagery."

"Just being honest."

"She's my *best* friend," Ella emphasized. "I didn't have much choice. But I can see now that maybe some of the things I was told were slanted, influenced by the hurt Rachel was combing through at the time."

Max crossed her arms. "I think that's entirely accurate."

"Doesn't mean I can kiss you again."

She felt her lips pull to the side. "No? Because we were pretty good at it."

"Likely award-winning, but it's probably best we not talk about it anymore."

"You're the one who brought it up."

"Stop pointing out the obvious."

Max could do this all damn day. There were people in this

world who threw sparks when they were within feet of each other, and not just through physical chemistry. The two of them had a give-and-take that made more than her body wake the hell up. Ella made her mind come alive. She made Max wonder if romance in all of its pageantry might be real after all. Because who else could make her feel so many little and big things at once? "How do you do that?"

"What?"

"Make every one of my emotions feel huge."

"Oh." She went quiet. "I do that?"

"Yes." She shoved a hand through her hair. "It's more than a little maddening."

"I'll stop."

Max opened her mouth and closed it, spotting Olive as she scooted by. "Hot date tonight, Olive?" Max asked.

"Yep." She slid into her car and slammed the door without another word, prompting them to exchange a curious look.

"I can't tell if she's serious," Ella said.

"That's Olive for you. She's either headed to a quiet house to climb under a quilt or on her way to a rave in Paris. It's one or the other."

Ella stepped closer as if sharing a secret. "So …"

"Yes?"

"I've seen her texting someone during book club, and she gets this saucy little smile on her face." She shrugged. "Maybe it's the kinds of stories we're discussing, but I feel like she has someone."

Max widened her eyes. "I've gotten that impression, too. I thought it was just me."

Ella laughed. "We're wholly onto something."

"Yeah?" The delicacy of the subject matter left them standing very close to each other. For a long moment, neither of them said anything, but their eye contact never wavered.

"Yeah," Ella said, finally watching Max like her world

depended on it. "You know, it's a shame we only kissed that one time."

"I completely agree." Without giving herself space to think, to change her mind, Max placed her palm on Ella's cheek, gratified when she pressed back. The world slowed down before finally disappearing altogether. The warmth of Ella's skin sent a tremor through Max, a quiet rebellion against every reason she shouldn't be doing this.

Ella's breath hitched, barely a sound, but Max felt it all over, felt the way Ella leaned into the touch like she was starved for it. Like they both were. Yes, it was reckless and self-ish, but for just this moment, the world outside didn't exist. Ella's eyes fluttered shut, just for a second, before she turned her face into Max's palm, pressing a kiss there, featherlight. It was a promise they couldn't keep. When Ella finally pulled away, the absence was unbearable.

"It's later than I thought." Ella closed her eyes, took a deep breath, and straightened.

"Yeah. I suppose it is." The spell was broken. The air felt different, no longer shimmering with that rare feeling of magic. Max shouldered the loss immediately, but joined Ella in the land of the logical. She had to face it. There was a giant obstacle between them, and no way around it. The code said you didn't fall for your best friend's ex, and that's precisely who Max was. In fact, she admired Ella for her decency. There wasn't enough of it in this world. "I probably shouldn't do things like that."

"And I probably shouldn't like it. Pact to stop?" Ella held out her pinkie finger. Max leaned back on her heels, trying to smile. The results were questionable because this wasn't a pact she wanted to enter into in the slightest. "Pact to stop or pact to stop liking it?" She met Ella's gaze. The moonlight high-lighted the slate blue of her eyes. "I don't think anyone's offered me their pinkie since the fourth grade."

"Then it's about time I'm here. You're welcome." Her smile lost wattage. "And it's a pact for *both*."

"I can agree to a pact to stop touching. There's no way I can erase the like part."

"Oh," Ella said, her lips holding the shape of the word for an extra moment. "Then maybe we'll just focus on," she shrugged, "becoming friends. Learning how to do a better job of that."

"That's a step up from coexisting."

"It is. I'm figuring this out as I go. I apologize."

"Accepted. And how will Rachel feel about us forging a friendship?"

"She already knows we're in the book club together. She's a mature adult."

"Most of the time," Max said and added a smile to soften the blow. Rachel wasn't an awful person, but she did strive to make the world tilt in her favor, sometimes at the expense of others. After a while, Max had to accept that about her and admit they were not meant for each other. She wondered about Rachel and Ella's dynamic because Ella emanated generosity and thoughtfulness. She imagined Rachel would step all over that if given the opportunity. But then maybe Ella brought out another side of Rachel. People weren't all one thing. She'd seen that in her work over and over again. "I don't mean to come down on Rachel."

"Then don't. She's the reason I'm still standing." That defensive spark was back. Ella seemed to recognize it and relax. "So, here's the thing. You two have your differences. I get that. But she was there for me when I lost my job, when even my parents blew me off. When my fiancée walked away, Rachel picked me back up again."

"I'm sorry those things happened. She seems to have been a good friend to you." Max had a lot of questions and chose to hold her tongue. The knowledge that Ella had been engaged and broken up with was surprising new information that snagged her focus.

"Yeah," Ella said quietly. Her gaze held Max's, wistful and laced with regret. It was the natural time to end the conversation, for Ella to say goodnight. Tell Max she'd see her next week. Yet, she hadn't moved.

Max did, though. She took a step into Ella's space, and for what felt like a minute, but also five hundred years, they breathed in the same air. "I'm going to do us a favor and get in my car and drive away before I do something I want to but shouldn't."

She took four steps before the sound of Ella's voice stopped her. "Max?"

"Yeah?" She said, turning back and offering a small smile.

Ella wrapped her arms around herself and shifted her weight. "Nothing."

Max drove home, wondering what Ella was about to say, hating that their moments together only existed within the narrow confines of what they were allowed to say or do. They were two grown people who seemed to want the same thing, and yet, they were sidelined. She allowed herself to drift back to that one night, not too long ago, where they'd shared a moment free of any external constraint. She turned up the song on the radio and let the music drown out the rest of the world so she could remember the feeling of Ella's lips pressed to hers, the sound of her laugh, and the tucked-away hope she'd carried with her in the days after. It had been so nice while it had lasted. She sat at the red light and closed her eyes. So very nice.

EIGHT

Cordially Yours

"So, there's something I wanted to talk to you about."
Why was Ella's heartbeat so prominent, banging on her chest like a door-to-door salesperson? Get outta here, heartbeat. It had no business in this conversation because she had zero reason to be nervous. She wasn't even digging her nails into her palms. *Stop that.* This was Rachel of all people. And all she had to do was put the cards on the table.

"Talk away. Everything all right?" Rachel, newly home from work, slid out of her shiny, gray pumps, which matched her belt perfectly. They must have been a matched set. She then pulled out the hairband and a variety of pins that had been holding her hair in the fancy swirly updo. She was de-Rachelfying. In the time they'd lived together, she'd come to know that the second Rachel walked in the door, she set about stripping herself out of work mode. The transition would start before Ella could count to ten.

"Everything is fine. But I've seen Max a couple of times. At book club."

"Of course." She winced. "Sorry about that."

"Once at the grocery store."

"Random. Did you at least say hi?"

"I did. She bought me grapes."

"What? That's so weird." Rachel tossed a final pin onto the swirly white granite countertop and gave her red hair a shake, forcing it to drop like a waterfall onto her shoulders. Rachel had always had beautiful waterfall hair. "Why in the world would she do that?"

"I think she saw that I was worried about my budget, and was shooting for a peace offering."

"Typical." She rolled her shoulders as if ordering her body to relax. "Don't fall for it."

"Right. No. I won't. But what I want is to, at least, try and keep things cordial between us, and I wanted to be up-front with you about that." She met Rachel's green eyes and waited.

"Right. Cordial, of course, which is different than friendly. I'm just looking out for you when I say that Max is …"

"What?" Ella asked, honestly wanting to hear Rachel's thoughts.

"Trouble. And I happen to be very protective of you. I think there's nothing wrong with cordial."

She watched as Rachel breezed past her, effectively ending the conversation with a fragrance-filled exit. Yet, there Ella still stood in the kitchen, wearing her Wonder Woman socks and trying to decode the tiny differences between friendly and cordial, and what kind of interaction was crossing a Rachel-drawn line in the sand. Why did everything have to be so hard?

As if on a rescue mission, Ella's phone began to scream from her pants. "Why couldn't something else cause screaming in my pants?" she murmured, checking her phone's readout. A smiling photo of her parents grinned at her, signaling their call from her mom's phone.

"Hey, you two," she said, accepting the FaceTime invite. "Where are we today? Is it Brussels?" Her parents, looking back at her, resembled near carbon copies of the ones in the photo, only these two were holding up fancy chocolates.

"Hi, sweetheart," her mother said. "We're stuffing our faces full of chocolates and saying cheers to you and your new adventure in Virginia."

"Ha. Kind of you, but you might hold off until we see if I sink or swim."

Her father shook his head. "You'd never sink. You have your mom's street smarts. Speaking of, she knows this place so well, she's already offering directions to lost tourists."

"Impressive. Hey, are we still on for next month?" After losing her job, they'd talked about a meetup when they got to London. Ella had always wanted to see Buckingham Palace, and with her parents already there, it seemed like the perfect time. Plus, she hadn't seen them in what seemed like forever.

Her mom frowned. "About that. We were talking, and our schedule is going to be jam-packed on the days we're there. Plus, Tom and Susan and Bill and Margaret will be with us."

Her father frowned, too. "We're so sad, but I'm thinking it's not going to be the best time."

"Oh," Ella said, her heart squeezing uncomfortably. "That's totally okay," she said, brightening. "I was only going to come if it was convenient."

"You are the most considerate," her mom said, hand to her heart. "I raised the sweetest girl. Oh! And we want to send you a little something, so text me Rachel's address."

"Unless you're so ahead of the game that you'll have a place soon," her dad said.

Ella closed her eyes, a part of her deflating because there was no way. "Not quite there, yet, Dad, but I do have some irons in the fire, as you used to say."

"I love it." He glanced behind them and yelled. "We'll be right over. Don't toast yet. James, I'm warning you." Laughter ensued. Ella tried to smile along, but hers felt wobbly at best.

"We'd better run," her mom said. As an afterthought, she dropped her shoulders. "I'm so sad London didn't work out."

"Me, too," Ella said. Her hand was shaking. That was

weird. She used her free one to steady her wrist so they wouldn't notice. "Maybe we can pick another date. Some other city." Her dad was already gone. He'd run off after their friends had jovially shouted something in the background.

"That is the best idea. Let's both brainstorm. Send me that address. I love you to the stars."

"I love you, too. Don't eat too much chocolate."

"Can you imagine? Bye!" And then she was gone, leaving Ella in the kitchen, still shakily holding the phone in front of her.

"Everything okay?" Rachel asked quietly. She'd slipped back into the kitchen at some point, work clothes now gone.

Ella turned to her, her eyes filling. "Yeah. For sure."

"No, it's not," Rachel said quietly.

Ella shook her head, a crumpled mess. "It's stupid. I don't know why I'm getting all—"

Rachel's arms were instantly around her, holding on tight. "It doesn't matter why, but I've got you."

Her throat ached, and her tears spilled hot and plentiful, making her every bit as embarrassed as she was sad. Her parents didn't want to see her. In fact, the idea of her joining them for even a few days seemed like an awful inconvenience. She didn't understand what it was about her that made her such an afterthought. Why was she so very inconsequential to the people she invested in?

Rachel guided her to the couch and plopped down next to her. "Sometimes a girl has to cry, right?"

Ella nodded, her voice not quite available yet. Rachel didn't seem to mind and even took the lead, chattering away, which allowed Ella the space to breathe and compose herself.

"I remember the last time I cried at work. It was two weeks ago when I'd been pushing myself so hard and working too many hours that my coping skills were drilled down to nubs. I knocked over my Venti half-caf oat milk caramel macchiato before I'd even gotten a second sip. The whole thing just gone. I wailed, channeling my inner three-year-old."

Ella wiped her cheeks as she listened, a small smile forming like a flame flickering to life in the dark. "That's awful," she mumbled, imagining the tantrum.

"I wanted to throw things at the wall. I would have if I didn't share it with Ben the Backstabber."

That's right. She'd heard of Backstabbing Ben. He wore the tightest pants in the East and heated salmon in the microwave. "You should have done it anyway. The salmon infraction alone would exonerate you."

"Damn right I should have," Rachel said, handing Ella a tissue from a box on the end table. "Now, what's made you cry tonight?"

Ella sighed, ready to speak on it. She appreciated Rachel giving her the space to find her way there. "I was supposed to visit my parents in London in a few weeks."

"I remember. You were shopping for that plaid raincoat. I still vote for the blue and red."

"Well, they don't think my coming is the best idea." She shrugged, embarrassed for even her best friend to hear that.

Rachel closed her eyes and shook her head. "Your parents can be selfish assholes."

Ella's brows flew to her forehead, and she laughed. "Tell me how you really feel."

"It's harsh," Rachel said, waving a hand. "But I'm going to level with you. They've always been self-involved, and I can say that because I'm self-involved, too. We can spot our kind in the wild."

"That's impressive, I guess. I've been feeling like a loser lately, and just when I started to get my footing with this new business, bam. Right back to Loser Central."

"Ella Baker, look me in the eyes." Reluctantly, she did. "You're not a loser. You're the most awesome person I know. The one human whom I can depend on, and laugh with, and simply chill next to for hours on end. No one makes me feel as comfortable or like myself as you."

Those words were in such need at that moment. "Thank you," she said quietly. Her silly little emotions welled up again.

Rachel slapped her knee. "And you can stand on your head and sing the alphabet backwards. I don't think I've ever seen that duplicated."

"I appreciate you acknowledging that," she mumbled.

"Now go put on leggings or sweatpants. Ditch your bra. We are going to eat so much popcorn on that couch and watch whatever the hell you want while we bash Ben."

That perked her the hell up. "What am I gonna do if I ever meet this guy? Will he know all the shit I've talked about him?"

"No. He's the most oblivious crumb of a person. He thinks he invented cool socks. Like the ones with the loud, colorful designs that people have been wearing for the last eight years. Credits himself."

"Dammit, Ben. You did not invent loud socks."

Rachel waited in front of the microwave while the bag inside rose up like a sleeping giant stirring awake. There would be buttery goodness soon, and she could wallow properly. The microwave beeped, and as Rachel dutifully assembled their feast, Ella threw herself onto her back and checked her email. It had become an obsessive habit since the faithful day she was laid off. She blinked at the top of her inbox and sat right back up.

"I think I just sold a cover. One of the first four pre-mades I listed on the website."

"What?" Rachel asked, swiveling. "How do people already know about you? Did you not just design that website a minute ago?"

"I ran a cheap little Instagram ad targeting romance authors. It cost exactly nine dollars and look!" She turned her phone around in victory. "It sold me a cover, and I didn't list them for cheap. Do you know how many groceries I can buy now? This is amazing." She stood on the couch and began walking its length back and forth like a wrestler who'd just trounced an opponent.

"I like the new, triumphant you." Rachel put a hand on her hip. "Things turn around fast in this house."

She dropped down onto her ass with a happy bounce. "I need to make more covers since it looks like this idea might just take off."

Rachel held out the bowl. "Do you want popcorn first or …"

"Oh, the popcorn is required fortification before I can create."

As they watched loud game shows from twenty years ago while wearing pajama pants and worn-out T-shirts, Ella let her mind drift. She looked forward to telling the Weepers about her sale, and specifically imagined Max's face softening to a grin, a sight to behold. She touched her cheeks, half realizing that they were warm.

"What is going on in that head of yours?" Rachel asked.

"Me?" She sat up straight, moving herself guiltily right out of the daydream. "I was just fantasizing about my new little job and all the ways I can spend the lavish sums of money I'm going to rake in."

"You can buy your own grapes now," Rachel said, rolling her eyes.

"Right. Thank God."

Rachel shook her head, ponytail swishing in judgment. "I still can't believe she did that. How desperate for attention do you have to be?"

"Yeah. It wasn't necessary." Inside, alarm bells sounded. She looked over at Rachel, the one person who had never let her down. She thought of Max and the grapes and the kernel of hope she'd been sheltering. She couldn't hold onto both. How was she supposed to stay away from Max when all she wanted to do was not stay away from Max? At the same time, she absolutely refused to throw her friend under the bus.

"Hummus!" Rachel yelled, startling Ella right out of her crisis of conscience. "Hummus!"

"What?"

"It's the answer to the question," she said, popping an M&M and gesturing to the TV with her chin. She'd forgotten all about the supermarket game show they'd been watching.

"I do love hummus," she said, attempting to rejoin the here and now.

"I have some in the fridge." Rachel hopped up, squeezing Ella's shoulder as she passed. She paused, fridge door open. "You know, I'm not the sentimental type, but I'm really happy you decided to move to Everly Springs."

She smiled up at Rachel, and everything in her inflated. She had to remember something hugely important. She wasn't alone or overlooked, not in this household. Gratitude stuck with her for the rest of the night, and she let her hang-ups with her family, her preoccupation with Maxine Wyler, and her own self-esteem issues float away in favor of a little much-needed friend time. It was salve to a wound.

"Hey, Rach." She squeezed her friend's ankle across the couch. "You've saved me in so many ways this year. I'm not sure how to go about repaying you."

Rachel relaxed into a warm grin. She dropped her cheek against the couch cushion and met Ella's gaze with purpose. "Nothing to repay me for at all. This is what friends do for each other."

Rachel was absolutely right. Friendship wasn't just text messages and inside jokes—it was about showing up. And Ella knew, without a doubt, she'd do the same for Rachel in a heartbeat. "Hey. I love you."

Rachel beamed. "I love you back."

NINE

Ride or Die (But Mostly Ride)

A slight shift in the vibrancy of the purple. Ella bit her lip and surveyed her work. *Better.* A couple of subtle lines to add detail to the woman's chestnut hair as it swished to the side, mid-swing. *Yes.* That most certainly worked. And finally, a pull back on the opacity of the ice rink in the background. There. Right *there.*

Ella sat back with a happy sigh, more than pleased with the cover illustration. Her shoulder blades ached, and her head held nothing but fuzz. Didn't matter. Her heart was ready to burst and run down the street in victory. She had just put the finishing touches on her very first commissioned cover, *No Pucks Given.* Who knew hockey romance was so hugely popular? She certainly hadn't, but had fallen down a rabbit hole and quickly educated herself. She'd been hugely happy slash shocked to accept the job from an indie romance author whose cover artist had left her high and dry on the cusp of her release date. The author at hand, Holly Sprockets (which couldn't have been her real name), had fallen in love with the rough draft version depicting a woman placing a hockey stick across a uniformed player's chest while she leaned into his space, determination in her eyes. Had she drawn the guy extra hot just for Holly? Most definitely. But she liked that she'd given the power on the cover to the female character.

"Headed your way, Sprockets," she murmured as she attached the file and uploaded it to their shared drive for Holly's approval, two hours before she'd promised to have it delivered. "Tell all your hockey writing friends." Once Holly signed off and had a chance to post a cover reveal, Ella would toss it up on her new Instagram page, which she'd noticed was growing steadily already. If she pulled in enough of these commissions, she might be able to sneak by without another job. Freelancing for herself would be the best thing that had ever happened to her. The cherry on top of the sundae was how much she loved the work, reveling in the creation process and celebrating her contribution to telling a brand-new story. She gave her shoulders a celebratory shimmy-shake just as her phone leapt to life and joined her. *Ariana*. "Dance, Ari. Dance," she said, continuing their duet with a bit of hip action.

She slid onto the call with a grin. "I just finished my first commissioned book cover, and you and I just danced."

"Because you're a badass. We should dance more." And pause. "How are you so quick to start taking over the romance world? You literally just walked in the door."

"Well, I'm not new to design. It was simply a matter of understanding how the work differs on a cover. Binging the books sure helped." She fell back onto her bed like a teenager and regretted it when her body screamed back like a woman in her thirties. "And I'm getting old."

"You're a toddler at best. So, here's the thing I'm calling about, you badass creative child, you."

Ella got serious. She sat up and rested her elbows on her knees. "Tell me."

"Remember how we pitched the very gay bar Sally Sue's Western Safari?"

"That name puzzles me at night."

"By design, I'm sure. I think you'll love it there. Everyone does once you're over the warring themes."

"That's a valid pitch." She'd been looking forward to checking it out.

"Well, find your boots. It's on. Can you be ready in an hour?"

"Tonight? It's happening now?"

"You just finished the cover, so the answer must be yes."

"Really, though? Must it?"

"I think Stevie could use a night out," she said in a less playful tone. This was down-to-business Ari. She was learning the difference. "She's guilt-ridden about the divorce and ruining Dominic's life. And now she's just staring at these shattered pieces of the past. I think she needs a taste of what's ahead to help her through."

"Okay, okay. So, we show her a good time." Ella's eyes darted around the room. She had three shirts on the bed, two on the floor, and one on the lampshade—beautiful, organized chaos. "Let me just get my bearings here. Fashion is important, but a struggle."

"Listen to me, you're gonna nail it. Want to ride with Max and me to the bar? She drives her black luxury car while I check my nails and secretly pretend like she's my chauffeur. It's the best kind of game."

Ella went still, lampshade-shirt frozen in her grip for examination. She didn't exactly want to drive thirty minutes on her own in the dark to a place she'd never been, but hopping in hot Max's Range Rover might not be the best idea, given her pledge to Rachel about cordiality. But hold the phone. With Ariana as a chaperone, they would have no choice but to keep their distance. That felt pretty cordial. Plus, she could let Ariana carry the conversation. "You know what? I'd love a ride. Sign me up."

"Done. Pick you up at nine."

Her brain screamed. "Nine? Did you just say nine? I'm in my thirties."

"Ella, you're going to be just fine."

"How old are you?"

"Twenty-eight."

"That's why. When you cross the thirty threshold, it's like a light switch. You can't hang with the late nights anymore. You physically feel the betrayal in your bones. It's like my joints just heard 'nine' and filed a formal complaint."

"Tell them we'll get back to them. And when the clock strikes midnight, maybe Max will hold onto your shoe for you."

She winced because it meant Ariana had picked up on the often sexy vibe that pinged between her and Max. She decided to dodge the insinuation. "Good thing I'm a night owl."

"Good thing, Buttercup. See you soon. I won't ask for directions because I'm confident Max knows how to get to the house."

"Very funny, Ari."

She headed to the small closet in the guest room and found her cute red top, which she paired with her brown booties, the closest thing she had to actual western boots. They'd have to do. Since Rachel was with coworkers for the night, she helped herself to her curling wand and added a few loose curls, anything to elevate her look beyond just sitting in front of a tablet all day. She surveyed herself in the mirror, adjusted a few strands, deciding that she'd done her best.

When 9:07 rolled around, there was Max's black Range Rover in the driveway. She headed into the cold night, approached the car, and paused because where in the world was Ariana, the pretend passenger who'd hired the car?

"Hey," Max said as Ella opened the door to the passenger side. She gestured to the center console. "I grabbed you a coffee for the ride. Just wagered a guess on what you might like."

"Thanks," Ella said, distracted. She slid into the passenger seat and glanced behind her like a cop looking for clues at a crime scene. "I thought Ariana was riding with us."

"That's true. She was. But then something happened with her aunt and a prescription at the pharmacy. She may or may not make it later."

"Oh." Chappell Roan played from the speakers as Ella sorted through her jagged thoughts. "So, just us."

Max studied her and hesitated. She was a people reader. Hell, it's what she did for a living. Ella was probably shooting off worried flares like a stressed-out rocket. "Is that okay? You can be honest. If you're uncomfortable, we don't have to ride together. Ari just told me you were expecting me, so I came."

"No," Ella said after a beat, not wanting to make this any more complicated or weird. "We're grown-ups capable of riding in a car. Right?"

"My thinking exactly. I tell myself to be a grown-up at least twice a day."

"Oh, no. And it still hasn't worked." After a brief pause for effect, Ella smiled triumphantly at Max, already feeling lighter. Why was it that when they were in the same space, all the issues between them felt conquerable? She should lean into that tonight. Keep things fun. And just like that, all the stress she'd been carrying around about how to handle the Max/Rachel debacle just lifted right off her chest.

"You've been in this car for less than three minutes and completely flamed me. Impressive."

"It's my job in life to keep you humble."

"You keep me a lot of things."

She pulled in air, allowed the comment to dissolve and settle, unsure what words to send back.

Max looked over at her as they approached a red light. "Too much?"

"No. I'm okay."

It wasn't the answer Max was expecting, and she seemed pleased. "Good. How was your week so far?" There was elegance in the way she asked even the most mundane of questions.

"I'll tell you, Max Wyler, it's been a series of ups and downs."

"Fair enough. Tell me a down."

It was a low-pressure command, and it sent a shiver winding through her body. Who'd ever heard of a winding shiver? "Okay, well, my parents broke up with me for the season."

"I'm sorry? I'm trying to translate. They broke up with you?"

She recounted the story to Max and sighed. "They mean well, but they have a whole big exciting life, and I'm usually not at the forefront of it."

"I see." She paused at a red light, which afforded her a moment to look at Ella fully. "This may not help, but after years of dealing with people and their interpersonal strife, I can tell you that it was likely more about them than about you."

Ella nodded, but it was hard to believe entirely. She decided to move them away from the subject matter that still made her chest ache. "Are you close with your parents?"

"Well, we talk every day, but close is not a word I'd use." The light changed, and they drove on. "Today, my mom asked me if I'd given any thought to a more dignified hairstyle. That's a pretty standard example of daily conversations."

Ella balked and didn't hide it. She couldn't. "Your hair is *gorgeous*. People pay tons of money to try and achieve what you have through genetics alone."

"Ella, I had no idea you felt this way." She shook her head in disbelief. "Wow. You're really into my hair."

Ella laughed. "Yeah, yeah. Enjoy your moment."

"I'm relishing every second. Do you see me over here?" The funny thing was that Max's version of relishing was still very much in control and polished. Everything about her was. Ella was getting good at reading the nuance, though. That slight smile that played on her lips. The small sparkle in those brown eyes. She also sat a little taller.

Ella laughed, enjoying their back-and-forth. "I do see you. But you'd better calm the hell down. Don't want you to crash the car with all that relishing." She watched Max drive for a beat longer, appreciating her profile, the way she focused on the road like she owned the damn thing. She tried to imagine Max being bad at something, and couldn't quite conjure the image.

"Weren't you supposed to keep me humble?"

Ella shrugged. "A blip. They happen. I'll get back to making your life hard in a minute. What's your mom's problem with your luscious locks?"

"That's not an awful nickname. Maybe we should keep it."

"No."

"She thinks I wear it down too often to be taken seriously, except, of course, when she wants me to woo a man and make him my lifelong mate. Then I'm free to toss at will."

If Ella had been drinking something, she would have spit it out all over the expensive windshield. "Woo a man? Woo a *man*?!" She hadn't meant to scream that last part. "Does she know you?"

"Ella. I think you just called me super gay."

"I did. I mean, you're like the most *lesbian* lesbian. It's not the way you look, it's the energy." She leaned in. "She must see that. You would be in Honors Gay if this were school."

"Oh, you've said some nice things to me before, but that one wins." She flashed Ella a wide-eyed glance and went back to the road. "And I *was* in all honors classes, by the way."

"Well, of course you were. I was not. Too busy doodling." She looked around. They seemed to be off the beaten path.

The familiar sights of Everly Springs were nowhere to be seen. Fewer streetlights and fewer cars. She had a feeling they were close to the bar. Or was it a club?

"You're an impressive bisexual, too," Max said. "I didn't mean to not return the compliment."

"Thank you for thinking of me and my fluidity."

Max lifted a shoulder. "Anytime, Ella. What's your middle name?"

"I'm not telling you."

"Fine."

When they arrived at Sally Sue's, Ella took in the scene because it wasn't at all as she had imagined it. The one-story building, all by itself down a dusty, dark road, didn't feel a part of the city at all. The parking lot around the back was a literal field, and the people heading inside and spilling out the entrance had all dressed the part.

"Now that's a lot of flannel," she said, rethinking her outfit. She came around the front of the car to wait for Max.

"Isn't it?" Max took off her coat, dropped it onto the front seat of the car, and gave the door a slam. Ella went still at the sight. *Whoa.* The sounds of The Chicks drifted into the parking lot, her underscore to the visual of Max fucking Wyler looking *like that* in jeans, black cowboy boots, and a red-and-black checkered shirt that made her the sexiest woman she'd ever seen. Since when was she into cowgirls? Since fucking now. With her hair down and her shirt unbuttoned to a generous neckline, Max looked like the October page of a sexy calendar, and honestly? She wasn't even showing that much skin. "What? Ella, you're staring."

"You didn't warn me."

"About what?"

"That you were ..." She had to reframe that thought because the sentence, "You were going to look so ridiculously hot tonight," wouldn't do. "Were, uh, going full Western."

"I had no idea you had opinions, or I would have."

"Well, I do!" she shouted without meaning to. The emotion had just burst straight out of her. A woman passing by turned abruptly at the sound of her voice. "Sorry," she told the woman in a much quieter voice.

"No, honey, you get it out."

"Right. I will. Thank you."

When she turned back, Max was watching her with an arched brow that only increased the reading on the sexy meter because now she looked like she was up to something.

"We should just go inside and find the others," Ella managed in a voice that, for some reason, sounded strangled.

"Whatever you want," Max said. "Right this way."

Ella made a point of hurrying so she could catch up to Max and walk toward the entrance side by side. No reason to check out her ass in those jeans. None of this was helping her turn over a new leaf.

"Why are you sighing?" Max asked.

Had she sighed? "Oh, it's the air quality. It seems poorer than usual. Climate change is such a bitch!" She'd added an extra shot of passion to her delivery, hoping to sell it. She was pretty sure that had been a mistake.

Max stared at her knowingly for an extended moment as they waited for the people in front of them to funnel through the double doors. "I had no idea you were a champion of the cause."

She nodded along. "Not too many people do."

"Twenty-dollar cover," the woman at the door said in a sultry voice. She wore a cowboy hat, jeans, and a textured, pink tube top. She also had binoculars around her neck, which is when Ella remembered the split theme. The bartenders behind them were dressed in safari shirts. Her friends hadn't been lying about the strange mash-up. The barstools were faux zebra print, but cowboy hats lined the back wall.

"Wow. This is … something."

The woman leaned in. "Never been to The Wild Frontier?

That's what we all call it. Only gay bar out this way, so we make a meal out of it."

"Never. My first time," Ella said.

Automatically, the woman pulled a free drink ticket in the shape of a boot and handed it over. "This'll get you started."

"Thank you." She already liked it here.

"There's a mechanical bull in the back room," Max said in her ear, likely because the music was so loud, she'd never hear her otherwise. Regardless, it caused Ella's stomach to tighten and her cheeks to flame hot at Max's proximity. She smelled like a raspberry popsicle. "I do love a good ride."

Oh, those words. Ella braced against the heat that now pulsed between her legs. She tried for cavalier anyway. This was all just fun and games, right? "It's like you keep trying to one-up yourself."

"I like a challenge." She met Ella's eyes and extended her hand for the woman to stamp it with what looked to be a dancing banana. Oh, this was going to be an interesting night. Ella followed Max inside and scanned the room, which featured a sizable dance floor filled with line-dancing women. *Oh, my.*

"Feel at home?" Max asked.

"Yeah, I dance like that in my living room nightly. I slay on area rugs."

Max waited her out.

"Okay. I've never tried line dancing in my life. I'm an abysmal dancer who should steer clear of rhythmic move-ment. I can own it." The amused look on Max's face had her playing back the sentence and closing her eyes at the implica-tion. Mortification was her new best friend, clinging to her like shrink-wrap.

"You're here!" Morgan said, throwing an arm around each of them from behind. "I just knew we'd find a way to make tonight happen. Stevie's over there looking gorgeous and terrified."

Ella and Max exchanged a nod of solidarity and followed Morgan to Stevie, who stood in the corner in her jeans and button-down white shirt. She looked downright lesbian tonight, and it made Ella's heart squeeze for her and the apparent effort she'd gone to. She desperately wanted Stevie to have a good night, or at the very least, not a bad one.

"Hi. So, I'm here," Stevie said, her blue eyes wide as if it was all a lot to take in. "It's not bad. A little loud and busy, but I'm good. Real good."

Max pulled her in for a squeeze. "See? Not as scary as you thought. And we'll be with you the whole time. You look great." She really did. These women were going to go nuts for Stevie.

"I don't mean to interrupt, but I would love to buy you a drink," a woman said, leaning into their conversation, her hand curved onto Max's shoulder from behind. Her nails were painted purple and her boobs were about an inch from coming out to play. She was staring at Max like she was lunch. Ella prickled and went still.

"You're sweet, but I think I'm gonna work up to it," Max said.

The woman shrugged. "Sounds good. I'll be around if you change your mind. You're gorgeous, by the way."

Once she was gone, Ella stood taller and took an involuntary step closer to Max, who, of course, noticed, because she was ridiculously obvious. What in the hell was she doing? *Back off.* Somehow, she didn't. Couldn't.

"Drink?" Max asked. Morgan and Stevie were waving at Olive, who had pulled out all the stops tonight. She looked inarguably sexy in a red dress, her dark brown hair flowing freely. She'd also left her glasses at home and didn't at all resemble the librarian Ella had come to know at book club. *Well, well.*

"Definitely will need a drink," she told Max. "Something refreshing but strong. Is that a thing?"

"It can be. Be right back," Max said as the group took turns complimenting Olive's nighttime look.

"I like to raise the volume on nights out," Olive told them, but the quiet voice in which she'd said it was a sweet juxta-position.

When Max returned a short time later, she had a rhythm to her step that matched the country song twanging away on the sound system. "This is called a Savannah Mule," Max said, presenting the fizzy-looking drink. Ella happily accepted the beverage and closed her eyes at the crispy ginger beer, vodka, and … "Is this some kind of citrus?"

"I believe the term melon was used."

"God bless melon," Ella said, taking another pull from the cute green straw. She decided she very much liked Sally Sue's.

Max watched the dance floor and halfway joined the line dance in progress.

"You're dying to get out there, aren't you?" Ella asked.

"What gave me away?" She turned in place at the same time as the group on the dance floor and then grapevined to the right along with them. This time, Ella did allow herself to check out Max's ass, which did not for one second disappoint.

"What is happening right now?" Ella asked.

"Come out there with me."

"That would be an epic mistake."

"Take another drink then."

She did. She was four swallows in and feeling a little looser. Maybe she could throw inhibition out the window and dance a little. There were worse things people could witness like that boobs-to-chin woman hitting on Max. She'd also been checking out Max's ass while she danced, which only bolstered Ella's determination to stay close.

"Ready now?"

"Fine, Max. I will shuffle around the dance floor. Happy?"

Max took her hand and gave her arm a tug. "Beyond."

Uh-oh. The song changed as they landed on the dance

floor. She quirked her head to the ceiling, listening. "Is this the 'Boot Scootin' Boogie'? My parents used to play this while they cooked chicken-fried chicken."

"You're going to have to educate me on what that is after this song. Ready?"

She didn't have time to answer because the dancers were moving toward her as one, and she had no option but to move with them if she didn't want to be flattened. "Oh, okay. We're going this way. And now we're turning. Sorry!" She told the woman with the braids and black cowboy hat. "I'm new."

"Follow me," Max said, executing the next turn around like a damn pro. How was she so calm? "Oh, it's faster here. Get ready."

But Ella wasn't ready, and to save her, Max took her hand and gave her a pull in the right direction, keeping her from ruining the spacing for the whole row of dancers headed their way.

"This is terrifying!" Ella shouted, but she was also laughing, the four swallows of alcohol having settled in and spread. Max gave her a quick twirl and let go of her hand, a real shame.

"You're killing it," Max said. "We're headed left. Lead with your left foot."

By the time the song wound down, Ella was out of breath, laughing more than she had in months, and convinced she was the least coordinated human in ten miles. What she'd also noticed? Max touched her with a quiet confidence she found unendingly attractive.

"You held your own," Max said, as they walked back to their friends. Ariana now stood next to Morgan, her arms crossed in front of her as they approached.

"You made it," Ella said, arms out, still riding the adrenaline from the terrifying impromptu dance routine.

"Just in time to witness that dose of foreplay," Ariana said in her ear as they hugged.

"Obvious?" She asked, still holding on.

"Probably just to me."

"Good," Ella said like the best kind of ventriloquist, releasing Ariana and remembering to keep her smile in full bloom. "Whatever happened to my drink?" she asked.

Stevie, who was now grinning happily, handed her the drink from the ledge along the wall. "I'm on my second," she proclaimed. "Catch me." She then did a little hip-shaking dance as she drank. Four women turned to watch. Yep, Stevie was going to do just fine.

Ella, who wasn't someone who consumed more than one or two at a time, raised her glass. It was Stevie's night, dammit. "Challenge accepted."

The only problem was that Stevie had a much higher tolerance. An hour later, Ella held drink number three and sipped from it passively, realizing her sobriety was slipping through her fingers like sand through the hourglass.

"You okay?" Max asked, sliding a strand of dark hair behind her ear. What Ella wouldn't give to run her fingers through it as she climbed on top.

"I'm actually having a really great time."

"*Actually* sounds like a qualifier. *Actually* means you didn't expect to."

"You are such a lawyer, aren't you?" Ella said around her straw.

"You've got to stop looking like that," she said with a playful grin and drifted away again. Max, she was finding, never lingered too long. She was approached by another woman, who seemed to be gesturing to the dance floor, and, aha, asking her to dance. Max shook her head, seeming to decline the invite, which made warmth gather in the center of Ella's chest.

"I had a great conversation with a woman."

Ella turned to find Stevie staring at her with wide eyes.

"That's great. Is this someone you'd like to talk to again?"

Stevie nodded. "If I sent over a drink, would that be, you know, cool?"

"It'd be very cool. You might even drop it off yourself, and see if there are any buying signs. If so, stick around for another chat."

Stevie continued to nod. It seemed to be her crutch. "I'm going to do that. The others are great, but I think you get me, Ella." She squeezed Ella's hand, offered a here-we-go wince, took a hearty swallow of her margarita for fortification, and headed to the bar.

"Well done," Max said, watching after Stevie. "I think you've been appointed coach."

"How long have you been standing there?"

"I caught the tail end. She trusts you."

"Good." There were so many things she wanted to say to Max. She wanted to tell her about all the feelings she had gathering and settling. And how her brain wanted to know everything about Max. How her body wanted to press into her and put an end to this torturous dance once and for all. And in this moment, she couldn't seem to cling to the very important reason *why she shouldn't* any longer.

"What? What are you thinking?"

She met Max's eyes and went up on her toes, her mouth close to Max's ear. "I want to know you. Is that wild? I just do."

When she went back down onto her heels, Max's smile faded into what can only be described as sincerity. "I want you to know me, too," she said back. The moment felt so simple, so easy, and so ridiculously clear. Why didn't she enjoy three drinks more often? In fact, she planned to, because the stressors that hung on her like a lead vest were now gone. She liked Max. Max liked her. They also happened to possess an intangible electricity that made her feel more alive than anything ever had. That didn't seem like something to be discounted.

"This is a good song. Let's go." Max grabbed her hand

and tugged. Before she knew it, Ella was on her way back to the dance floor, where her reputation as an uncoordinated sheep surely preceded her. Only this time, she did move a little bit easier. She'd loosened up, which was helpful. Also helpful was Max's hand on the small of her back when she didn't move fast enough to the left.

Which Ella made sure happened a whole hell of a lot.

TEN

Line? What Line?

They were laughing a lot more this time around on the dance floor. Max hadn't had this much fun with someone in a long time.

"Turn! Turn, Wyler!" Ella howled, scurrying along with the crowd as if they were a mob chasing her to the right. "Oh, and forward we go. Keep up," she shouted. "Hurry!"

Max easily did as she was shouted at, enjoying Ella's newfound dance floor confidence. "Watch out," she said, taking Ella's hand and dragging her along three steps backward.

"How are you predicting all this?" Ella shrieked. "These people are so coordinated." The group turned in unison, and Max did, too. Ella joined them two beats later, seeming pleased with herself.

"Probably because this is the fifth time we've repeated this section."

Ella placed her hands on her hips and dipped them, this time perfectly. "Don't be a know-it-all."

They grapevined to the right. "But have you considered that I might actually know all of it?"

"No. There is no room for that in my brain."

"Then I suppose I have to keep proving myself."

"Oh, Counselor, you do."

"Say it again," she said with a wink because she liked the sound of the nickname on Ella's lips. In fact, she liked her lips in general. She remembered how they tasted the night they'd kissed—sweet like wine and chocolate. Tonight, dancing with strangers in a darkened room, music too loud, touches more than a little free, Max couldn't rationalize not kissing those lips again. How would they taste tonight?

"That was a much better dance," Ella said, as they stepped off the dance floor. The part in her hair had flipped halfway through the song—correction, Ella had flipped it in a move that pulled Max's entire focus, leaving it wild-looking and unkempt. "I'm getting good."

"You only slammed into me seven times this go round. I didn't even count the eighth and ninth because I'm benevolent and kind."

Ella's jaw dropped in offense. "Either way, that's an improvement, Max. Give me my credit."

"That's what I was doing." When she'd said it, she'd stepped into Ella's space near the stretch of wall they'd claimed a safe distance from the rest of the world. It probably had looked like she'd moved closer to hear Ella better, but the truth was quite different. She craved proximity to the woman she felt drawn to like a magnet and took it. She must have been wearing that citrus and vanilla lotion combination that Max would always associate with this moment. The sweet scent made her want to bury her face against Ella's neck.

Ella must have been able to tell because the amusement slid right off her face. They locked eyes and held, activating that superpower they had to erase the rest of the world. Max wasn't even sure the music was playing anymore. Were the walls still standing around them? She didn't care. Lost in the unravelling, she couldn't stop if she wanted to. Her defenses had been hammered away, and she was no longer able to stop herself from leaning down and taking what she wanted, what she needed. When her lips pressed to Ella's, the world, flat and lifeless, sparked into three-dimensional color. Ella went up on her toes, her hands moved to cradle Max's face. It wasn't a soft kiss in the slightest, but came with the brand of urgency that said they were making up for a lifetime of not doing exactly this. And, sweet fucking heaven, they really should have been. Max was gently pressed to the wall as she sank further into the kiss that deserved its own damn plaque. Caught between living in the moment and emblazoning every single detail of kissing Ella into her memory in case they didn't have this opportunity again, Max went with the latter. First was the taste of vodka and something sweeter on Ella's lips. The soft, uneven hitch in her breath when Max traced the shape of her mouth with her tongue. The way Ella's hands, tentative at first, slid to Max's waist, fingers curling into the fabric of her shirt like she was afraid to let go. And the way Ella kissed her, like she was both terrified and desperate. She knew they were stealing some-thing that wasn't theirs to keep, but couldn't help taking it anyway.

When Ella finally pulled back, the absence was immediate, sharp. Max kept her eyes closed a second longer, holding onto the ghost of Ella's lips, the press of her body, the impossible heat between them. Because if this was the only time, she needed to remember *everything*.

"Uh-oh," Ella whispered, her eyes still on Max's mouth.

"We weren't supposed to do that," Max said. "Now what?" She'd done this. She'd taken the liberty, initiated that kiss, and crossed them over the line of—

Ella's mouth caught hers again in a lip-lock that said none of this was in the past tense. If they'd crossed a line, they were apparently living on this side of it for now. As her mouth moved perfectly with Ella's, the rest of her body lit up with the desire she'd shoved to the side for far too long, now demanding to be recognized.

"This is too good," she murmured against Ella's mouth, angling and going in for more. The problem was her hands. They wanted to slip under the hem of Ella's blouse, touch her heated skin, run down her body, slide through her hair. Yet, they were in a public place, which meant combustion was not an option. And if left unchecked, that's exactly what they would do.

"So much better than dancing," Ella murmured back. She stole another kiss, the kind where their lips clung for an extra moment, reveling in connection. "And I tried so hard not to do this. But there's only so much a person is capable of. Also, I'm largely innocent. This is your fault." Another kiss. This one quick.

"All mine? How come?" Max asked, after pulling back and taking a breath.

"Looking like this. Talking like that. Quirking sideways smiles."

Max arched a brow. "I wasn't expecting a whole list."

"There's a dissertation."

She blinked and let the meaning settle. Ella thought about her a lot. The deeply satisfying understanding settled and spread out. "What do we do now?" Max asked because the world felt different; they did.

"I have no idea." They stared at each other with the firm understanding that this was going to be too hard to put back in the box. The box would surely catch on fire if they tried. "Can we just figure it out as we go?"

That wasn't easy to answer for someone like Max, who dealt in logic, plans, and strategies on a daily basis. Shooting from the hip was not her strong suit. She had backup plans for her backup plans, and many of them were organized in spreadsheet form. "Figure it out," she repeated. "Sure. We could try that."

They eyed each other, and Max felt the intense pull. What she wanted more than anything was to step right back into

Ella's arms and pick up where they'd left off. She wanted to explore Ella's body, trace her curves, and make her call out in pleasure beneath Max's touch.

"Maybe we should find the others," Ella said, the look on her face mirroring Max's warring desires. At least now she knew unequivocally that they were on the same ridiculously turned-on page. Commiseration helped. "I'm still shaking," she confessed.

And then Max saw the slight tremor, struck and more than a little honored to know that she'd been the cause. "I'm all over the place, too."

"Yeah?" Ella asked, her lips tugging into a relieved smile.

"Yeah. I guess we'll know pretty quickly what they saw," Max said and pushed off the wall. "Those women don't have impressive poker faces." She led the way through the bar that felt exponentially more crowded than when they'd arrived. She turned to the side to dodge a group of women waving their drinks around freely as they walked. "You're hot," one of them said.

"Thank you," she said and reached behind her for Ella's hand, afraid she'd lose her in the chaos. Their hands linked, and Max felt that connection click into place. With Ella's hand in hers, something important anchored within her. She felt confident, steadier, as if a missing piece of herself had returned. She took note, realizing the significance and refusing to discard the moment as a fun night at a club.

"That happens to you a lot, doesn't it?"

"What? Almost getting drinks sloshed on me? Not as often as you'd think."

"Try women hitting on you," Ella called above the music.

She reflected. Women approached her a fair amount. "Here and there. Isn't that standard?"

"No. What I've witnessed tonight is definitely above average. You're a chick magnet, Max. So, what are you even doing with me?" She sounded like she was only half joking.

Max paused, not liking the framing. She turned around, stopping them right there in the middle of the bustling walkway to the dance floor. "You're by far the most beautiful woman here," she said in Ella's ear. Determination drove her. "And that's not even a question." Ella went still and she studied Max's face, perhaps searching for hints of sincerity. The idea that Ella might have a shred of skepticism about that was ludicrous, and Max wanted to do everything within her power to correct her awareness.

Morgan beamed as she approached. "Did the dance floor swallow you up?"

Nope. She hadn't seen a thing. Max brightened. "This one had to be dragged off. She's getting really good at stepping on feet."

She felt an elbow to her ribs. "Hey. Back up. I've improved noticeably," Ella said in emphatic defense of her dancing skills. The bonus was the playful stare she shot Max that made her want to tease her more.

"Well, the tea is that Stevie is giddy, talking to all sorts of women. She's made friends with groups of them at the bar."

"As we knew she would," Max said.

Ella nodded happily. "Good for her."

"The downside is she's a little overserved, and we should get her out of here sooner rather than later. She told the bartender that spiders should live in tiny apartments."

"It's not the worst idea," Ella said. "What about her car?"

"That's the thing," Morgan said. "It's a whole shuffle. Stevie can't drive, and we might have to leave her car and—"

"We can take her," Ella said without a shred of hesitation. "And I can bring her back tomorrow to pick up her car. I don't mind." She shrugged, stepping out of the way of a muscular woman in a green cowboy hat, who tipped it to Max. Ella sent her a see-what-I-mean stare before turning back to Morgan. "I'm the one without a nine-to-five."

"If you two don't mind, that would be great."

"This is the best place I've ever visited," Stevie shouted and danced in a circle, rejoining the group. "The way people dance this way and then that way is my favorite. Like a movie just for me." She offered a demonstration, hooking her thumbs through her belt loops.

"Glad you had a good time," Max said, placing an arm around her shoulders. "We'll drive you home since you've had a couple." *Or eight.* Stevie had clearly imbibed away her anxieties. Luckily, Max's two drinks had long fled her system with all the dancing. And kissing.

"You are the nicest," Stevie gushed. "And we've never talked about it, but you are a hot cookie." She touched Max's arm. "OW! Dammit. You got me." That was followed by Stevie's extra throaty laugh. Across the friend group, Ariana's face came into focus. She folded her arms and regarded Max with a knowing smirk. *Well, fuck.* When Max met her gaze, Ariana raised an eyebrow in a challenge that said *just what are you up to?*

Max sent back a wide-eyed stare that said *calm down, I'll tell you later,* which seemed to appease Ariana. At least, temporarily.

"Shall we get Stevie home before she takes that woman's hat again?" Ella asked, interrupting their silent exchange.

Max followed her gaze to Stevie, who was returning a backwards baseball cap to its frowning owner. "Oh, don't pout. You look cuter in it than I do," Stevie called and then danced what could only be described as an Irish jig.

"Yeah, I'd say it's time to go."

Once they'd said goodbye to Ariana, Morgan, and Olive, they ushered a very chatty Stevie to the car. "Lesbians in that bar are way nicer than I ever would have expected. There was the woman who knew about all the different types of beer. The one who was too pretty to be believed. I really liked the one who gave me her number."

"Wait," Ella said, turning around in the car. "You got a number? Stevie!"

"I did. She put it right in my phone. Is that good? These seats are so comfortable, Max. I might sleep here tonight."

"No need," Max said. "I know exactly where your bed is. Tell us about the woman you met."

"She seemed like she was around my age. I liked her eyes. Goodnight."

Ella swung around to Max, beaming, hand on her heart. "She met someone."

"Is that the naive romantic in you lighting up all over?" Max winked.

"Yes, as a matter of fact, it is, Maxine. Is your cold, logic-driven heart even in there anymore?" She made a show of craning her neck to find out.

Max pretended to be fixated on the road. "Stevie's story might have made it grow a size or two."

"I'm so impressed with you right now," Ella said in what sounded like her most earnest delivery. "Having actual feelings."

"I can't tell if you two are flirting," Stevie's voice said, floating in from the back seat. "If so, I say go for it. Whole hog it, Max. Life is too short. Ella is a catch."

"Thank you, Stevie," Ella said. "We're a complicated mess, though."

"I'm going back to sleep now."

"You do that." Max grinned as they pulled into Stevie's driveway. "I agree, by the way."

"You agree that I'm a catch or that we're a complicated mess?" Ella asked. Her makeup had faded, and she stole Max's breath in a whole new way.

"Yes," Max said, and slid the car into park. She turned around to see Stevie in her cowboy boots, full-on snoring in the back. "Hey, Stevie. Guess what? We're home."

"Hallelujah. So done for. I haven't moved this much since 1998. I'm dying to get naked and get into bed."

Ella's eyebrows shot to the ceiling, and she turned to Max. "Well, well."

"We'll get you as far as your bedroom," Max said, regarding Stevie in the rearview. "But we'll leave the naked portion to you."

"You're good people and kind girls. I can't believe you did all of this for me. Family," she said. "That's what it feels like."

"Well, that's what we are," Max said.

She and Ella shared a private smile before exiting the car. The moon was brighter than it had any right to be, making the cool, crisp night a beautiful one. Stevie, moving a little slower than Max was used to, ambled from the car to the house as they followed, making sure she found her footing. Once they were inside, she waved to the two of them as they stood in her darkened living room. The digital clock on the end table read 1:03 in a bright-green glow. "You get out of here. You've done your job." She turned to head down the hall, paused, and grinned, immediately sending warmth through the room. "It was a really good night, wasn't it?"

"It was the best," Max said. "Proud of you, Stevie. You took a big step."

"And now you've been on your first super gay outing," Ella tossed in. "You're a pro now. And maybe someday when you're ready, you can message that number you scored."

"I just might. Sylvia. That was her name." Another smile. "Night, you two."

"Night," they each whispered back.

In the darkened room, Ella turned to her. "I honestly thought tonight would be me alone in my pajama bottoms and a Diet Coke with lime."

"That honestly doesn't sound terrible." A beat. "This was better."

"And enlightening. I think you're hot, but I had no idea

how forcefully the rest of the world agreed with me." She grinned and held up a conciliatory finger. "Well, maybe I did."

"I didn't notice," Max said without taking her eyes off of Ella. The comment made the smile fade right off her face.

"When you say things like that, all I want to do is kiss you." Her voice was quiet. She was trying not to disturb Stevie. But her words slid up Max's spine and inspired action.

She was close enough to Ella to reach out and catch her wrist. She pulled her in until they were pressed together. Ella's breath hitched, her hands finding Max's waist as if drawn there by instinct. For a moment, they hovered in the space between anticipation and certainty, the air charged with the weight of what was about to transpire.

Then Max closed the distance, her lips brushing Ella's in a kiss that was slow and deliberate, filled with the longing of things she felt but didn't say. Ella sighed against her mouth, melting into her, and Max felt it again—that deep, undeniable rightness. Like she'd been waiting for this, for her, all along.

Alone in the darkened living room, everything felt different. There were no eyes on them. The boundaries were limitless, other than the voice inside Max's head warning her quietly. She nudged it away. In the same room where they'd shared laughs, ideas, and even argued over the pages of a book, they could now kiss with abandon, disregarding time and space and the rest of the world. Heat licked its way from Max's ankles to her elbows to her shoulders to her breasts and beyond. She savored the warmth of Ella's mouth, kissing her deeper, exploring with her tongue, ever so slightly at first and then more purposefully. She pulled back from the kiss and, with one finger, traced the column of Ella's neck, listening to the quiet sound of her breathing. She kissed the underside of her jaw and met her gaze in the small patch of moonlight streaming in from the back window.

"Come back here," Ella murmured, guiding Max's lips to

hers for more. This time, Max's hands didn't obey her instructions, slipping beneath Ella's shirt to the warm skin of her back. She needed to feel just some portion of her right this moment. When she heard Ella murmur encouragement against Max's mouth, she wanted to touch more. She palmed Ella's breast through her shirt, completely turned on by the weight of it, her nipple pressing into her hand through the fabric. Sexiest fucking thing ever. Her center ached now, and she wasn't sure what to do about it. As they kissed, she cupped Ella's ass, satisfied yet hungry at the same time. Ella nodded, propelling her. Were they doing this? Could she actually take things further in Stevie's living room, of all places? "You're a bad influence," she murmured in Ella's ear. "But I can't seem to get enough of you."

"I blame you for all of this." Ella nipped her jaw, the sound of her accelerated breathing intensifying the urgency with which Max moved. She undid the button on Ella's pants and slowly slid the zipper down as they kissed. The forbidden nature of their surroundings somehow only intensified her drive. When Ella nodded again, she had all the confirmation she needed. She slid her hand down the front of Ella's pants into warmth, honored by how wet she was, and determined to make her see stars. Ella immediately moaned ever so quietly and covered her mouth, remembering Stevie in the next room. Max nodded and settled a hand behind Ella's back. She allowed her fingers to explore, moving through damp folds, relying on soft touches. Ella's facial features served as her silent guide. As Max began to stroke, they found their own hypnotic rhythm. Ella's hips began to rock, and her eyes closed. It was only a short time before her head fell back and her lips parted, their pace now quicker. Their eyes locked and held just as Ella's muscles went tight and still in Max's arms. Her lips rolled in, a shout of pleasure contained. The moonlight spilled over them like a secret, illuminating the raw, tender intimacy, a soft glow that seemed to seal their bond in that fragile, fleeting moment.

"You're beautiful when you come," Max said simply, holding Ella, watching her float back to herself. "I've never seen anything like it."

Ella exhaled, her hands shaking. "I've never done anything like that." She looked around. "At book club even."

Max laughed quietly in her ear. "This is so not book club."

"We're scandalous," she hissed, a smile on her face. "But that was a satisfying scandal." Another exhale and a head-shake. "Let me tell you."

"We need more time and privacy. And soon."

"What are we doing?" Ella said, going up on her toes and wrapping her arms around Max's neck. "I feel entirely out of control."

"In a bad way?"

She met Max's gaze, her blue eyes reflecting the moon-light. An angel on earth. She slowly shook her head, her hands sliding into Max's hair as she guided her mouth back down. She brushed Max's lips with hers once, twice, and then kissed her deeply.

"I should take you home," Max said when they came up for air. "Because if I don't, I'm not going to be able to control myself."

"Should I return the favor?" Ella whispered in her ear. "I want to. I want my hands all over you."

The words sent an intense wave of heat through Max's already overloaded system. She closed her eyes, taking a minute to absorb the sensations that moved through her, and opened them again. The two of them, simply put, combustible. More so than Max had even planned on. "If we start again, we won't stop. We both know it." Reluctantly, Max kissed the inside of Ella's wrist, returned Ella's hands to her sides, and took a step back. "See? I keep kissing you."

Ella laughed. "Then I guess we'd better get out of here." God, even her whisper was sexy.

"What are you doing to me?" Max murmured, watching Ella walk to the door, buttoning her jeans as she went. Their interactions tonight had been totally unexpected until she thought about the fact that they'd been navigating a crash course toward each other from the moment they'd first laid eyes on each other. She didn't know how this whole thing was going to play out, but there were land mines scattered all around them. They weren't a good idea. But Max knew one thing for sure—whatever sparked between them was as irresistible as it was dangerous. They could go up in flames just as easily from passion as from destruction, and, somehow, that only made the pull between them stronger. Plain and simple, Max Wyler, who knew exactly who she was and what she wanted, didn't know how to say no to this.

ELEVEN

Text Messages and Tagines

"You never told me about your night at Sally Sue's." Rachel sat in the middle of the living room, painting her toes a deep plum. She believed that biting her lower lip improved her accuracy, and, honestly, it probably did.

With that question, Ella was immediately transported back in time. It had been two days since the night out to Sally Sue's with the book club. Two days since Max had turned her world upside down with that sexy encounter in Stevie's living room.

And now Rachel was looking at her while she thought about kissing Max. Alarm bells blared, and her bowl of Oatmeal Hoopties went still in her grasp. "Right. The other night happened." A pause because hell, what should she say? "Yeah. It was great. I can't believe you haven't mentioned that place before. The whole scene is like something out of a dream ... or a very western acid trip."

"Thank you for getting that." Rachel looked up from her toe-painting. "It's a good time, yes. And a highly effective venue for picking up chicks, but I can't get past the gaudy theming that borders on aesthetically criminal, ya know? At least *try* for complementary colors."

"Maybe Sally Sue wasn't a design major in school."

Ella felt a little defensive about little Sally Sue's Western Safari. It now had a special place in her heart after the whirlwind night with Max and the Weepers. Had she thought of anything else since? Of course she hadn't. Max seemed to edge her way into every other topic like she owned all of Ella's thoughts.

"Maybe she should have been," Rachel said and went back to her toes. "Who was there?"

And here we go. "Oh. Just book club people. The same group as always. Remember I told you about Stevie, who came out after twenty-some years of marriage? Well, this was her informal debut on the scene."

"I love that for her." A pause. "But I take it you had to deal with Max."

"She was there," Ella said, placing her bowl in the dishwasher. "Do you work today?" It was later than usual for Rachel to be home, and the tidbit seemed like a great segue out of the dangerously loaded Max conversation.

"Yeah, but I've stayed late all week. I'm taking a leisurely morning. I've earned it."

"Nice! I think I'm gonna invest some time in social media today. See if I can drum up some more business for Cover Crush."

"I'm so impressed with you, Ella. You're dealt this blow, you move across the country, and you're already carving out not just a new social world, but also a whole new career trajectory." She took a moment to apply a quick coat of lip gloss. "We could all take a page from your book."

The vote of confidence and the way Rachel framed her past few months really did make Ella feel like she'd accomplished something important. Her life was by no means a success just yet, but she was on her way, and someone else had noticed, too. "I think you just made my morning. Thank you. Sincerely."

"You're welcome. Now, can you make mine by hitting

brew on a cup of coffee for me while I change into my work ensemble?"

"You got it, Rach," Ella said like a woman on a mission and grabbed for one of Rachel's expensive sage travel mugs. She had exactly four and kept them lined up in the cupboard, like soldiers ready for a department store skirmish.

It was in that exact moment that a text came in. She checked the readout. *Max.* She leaned against the counter, unable to suppress her smile. She'd wondered if she'd hear from Max this morning, and here she was.

> I hope your morning is a good one. BTW, I'm sitting at my desk thinking about you whether I should be or not.

Well, that did it. Ella read the words a second time, her heart rate already climbing as she remembered Max's mouth on hers. The way her gaze had searched Ella's face in the moonlight. Her stroking gently between Ella's legs. *God help her.* She'd never been this sexually invested in someone she'd never even gotten naked with. She waited as the Keurig sputtered and hissed, its warm-up routine now sounding decidedly sexy in its own right. What was happening to her? The pent-up energy had her sexualizing kitchen appliances. Fantastic.

"What's going on over there?" Rachel asked, dancing on one foot as she slid the other into a light-blue pump that perfectly matched her dress. She looked soft yet sophisticated. "You seem somewhere far away and awesome. How do I get there?"

"Me?" Ella stood ramrod straight, a first grader caught with a handful of stolen cookies in her mouth. She placed her phone on the counter. "Oh. Just thinking about the weather forecast because it's supposed to be about five degrees warmer today and that just, uh, fucking rocks. I'm ready."

"I'll take warmer weather," Rachel said, and breezed past Ella just as her phone buzzed again. Rachel picked it up, given that she was closest. "Message for you. Well, this is certainly interesting."

Ella's blood turned to ice. Dammit. Why had she set her phone down? "Oh yeah?" She braced.

Rachel flipped around and showed Ella her screen. "Your brother wants to know why your mom always insists on French restaurants."

Every muscle in her body went slack with relief. "That's Mom for you. A big fan of all things butter."

"God, I can get behind that. Gotta run. Love you," she said and placed a smacking kiss on Ella's cheek. "See you after work if it doesn't kill me first. We have corporate visiting, so everything has to be perfect down to mannequin feet."

"It will be," Ella said, still celebrating the bullet dodging from moments ago. "And I never thought about the fact that mannequins even have feet."

Rachel quirked her head. "Ella. How in the world do you think they stand up?"

"Rachel. I've never bothered with mannequin magic. I just assumed there was some sort of stand or something."

"Well, they have feet, and those feet must be styled. That's where I come in."

"Well, make the mannequin feet pop, okay? Montclair's depends on it."

"Now you understand my life. Bye. Make good choices."

Rachel had meant that last part as a joke, but the sentiment zinged Ella all the same. Because she wasn't sure she was doing that at all. She also wasn't sure she had any control over those choices when it came to Max. The two of them were careening toward each other like two stars caught in each other's gravity, drawn closer with every passing moment. She wasn't sure there was anything she could do to intervene, but it was getting to the point where she wasn't sure she wanted to. So, where did that leave her with Rachel? This was a situation she was going to have to deal with sooner rather than later, or face the flammable repercussions. She grabbed her phone, biting her bottom lip as she typed.

> I was thinking about you, too.

She would sort it all out in time. She would.

MAX FIDGETED with the cuffs of her dress shirt as she entered the restaurant her mother had selected for their lunch. She was six minutes late, despite leaving a ten-minute window in case of traffic. There'd also been an emergency call from Sonya that one of her clients desperately needed to move up their next session because her soon-to-be ex was making all kinds of uncharacteristic threats that involved the destruction of property.

She'd pinched the bridge of her nose, realizing she was going to be late now, acutely aware of their noon reservation and her mother's penchant for timeliness. She'd had the lesson drilled into her head from an early age and had paid the heavy price for receiving a tardy on her attendance record in high school exactly twice before she never made the mistake again.

"What should I do with them?" Sonya asked on speaker.

Max raised her gaze, letting her hand drop. "See if you can squeeze them in on Friday. If it doesn't seem like a settlement is imminent, I will have both parties schedule a hearing before Judge Wheeler. There's only so much I can do."

"I think you're going to get him back to the bargaining table. Give him No-Nonsense-Max."

"She's definitely next. He's trying to run right over the reasonable version."

"His poor wife."

"My thoughts exactly. How do these people end up in

these marriages?" It had been a lesson she'd learned time and time again. Love only lasted so long before you sat across the table from your significant other, trying to figure out who got custody of the forks. But then she thought of Ella and something in her shifted. Ella made her wonder. She challenged Max's sense of what might be possible and threw her preconceived notions about the long term out the window. After the debacle that was her and Rachel, she was pretty sure her exclusive entanglement days were over. But for Ella, she might be willing to step out onto a limb again. The *what-if* dangled and tempted.

She'd finished up the call with Sonya and took a moment to gather herself in the waiting area of the restaurant, which meant fidgeting, something she only did when in her mother's presence.

"There you are," she'd said dismissively when the host deposited her at the table.

She kissed her mother's incredibly soft cheek and took in the familiar scent of her jasmine perfume, a gift her father presented her dutifully every Christmas.

"I am so sorry I'm late. I had a client who needed a last-minute scheduling miracle, but Sonya and I managed to work it out. Did you have a chance to look over the menu?"

"I already know the menu. Don't you?" The Moroccan-inspired café was a favorite of her mother's.

"Yes, actually, I do." She swallowed her defenses, knowing they'd be no good to her here.

"Next time, I'd like it very much if you valued my time as much as you do your own." She was still upset about Max's late arrival. That was likely to last another ten minutes. She'd suck it up.

"Again, I'm sorry about that." She moved them past it. "How have you been?"

"Busy. I've scaled back patient hours and want to spend more time on the research front."

She smiled. "I know you love to lose yourself in a good trial."

"We have three on the way, and I'm optimistic about the prospects of one in particular. I won't bore you with the specifics."

"You don't bore me. I'm interested in hearing about your work."

"I can't imagine you want to talk about skin cell regrowth over lunch. Tell me about divorce. Surely, there are some dramatic stories from this week."

"I do have one guy threatening to destroy property."

"Barbaric. So is divorce by the way." It was the same old tune. Not only was her mother unhappy about her journey into law, but she also hated her specialty. "Even if your father and I were at odds, we'd work it out. You don't just quit."

"That philosophy is not always practical or safe."

She shrugged and sipped her water with fresh lemon. "People abuse the option. That's my opinion. We'll take the bread service, please." She told the server. They paused to order the rest of their meal, and Max took a deep breath, preparing herself for the next hour of what would probably be small talk mixed with incremental judgment about various aspects of her life.

"I do have one piece of news," her mother said once they were alone. She pursed her lips, which was a tell that she was uncomfortable.

"All right."

"It seems that I'll be the patient. At least for a little while."

Max frowned. "You'll be the patient. I don't understand. Does that mean you're sick?" The idea was so foreign. She'd never known her mother to have so much as a bad cold. She was immune to everything.

"It seems the cancer doctor has cancer." She shook her head, a slight smile playing on her lips as she raised her glass for another sip.

"That's not funny. I can't tell if you're serious."

"I most certainly am. I was diagnosed with a rare form of liver cancer last month and will meet with my doctor quite soon."

"And you're just now telling me?" Max was as stunned as she'd ever been. "After a month?"

"Three weeks. I needed time to organize my life, my thoughts, and prepare for what's ahead. I've done that and here we are."

"Is it treatable?"

"Yes. The treatment plan is very sound, and I have every reason to believe my doctor's protocol will go according to plan and we'll put this behind us." She delivered the information with the same matter-of-fact calm she would her afternoon grocery list.

"I'm so sorry," Max said. It was all she had. "If you're scared, that's okay, Mom."

"Thank you for saying so."

"You don't have to be brave for me."

"I'm not." She sat taller. "I'm realistic. I've seen the data. My chances of overcoming this obstacle are favorable, and I'll lean into the sentiment."

Max blinked, unsure whether to mimic her stoicism or shake her mother until a shred of emotion eked out. Surely, she was feeling *something*. "Mom, this brand of news would probably be a lot for any person. It's a lot for me right now, so I can only imagine how it must feel for you, someone used to being on the other side of the prescription pad."

"Nothing I can't handle." She placed a hand on the table. "I was brought up to be strong. And I will be. Oh, and here are our entrees." She smiled politely at the server and her approaching salad.

As the chicken tagine that Max no longer wanted was placed in front of her, she looked to her right and absorbed the room's activity. People were dining casually as if it were any other afternoon. In fact, she'd been doing the same just five minutes ago. She swallowed, forced herself to think logically, and press on, pretending her heart wasn't pounding uncomfortably, that her world didn't feel wildly chaotic, upside down, and, quite frankly, overwhelming. She and her mother had a rocky relationship, but no amount of interpersonal clashing could topple the tether she felt to her family.

"What do you need?"

"Grandchildren?" her mother said with a sly smile.

"You still have your sense of humor, I see." Max sat back in her chair, ready to absorb and regroup. This was no longer lunch; it was the two of them going into battle. "What do you need today? Next week?"

The smile dimmed on her mother's lips. "Maybe a ride to my treatment if I'm not feeling well. Your father will help some, but he doesn't have the stomach for hospitals. Never has."

"Of course. Do you have a schedule you can send me?"

She reached into her bag beneath the table and produced a folded, printed copy with Max's name written on the outside. Her hand shook slightly as she handed it across the table. She'd come prepared. Max had to wonder if the schedule would have remained in the bag had she not asked for it. Her mother's stiff pride had always eclipsed everything else, including logic. As they moved into this more difficult season, Max would have to figure out how to break through somehow. They had to be able to communicate freely.

"Thank you," she said, looking it over. "I can clear my schedule on Monday afternoons. That should knock out a good portion of these infusion days."

Her mother nodded solemnly. "Thank you. I know your calendar is so full, and I hate being in the way."

"But this is important. Would you clear your schedule for me?"

"Easily." She frowned as if the question was ridiculous. "You're my child."

"And you're my mother. So, you get it."

Another nod. Acceptance.

They ate mostly in silence, Max lost in a jumble of raw feelings she swallowed in the presence of a woman who looked down on emotion and viewed it as a weakness. Finally, when the credit card slip was returned to them, her mother met her gaze before signing. "I'm turning sixty-five this year."

"I know." She offered a soft smile.

"I think I'm going to have a party."

"You should. I'll help." Milestones like that one seemed much more poignant now. Time was no longer something she could take for granted. It wasn't just moving forward—it was quite possibly running *out*. And for the first time, Max wondered if there was still enough of it left to bridge the distance between them.

TWELVE

Cracker Tray Confidential

Doug's Books was becoming the equivalent of a cozy coffee shop for Ella. She'd set herself up at the shiny wooden table at the back of the store, sip the best brew in town, and watch all the locals stroll the haphazard aisles looking for the perfect book to take home. She vacillated between reading whatever romance novel she was knee-deep in or designing a cover. Three more commissions had arrived in her inbox after she'd posted the cover for *No Pucks Given*. Two contemporary romances and one delicious romantasy, a genre she was quickly educating herself on.

"How are the Weepers?" Doug asked as he passed by with a stack of books to shelve. He wore a blue cardigan today that was a replica of the maroon one he'd worn the last time she saw him. He fit the part of bookishly cozy to a ridiculous tee and preferred to do it in various shades.

She glanced down at the book in her hands, realizing he recognized it as the selection of the week. "Scrappy. Ariana sent a message to the group that she had a bulleted list of grievances for this one. I happen to enjoy it and am prepared to defend its honor."

"I thought the grump was a bit too grumpy. She should have let the happy sunshine give her the tour of the rooftop."

She paused. "Wait. Doug. Are you saying you've read *The Plot Twist*?" She held up the book and turned it to face him. She loved the pink cover with the script typography.

He shrugged. "I was here late one night, and it was the closest book within reach because Stevie always demands a register display and she's bossy."

"She is."

"She's a lesbian now, too. She told me."

"She did?" Ella grinned and sat taller. "That's a compliment that she felt comfortable enough to come out to you. Not everyone in her life is up to speed, you know."

A tiny smile played on Doug's lips. "I had no idea." He wiggled out of the sentimentality. "It's just that we've known each other for years. That's probably the only reason."

"Yeah. Nothing to do with her thinking you're rad or anything. Blech. Friendship."

"You're teasing me. You've been teasing me ever since you got to town. And drinking my coffee like it's milk."

"All of those things are true. You're stuck with me, Doug. Is there more coffee?"

He grumbled something and shuffled away, which was Doug's code for *I like you, too.*

She placed her book face down on the table, her leisurely reading/research on pause, while she went back to a little cover design. She was experimenting with a new color palette for this particular client who was seeking a fun and flirty look while also grounding it in the essence of autumn. Chestnuts, coppers, crimsons, and ochres were all up for grabs, and playing with the color combinations was her favorite.

"Well, well. What's going on back here? Are you holding office hours?"

Ella went still at the very familiar voice and peered up from behind her tablet. There, next to the mystery section, stood Max in a black suit and white dress shirt holding an identical copy of the book Ella was reading. Her dark hair was down and tumbled onto one shoulder, which made Ella forget what words were. *Holy hell.*

Max raised a brow. "You may not be happy to see me. I'm trying to decide. You haven't spoken."

"What?" Ella gave her head a shake. Was her face hot? "Sorry. Not on purpose. It's, uh, the thing was … my tablet. Hi."

"That's a good starter. Hi, back." She brightened to a smile. "I had no idea I would run into you here." She turned to her right as if still trying to piece it together. It would be cute if she weren't so fucking hot right now. "I was stopping by for this week's book, but no one's at the counter."

Ella hooked a thumb. "Doug is that way, shelving books. I'm working." She shrugged. "I like it here and am racking up the hours. He's going to charge me rent soon."

Max set her book on the table and came around behind Ella. "Show me what you're working on."

"No way. It's pretty early in the process and—"

"What's this?" Max asked, picking up her Apple Pencil.

"That's my pencil. I use it to illustrate."

Her mouth fell open. "You do that on your screen? I'm learning so much, and I'm more than a little impressed. I just figured you'd sketch out your illustrations on a piece of paper."

"Sometimes I do, and scan them in later. Other times they're just jumping-off points." Ella gestured to her screen. "But the illustrating apps I use on my tablet offer me a lot of versatility to make my sketches leap to more vibrancy. Does that make sense?"

Max shook her head, biting her lip. Ella wanted to bite it, too. "Not yet. You'll have to let me watch you work some night."

"Night?"

"That's exactly what I said. Where's Doug?"

"Who's Doug?"

Max placed a hand on the back of her head and gave her hair an affectionate smooth. There was a quiet domesticity to the gesture that made Ella curl her toes and imagine bacon and eggs on a Saturday morning, quiet walks around the neighborhood, and mad, passionate sex in multiple portions of the house.

"Did you hear me?" Max asked, folding her arms in amusement. "You're a million miles away right now."

"How do you feel about bacon?"

"The smell of it sizzling in the morning ranks really high."

Ella smiled, satisfied. "Good answer." She knew she was eons ahead of herself, and the concept of her and Max as endgame was a long shot at best. But it was fun to play make-believe and imagine a world where they stared at each other over long dinners, talking for hours, kissing for days, and losing themselves in the tangled sheets. She was doing it again.

"Oh, and now I've lost you a second time," Max said and dropped her head to the side in a whimsical display. Her eyes danced, and the sides of her mouth tugged. Everything between them felt light and promising today, like a cool glass of ice water after a long run. "You're adorable when you daydream."

Ella perched her chin on her hand, reveling in the ease of their back-and-forth. "You seem to inspire it."

"I do?" She watched understanding transform Max's beautiful face, making her seem both surprised and satisfied. "Even better."

God, she wanted to kiss her into their next chapter, lose herself in those lips, and taste the sweetness of her lip gloss again. She had no idea what was next in their story, but she knew this wasn't the end. "You better go find Doug before this gets any worse."

"But maybe I want it to get worse. Who knows what could happen?"

"Max."

"Yes?"

"Exactly my sentiment," she said, dropping her tone. "We're in a bookstore."

Max leveled a stare. "In my experience, we do well when books are involved. It's how I met you."

"Find Doug."

"No need," Doug called out. "I'm just over here working and listening to you two dance around each other."

Max's eyes went wide. "Point taken."

"And don't come to my office looking like that," Ella said.

"Like what?"

"A lawyer."

Max strolled back, hands in her suit pockets, which wasn't helping. "Do you have a thing for corporate executives, ma'am?"

Ella sucked in air. "You could say it checks a lot of my boxes."

Max arched a brow. "Good to know," she said in a breezy voice. Too much. Max, if Ella wasn't careful, would be the death of her rational thought and productivity. Ever since she'd given in to her desire, the world had become a much happier place. Well, as long as she pushed thoughts of her best friend and her feelings aside. That part was still a big problem. It was too early, she told herself, to bother Rachel with something that could turn out to be frivolous in the end. She and Max had a lot of potential, but they didn't know each other very well at this point. Maybe their bond was purely physical, likely to fizzle and burn itself out. Wouldn't it be wiser to wait and see if there was anything worth making waves about first? Yep, that's what she was going to go with.

TUESDAY NIGHT HAD SEEMED SO FAR AWAY. All week, Max had waited, knowing it was the next time she'd get to share space with Ella. The news about her mother hung over her, heavy and thick, leaving everything coated in regret and sadness, except Ella. She was the one bright spot in Max's life. When things felt alarming or overwhelming, it was thoughts of her that Max turned to for a short respite. Seeing Ella in person, after several days away, was like taking a deep breath after being underwater for too long, necessary and urgent, the only thing keeping her from sinking.

"You're a very forgiving person. I'll say that for you," Ariana said across the room to Ella, flipping through the book and turning it around with noticeable vehemence. They were forty-five minutes in, and the polite agreement had moved to the back burner in favor of friendly spars. It was, honestly, Max's favorite part of book club. The Weepers didn't mess around when it came to expressing their varied viewpoints. "But Chapter Fourteen was criminal. I wanted to call the author's mother and personally tattle."

"I hear you," Ella said, the picture of calm. She was often that, a quality Max admired. She had her hair in a ponytail tonight with just the right amount of hair escaping and framing her face. Her lips carried a hint of pink lip gloss, and her lashes a slight touch of mascara. Unintentionally gorgeous. "I'm thinking this is about the rooftop tour gone wrong. It crushed me as well, but I love a good crushing. It makes me long for that romantic little payoff all the more, and who doesn't love it when their own emotions get entangled in the story?"

Ariana went up on her knees, and Morgan's eyebrows hit her hairline. "She's gearing up for battle, folks. Hold onto your merlot."

"But the crushing was unnecessary in this sense," Ariana explained. "These women were on such a fantastic trajectory that she could have ridden that wave and crushed us like reader-bugs later on. It would have been a much more epic crushing, too."

Stevie nodded and popped a grape. "Reader-bugs. I like it." She seemed a lot lighter these days, smiling her way through the meeting. Max had to wonder if she'd quietly messaged that woman from Sally Sue's after all. Maybe Stevie just needed a little breathing room to explore this whole new world on her own—a concept she'd mention to the others.

Olive sat forward. "But maybe that's why it worked so well for Ella and her entangled feelings. It was a surprise crushing." She nodded at her own quiet suggestion, always treading so delicately. Leave it to Olive to say very little all night and then bust out with an impressive nugget of wisdom.

"I have to agree," Max said. Ella turned in her direction and they connected, holding each other's gaze with a palpable intensity before Max reminded herself that they were in a room full of their friends and couldn't spontaneously combust and take the whole place down in flames with them. Would be rude. It wasn't her home.

"Are you going to say why?" Morgan asked, and that's when Max realized she'd trailed off, her gaze still locked on Ella, who'd had the self-awareness to glance away. She'd just looked so fucking edible today. The way her silver necklace with the flower rested on her collarbone. The slight wave of her hair, and that damn shade of blond Max hadn't quite been able to duplicate in her mind's eye until she laid eyes on the real thing and went soft all over again. Ella had stolen her attention in a way no other woman ever had, and Max's only explanation was the intricate combination of traits woven together that made Ella, well ... *Ella*. The cumulative effect mystified, terrified, and excited Max all at once. She was lust drunk these days, admittedly.

"I am going to say why," Max said, ordering herself to behave and focus. "But I need a minute to organize my thoughts."

Ariana shot Morgan a knowing glance, as if to say, *See what I mean?* She swiveled back to Max and raised a brow (and Ariana had good ones). "You're off your game these days."

"Work is killer. Two long mediation sessions today."

"You sure that's all? Anything you want to share with the class?"

Max pretended to think it over. "Hmm. No. Nothing I can think of."

"Ella, what about you?" Ariana asked. "You seem engrossed in the leaves of that plant."

"I got it at Lowe's," Stevie said proudly. "And it's still alive even with me being distracted lately. Bless its sweet heart."

"What about me?" Ella asked.

"Anything new going on these days?" Ari asked.

"Other than the move, the new town, new job, and recent fascination with these awesome books, thanks to you all? No. I think I'm at my fill," she said with a winsome smile.

Max grinned. Proud. Amused. All of it. She raised a finger. "I have my thoughts composed."

"Ah! Tell us all about it," Ariana said, and folded her arms as if she couldn't wait. She clearly knew way too much and enjoyed every delicious second of her triumph.

"I think the dark moment came earlier than anyone was expecting, and by exercising that early pounce, the author," she turned her copy of the book to remind herself of the author's name, "Amber Elton, caught us unarmed and emotionally vulnerable, and that made the cut much deeper. I thought we had more good days to explore with these characters, and they were viciously ripped from me."

"So vicious," Ella said with a dark nod.

She happened to enjoy that she and Ella were united on this one, even if her opinion might have been easily swayed by her newfound preoccupation with Ella's lips, hands, and body.

As the book club discussion continued, Max slipped her phone out of her back pocket and typed quickly.

I want my hands on you.

A minute later, she noticed Ella look down at her phone, roll her lips in, and type something before leaping back into the conversation.

Kitchen.

Max understood the assignment, downed her wine, and gestured to the kitchen as if going to open a new bottle. It was only a couple of moments until Ella appeared with an empty cracker tray. Laughter floated into the kitchen through the open window that divided the two rooms. She and Ella exchanged a charged look, full of the pent-up tension that had been ping-ponging between them all night, and went about busying themselves in clear view of the others. Max subtly inclined her head in the direction of the laundry room off the back of the kitchen and casually walked that way. On board with the mission, Ella followed.

The second the door clicked shut, Max had Ella backed against it, her hands already dragging up beneath the hem of Ella's sweater, fingers greedy against warm skin. Ella gasped, but it melted into a sigh of appreciation as Max's mouth crashed against hers, the kiss desperate and deep, all tongues and need. Ella clutched at Max's shirt, yanking her closer, as if she could press them into one, as if that would somehow be enough. It wouldn't be. Not even close.

Max nipped at Ella's lower lip, swallowed the quiet sound she made, and then Ella's hands were everywhere—tangling in her hair, clawing at her back, sliding down to her hips. She was aroused and very aware of it, a distinct throbbing settled between her legs that she'd give anything to satisfy. A low groan rumbled through Max as she pressed Ella harder against the door, but then laughter from the other room. A reminder. An unfortunate one.

161

They stilled, panting. Ella's hands went soft against Max's spine. "We should—"

"I know," Max muttered, but she stole one more kiss anyway, deep and slow, before forcing herself to step back.

"Dammit." Ella exhaled sharply, eyes still dark with want. Then, with a smirk, she grabbed the cracker tray off the shelf where she'd set it. "Think they'll notice I forgot to come back with the crackers?"

Max huffed a breathless laugh, swiped her thumb across Ella's kiss-swollen lips, and let her go first—because watching her walk away was its own kind of reward.

THIRTEEN

Garlic, Vinegar, and Dread

F ive days later, and Ella couldn't read any more of these steamy books in fear of what kind of sex monster she'd create. She set her newest client's most recent release on the end table and closed her eyes. The hot and heavy scenes were too much for someone who, ahem, had a lot of pent-up sexual energy and no actual means to expend it.

She thought about Max and their various encounters more than she'd care to admit. She fantasized about what would have happened if each one of those illicit moments had been allowed to play out without interruption. The practice generally left her dizzy, hot, and a whole lot bothered.

The truth was that either one of them could have reached out to the other and suggested a meetup. Neither had. But they hadn't exactly stayed away either. There were good morning text messages—flirtatious exchanges and sometimes, at night, naughtier ones.

"So, who's the woman?"

"What?"

Rachel stood in the doorway of her room, watching her with folded arms and a smile.

"The woman you're thinking about, and don't for a

second say that's not what you're doing. I've known you your entire adult life, and that's exactly who you're thinking about."

A quick calculation told Ella that there was no way out of this one. Rachel was right. She knew her too well. She swallowed and decided to be honest.

"Okay, here's the deal." She took a deep breath, unsure of how to go about this, but feeling compelled to try. She was stuck in neutral with both Rachel and Max and had to find a way forward. "There is a woman. From my book club—"

"Ariana. I knew it. You mentioned her name the other day. Plus, I heard you on the phone with her and caught the tone in your voice."

"When she called about food allergies?"

"Yes. You also had this look on your face." It was such an inconsequential call and it had lasted all of two minutes. Ari had been preparing a dessert for book club two weeks prior and wanted to ensure Ella wasn't allergic to any of the ingredients, given that she was new. How in the world had Rachel inferred that she was into Ariana? "No. It's not like—"

"It's pointless to deny it. It's cute, is all." She hopped onto the bed next to Ella and bumped her shoulder. "Give it time, and I guarantee you'll get more comfortable with her. You always were a little awkward and timid when it came to meeting women. A sweet little underdog."

Ella swallowed. She didn't love the characterization, but, honestly, maybe that's who she was. Wouldn't Rachel know? The unassuming wallflower that people had to reassure and pat on the head. "That's me. Work in progress." She attempted a smile because sometimes those made you feel better when slugged.

"But you settled in with Britney eventually, right?"

"Except she left me."

"Right, that bitch. Well, you can do this, Ella Bella. I promise." She popped up like a groundhog. "Hey, speaking of women, I got hit on again today. Not my type at all, but she had beautiful green eyes, so I gave her my number anyway. Who doesn't love a free martini?"

"But you want to get to know her, too, right? Maybe she's nice."

Rachel stood and shrugged. "Maybe. Gonna make a big salad with those amazing feta sprinkles. Low calorie. Amazing. Want one?"

She didn't. She'd had a cheeseburger like the underdog she likely was. "That sounds awesome, but no, thank you, madam."

"Suit yourself, madam. I'll leave you to think about sex with Ariana."

"Rach! No!"

"You know I'm right." With a final circle of her shoulder, she disappeared, bound for the land of healthy salads and women who asked her out randomly at department stores.

The entire conversation had sucker punched Ella's ego and distracted her from the cause. She hadn't had the chance to set the record straight about what was going on with her and Max, and now it felt like the moment had passed. Dammit. What was wrong with her? What kind of friend makes out with an off-limits ex and then doesn't have the courage to be up-front about it?

"Hey, do you want to watch a randomly selected Sandra Bullock movie and stare at her?"

"Yes. Obviously," Ella shouted back.

"Then get your ass in here already. I'm gonna make my phone bot pick one for us and pray to God it's the outer space one where she looks so hot I melt into the couch like a Slurpee in summer."

"Honestly, it can't go wrong with any of them," Ella said, glaring at the discarded romance novel that tortured her as she trudged into the living room, her pillow clutched to her chest. Surely, a really attractive brunette on the screen wouldn't lead her to lustful thoughts about Max pressed up against a wall. That was definitely not a possibility. No daydreams about Max's perfect mouth. Or her annoyingly sexy confidence. Or the way she always smelled like raspberries and something just a little bit spicy. Nope. No thoughts like that at all …

Ella dropped onto the couch, tucking her legs under her, and watched as Rachel held up her phone like it was a magic wand about to dictate their fate.

"Okay, here we go," Rachel announced. "Random Sandra Bullock selection commencing in three … two … one …"

A beat of silence. Then Rachel pouted dramatically. *"Miss Congeniality."*

Ella balked. "What's wrong with you? That's a bad thing?"

Rachel sighed. "No, but I was hoping for *Gravity* so I could be emotionally devastated while also very attracted to her."

"Fair. But this one has a makeover montage, and I know you love those."

Rachel waggled her brows. "I forgot about that. You know me too well."

Yeah. That was the problem.

She knew *exactly* how Rachel would feel if she had all the details of Ella's recent history. She hugged her pillow tighter as Rachel hit play, and Sandra filled the screen, charming and a complete klutz.

Rachel has no idea.

No idea that Ella had been making out with her ex behind her back. No idea that every stolen moment with Max made Ella crave more. No idea that, right now, as Rachel laughed at the screen and lusted after Sandra, Ella was lusting after someone else entirely.

She was so very screwed.

~

Max's childhood home hadn't changed very much since she'd last lived in it nine years ago, when she started law school. Her dad's dark-blue La-Z-Boy sat in the corner of the living room, worn in and soft. Her mother hated that chair but tolerated it all the same because she loved the man who came with it. Her parents were affectionate in unconventional ways. A smack to her father's arm. A ruffling of her father's hair. A loud smack to her mother's cheek. Nothing too sincere. They nagged, as well, in their own unique way of showing they paid attention to each other's trajectories.

When Max arrived at the narrow two-story house, her mother must have been well into dinner preparation, because the rich, garlicky scent of chicken adobo filled the house, intermingling with the sharp tang of vinegar and soy sauce in a way that instantly transported Max back in time. On the stove, her mother stirred a pot of sinigang, the tamarind broth bubbling as it embraced tender pork and a scattering of bright-green kangkong. The interesting part of the whole scene was the Taylor Swift music playing loudly from the speaker in the corner. As she rounded the corner into the kitchen, Max was surprised to see her mother not just bopping along to the music but shaking her hips and shoulders. And who knew she was such a good dancer?

"Hey, there. I was going to ask if you need any help, but I don't want to interrupt a full-blown Beyoncé *Renaissance* moment," she said, placing her bag on the back of one of the chairs.

"The what?" Her mother turned, hand on hip. "I'm dancing in the kitchen," she shouted above the music.

"I'm aware."

"I'll set you a place! You'll eat with us."

"That would be fantastic."

Her mother offered another hip shake and went back to the stove.

The whole scene had caught Max wildly off guard and,

honestly, left her a little relieved. It was not at all what she had expected in the days following the news of her mom's diagnosis. Max had worried endlessly about how her mother might be feeling, both physically and emotionally, which is why she'd made a point to swing by, despite the mountains of paperwork that'd have her up until midnight tonight. But this chipper, dare she say, sassy woman in front of her was the opposite of what she'd been expecting.

Her dad, wearing his Commanders ball cap, wandered into the kitchen for a soda refill and broke into a smile when he saw her. "Hey, hey. You staying?"

"I'm staying. What's going on?" she asked, and jutted her chin in her mother's direction.

"She's just decided this thing is not gonna get her down."

"Oh. Well, that's a good thing. Don't you think?"

He gave her a sideways squeeze. "I do. I do. How's the busted-up marriage business?"

"Today I had a pair of husbands. One is accusing the other of stealing his style and demanding that he return it promptly. That kind of thing is a little harder to enforce on paper."

"If somebody steals my sporty chic look, they'll pay," he said with the darkened look of someone who means business.

"But … who would do that?"

"Oh, you wanna wrestle?" he asked, and hooked Max into a headlock she was all too familiar with. Her arms immediately went around his waist, and she squeezed like the wrestler he'd taught her to be, which often made him drop his hold. If he'd wanted a son, he'd never let on, teaching Max how to roughhouse and watch sports like a champ. Was he an emotional guy? No. Not at all. He wasn't there to talk to when things were rough at school, or when she started to understand she liked girls. But he showed up for fun like clockwork, which counted for something.

"Get your hands off my child!" her mom called, hands on

her hips. Always in charge, her voice rose above the chaos and was all the prompting her dad needed to let go of Max, hold his palms up, and return to the fridge for his refill. He knew the pecking order.

"You got off easy this time," he said, pointing at Max.

"Yeah, yeah. But I have to tell you, I think your muscles are wasting away," she said with a shrug. "Age." That made him lunge for her, prompting her to duck and weave.

"You two stop that," her mom yelled, pointing at them with her stirring spoon. "Dinner is in five minutes. Maxine put out the napkins. You," she said to her husband, "come back in five minutes and don't be late."

He did as he was told and slunk away, returning the kitchen to his wife, who offered an uncharacteristically warm smile. This was all so … nice. Was there a second shoe waiting to plummet onto Max's head?

"How are you feeling?" she asked as she set the table.

"Tired, but not too bad. I can't complain."

"You seem to be in great spirits."

"I am. I have everything to lose, so I'm going to enjoy my time even if there's not much."

Max paused, salt-and-pepper shakers in hand. "Mom. No. You're not going anywhere. You told me yourself, the numbers are on your side."

"But not everyone is lucky. I'm going to get my life in order and make sure everyone I love is cared for and happy, and you are at the top of that list." She deposited a serving platter of chicken adobo on the table, placed a kiss on Max's shoulder, and went back to the stove. What was happening? A shoulder kiss? Since when? Surrendering to fate instead of staying strong? Max frowned, feeling uneven.

"Are we still on for your appointment tomorrow?" she asked, adjusting the forks just so, the way her mother had always insisted. No large gaps at the bottom. *Silverware should never float toward the center of the table, Maxine!*

"I've been thinking, and you don't have to accompany me."

Max straightened. "Well, I am. I cleared my calendar."

"I refuse to be a burden," she said in a singsongy voice, almost as if she'd just declared it was Wine Down Wednesday.

"You're not a burden."

"Good. Then I'll go alone." She adjusted one of the knives, probably because it wasn't just so, and then on second thought, knocked the sucker askew.

"Who are you and what have you done with my mother?"

"I'm a fun mom now. I'm dying."

"Hey. You are not. Stop that."

But nothing she said stopped it. Throughout dinner, her mother oohed and aahed over how vibrant the food tasted, how Max's top made her eyes look especially beautiful, and how her father had smartly figured out how to fix the leaf blower without having to take it in for repairs. In other words, this woman bore no resemblance to her actual mother. Next to them, her father ate his meal happily, enjoying all the new compliments, while Max moved her food around her plate, taking it all in with concern. A sense of doom had fallen over her in the past thirty minutes. Her hands trembled, and her skin felt clammy. Her mother was sick and no longer herself, and her father didn't seem to register the shift on either front. It fell to her to steer the ship.

By the time she kissed her mother's cheek and gave her father an affectionate smack on the arm, she was almost overcome with fear, and her mind moved at a rapid pace, conjuring all sorts of horrific scenarios and playing them out one at a time. She needed a distraction or a salve. Honestly, she knew how to achieve both. There was only one place she wanted to be, and that was next to Ella Baker.

FOURTEEN

The Green Sweater Incident

T he house was quiet, the kind of quiet that settled in only after dark in a sleepy neighborhood like this one with just the occasional hum of a passing car. Ella sat cross-legged at the desk in her makeshift office, a half-empty mug of tea cooling beside her. She was deep in the early stages of her second commissioned cover, sketching lines with careful precision, the glow of her tablet the only real light in the room.

That is, until her phone lit up with a soft buzz. Max.

Can I see you tonight?

Her skin prickled, and her stomach tightened; the idea of seeing Max sent a rush of anticipation through her, eclipsing the fatigue of the day. She dropped her stylus, barely noticing as it rolled off the edge of her desk, her entire focus narrowing to the three little dots flickering on the screen—Max was still typing.

Please.

She swallowed. That single word unraveled something inside her. Max wasn't just asking. She needed this. Needed *her*.

Ella's pulse pounded as she typed back.

> Tell me where.

Max's response came instantly.

> My place.

An address followed.

Ella was already reaching for her keys, somehow aware of the gravity of the request.

> On my way.

She didn't check her hair or change her outfit. The hunter-green cardigan thrown on over her white T-shirt and jeans would have to do.

"Wow. Where are you off to so fast?" Rachel asked from her spot in front of the fridge. She lifted her shoulder and turned her chin into it in a playful pose.

"Oh." Record scratch. "Me?"

"Well, I wasn't asking the couch."

"Valid." Ella pointed at the door and swiveled back to Rachel. Her heart thudded. Her thoughts chased themselves in chaotic patterns, making it difficult to snatch one. "I just got a text that this friend needs me to—You know, when someone—"

"Say no more." Rachel grinned around the open fridge door and wiggled four fingers in farewell. "And tell Ariana I said hi. I won't wait up."

She sighed, opened her mouth, and closed it again because this wasn't the moment to correct her. Max had said very little in her message, but Ella had the overwhelming sense that something was off. "Enjoy your night."

"Not as much as you will," Rachel called after her just as she swung open the door. Guilt threatened to topple Ella like a boulder teetering on the edge of a cliff. If she ran fast enough, maybe she could avoid being smashed.

Once inside the Mini, she cranked the volume, letting the music consume her as thoughts of Max surged through her mind like a riptide, pulling her under. Kelly Clarkson's husky belt tore through the silence, a perfect storm against the heavy, brooding sky. The need she'd buried for what felt like a lifetime clawed its way to the surface, raw and insistent. If Max needed her tonight, she needed Max just as desperately—no more second-guessing, no more holding back. After so many false starts, she was done resisting. This thing wasn't going away. Max wasn't. It was time to dive headfirst into whatever this was between them, once and for all.

She found her way to Max's condominium complex, which was definitely above her pay grade and possibly her sophistication level. She took in each detail as she made her way to the interior hallways. Shiny silver doorknobs and perfectly spaced sconces spoke of elegance and an expensive designer. This was Max's world. And for the first time, she wondered just how much she really knew about the woman waiting for her upstairs. She took the elevator to the second floor and easily located Apartment 212. With a deep breath and a jittery stomach, she knocked and waited.

When the door swung open, there was Max. Dress slacks, shirt untucked, and barefoot. Her dark hair was piled on top of her head and held in place by a clip that, well, really worked for her. Ella forgot to inflate her lungs. She resisted the urge to look behind her to see if this was, in fact, the right door and her real life. A woman this beautiful, smart, and into her seemed too good to be true. That's when she saw it, a bottle of wine dangling in one hand.

"Get in here and have a glass," Max said with a soft smile. But her eyes didn't dance the way they did when she was happy. Ella couldn't quite tell what was behind them, but there was something new.

"Big moment. I'm about to see your place for the first time. This is going to be very telling," she said, following Max into a small entryway where she slipped out of her shoes and left them next to a pair of black and pink running shoes. She certainly wouldn't mind seeing Max in a sports bra. Better yet, running in one. "Are you a runner?"

"I try to be. Exercise is where I work out a lot of my thoughts on stressful days."

The floor was gorgeous—gray-scale hardwood with planks that ran the length of the space, sleek yet inviting. Soft lighting cast a warm glow over the entryway, where a minimalist console table sat against the wall, topped with a small ceramic dish for keys and a framed black-and-white photograph of Max and two people who had to be her parents—a nice touch.

As Max led the way further into the condo, Ella took it all in—the clean lines, the intentional simplicity. She nodded along, impressed by the level of sophistication. Max was a grown-up. "Okay, Wyler. I see you."

Max gestured to the space and made her way to the open kitchen to free the wine from its bottle. "Take your time. Explore. Frolic, if necessary. I won't hold you back."

"Oh, I will, Maxine. Don't you worry."

The living room opened up beyond the entry, its high ceilings giving an airy, effortless feel. A deep, gray and white sectional faced a sleek fireplace, above which hung an abstract piece of art in muted blues and whites, reminiscent of crashing waves. Mad good taste in art. Who would have guessed? She grinned because she would have. A built-in bookshelf framed one side of the room, lined with an eclectic mix of legal casebooks, fiction, and the occasional vinyl record. The space was stylish but lived-in, refined but comfort-able. A soft throw was casually draped over the arm of the couch, and an empty mug sat forgotten on the coffee table beside a face-down pile of papers. *Work*, she thought to herself.

Ella grinned, leaning against the doorway. "Okay, this is exactly what I would have guessed. A mix of sophistication and just enough mess to prove you genuinely live here."

"Very astute. I purposefully created a mess knowing you were on your way and might doubt my residency."

"The lengths we go." She moved back to Max at the kitchen counter. "How long has this been your place?"

Max looked skyward, her big brown eyes searching through the records of her life, a life Ella wanted to know all about in unflinching detail. "Coming on four years."

"Staying power."

Max popped the cork on the bottle. "I think that's a compliment. You're cute in that sweater."

She glanced down at the hunter-green cardigan that she regretted now. "This old thing?" She laughed. "I'm embar-rassed I showed up in it, given that you're still dressed for what looks like a big day in court, and I'm a rumpled librarian who can't find her reading glasses that are likely on top of her head."

"You're the hottest librarian I've ever seen." She said it unequivocally. Zero hesitation. Without even a smirk.

Ella swallowed, not having expected the comment. Max had a way of making her feel significant in a world that didn't.

"Way to steal the air in the room."

Max's mouth eased to one side in a half-smile, the very one Ella couldn't get enough of. She had such expressive lips. Bow-shaped when she was unsuspecting, curling like a secret when she was cheeky. "But in fairness, I'm untucked and without shoes." She pointed to her feet. Plum nail polish on pedicured toes. "And I'm only still dressed for work because I swung by my parents' house after my last session."

Aha. Maybe they'd argued. Is that why Max carried an uncharacteristic heaviness? "And how was the visit?"

Max sighed. She slid Ella one of the glasses of wine and picked up her own. "Surreal. I should probably tell you that my mother was recently diagnosed with cancer." She paused. "Sorry. I'm still working on processing that, and it's entirely different saying the words out loud."

Ella's hand went still, glass frozen midway to her mouth. "Oh, shit. That's awful."

"It is." She lifted a shoulder. "The statistics are in her favor, but she seems to be preparing herself for the end of her life, and it's … jarring. She's never been someone who gives up easily." Max stared at the wall behind Ella and shook her head. "It's not in her DNA."

"I'm sure this has you rattled."

"Understatement." Max nodded. "I think I needed … someone tonight. No. Not someone. You."

Ella came around the gray and white marbled island and faced Max. "Well, I'm glad you called." They stared at each other for a long moment, the tension prickling Ella's neck. "Do you want to talk about it or talk about anything but? Maybe we could—"

Max's lips silenced her as they pressed to Ella's, insistent and mixed with something deeper, something she wasn't sure how to name. Max paused for a moment, giving Ella the chance to pull away or step out of her space. She did neither. The kiss had sparked something primal in Ella, and she went up on her toes, wrapped her arms around Max's neck, and crushed her mouth to Max's. As their lips tangled, fitting together just as perfectly as before, the spark turned to flames, and the heat licked its way from her toes to her midsection before dipping lower. She was already aching for Max, the throbbing between her legs incessant. She slid her tongue into

Max's mouth and explored, greeted by the soft press of Max's nails. She was quickly wet and longing to be touched, licked, fucked, all of it.

The cardigan hit the floor. *Good.*

Max's fingertips skated down her arms, highlighting the sensitivity of her skin. Her whole body came alive at just that slightest touch from Max, like it had been waiting for her. In so many ways, it had. Their breasts pressed together as Max walked them backward, and Ella loved every second of that sensation. When her ass hit the back of the couch, Max paused and cradled Ella's face, holding her there as she good and kissed her into next week. Her tongue touched Ella's bottom lip, a request. She granted it, and Max's tongue was in her mouth, exploring expertly, devouring. It was everything holy in this world.

"You are so fucking hot," Max said, coming up for air.

Ella, lust drunk and wanting more, nodded. "Do you know what would be even hotter?" Her fingertips found the hem of Max's dress shirt. "You with no shirt on."

Ella unbuttoned the first button, which offered her a glimpse of cleavage. The second showed off Max's baby-blue bra and the tops of her breasts. Ella swallowed, and her mouth watered. Low cut and sexy as hell. Max conducted business in a boardroom wearing that thing? Ella's cheeks flamed, and her center ached. "Fucking look at you," she murmured, watching as Max's eyes flashed dark. She didn't say a word, waiting patiently for Ella to continue, and she did. The fourth and fifth buttons left the shirt hanging open, exposing the soft skin of Max's stomach. Ella pulled the shirt down Max's shoulders, met her gaze, and then placed a kiss on one of them. It was Max who reached behind and unclasped the bra, setting it on the top of the couch behind them. Ella exhaled slowly, trying to keep her thoughts clear. With Max now standing topless in front of her, the world was less steady. Ella wanted to touch, taste, and stare all at the same time. The jumble of feelings, emotions, and primal impulses assaulted her senses, overwhelming. She knew one thing with certainty. There had never been a more gorgeous woman than Maxine Wyler. Her breasts were round and perfect, medium in size, with rose-colored nipples. Ella's hands trembled slightly as she touched one, tracing the perimeter of a nipple. Max sucked in air, which pulled Ella's focus from her breasts to her face as she continued to touch her intimately. Max's lips were parted, her eyes luminous. Ella's featherlight touches gave way to a more assured massage as she watched each tiny reaction play out on Max's features. The kind of movie she could watch all day long. She rolled the nipples between her thumbs and forefingers, prompting Max's eyes to slam shut and the word *fuck* to escape her lips.

"They're sensitive," Ella said, her own voice emerging with a rasp she didn't recognize. Max bit her bottom lip and nodded. On a power trip now, Ella wanted to see more of Max, to spend time with every inch of her body, make her writhe beneath Ella's touch before eventually breaking into a free fall to pleasure. But then she had a thought. "What do you want?" she asked, afraid to race ahead of Max. It was an important question.

"That's my bedroom. I want to go in there with you," Max said, indicating a doorway beyond the living space. "And explore every part of us. Finally."

Ella nodded, and within a millisecond, they were kissing again, unable to keep their hands and mouths off of each other for more than a couple of beats. "Let's go," Ella said around kisses. Max led the way to her bedroom, but they took frequent kissing breaks. And ones for touching, groping, and pressing. Up against the wall was her favorite, and it was very quickly determined that clothing was their enemy. They lost a few more items as they traveled to Max's absolutely gorgeous bedroom. She had a cream and lavender bed, lower to the floor than was traditional. Ella liked the uniqueness—very

Max. She'd only glimpsed the furniture before the lights went out—Max's doing. But it was a deep gray with long silver handles. She liked those very much, but was too lust drunk to think beyond that. A bolt of pleasure slid up her thighs because there was a hand between her legs, touching her through her underwear, stroking her slowly from behind. The attention sent shockwaves straight to her center, causing her knees to go weak and her words to disappear. Her pants had been lost somewhere en route to the room, leaving her bare-thighed and trembling—all Max's adept work. Hypnotized with longing, Ella closed her eyes, lost in the sensations that overtook everything. She dropped her head back, reveling, enjoying, and craving so much more with each passing second. She wanted their bodies naked and pressed together on Max's bed. She wanted to learn Max's body and use that knowledge to make her whimper and claw that beautiful bedspread. She wanted Max's fingers curled inside of her, carrying her higher and higher. That's when she felt the pressure start to build. She was making sounds she didn't remember choosing to make, which meant she wasn't in charge of her own body at this point, but was merely along for the ride. There was something so incredibly freeing about that knowledge.

"I want to do so many things to you," Max said in her ear as she continued to touch her, stroking with more purpose. Her underwear was soaked. "I want you to want. And I want you to come so hard. To cry out. And then I want to do it to you all over again."

Ella swallowed, thick with need, pressing herself against Max's hand, which had withdrawn to light touches, avoiding the one spot that so desperately craved attention.

"Show me you," Ella managed. She'd waited long enough and fantasized too often.

Max straightened and crossed to the lamp on the bedside table. She clicked it on, casting a warm glow across the room. She turned around and faced Ella, whose gaze fell immediately to the breasts she was only just getting to know. Ella watched in captivation as Max dropped her black pants to the floor and effortlessly stepped out of her underwear. She was exquisite. A woman to be painted and hung on a wall, yet here she stood in front of Ella, hers. At least for tonight.

"How are you so perfect?" she asked, moving immediately to Max with purpose. She captured her mouth with a hungry kiss before Max could answer. It was only moments before her bikinis were slid halfway down her legs, and without pulling her lips from Max's, she stepped out of them. Her bra hit the floor right after, and skin on skin was a sensation Ella hadn't been prepared for. The intense pulses of pleasure tripled when she was pushed onto her back, and Max crawled on top. As her weight settled, the world changed forever. This. It was everything Ella had longed for and craved for so damn long. The warmth, the curves, the smooth expanse of Max's skin beneath her fingertips left Ella throbbing and in absolute heaven.

"Dear God, you feel amazing," Max said, closing her eyes. She pressed her thigh between Ella's and lifted, causing her to see stars. Ella pressed her nails into Max's back as she absorbed the pinpricks of desire coursing through her.

"Please always do that," Max said with her eyes still closed. Max liked nails on her back.

Ella nodded, taking note, lost in her body's overt reaction to Max's. She pressed closer against Max's thigh, rocking her hips to inch closer to release. Accommodating her, Max removed the thigh and slid her hips between Ella's legs instead, rubbing herself back and forth like a gift. "Oh, fuck," and then pumping her hips, matching Ella's rhythm. There was no way she could come from this alone, but to her utter shock, the pressure at her core began to climb. What was happening? The friction became a relentless beat, a pulse that vibrated through Ella's every nerve ending. Max's breath hitched, a soft moan escaping her lips, the noise so incredibly sexy that Ella undoubtedly became wetter. Her earlier disbelief began to crumble, giving way to a singular focus on the rising tide within. Then something shifted. The shooting sensations skyrocketed, and cool air caressed her skin. Max had slid down her body and was sucking her clit. God. She clawed the bedding beneath her like a lifeline. Desperately reaching, she arched up in search of what was so close, rushing to her. With Max's arms around her thighs, she pumped her hips rapidly until finally, the pressure broke like a speeding train, and she was rocked by a staggering wave of pleasure that moved from her center outward to every inch of her body. She shook against it, falling into a wonderful oblivion. When she opened her eyes, Max was straddling her stomach, watching her with reverence, as she rode out the remaining shockwaves.

"You are so beautiful." She leaned down and placed a slow kiss beneath Ella's jaw, her hair tickling Ella's bare skin. "And that was worth every moment I had to wait."

"You were waiting for me?"

"Are you kidding me? Since the first night we met. Couldn't get you out of my mind. I wanted you right here."

Holding Max right where she was, Ella pushed into a sitting position and stared up at Max, now in her arms. "We are such a storm. That was unreal."

Max nodded, her eyes darker than Ella had ever seen them. "Complicated and powerful, but it's sexy as hell."

They came together again in a kiss fueled by passion and the kind of desire that Ella had only read about until Max. Their mouths moved in hunger, tasting, nipping, exploring. She kneaded Max's breasts, loving the weight of them in her hands, realizing that she was now very much a breast girl. With Max's nipple in her mouth, she slipped her hand between her legs and smiled at how so very ready she already was.

She began to stroke, moving through wet folds that felt so

fucking wonderful. Max moaned and went up on her knees, granting Ella even better access. She joined her there, kissing Max's neck, the same expanse of skin that had her captivated at book club for weeks. "Lie down," she whispered, "and open your legs for me."

Max complied, and Ella followed her to the now rumpled sheets beneath them. She stretched out on one forearm alongside Max, letting her breasts sway as she continued to touch, play, and explore with her hand to the sounds Max offered up like signposts. That is, until she followed her urge and slipped inside. Max gasped as she entered her, her eyes slamming shut as Ella began to move, pressing deeper and sliding out, seeking out a rhythm she let Max set. "Yes. More. God. Just like that," Max said, her voice a ghost of what it usually was. Ella moved faster and let her thumb glide gently over Max's clit. Max whimpered beneath the touch, and Ella felt the way her body opened further, welcoming her in. It was heady—how responsive Max was. Ella moved with slow, deliberate thrusts, watching the muscles in Max's stomach shift, the way her hands gripped the sheets for something to hold on to.

All the while, Ella couldn't stop looking at her. Max—naked, vulnerable, and utterly gorgeous in the low light—was a vision Ella knew she'd never be able to forget. She kissed along her shoulder, tasting salt and skin, letting her lips linger as her hand kept working in a rhythm that made Max's hips press back into her.

The sounds Max made were addictive. Ella found herself chasing them, adjusting her angle, pressing a little deeper just to hear more. Her own center ached all over again, but this moment wasn't about that. It was about Max and the way she fell apart under Ella's touch.

She could live right here.

Ella pressed her forehead to Max's chest, breath catching. "You feel so good," she whispered, her voice rough with want.

"God, Max, you're perfect. I love fucking you. I want to see what you look like when you come."

Max nodded, obedient, breathing rapidly. Ella lowered herself between Max's legs and pulled Max into her mouth, swirling her clit with the tip of her tongue. Skating it with her teeth, sucking gently until the sounds Max made grew louder and louder.

Ella raised her gaze to watch, not stopping, but not wanting to miss a second. Max's head tipped back, her lips parted in a gasp. Each movement, each sound, felt like a gift Ella had somehow earned. She adjusted her rhythm, paying attention to every tremble of Max's thighs, every breath that caught.

She slipped her fingers back inside, curling just right, and felt the way Max's body tightened around her. It was happening. Ella could feel it in the way Max's whole frame arched toward her, in the broken way she whispered Ella's name.

And then Max came—hard, beautiful, shaking—and Ella watched it all. The rush of it. The surrender. The way Max's eyes fluttered shut and her mouth opened on a moan so raw it left Ella breathless.

Ella stayed there, pressing kisses to her hip, her stomach, letting Max come down gently while her own heart thundered in her chest.

"Where are you?" Max asked, prompting her to join Max on the pillow. "I need you."

"I'm here," she said, sliding a dark strand of hair behind Max's ear. She pressed her body up against Max's, not wanting to be apart even for a moment. She kissed the side of her face, her heart full.

"Better than I'd even dreamed," Max said, pulling her even closer. "Pretty sure you just played me like a fiddle."

Ella laughed and pushed up on her forearms. "Yeah, well, who played who first?"

"I couldn't help it. I really like you naked."

"Well, I was undressing you with my eyes before I even learned your name."

Max laughed as she slid on top, which seemed to be her favorite place to be. "I don't think I'm done with you yet."

"No?"

She pressed her hips into Ella. "Definitely not."

"Good," Ella said, struck by newfound desire and the sudden, unshakable thought that this—whatever it was—had just changed everything.

FIFTEEN

Yip!

E lla stretched like a cat and smiled without opening her eyes. She'd had sex last night. Mhmm. She sure as hell had. She hugged her sheets and took a moment to revel because *damn, it had been good.* Every inch of her sore and satisfied body reminded her of that. She finally opened her eyes and took in the beautiful sunlight streaming in through the slanted blinds of her room, mirroring the high she was still on.

Not only that, but she had *work* waiting for her that morning. Actual paying work that she'd been personally selected for, which, quite honestly, had done wonders for her self-worth in the wake of her unceremonious dismissal.

Floating on air, she made her way to the kitchen, realizing it was nearly nine and Rachel would have long ago left for work. She poured herself a bowl of Hoopties and moved to the fridge for milk. Hanging on the fridge was a light-blue Post-it with Rachel's friendly and rounded handwriting on the front.

Hope it was good last night. -R

Next to the sentence was a rudimentary sketch of a pair of boobs. Forgetting for a moment that she was one hundred percent betraying her best friend, Ella laughed and pulled the

Post-it off the door. Reality set in as she walked to the trash can and discarded it. Rach would have had a very different response if she'd known the truth. Ella rolled her lips in, sobering significantly. None of this was okay. She was focusing on her own happiness with blinders on, because, apparently, it had been so damn long since she'd experienced that emotion.

Ella felt like the main character for once and didn't want this moment in time to end. Maybe she was reading too many romance novels and allowing herself to dream about love finding its way to her. Is that what was happening with Max? Surely, it was too premature to say, but the question, what if, certainly played on repeat in the back of her head this morning.

However, the situation was nearing a precipice, and she needed to act before she fell off entirely.

She didn't have an exit strategy for this situation and needed one fast. She could walk away from Max forever and bury this secret, which would likely find its way to the surface anyway. No, thank you. Or, she could be an adult and come clean to Rachel for real this time. Maybe even today. Definitely today.

After breakfast and a quick shower, Ella stood barefoot with wet hair in the middle of the bedroom, scanning her email. Mostly junk. An ad or two she might be interested in. And then there it was. A familiar name in the subject line: Inquiry Re: Alexandra Raymond. She opened the email and read in mystification. It was someone from the publishing company checking on her availability for an upcoming cover design. Alexandra was impressed with her work and had requested her personally. Holy hell. She whirled around to the empty room and said it out loud. "Holy hell, empty room."

She spun back and typed a quick response, which she, of course, reworded in a panicked frenzy, because the Raymond books were in all the major big-box stores and these people were trusting her quite a bit, not that they shouldn't, but *oh my God.*

It was only an hour later when she heard back from the woman, Stacey, with a firm booking and a deposit to secure the spot on her calendar. What was happening? A big-time publisher in her inbox already? All because she'd been standing in Doug's Books at the exact right moment. Life was such a shocking place to live.

Stacey set up a consultation and would share the publisher's drive to go over inspiration and direction. Ella was so over the moon that she wanted to yip or scream. No, definitely yip because it seemed unique, and so did today. "Yip!"

She called Max because she couldn't imagine not in this moment, an urge she would examine more fully later. Max picked up on the third ring.

"You call me at work now? I think I like it." God, how was her voice this sexy? It was just last night that she was naked and on top of Ella, too.

"You don't even say hello?"

"I don't have to. The readout told me in advance it was you. Hot Blond Woman From Last Night, it said. I'll have to change it tomorrow."

"You go to a lot of trouble."

"It's like you haven't even met me."

"I've more than met you now. And we'll circle back to that because I have news. Do you have time?"

"I'll make it."

She heard the sound of shuffling papers and grinned. Max was working, which was mundane on anyone else. Incredibly sexy on *her.* "So … I just got hired to design the cover of Alexandra Raymond's next release." She covered her mouth, marveling at hearing the words said out loud. Telling someone just made the whole thing that much more real.

"What? How in hell did you manage that?!" Max shouted

into the phone. As someone who played most everything cool, her show of emotion made the moment extra fun.

"That's what I'm sitting over here screaming!"

"Well, now we're screaming together!" A pause. "Sorry. No. Everything is fine, Sonya. We're just celebrating a minute. Tell the Simons I'll be right in." Another pause. "Maybe you should chaperone in the meantime."

"Oh, wow. You'd better get in there. They might kill each other."

"Wouldn't be the first time. Marriage, am I right?" Max laughed, and Ella started to laugh along with her, but she honestly wasn't sure if they were being serious or not. They'd never discussed things like hopes, dreams, beliefs, and values. She was startled to realize that someone who read romance novels regularly might not actually believe in romance. But then, she spent most of her hours helping them unravel in a conference room.

She blinked and shook herself out of it. They'd slept together once. Twice if you counted Stevie's living room. No one was proposing. The rest of the details would come in time, or they wouldn't—no reason to burn the house down because there was a spider in the kitchen.

"I'll let you return to work, but thank you for taking a moment to scream with me."

"My favorite part of the day so far. I promise. I'm super excited for you. You need to put this news on the Weepers group thread."

"You think it's worthy?"

"More than worthy. Stevie updated us an hour ago on her bacon crisping technique."

"Yeah, but it's bacon."

"Tell them."

Ella grinned, giddy again. "Fine. I will! Bye! Go be a hot lawyer!"

"Well, now I'm motivated. I'll message you later."

Ella slid off the call, leaned against the counter, and sighed in that dreamy way people did in the movies. Her phone began to vibrate in her hand. Max, again. "You couldn't stay away. I knew this was bound to happen."

"Let me buy you lunch."

"What? Really?"

"To celebrate. Come downtown. There's a little place around the corner from my office that I think you'll love. Every time I pass it, I think of you. Today would be the perfect day to sit by the window and enjoy the gorgeous sunshine."

"Listen to you. Why are you so cheerful today?" Ella asked, but she knew. She felt it, too, and kept checking her shoulder for bluebirds. None yet.

"Let's just say it's been a much-needed fifteen hours. Are you coming downtown?"

"I'll be there. A corporate lunch."

"If you ask a few legal questions, it certainly could be."

The thought of Max explaining the law to her made her have to adjust the way she was standing. It took so very little to set off the sexual energy that bopped between them to its own unpredictable rhythm. "Well, now I have to. How about noon?"

"You're on. I'd better go so Sonya can stop tap dancing for this couple. Today we're discussing their Disney points and who should retain them."

"Don't give them to the wrong person either, Max. Make the mouse proud."

"Says the real-life Disney princess."

"Gasp out loud. Me?" She grinned, amazed that's how Max saw her.

"Don't get me started on the fantasies I'm not going to have the second we hang up."

"Just know they're encouraged," Ella said, leaning in. "How are your boobs, by the way? Do they miss me?"

She was greeted with silence. Until finally, "You know they do. You are going to be the death of me in the best way."

She grinned. "And on that note, I'd better go."

"If you say so. Bye, Cinder-Ella."

For good measure, she picked up her imaginary gown and walked sideways through the kitchen.

MAX PUSHED OPEN the café's glass-paned door, and a soft chime rang overhead, a delicate sound that suited the place perfectly. Inside Sugar and Bloom, the air was warm and rich with the scent of espresso and something buttery, like fresh croissants just pulled from the oven. Sunlight spilled through lace-curtained windows, casting patterns onto the checkered tile floor. Tiny tables, each adorned with a single bud vase holding a fresh flower, were arranged in cozy corners, and the walls were lined with shelves of mismatched teacups and framed sketches of Parisian streets.

It was the kind of place that felt tucked away, like the sort of café a romantic would stumble into while wandering a charming European side street. And it was exactly the kind of place that made Max think of Ella.

She glanced around, feeling just a little out of place in her usual business suit, but at least it was cream today and not black. She exhaled. There was something about the whimsy of it all—the delicate china, the handwritten menu on a chalkboard, the soft hum of French music—that made her smile. She hoped Ella would feel the same way. This was kind of fun, an impromptu lunch.

She found a table in the corner, ordered herself a club soda with lime, and reflected on the upside-down week she had going. The bizarre dinner with her parents. The night she'd shared with Ella that felt like it had catapulted them into somewhere new and unexpected. The doctor's appointment that loomed the next day with her mother. Then there was the still-dangling issue of her past with Rachel and Rachel's friendship with Ella. In the midst of a whole lot going on, she chose to focus on the here, now, and the woman who just walked through the door and lit up the entire room.

Ella's eyes roamed every inch of the place, taking in the detail with a childlike wonder that was so very her. She had a way of relishing the happy details. It made Max want to do the same.

"I love this place," she said, depositing her bag on the table with a thunk. "Oh. Sorry about that." She removed it. "Probably not my best Parisian manners."

"The French are forgiving," Max said with no knowledge of whether that was true or not.

"You scored us a table by the window, even. This day gets better and better." She sank into the chair across from Max just as the sunlight lit up her blue eyes.

"I find if you ask for what you want, people are inclined to try and give it to you."

Ella nodded and rested her chin on her hand. "That's a tip I should pocket and use. I tend to make myself smaller when I'm intimidated." She sighed. "I don't think I advocate for myself as much as I should."

"Well, you've certainly put me in my place a few times. It was a master class."

"That's different. You're an entirely different example."

Max quirked her head. "How so?" This was getting good.

Ella leaned in as if about to share something that wasn't for public consumption. "You bring out a different side of me. You," she searched for words on the tablecloth before shooting her gaze back to Max, "slam me with big, overreaching emotions—hyperbolic ones. When I'm mad at you, I'm furious. When I'm calm, I'm the most serene person on earth. When I'm happy to see you, I could lasso the stars. It's all very trippy."

"And when you're turned on?" Max asked around her glass of ice water.

Ella's blue eyes went dark. "I think you can see the pattern."

"And I identify more than you realize."

Ella sat back in her chair, mystified. It was adorable. "Really? Because at all times you seem like a cool cucumber, unaffected and completely in control of not only your emotions, but the room in general."

She nodded along, having heard it all before. "I think that all goes back to how I was raised, essentially by a mother who demanded excellence. And how do you achieve it? Learning to be unflappable in the face of pressure, competition, or any challenge. It was drilled into my head that if I exert energy entertaining emotion, well, then I'd already lost half the battle."

"Emotions make you weak. Was it kind of like that?"

"Another good way to put it."

"Add in a father who was so good-natured and optimistic that if a tornado were ripping through our house, he'd probably hold his spot in front of the TV and wave it off with a no-big-deal grin." She fiddled with her spoon. "Two very different approaches to not actually emoting. Needless to say, it's taken some work to undo some of that."

"So, you're telling me that you're a bottler." She smiled at the server who placed a basket of warm bread between them. "Bless you and your extended family," Ella told him and took a deep inhale.

Max laughed because there Ella went again, appreciating all that was placed in front of her. "I don't know if bottler is the right characterization. I do feel all of the things very acutely. I toss and turn at night when I'm stressed. I cry, not a lot, but sometimes, when I'm alone. I think what you're picking up on is my determination not to show those feelings in a public venue."

"What about to someone you're very close to?" Ella asked and took a sip of water.

Max mimicked her with her own glass. "I think it would depend on the person."

"Fair enough."

Their server, Brielle, returned to take their order. The quiche Lorraine for Ella. The endive salad with pears for Max. "You don't eat Oatmeal Hoopties, do you?" She said it as if she knew the answer, and it was a shame.

Max squinted, not following the thread. "I don't think I have."

"I figured as much when you ordered the very adult salad at the restaurant that specializes in butter and more butter."

"Did I just break your heart?"

Ella took a moment to chew her bread, and Max took a moment to watch. "Only on your behalf. I'm starting to feel like I might have been called into your life for a reason."

"You're going to teach me about hoopty things?"

She nodded and hooked a strand of that blond hair behind her ear like a bread-eating pro. "I like the way you put that. Yes. Hoopties and all things silly should maybe go on our to-do list."

"I'm all for lists. They are highly instrumental in making my workday happen."

"See? I had a feeling you kept those. I do, too, but mainly just in my chaotic little head, and sometimes I misplace them there." She shrugged. "I'd just like to see you enjoy your life more and feel okay about doing so."

"I think you just told me I'm boring."

"Listen." Ella let her head drop back. "You are the least boring person I've met, and you need to understand how seriously I mean that." She took a beat. "But you are stoic. Not that it isn't hot."

"I can plead guilty to this charge." Their lunches arrived, and Max sat back, allowing her perfectly plated salad to be slid in front of her. "I like that you're not. How about you help me emote and I help you advocate for yourself more often?"

Ella pointed at her with her fork. "I like that. I applaud the idea."

"Then we've struck a deal, and I'll have Sonya draw up the contract."

"Hanging out with a lawyer is going to take some getting used to."

"I'll teach you what you need to know."

They shared a moment of eye contact before Ella's cheeks dusted pink and she shook her head. "Oh, Max Wyler. Where in the world did you come from?"

She slid a bite of salad into her mouth as if to say *I'll never tell*. They took a moment with their lunches as more of the tables around them filled up. Popular place. In the midst, Max ordered herself to truly relax and enjoy the restaurant, the ambiance, and the company the way Ella would. It was … freeing in many ways. And while she didn't want to allow her thoughts to drift to the stresses at work, there was one topic that begged their immediate attention.

"Have you talked with Rachel yet?"

Ella finished chewing, set down her fork, and met Max's gaze. "I need to. I think the sooner the better."

"I completely agree," Max said. "And it's not like—"

"We're in some kind of committed relationship."

"No."

"Or eloping or declaring our love."

"We're hanging out."

Ella nodded. "And she should know that."

They were on the same page, and Max was relieved to hear it. "Can I offer you some advice?" She moved a pear slice around on her plate.

"Yes. In fact, I welcome it, Counselor."

"When you loop her in, include your own story in the mix."

"Oh, this is my first lesson in advocacy, isn't it?"

"In fact, it is. Let Rachel hear all the things you've gone through. The reason you made certain decisions, or acted when maybe you hadn't planned on acting. Include how it all made you feel. She needs all of the information so she doesn't jump to conclusions about your motives but can see you as someone in a very human predicament."

Ella sighed, her gaze falling to the table. "This isn't going to be easy. I'll tell you that."

"No." Max frowned, wishing she could take Ella's place. "I'm afraid it's not."

SIXTEEN

The Cutest Little Red Car in Virginia

"You've got to be kidding me."

Perhaps Ella had been on too big of a winning streak, because once she returned to her car after lunch, she was brought straight back down to earth when her beloved Mini made pathetic choking sounds instead of starting. This wasn't good. After a few more minutes and soft words of encouragement like, "You are the cutest little red car in Virginia, and you definitely have another ride in you. You've got this," Ella had to admit the car was not coming back to life.

She took out her phone and typed a quick message to Max, whom she'd just shared a sweet goodbye with on the corner before she walked back to work.

> You know anything about cars?

Her reply came almost immediately.

> Incredibly useful. Fast. Can be chick magnets.
> But not how to fix them, no. Trouble?

Mine gave up on life.

Give me five minutes.

True to her word, Max, in her beautiful black Range Rover, pulled up alongside the small paid lot near the restaurant. "Hop in. We can wait in the climate-controlled splendor for the tow truck."

"You did not have to do this."

"I wanted to." There was something sweet in the way she'd said it, and Ella glimpsed a strand of vulnerability. Rare and a little startling. She had a feeling that the more time they spent together, the more she'd glimpse the Max beneath the ultra-put-together exterior. She couldn't help but crave just that. She wanted to know every facet of Max.

The tow truck arrived even faster than the woman on the phone had promised, and once the Mini was on its way to the shop, Max rescheduled a meeting and offered to take Ella home.

"It might seem like I staged this whole thing to spend an extra twenty minutes in your presence."

Max tossed her a glance, holding the wheel with one hand, shades on, totally looking like the sexy corporate boss she was in life. "It had crossed my mind." She added a smile and went back to the road. "If so, I applaud the commitment to the charade. Tow trucks aren't cheap. Good thing you're sought after by famous authors."

"That's right. I am! I almost forgot."

They drove to the up-tempo sounds of Dua Lipa dancing the night away as Ella began to brainstorm ideas for Alexandra Raymond's next contemporary small-town cover. The assistant had offered her a one-page description to get her started on the brainstorming path.

"Two impromptu adventures with you in a row," Ella said,

as Max coasted them into the driveway. Then she raised a brow. "Well, three if we count last night."

"Why would we not count last night?"

"I don't know the rules for these things, Maxine. I'm shooting from the hip." She hopped out of the car and grinned when Max quickly followed her.

"I really like your hip. Both of them, by the way."

Ella turned as Max covered the steps to the porch and slid her arms around her neck. "You sure you have a meeting? Because today's been fun, but we can probably make it more fun."

"What's a meeting again?" Max asked and caught Ella's lips with her own, and it felt like all was exactly as it was supposed to be. Her heart rate escalated, her toes curled, and her body went warm. That's what happened when the two of them were together. Everything just *worked*.

"I thought I heard voices out here," Rachel said, emerging with a proud smile. They froze. Ella felt the blood retreat from her face. Her fingertips went numb, and the effect crept across her skin. *No, no, no.* This couldn't be happening. The smile faded right from Rachel's face. Automatically, Ella took a step back from Max and searched Rachel's eyes, trying to communicate that this wasn't all it seemed. Except it was. Rachel pursed her lips, her eyes wide with understanding. "I see. It was never Ariana, was it?"

This was a nightmare playing out in slow motion, and all Ella wanted was to wake up, rewind the last three minutes of her life, and do them all over again another way. "No." She took in air. "And I've wanted to talk to you about that. I was planning on—"

"Don't. It doesn't matter at this point." She looked around. "And I'm obviously in the way here."

Max took off her sunglasses. "Rachel, I think—"

"I honestly don't need to hear a word from you, who was kissing my best friend on my porch just seconds ago." She turned back to Ella, and the hurt slashed across her features shook Ella to her core. "And I'm not sure what to say to you, except this: I thought we were friends."

"I know." She nodded. "And we are, Rach. God, I'm just—"

"I can't listen to this. Not right now."

"Okay." She rolled her lips in and dropped her head to her chest, surrendering to Rachel's wishes. Max stood off to the side, seeming to understand that less was more. But all Ella could think about was fixing this immediately. While she did what she could to compose her thoughts and come up with the magical words that would do just that, Rachel went inside, grabbed a bag, and walked to her car, which was parked on the street. That's why they hadn't seen it in the driveway. She must have come home for lunch and hadn't wanted to be blocked in.

With Rachel about to drive away, Ella couldn't stand it another minute longer. She hurried down the driveway and stood next to Rachel's window, panic rising in her chest making it hard to breathe. "I love you, and I'm sorry, and I want the chance to explain everything. Can we take a minute? Just the two of us inside?"

Rachel rolled down her window and looked Ella straight in the eyes. That's when she saw them, the tears, big and plentiful, wet on Rachel's cheeks. She'd done that. She'd hurt her friend, and she hated herself for it. In an instant, none of the reasoning, none of the justifications she'd given herself recently made sense. It was like a light had just been turned on in a dark room, and she saw the error of her ways so clearly now. She should have communicated, been honest, and allowed Rachel to hear her out. She'd crossed a line that she couldn't uncross, and in the process, had done actual damage to the one relationship she'd always been able to count on.

"I need to get out of here, Ella." Her voice was low and

raspy. She hit her steering wheel. "And I have a damn director's meeting in an hour and I can't look like this."

"Come back inside. I'll get you a tissue. We can touch up your eye makeup."

"Do you not get it? I don't want anything from you. You're a traitor. And a damn good one. Please step away from my fucking car."

Ella, with tears of her own threatening, did as she was asked and watched Rachel pull away, driving faster than she usually did. That left Ella standing in the middle of the street, lost, guilt-ridden, and not sure what to do with herself.

Max arrived quickly and pulled her into a hug. She wanted to resist, to insist that everything about them felt wrong now, yet, somehow, she didn't. Couldn't. She needed Max in this moment, especially knowing it might be their last.

"It doesn't feel like it right now, but it's going to be okay," Max murmured. Her warm breath against the side of Ella's face was comforting. Being held was. Not that she deserved it. "You two are friends. You have some things to work out, but you will."

Ella straightened out of the embrace and nodded. "I hope you're right." She looked down the now-empty street in the direction Rachel had driven. "But you didn't see the look on her face just now. She's never looked at me like that before." Her voice had been reduced to a whisper, emotion having strangled what was left of it. The ache in her chest was near unbearable. "And she's right. I'm the definition of a traitor."

"No, you're not," Max said. "You were put in a difficult spot and reacted in a very human manner."

"Don't let me off the hook."

"Us. I was right there with you."

"Yeah, well, my duty to my friend certainly outweighed yours."

"Still."

"Yeah." Silence. "Still."

"What now?" Max asked, squeezing her hand. It was supportive at most and not at all romantic. Didn't matter. Instinctively, Ella pulled hers back because they just couldn't.

"You go. I stay."

Max nodded. "Are you going to answer me when I check on you later?"

"I don't know," she said, wrapping her arms around herself. "And I only say that because my brain is not exactly working at the moment."

"I know." She tilted her head in the direction of the house. "Let's get off the street."

They walked back to the house together with the weight of fifty lead balloons tethered to them, a complete contrast to the spring in their step just fifteen minutes ago. How quickly the world could flip on its end. There was a valuable lesson here, and when Ella returned to herself, she vowed to learn it.

THIS WAS BAD. This was really bad.

Rachel hadn't come home from work, and it was close to eleven. Ella knew because she'd checked the time on her phone every time she'd looked to see if a text from Rachel had snuck in without her hearing it.

She'd tried to work. She'd tried to eat. She'd tried to come up with the perfect words to make this whole situation better. Even sitting with a pad and pen hadn't helped her find them. It felt like her abilities were broken in every sense of the word.

One of Rachel's friends had posted a photo on Instagram of them at Dirty Little Secret holding up lemon drop martinis. Rachel looked like she'd had a couple, which made sense, Ella having stomped on their entire friendship and all. However, it was late, and she would usually have been home by now.

Even though Ella felt like she'd been run over by a truck with a crying-induced headache and a sour stomach, there was no way she was going to bed until Rachel was safe back home where she belonged. They didn't have to talk. She just needed to see that she was safely in bed.

An hour passed.

Then another.

Why hadn't she added Rachel to Find My Friends once she'd moved to town? It seemed like such a stupid thing to miss now. She walked to the front window and stared at the driveway, willing her friend to arrive. Self-recriminations pinged from every part of Ella as she slid to the floor in front of the armchair that had once belonged to Rachel's grandmother. She'd relegated it to the front room because she didn't want to get rid of it, but it hadn't matched the rest of the decor.

It was now after 1 a.m., and something had to be wrong. If this had been one of the romance novels she read for Weepers, Rachel's car would have veered off the road, or she'd have been kidnapped or robbed. Her victim status alone qualified her for tragedy on a night like this one, but Ella couldn't let herself think that way. Her mind was already running away with itself when a pair of headlights lit up the entire room. She exhaled, harnessing the relief that came over her.

Rachel. Finally. Relief spilled from her chest to her limbs.

Her heart hammered as she stood at the window, watching her friend exit an unfamiliar car, likely an Uber, and make her way up the walk with a less-than-perfect gait. She'd definitely been drinking, but had done the responsible thing and gotten a ride home. Thank God, Ella wouldn't be calling hospitals all night. She turned on the small blue lamp and stood just as the front door opened with a whine. They'd needed to oil the hinges for weeks.

"Hi," Ella said. "Um, you don't have to talk to me, but I just want to make sure you're okay." She was shaking again, nauseous, too.

Rachel turned at the sound of her voice, and when they

made eye contact in the dimly lit space, Rachel went still. "You're still crying." The tone in her voice was flat but not combative.

Ella shrugged. "You don't have to worry about me."

"Trust me when I say I don't want to." A pause. "But I do."

Ella waited, absorbing the unexpected words.

"I know I can be a selfish bitch."

"I would never call you that."

"Well, you wouldn't be the first. And maybe I need to work on that and become a more thoughtful friend, but I never would have gone behind your back." She'd said that last part with a bite.

"I know." Ella nodded, taking in every word and emotion. This was a moment for her to listen, rather than explain.

"Here's the thing. I would have fucking hated hearing you and Max had something going, but I would have dealt with it."

"I know."

"What I can't handle is you hiding the truth, walling me off from your actual life like I'm this child." She closed her eyes and shook her head. "Sorry, the room is spinning."

"That's okay. And you're right. I completely decided how you would react and panicked. I screwed up and am not sure how to fix it."

"I don't know if we can," Rachel said, her voice steady but edged with the lingering weight of hurt. She turned and walked out, her footsteps fading down the hall, probably en route to her room, to the quiet refuge of space and distance.

But then, just as Ella braced herself for the cold finality of that exit, Rachel reappeared. She strode back in without hesitation, her expression unreadable, and before Ella could say a word, Rachel pulled her into a tight, unwavering embrace.

Ella froze for a heartbeat, then shattered. The dam inside her broke, and a fresh wave of tears spilled down her cheeks as she clung to Rachel, her fingers fisting into the back of her sweater like she might disappear again if she let go.

Rachel said nothing—she didn't need to. The warmth of her hold, the strength of it, was enough. It was a balm, an unspoken promise that maybe, just maybe, forgiveness wasn't out of reach.

That moment of grace was everything to Ella. It was oxygen in a suffocating room, a flicker of light in the wreckage of guilt and regret. And for the first time in hours, she could breathe again.

Rachel hadn't ended their friendship or kicked her out, which she had every right to do. Time was what Rachel needed. Ella could certainly put in the time and work required to rebuild her trust. It was a kernel of hope that Ella wasn't sure she deserved, but promised to pay forward one day.

SEVENTEEN

Soft Pants Required

S ome days passed without much notice. Some days
embedded themselves in Max's memory for all the right
reasons, happy and full of joyful exchanges. And then, there
were the days that fucking ate her alive. That had been
yesterday.

Max slammed her locker shut, the metallic clang echoing
through the nearly empty gym. *Good.* She rolled her shoulders
back, forcing herself to focus on the weight of her own body
instead of the weight of everything else.

Rachel's tear-streaked face. Ella's trembling hands pulling
away. The way the world seemed to tilt on its axis in a matter
of seconds. Not that she was innocent, or a victim. That part
made it worse.

She exhaled sharply, yanking her wraps tight around her
knuckles.

It wasn't supposed to feel like this. Today.

Two nights ago, she had Ella's laughter in her ear, warm
fingers tracing absent patterns on her skin. And now, she
wasn't sure if she had her at all.

But, of course, that wasn't the last of it. Earlier in the day,
she'd accompanied her mother to her doctor's appointment,

where her family's future had rested in the hands of an oncologist with a clipboard. Max hadn't been ready for that, either.

"We're going to do what we can to get ahead of this thing, Mayumi." Dr. Rivera scratched his head, a gesture that was so commonplace. It reminded her that these doctors were just human beings, who might be able to help and might not. She swallowed, ignoring the slight nausea that peeked its head in now and then.

Her mother nodded. "I'll do whatever you say, Carlos. You know that I have a great deal of respect for you," her mother said with a wave of her hand. Max only caught that it was trembling when she placed it back in her lap. Apparently, the two were acquainted through a professional organization of physicians in the area. They had a shorthand and spoke medical jargon that was sometimes over Max's head. She did her best to take notes and keep up, knowing her primary role was to provide moral support and serve as a second pair of ears.

"I think our best move is to move forward with chemo," Dr. Rivera said. "The sooner, the better. We'll see how you respond after six weeks, and go from there."

Her mother nodded and offered a wobbly smile—another example of her vulnerability. "Either way, everything will be okay, right? I've lived a good life." Max didn't like the sound of those words, but she was also coming to understand that there was no right or wrong way to cope with fear, and if this was her mother's method, she'd support her.

"Well, let's get you many more good years." He covered her hand with his, gave it a squeeze, and rolled back to his screen to put in the order. The clickety-clack of the keyboard echoing in the stark exam room had plucked every anxious nerve ending Max had like she was a tightly strung guitar. She pulled her focus away and instead passed her mom a smile, absorbing the small one she sent back.

All these hours later, the punching bag swayed gently in front of Max, waiting.

Max didn't.

Her first strike sent a satisfying shock up her arm. She closed her eyes and experienced the much-needed discomfort. Somehow, it helped. The second came harder, the third harder still. The rhythm took over, demanding more force, more focus, more of her breath until she didn't have space for anything else. Not for the guilt or the ache. Not for the impossible unknowns hanging over her like a storm about to break.

Fists met leather, over and over, until her muscles screamed and the burn in her lungs reminded her she was still here. Still fighting.

Still standing.

"You haven't been in here for a while. I'd say I missed you, but I can't stand a big head."

Max smiled through her recovery. Amanda. Their workout times apparently still coincided, even though Max had been missing hers lately. She straightened, giving Amanda a chance to see her face.

The smile fell away. "Oh, fuck. Are you okay?"

"I'm fine," Max said. "Always. Why?"

"You are not. Don't bullshit me. I've known you since Jesus was in junior high school." She placed a hand on her hip, her trim and spray-tanned midsection on display as always. In a new twist, Max barely noticed, and she certainly didn't check her out the way she might have in the past, which meant she really wasn't herself. Or was it a reach to think that she was simply a new version of herself? There was before Ella and after, a phenomenon she was still getting used to.

"Fine. I had a crap week and it's likely to continue."

"What happened?"

Max began to unwrap her hands. "Oh, we're doing a deep dive today?" Their relationship was built on flirting, teasing, and an occasional actual conversation.

"Yes," Amanda said without budging an inch. "What you don't seem to get about me is that I give the best advice in the history of the fucking gym."

Max looked up, arched a brow, and surveyed the gym for those she'd beaten out. "You think highly of your ability."

"Listen to me carefully," Amanda said, taking a seat along the wall and pulling a knee to her chest. "I don't think. I know."

Amanda, as always, was a force. And maybe Max could benefit from the insight of someone on the outside looking in. Perspective was a valuable commodity, and perhaps she'd lost hers.

"My mom is sick. It's cancer."

"Fuck. I'm so sorry."

"And my personal life is crumbling like a condemned building. That's probably where I could use a little wisdom."

"Perfect. Tell me more."

"There's this woman who's moved to town, and I've developed this," she searched for the words that fit, "crush."

"Mhmm. I'm waiting for more, because crush sounds so incredibly innocuous, and what I just witnessed cross your face was anything but."

"Fine. She's different. I feel differently than I have in the past, but I didn't get the chance even to figure out what that might mean because she's best friends with my ex."

Amanda's mouth fell open. "She's best friends with Rachel?"

"I forgot that you know her."

"Everyone in this community knows everyone. I bought her a martini once because she's pretty."

"She's definitely that."

Amanda paused. "This isn't going to go well, Max."

"Now you're with me."

Amanda ruminated on the information and took a swig from her water bottle. "Rachel knows?"

"As of yesterday. She saw us kissing."

"Oh, fuck. This is a sophisticated sapphic soap opera in the making." She stood. "Here's what you're going to do."

"Listening. What am I gonna do?"

"Very little. Be responsive if she reaches out, but give the two of them their space to work through the friendship. It's not about you right now. It's about them. She'll get to you in time."

"And if she doesn't? If I never hear from her again?"

"Better to have loved and lost?"

Max sighed. "I don't know that I subscribe to that theory, given what I'm feeling right now." She eyed the bag. "Maybe I should hit more things."

"Only if I can watch." Amanda held up her hands. "Kidding. Your attention is spoken for, and I respect you for it. I'm also here if you want to talk it out some more. You have my number."

Max turned. "You really think less is more?"

"Right now, I do."

She exhaled, swallowing the pill. "I hear you."

When she got home an hour later, she allowed herself to check her phone, something she'd forbidden herself from doing every five minutes. Nothing from Ella. Max set the phone on the counter and stared at it like she could will a message into existence.

She braced her hands against the cool surface, exhaling slowly. The house felt too quiet, her thoughts too loud. She grabbed a glass of water and took a long sip, then clapped her hands a couple of times, as if physically resetting the vibes in the room might help.

One day at a time.

One hour at a time, if that's what it took.

She pushed off the counter and headed for the shower, letting the night wash over her.

The Weepers were meeting that night, and Ella wouldn't be there. That was hard, but necessary, at least for now. She and Max had exchanged messages only twice since the porch debacle. In the first, Max had asked if she was okay and if there was anything she could do. In the second, she said she'd hoped to see Ella at book club and inquired if she'd be there. Ella had answered both texts as politely as possible, but gave very little of herself, which Max had picked up on.

As the days passed, she began to truly feel the loss of Max in her life. "It was the right thing to do," she said quietly to herself as she made a quick sandwich between work sessions.

Even if she missed the way Max's laughter could pull her out of the heaviest moods. Even if she missed the warmth of her hand resting casually on Ella's knee, like she belonged there. Even if she missed the late-night conversations that stretched until dawn, where Max saw through all of her walls and made her feel understood in a way no one else ever had.

Even if she missed *her*.

"I lost my job," Rachel said, dropping her Prada bag on the kitchen counter with a decided thump.

"What?" The two of them hadn't done a lot of talking in the last few days. They exchanged pleasantries, but kept their interactions at surface level for Rachel's comfort. But this was different. This was life stuff that demanded an immediate pause to the new dynamic.

Her face was blank. "My director of sales is bringing in her niece, who is moving here after graduating from design school in Paris. I'm not making this up."

"This is exactly the kind of romance novel victim status I thought we'd sidestepped."

"What?" Rachel turned to her, brows down. She looked exhausted, as if she'd spent the week wrestling ghosts no one else could see. "I don't know what that means."

"Nor should you." Ella leaned back against the counter. "What do you need?"

"Um, maybe those hoopty things you like." She looked around the kitchen, as if unsure where the box might be. Her voice had taken on a childlike quality, which made sense. "In a big bowl."

Ella whirled into action. "Excellent choice. I'm on it."

"Can I maybe have some sugar on top?"

"Goes without saying. I'm not a heathen." She ushered Rachel out of the kitchen. "Tell you what. I'll make the snack. You go get comfy pants on. The bigger, the better."

"You think?"

Ella turned back and met her eyes. "I know."

"Okay, yeah, this probably warrants the big, soft pants. It's like my brain's not even working."

"It doesn't have to, okay?"

Rachel paused on the way to her room and met Ella's gaze. Her features softened. Whatever issues they had between them, Ella was still a familiar face, which Rachel likely needed right now. "You've had a rough go of it and just need a soft place to fall. Let's just give you that. You can hate me again, after. I promise."

"Ella."

"Yeah?"

A longer pause. Her stomach tightened. "Nothing. You're right. Thank you."

She nodded and watched her wounded friend head out on a comfy pant mission while she prepared a bowl of Hoopties with care.

The afternoon was a quiet one. Ella shelved her cover, knowing she could pick it back up again and work as late as she needed, the beauty of self-employment. They popped on Netflix, and she let Rachel have the remote. They navigated between trashy reality TV and vintage rom-coms. Once they finished one, Rachel navigated them to another. After the first hour of mostly silence, Rachel started to make occasional comments.

"I never get tired of that part," she said when Kate Hudson finished singing "You're So Vain" with Matthew McConaughey at the party.

"I love that Carly Simon let them tear that song apart for this film."

"She should thank them. I didn't even know the song until this scene."

"Don't tell my parents."

A few more moments of silence. "How are they?" Rachel asked.

Ella thought about the question. The truth was, she didn't exactly know. Her brother had joined them in Greece, but she wasn't sure if they were all still together. She often reached out when she hadn't heard from them, but this time, she decided to wait. "I'll find out the next time they remember I'm out here."

"They don't forget about you. They just get caught up in their adventures." She sighed. "Sometimes people just fall for their own bullshit. I do." She turned back to the film, a heaviness still hanging off of her.

"Well," Ella said, finally. "You're not the only one with things to work on."

Rachel leveled her with a pointed look. "Trust me. I know."

"Touché."

They watched the rest of the film in silence. Ella checked the clock, sometimes wondering what the Weepers were discussing in this parallel moment. Had Max explained away her absence? Had their friends believed her? It was likely that if she wanted to maintain her friendship with Rachel, which she did, she would need to keep her distance from Max. She hadn't thoroughly examined the impact of that reality, but it likely meant stepping away from the Weepers altogether, a thought that made her chest ache. The club had been her first true home base since landing in Everly Springs.

After one last episode of *The Traitors*, Rachel powered down the TV and dropped off her empty popcorn bowl in the sink. "You didn't have book club tonight?"

"I skipped it. I probably won't be attending anymore." She wanted Rachel to know that she took repairing their friendship seriously. If that meant sacrificing herself, so be it.

"Oh. Well, if you—"

"It's a bad idea. I'm going to keep my distance from Max. The whole thing was out of line and never should have happened."

She nodded as she rinsed out her dish, but said nothing.

"I didn't ask a lot of questions about work because I thought you needed some time away from the whole topic. But if you want to talk about what happened today or what your future plans might be, we can. As you know, I've been there."

Rachel paused, placed her bowl in the dishwasher, and met Ella's gaze with closed-off green eyes. "I don't think so."

"Okay. No problem. Well, the offer stands."

"I think I just want some sleep."

"Understandable."

The wall was still up between them, and Ella couldn't help but wonder if it would be permanent. The thought made her uneasy. She watched Rachel extinguish every light except the one above Ella's head and leave the room without another word. That's when Ella felt the hopelessness descend, the overt loneliness she had no one to blame for but herself. Without Max, the Weepers, or Rachel, she honestly had no one. Her other friends were acquaintances, and most of them were back in Tulsa. Her family would surface again someday with a bubbly update before flitting off into their bright and cheerful lives without her. And here she would be, Ella Baker—party of one. Forever and always.

EIGHTEEN

Pajamas and Pop-Ups

S he wasn't supposed to reach out. Max had promised herself that she'd take Amanda's advice and give Ella the space to work through her turmoil with Rachel and take the lead on whatever happened between her and Max. The problem was that Max was not a passive person, but rather someone who preferred to take charge of her destiny, which led her to text Ella several days after the last book club meeting, the one without Ella.

> I miss you. So very much.

It had been a simple text, but the words were from her heart. There was so much more that she wanted to say, too. That she missed the way Ella's eyes lit up when she talked about something she liked. Or the fire that crept into them when she spoke with conviction. The way her presence felt like a satisfying breath after a long day. How her fingers found Max's when they were close, even when they weren't supposed to touch. She also missed all of the memories they could have been making right this very moment if circumstances had been different. Even the book club, which had been a part of

Max's life long before laying eyes on Ella Baker, now felt incomplete without her presence.

A day went by. Two. Three. Unfortunately, Ella didn't return the message.

Max drove home from work well after nine, having stayed late at the office on purpose. Distraction was her best friend, keeping her from overthinking. Maybe she'd been right about the whole love game all along. Letting her heart even tentatively hope had been a bold move. Love was never the gentle thing that poets promised.

"You're being dramatic," she said as she stood in front of the elevator to her apartment.

"Me?" her neighbor asked when the doors opened.

"Sorry, Tom. No. But you should know, love sucks."

Tom exited the elevator, and she entered it, switching spots. "I don't know," he said. "Meg and I have been married for eighteen years."

"So far," she said with a shrug as the elevator doors closed.

"That was dark. Even for you, Max," Tom's voice called as the elevator began to move. It wasn't until she got to her apartment that she saw she had a message on her phone from Stevie.

Awful news. Doug's is on fire. Fire department there now.

What the hell?

The news smacked Max square in the face. It wasn't the kind of message you ever expected to receive. Some things in life feel sacred, off-limits for anything unlucky or tragic to ever touch them. Doug's was one of those entities. She prayed the damage was minor while wondering what had gone wrong and what she could do to help. As thoughts raced and swirled, one concept rose to the top of her mind. A business as beloved as Doug's would be more than just a loss to this city. There was, quite simply, no place like that little bookstore, unique and chock-full of character. The corkboard at the back of the store was responsible for the inception of Read It and Weep Book Club, which gave way to the important friendships Max now treasured.

Rumors flew on social media about what had caused the place to ignite. Some people said that a specific group of kids had a grudge against Doug and had intentionally set fire to the place. Others felt that Doug seemed the type to light candles, and maybe he'd left one burning after hours. It took the fire department two days to determine that a power surge had likely caused the coffee maker to overheat and spark. *The damned coffee maker of all things.*

Max drove by the store later that week. The building still stood, but its heart had been hollowed out by fire. Through the veil of soot and char, she could make out slouching shelves, their warped frames leaning on each other like fallen warriors. The sight twisted something deep inside her. Doug had poured himself into this place, and now it was a ruin, and Max couldn't stop wondering how Ella was holding up.

Everything in her wanted to ask—to hear Ella's voice, to be the person she turned to. But reaching out meant opening a door Ella might not be ready to walk through, and Max would never be the one to push her through it.

With a slow breath, she pressed the gas, driving on but not away. She didn't have answers, but she'd find a way to help. Letting this bookstore disappear, letting Doug lose everything, letting Ella carry it alone? Unthinkable.

IT WAS THURSDAY, but it didn't feel like it. On Thursdays, Ella generally swung into Doug's in the mid-morning and worked there until mid-afternoon when she got hungry and returned home for a sandwich. She'd design for most of the morning until Doug hit a lull, and then she'd work with him on his social media. He was actually becoming quite adept at Instagram and had even started following a few independent bookstores and a couple of authors he wanted to attract to the store.

This first Thursday since the fire was Ella's least favorite Thursday ever. She was listless, depressed, and a little pissed off about it. The overcast skies did little to improve her mood, which even coffee couldn't help at this point.

"If you were a cartoon, there would be spiky lines flying off of you," Rachel said, watching her from the fridge.

"That tracks." She eyed Rachel, who wore a cream-colored skirt and a white blouse. "Why are you dressed up for the living room?"

"I have an interview."

"That's awesome!" She might have shouted that too loudly, based on the fact that Rachel launched herself into the air and spilled a little bit of half-and-half from the carton in her hand. "Sorry. I felt a rush of positive energy and had to act before it was gone."

"Clearly." Rachel still wasn't her bubbly self in Ella's presence, but they'd worked out a decent rhythm of civility, and maybe one day they'd get there.

"Is it a retail job? Should we pack you a lunch?" She glanced around the kitchen for supplies. "What do you need?"

"Ella. Slow down. I don't need anything."

She froze. "Got it. No. You're right. I'm just jumpy today. In my head."

"Well, you've been in those pajamas for a couple of days. Why don't you get dressed? Touch some grass."

"I should be at Doug's right now."

Rachel kicked a hip against the counter, bag on her shoulder. "How is he?"

"Quiet. Not that he's a verbose person to begin with, but the two times that I've spoken with him since the fire, his judgmental little quips are gone. He's lost his spark, which makes sense."

"And what's your plan? For Doug."

Ella blinked. "I don't have one."

"Hmm. I wasn't expecting that." She turned to go. "Give it some thought. Maybe a goal will get you out of those plaid pants."

Ella looked down at her baggy ensemble, understanding Rachel's meaning. Instead of moping in her kitchen, she should channel her emotions and mobilize. She was fantastic at project work, and although she couldn't take back what happened to Doug's, she could do everything in her power to help rebuild the store bigger and better than ever. It was the jump start she needed. Without delay, she hopped in the shower, blasted her music, and settled in in front of her laptop, making list after list of ideas.

"A pop-up shop?" Ariana asked from across the table at Gizmo's, the coffee shop she'd recommended, which seemed to be patronized by college students much cooler than Ella. If only she'd known there was a beanie requirement, she could have swung by the store.

"Yes. Doug said that the insurance claim is in process, but won't cover the full range of damage, so I've been brainstorming ways we can help him, and a pop-up store is my favorite option. Hear me out."

"Listening."

"Doug says he has some leftover inventory safely living in his storage unit. We set up the shop, but without prices. People pay whatever they want for the books."

Ariana nodded, understanding the concept. "But if they know it's to help Doug, they're likely to add on a little."

"Or a lot."

"This is an excellent idea. And Doug's on board?" Ariana, with her bright-green eyes and shiny brown hair, sat back, sipped her cappuccino, and looked cool doing it. No wonder she frequented this coffee shop. She was the type who'd fit in anywhere.

"I haven't told him, but I will. He'll listen to me. I doubled his sixty-person Instagram following and now he thinks I have magical unicorn powers."

"Then we capitalize on that." Ariana shook her finger, gathering a thought in real time. "So, if people are setting their own price, we need to curate our special invite list."

"Exactly that."

"We need the financially comfortable. Who do we know that's connected? Isn't Max on the board of some bigwig attorney association?"

"Yes, she definitely is." Ella dropped her gaze to the beige and white swirling pattern on the table, swallowing the swarm of feelings that came with thinking about Max after refusing to let herself for so long. "You want to give her a call?" She looked up.

Ariana watched her with interest. "You know, I think you'd be better suited."

They stared at each other. She knew too damned much. That smug expression said so.

"Ella." The use of her name in that level-with-me tone and wide-eyed look confirmed it.

"She and I haven't spoken in … a while."

"Why is that? Because I don't think I've ever seen two people look at each other the way the two of you do. So, something went wrong, and I'm going to imagine it had some-thing to do with the Rachel factor."

Ella rolled her lips in, considering how much to share, but then realized that it was stupid to withhold when she'd felt so isolated and desperately needed a friend. Well, here was Ariana, presenting herself on cue.

"You can just say it," Ariana said around her mug. "You know you want to."

Ella raised a casual shoulder. "I like Max a lot."

Ariana shook her head and made the sound of a game show buzzer. "Nope. We all like Max. Max is great. Try again."

"Fine. I'm wildly attracted to Max."

She made the come here gesture. "More."

Unable to resist, the dam broke. "Fine. I enjoy every moment I spend with her. I think about her when we're apart. And even when we're debating books with the passion of a thousand suns, I'm also imagining her naked." Ella exhaled slowly, feeling a little better for having said it out loud without downplaying it.

Ariana broke out in a slow smile. "And there it is. Now tell me something shocking, like water is incredibly wet."

"Stop it." Ella grinned. She shook her head, clearing it entirely so she could come at this fresh. "So you *did* know?"

Ariana dropped her chin in pouty sympathy. "Oh, sweet little kitten in a box, the whole book club knows."

"Seriously? Even sweet, innocent Morgan?" She clapped her forehead with one hand.

"Did you not notice the whispering when you snuck into the laundry room together at Stevie's?"

The embarrassment swooped and swarmed. "I had no idea you all were aware of that. I need to move to another country by this afternoon."

"Completely unnecessary. We were rooting for you. The two of you don't do a good job of hiding how you feel. Max might as well have had little fireworks going off in her eyes every time you walked in the room."

"And here I thought we were subtle."

"As a skywriter spelling out 'Max is my one true love' above the city."

"Hold on right there. We're not *in love*. Let's not leap to hyperbole."

"Fair enough." Ariana nodded, moving forward. "And so there's trouble brewing?"

"Brewed. Past tense."

"Rachel is not happy? Is this one of those girl code things? I never understood them. Everyone should want their friends to be happy as long as they treat everyone else with respect."

"That's the problem. I could have been more respectful. I didn't tell her about my feelings for Max or that we were ..."

"Making out in small rooms at book club?"

"Yes, Ari." She raised her eyebrows and stared at her cup. "That."

"I kept putting off the moment to tell Rachel everything, and then she saw us kissing."

"Dammit. I'm so sorry all three of you had to experience that moment."

"It was awful and not the way I wanted her to find out we were—"

"On absolute fire for each other."

Ella closed her eyes. "So many bold statements in this conversation, though I can't entirely argue with that one," she said with a sigh. But Ariana was speaking the absolute truth, whether Ella wanted to admit it or not. She and Max *had been* on fire, and not just in the bedroom. They challenged each other and teased with the best of them. They came with the perfect amount of camaraderie with the right blend of friction built in. And now they were two islands separated by a virtual ocean, and it made Ella want to throw her napkin at the boy playing his guitar badly two tables over. Double justice. "But I'd be lying if I said I didn't miss her now that we're purposefully keeping our distance."

Ariana frowned, clearly disliking the ending of the story. "What are you going to do about it?"

She shook her head. "Nothing. Because in good conscience, I can't."

"This is girl code, right? That's what's holding you back from Max."

"Friendship is another term. But girl code, sure."

"I get it. I do, but," Ariana pondered her cappuccino a moment. "At what point, Madam Romantic," she asked, meeting Ella's eyes, "does girl code get walloped in the name of love?"

Ella sat with the words, turning them over in her mind. "I think that's an answer I just don't have, which is why I need you to call Max about the pop-up and not me. Ari, I'm trying to right my wrong and make the best choice for everyone. Rachel's the best friend I've ever had."

Ariana's eyes softened, and her features relaxed in understanding. "I hear you. And I will reach out to Max about leveraging some of her big fish connections."

"Thank you. I think what we're doing for Doug could turn into a really good thing. I just want him to be okay again. The light's gone from his eyes."

"And what about the light that used to be in yours? Will you be okay again?"

"Yes. I will." Her resolve weakened. Those very eyes felt hot with the prickle of tears. "I hope so."

NINETEEN

A Novel Evening

M ax grasped the hem of her black cocktail dress, protecting it as she traversed the rotating glass doors. She was impressed. The museum lobby was not the museum lobby. She paused to take in the fully decorated space in front of her and gave her hair a subsequent shake, hoping the wind hadn't whipped up too much chaos. She'd chosen to wear it down in a less-is-more style. But, wow. The pop-up bookstore event was anything but.

The lobby of the Sinclair Museum of Art had never looked so downright swanky, as if a group of elves with design degrees had descended in the night and had their way with the space. Ella, with Ariana assisting her, had really made a meal of their concept. Max had done what she could to further their efforts. She'd been the one to secure the location, calling in a favor from her friend Barney, the museum's director. He'd agreed to waive the usual rental fee for the event Ella and Ariana had affectionately named *A Novel Evening*. The title was printed in gold on all the little black napkins they'd managed to have donated, matching the shimmer of silver and gold balloons clustered around the room.

The sponsored bar stood in one corner, flanked by high-top tables draped in black linens—courtesy of Fork, Yeah Catering Company, who'd generously supplied them pro bono. Overhead, the museum's tall lobby ceilings gave the space an air of elegance. And at the entrance, Tony, the classical guitarist, filled the air with soft music that made browsing the shelves of books feel like something special.

"Thank you for your attendance, madam," Morgan said in her most official voice, stepping forward with a black card that informed her that all proceeds would go exclusively to rebuild Doug's Books. "How did I do?" she asked Max in an adorable whisper. "I'm the door person. I greet the guests."

"Morg, it was one of the better greetings I've had in life," Max said, and gave Morgan a sideways squeeze. "This place looks amazing." She scanned the room that had yet to fill up. It was early, however, so it was only a matter of time. "I'm serious. Live music. Passed hors d'oeuvres. I was expecting paper plates and cake."

"It's all Ella. She's barely slept, putting all of this together. Lists upon lists. The group texts. I think you're on the one about the venue." It was the only lengthy communication she had received from Ella since everything came apart. "Literally everything is donated."

She marveled, just now noticing the display at the back of the room, which featured a collage of photos of Doug and the bookstore. A brilliant idea to show everyone what was lost and what was to be gained. "That's nothing short of amazing."

"Remind me never to underestimate that one." She nudged Max with her elbow. "Go grab a glass of bubbly and pick out a book or eighty-five. Doug had a lot of inventory in that unit. I'm hoping for a lesbian hockey romance, myself."

"Does that exist?"

Her blue eyes went wide. "Oh, sweet Max. You're in for a treat."

"I hear you. Hockey romance. I'll seek one out. You don't have to tell me twice."

Max moved into the room, looking for a place where she could plug in, assist, or be helpful. But the serene smiles on the faces of absolutely everyone in the room told her all was under control. She strolled to the bar, scanning the room until she found the one person who slipped into nearly every thought she had. There she was. Max exhaled slowly, anchored in a manner she couldn't have predicted just seeing Ella a few yards away. She calmed Max's storm every damn time, even when they weren't exactly speaking. She could almost set her watch by the effect. Gorgeous, Ella stood in the middle of the shelves wearing a red dress that came in at the waist and flared. Her hair was pulled partially back and fastened with a silver clasp that matched her three-inch heels. Max swallowed. Of course she'd look incredible. It was impossible for her not to. Next to Ella, Doug squeezed his hands in front of him, wearing a black blazer and a red and black checkered bow tie. Of all the unbothered faces in the room, his was not one of them. Not exactly a socialite, Max would imagine that having the spotlight square in his face was not his idea of a good time.

"I'm so grateful," he told Max a few minutes later when she caught him on one of the laps he started making. "I'll never be able to say thank you enough to this town," he said, shaking his head. "I just hate that everyone is having to go to so much trouble over me."

"Tell yourself it's for the books. Does that help at all?"

He paused, nodding, as he internalized the advice. "I like it better, actually."

"See? It works, and it's true, too."

She saw Ella steal a glance in their direction and then choose to take the long way to the silent auction table. That was okay, too. Max could sadly give her space, even though all she wanted to do was sit with her at one of those tables in the corner and hear all about what she'd been up to lately. How the business was going, if she'd picked up any new clients, or eaten at a new restaurant she'd enjoyed. But sharing the same space was better than nothing, right?

"Max."

She turned and found herself standing in front of none other than Rachel herself. Her red hair was up in a twist, and she wore a forest-green designer something or other that made her look like she was walking a runway rather than attending a charity event. But that was Rachel, fashion first. Always. "Hey, Rachel. How are you?"

"I've pretty much had the worst year of my life. What about you?" She held her martini off to the side in a dangle. Though Max wasn't entirely happy to see her, she could also admit that none of this was Rachel's actual fault.

"Ups and downs for sure."

"I'm guessing the ups had to do with my best friend."

She paused, absorbing the pointed stare. She placed her drink on a nearby high-top and went with honesty. "I'd be lying if I said otherwise."

"Good. I want you to realize how amazing she is. But maybe rein in those longing stares across the room like you're watching a ship sail away." Rachel's voice was gentle as if offering legitimate advice. She turned to go.

"That noticeable?"

Rachel paused and raised one bare shoulder. "Might as well fly a blimp outside with her photo on it."

"Good tip. Thanks, Rach."

"Anytime," Rachel said, about to breeze her way to someone new. "Now let's raise some money and make our girl proud."

"I'm 100 percent on board. It's why I'm here."

Rachel nodded and disappeared into the crowd that had grown considerably in the last fifteen minutes. The line at the point-of-sale stand now snaked around the side of the book-store and contained several of her colleagues from the local bar association. Not only was she proud of Ella and Ariana, but relieved for Doug and the boost he was about to receive to his rebuilding fund. There was only one thing left to do: buy a book or two and quietly exit the event. Why did the thought make her heart tug uncomfortably?

"AND WHAT ARE we paying for this pristine copy of *Knot Today, Cupid?*" Ella asked the woman with long gray hair and pearls clutching the newest Parker Bristow. Ella had read that one earlier this month, and the wedding planner romance was an emotional roller coaster for the ages. Bristow was getting more daring in her career.

"I was thinking a hundred and eighteen," the woman said with a definitive nod.

"I applaud your specificity."

That seemed to make her happy, and her cheeks glowed pink. "Doug and I went on a date in 1997 and now I show up at his store once in a while just to give him shit. It's my favorite hobby."

"Then you and I are a lot alike."

"Don't go gabbing about me, you two," Doug said, looming over Ella's shoulder. He just looked so cute in his bow tie, even when he griped and scowled in that Doug way he had. "And Beverly, you don't have to buy anything! I already told you that. You never listen when I speak."

"I do, too. I just do what I want, you old fool!" Beverly shot back.

"That's because you're hardheaded like your sister."

"He always had a crush on her," Beverly told Ella. "I'm afraid it went unrequited."

"I absolutely did not. I just thought she made a mean White Russian, so I hung around to have some. Who wouldn't?"

Oh, wow. Ella realized that she really liked these two.

They needed a sitcom or maybe a candlelit dinner for two. Just the thought of romance made her heart sink the minute she remembered hers was kaput. Seeing Max across the room had her shaken in a manner she hadn't been able to prepare for, and she'd done lots of emotional prep work for tonight. Max stunned in that black dress, making Ella's mouth go dry.

"Do you need more bags?" Rachel asked, approaching. Ella had recruited her as an extra pair of hands behind the counter when the line began to overwhelm the group.

"Um, actually yes. That would be incredibly helpful."

She and Rachel seemed to be in a better place. They weren't exactly cuddling and swapping funny stories from their days quite yet, but they were laughing on occasion. Rachel had even asked her if she needed anything at the grocery store, which felt like a huge victory. With each passing day, another chunk of ice fell off their friendship, and they took a small step forward. In fact—*oh shit*. Hold all thoughts. Ella swallowed and lightly touched the counter, then untouched it because Max was in the book line. This was no big deal. Air would show up momentarily. Max *should* be in the book line. She was here to help, like all the rest of them. Moreover, she'd been responsible for securing the space and for many of the evening's biggest donors. *Exhale, and in again.* It was just that Ella hadn't seen her face-to-face since that last day when everything came apart, and her heart squeezed uncomfortably, reaching for Max automatically, because how did you tell a heart not to reach?

Two quick sales from two very generous buyers, and she stood facing Max. She could have stepped aside and let Doug handle the sale, or switched spots with Ariana, who floated through the store. The truth was she didn't want to. She wanted a moment with Max, even if it was just that.

And then the moment was upon them, and those soulful brown eyes were on hers. "Hi," Ella said. "It's nice to see you." Anything else would have been a lie.

Max's smile was small, hesitant at the edges, like it wasn't sure it was allowed to stay. But it was real. It was Max. "Hey, El." Soft and familiar in a way that made Ella's chest go tight.

God, she'd missed that voice.

Up close like this, Max looked the same and not the same. There was a weariness to her now, maybe the same weariness Ella carried. Perhaps you didn't come out of something like what they'd been through unmarked. But, underneath, she was still Max. Still achingly, impossibly Max.

"I didn't know if I should—" Max started, then stopped, glancing down at the book in her hands like it had the ability to tell her what came next.

Ella shook her head before she thought better of it. "I'm glad you did." And it was the truth. Wildly inconvenient, probably unwise—but true.

For a beat, neither of them moved. The room went on around them—laughter, the low hum of conversation, the rustle of shopping bags, and the clink of wineglasses—but Ella's whole world had narrowed to the woman standing just in front of her. The woman she wasn't supposed to want. The woman she still did.

Max's fingers traced the edge of the book absentmindedly, like nervous energy that needed somewhere to go. "You look —" She huffed a quiet laugh, self-conscious. "You look great."

Ella's laugh caught somewhere between nerves and wanting to cry. "So do you."

There was so much more lingering in the space between them, everything they couldn't say, everything they maybe still wanted to, but all Ella could do was press her palm lightly to the cover of the book between them. A touch without really touching.

"Can I ring that up for you?" she asked gently.

Max's answering smile was barely there. But God, it still knocked the air right out of her.

"Yeah, let's do that."

Max's donation had been a generous one, but she had a similar affinity for Doug's. They all did. And then with one final conservative smile and nod, she disappeared into the mingling attendees, leaving Ella in a very different state than she'd found her.

She helped the next two customers, attempting to smile and interact, and let them know about all the ways their purchase would contribute to assisting Doug in first cleaning out the store and then slowly inviting contractors in to start the rebuild. She was failing miserably with phrases like *What was I saying again?* and *Um, what I mean is ...* infiltrating her speech.

Finally, she tapped Morgan in and stepped back, attempting to reset herself. It was only a moment until Rachel was by her side. "So, that was brutal."

"What was?"

"Watching the two of you dance around each other."

Ella closed her eyes, absorbing the information. It still hurt Rachel to see them interact. "I'm really sorry."

"No. I didn't mean brutal in that sense." She shrugged. "More like I don't want to see you go out of your way to be unhappy. And that's what staying away from Max is doing to you."

Ella turned to her, head tilted as she tried to understand. She searched Rachel's face and saw a newfound softness to her features and what seemed to be the beginnings of a brave smile. "Here's what I think. You stop circling each other and put us all out of our misery."

"No. Rachel, if you're at all—"

"Did you hear me? Max is standing right over there like a wounded puppy lost on a busy street." Ella followed her gaze to see Max holding her drink and watching the crowd from the perimeter. "And you're standing over here like a broken copy of yourself glitching all over the place. I'm certainly no better off for either of those things."

"I don't know what the solution is here."

"I do," Rachel said quietly. "I'm going to have to put my big girl pants on and remind myself to, every once in a while, think of other people. Girl code is way less important than my best friend's happiness." She shrugged with a wry smile. "Now, go talk to Max Wyler before I change my mind and become incredibly selfish again."

It was a gesture that Ella wasn't sure she deserved. This new reflective Rachel was a little bit jarring. But when someone extended kindness, it was important to acknowledge it. "I don't know what to say other than thank you, and are you sure? You're my friend, and I want you to be comfortable. I want you and me to be okay."

"Shut up," she said with a half-smile. "It's the right thing, and we will be. Go. And then get back to this line already. We need you to close out the night strong."

An automatic smile appeared on Ella's face and slowly grew. "I guess I'll be right back." She took a few steps into the crowd, then turned back to Rachel, only to receive a dramatic shooing gesture. This felt like the biggest improvise ever, but she surfed her way to Max, arriving behind her.

"Excuse me," she said, going up on her tiptoes and positioning her mouth close to Max's ear so she'd hear her over the chatter all around them. Max turned, and her eyebrows rose when she saw Ella there. "I don't know what your week looks like, but I was hoping we could grab a coffee or a glass of wine. If you have time."

She watched every muscle in Max's face relax. A small smile emerged. "If I have time? Of course I have time, but …" She trailed off, and her eyes shifted to where Ella had left Rachel. She was attempting to piece together the series of events.

"Yeah. Rachel and I are working things out. And I want to see you. Very much."

"Then, yes."

Ella laughed, feeling lighter, as if she might float away at any moment. "When are you free?"

"Right now. Later tonight. Tomorrow."

"Oh." They shared a smile, and a nervous flutter hit her midsection as if she'd swallowed Tinkerbell. She was a teenager all over again. "Well, um, I have the event."

Max didn't waver. "I'll wait. I'll help clean up. I'll sit in my car. Whatever you want."

"Really? You're willing to wait? Don't you have work in the morning?" The gesture was a big one.

Max stepped closer, the determination in her eyes bypassing flutter and sending a full-on shiver. "I've waited this long. Waiting a few more hours just means I get to want you more. I'll wait all night." Her voice was low and quiet. Sexy for days. Ella blinked, but words had fled the scene. She swallowed, rebounding, searching for even ground because she'd almost forgotten the potency of Max's presence.

"I bet I'm done by 10:30. I just have to offer some instructions to the volunteers from the museum, but with everyone helping, we should have the books packed up in no time."

Max smiled. "You're not going to have any books left."

Ella looked behind her. "I don't know. We brought so many."

"There's an hour left. Just wait."

Not only was Max correct about every last book leaving the event with a new owner, but their grand total was three times the goal they'd set going into tonight.

Doug was shaking as the caterers broke down the little cocktail tables to haul away. "Why would they buy all of them?" he asked, still in disbelief. In between the cleanup, he'd walk one direction and then the other, still in shock and unsure what to do with himself. It had been a tumultuous period in his life, and he was clearly working through the bad and now the good.

"Because this town loves you and the store," Stevie said,

hands on hips. "There wasn't a single chance they'd let you go down because of a ridiculous power surge." She studied the Weepers, who'd all stayed back to help. "And now that you've covered the gap in your funding, we can get started on cleanup. I'll be there on Monday."

"I'll be by after work," Morgan said. "There's a faculty meeting, but I plan to steal the agenda and sneak away. Don't turn me in."

"I know a lawyer if you need one," Max said with a wink.

The others chimed in, having all made arrangements to pitch in, and the whole thing just brought a big ole lump to Ella's throat, because this was what real life was all about, coming together when a neighbor needed help. She knew they wouldn't rest until Doug was back behind the counter, passive-aggressively judging every book placed on his checkout counter and mumbling to himself, while loving every minute of his time with his customers.

Tonight had been the first truly good night in a long time, and it wasn't even over yet. "Get in here, Weepers," Ella said, placing her flat hand in the center of their circle. "You too, Doug. You're an honorary Weeper tonight."

"Oh, good," he said, wandering over.

Each member of the group tossed their hand on top, including Doug, and Ella beamed. "We came. We mingled. We sold every damn book in this place. There's nothing we can't do. Weepers on three. One, two, three."

"Weepers," shouted the group.

And that brought the night to a close.

Ariana and Morgan began to dance to the club music that one of the caterers played from her phone. Stevie, Olive, and Doug were carpooling and gathered their belongings, along with an extra tray of brownies that the catering company had gifted them.

That left her and Max.

TWENTY

The Great Martini Swap

Noticing the charged glances passing between Max and Ella, the rest of the group got the message. With a flurry of friendly goodbyes and quick packing, they filtered out one by one, leaving the two of them alone in the quiet hum of the nearly empty room. Only the custodial staff remained, their movements methodical as they tidied the last traces of the event.

Max stood there for a beat, heart ticking faster than she let on. "So ..." she said, a soft smile playing on her lips as she let out a breath. "There's a bar two blocks from here that stays open late during the week. Totally walkable." Max tilted her head slightly, the corner of her mouth lifting in invitation. "I'm buying, if you're up for it. What do you think?" She held her breath, unsure if she'd been too forward. It felt like a moment balanced on the edge of something hopeful and terrifying all at once.

Ella's eyes lit up, and the visual was an anchor in the storm. She relaxed and smiled without trying. "I skipped all the champagne opportunities tonight simply because I didn't have a spare second to enjoy a glass, so I would love a drink, actually, and am refusing to pay a cent."

"Sounds like a match to me."

Downtown was in that late-night lull, the space between the late dinner crowd and last call. Some places had gone dark already—boutique windows empty, chairs flipped onto tables —but others still glowed soft and inviting. The coffee shop on the corner was open late, and a couple of college kids hunched over laptops in the window. Somewhere farther down the block, music spilled out of the cracked door of a dive bar, laughter trailing after it.

Max didn't let herself reach for Ella. Not yet. But every step they took together down Main Street felt like easing pressure off a bruise she'd been pretending didn't hurt.

She'd missed this. Not just Ella, though, yeah, that was a constant ache—but this *with* her. Walking side by side like it was easy. Like it was allowed.

Dirty Little Secret was a popular martini bar in town, and it was still bustling when they walked through the main room, which housed the bar. The plastic high-top tables were all occupied, and they waited at the host stand for directions.

"Hey there, Max. Please feel free to seat yourself," Peter said. She'd gone to high school with Peter (Go Huskies!) and had handled his sister's divorce two years prior.

"Thanks, Peter. Busy tonight."

"Everyone knows Peter," Ella murmured.

"Oh, you've been here before?"

She nodded. "With Rachel. Many a cucumber martini. Mild headache the next day."

"Well, Marco makes the best. Want to see if there's space in the back? It's likely quieter. We can … talk."

"I'll follow you."

The sentence was innocuous but sent a shiver down Max's spine, signaling that her body was ready to catch up to what her heart was already reaching for. Hope was a tricky thing. She wasn't sure whether to tamp it down or release it more fully.

They found an available, but less-than-comfortable-looking couch in a dimly lit section of the bar. It was shaped like an elongated clamshell and probably cost more than most people paid in rent.

"Is this the hardest couch you've ever sat on as well?" Ella asked, hopping a little to try and get comfortable.

"It's the literal worst," Max said with a laugh, giving her hips a shake to see if she could wiggle her way into the cushion a little. No go. "Can you imagine curling up with a good book on this thing?"

"It would be a total mistake." Ella smacked the couch's rigid backing to absolutely zero give. "I guess the upside is you wouldn't fall asleep in the middle of the chapter."

"Remind me not to try to seduce someone on this thing."

"Well, there goes my entire evening," Ella said, her eyes dancing. They were loosening up around each other, and it felt so damn good, like water to someone parched.

"How have you been?"

Ella shrugged, the emotion she'd held back in regards to all that had happened came rushing up on her in a whoosh of untethered feelings. "I'll say this. It wasn't my favorite period."

"No. Mine neither. So, tell me what shifted for you and Rachel?"

Ella quickly relayed the conversation they'd had at the pop-up and sat back on the couch, shaking her head. "Between losing her job and potentially her best friend, I think Rachel is on a journey of rediscovery. Maybe forgiveness is a part of that."

"I think maybe we all are," Max said, smiling up at the server who delivered their drinks. "Thank you so much."

Ella was watching her with interest and a small smile.

"What?"

"You're always so polite. I appreciate that about you."

"Really? I've always worried I was too direct. I blame law school and my no-nonsense mother."

Ella leaned her head on her hand, which was propped up on the back of the couch. "Well, you are direct. And confident. I'll give you those. But there's an undercurrent of kindness woven into your interactions, too. Best of both worlds. Don't get a big head, either."

Max smiled, feeling seen and understood in a manner she wasn't entirely used to. "Only temporarily. I'll surely do something to get trolled before this conversation is over."

"We can only hope." They shared a smile, and Max reminded herself to breathe, taking in air beyond the nervous, shallow intakes. She knew the reason. She was excited but also so very ready to flip the pages to see where they ended up. She wanted more than anything to skip ahead to a moment of certainty where she knew exactly what they were to each other and what the future held. She also understood that the ground beneath their feet felt a little different than it had before their time apart, and she had to be prepared for feelings to have shifted. She wanted Ella to give them a shot, but she also wanted her to be sure. And what an ask that was. How many times had she cursed and sworn off romance herself recently?

Yet, sitting here in close proximity to Ella fucking Baker, she was falling all over again, the cynicism sliding off of her like a long day at work. Was it dangerous to shove her chips to the middle of the table? Definitely. Maybe she slid one stack at a time and went from there. She reached for her passion fruit martini and winced a tad at the sweetness. Ella made a similar face at her dirty martini, which came with blue cheese olives. Without a word, they switched drinks, an unspoken understanding that it might go better the other way around, and it was the most clichéd couple thing Max had maybe ever experienced.

"Much better," Ella said, brightening.

"I can safely say the same." It was a metaphor if she'd ever encountered one. The right drink and the right person made all the difference. Maybe romance was only problematic when you'd ordered the wrong drink for yourself.

"What's going on in that head over there?" Ella asked, sitting up taller and enjoying her newly acquired colorful drink.

"I'm happy to be sitting here with you, and I'm also wondering what it all means."

"Because you're an absolute type A control freak."

"Who really likes these olives." She grinned around a bite. "Good lord."

Ella's eyes were on her mouth, and that was more than okay. "Good lord is right." They shared a smile and maintained eye contact that neither seemed in a hurry to break.

"I think we need a plan," Max said, sliding a little closer to Ella on the couch.

"I thought you might say that." Ella took a sip of her drink, then held it up in a small toast. "How about two drinks, then home? I'll grab an Uber, sneak in six hours of sleep, and pretend I'm a well-adjusted adult tomorrow. You?"

She flashed a cheeky grin that Max had half a mind to kiss right off her face. Instead, she just looked at her—really looked—and waited.

"What?" Ella asked, setting her glass on the low table in front of them. A group shuffled past their couch on the way out of the restaurant, forcing a brief pause. When they were gone, Ella turned back to Max. "Not the kind of plan you had in mind?"

"Not exactly," Max said, her voice low.

Ella's smile softened. "Well … I'll say this. I've missed you. I've missed your words. I've missed your laugh. Your body."

Max's heart thudded, but she waited, needing to hear everything else Ella had to say.

"I'm feeling rather hopeful," Ella continued, sincerity lacing her delivery. "Of course, I want to be sensitive to

Rachel's feelings. But I also really want to spend time with you."

Max nodded, her voice steady. "I hear you. And I'm going to take it one step further."

"Do," Ella said, giving a gracious little take-the-floor gesture.

"I want us to give this a real shot. Officially. If I had my way, you wouldn't be catching a ride home tonight. You'd be coming back with me." She paused, studying Ella's face. "But I get the need to take it slow. I do. Especially after … everything."

"We were a twister," Ella said, awe in her voice. "Tearing through everything in our path."

Max smiled at the image. "Powerful and focused. That's us."

Ella inhaled like she needed a moment to ground herself. "I admit that it's hard to focus on anything else when you're in the room."

Without thinking, Max reached for her hand and tugged it gently into her lap, lacing their fingers together. "I can't recall much about the last few Weepers meetings we attended together. But I can tell you exactly what you wore and thought about each book."

"Good," Ella said, her grin returning. She leaned in. "Because I happen to have opinions, ma'am."

"You don't have to remind me." Max's chest tightened with the urge to close the space between them, but she held back. "So. About us. What I tossed out there."

"You want to date me officially," Ella said.

Max raised a finger. "And exclusively."

"I love it when your hair's down." Ella's gaze then dipped briefly to Max's lips.

"Focus."

"Sorry. Recurring issue, remember?" She gave a tiny

headshake, as if rebooting herself. "Right. So ... in that case, we'd be ... an item?" She seemed to be turning the information over in her mind, employing a total poker face. That was new.

Max leaned her head against the back of the couch, her thumb brushing over Ella's knuckles. "That's kind of what I was angling for." Her heart thudded, wondering what Ella's response might be, nervous she'd say no. Nervous she'd say yes, because this was scary territory for the romantically cautious.

Ella searched her eyes for a long moment, then said simply, "I think we do it." Ella nodded, agreeing with her own declaration.

Max felt the spark of anxiety beneath her happiness, but it was steadying as well. Because this was Ella. And there was no one else she could imagine taking this leap with. "Now we're always going to remember this hard couch as the moment we decided to go for it."

A pause. "You mean our *hard* launch?" Ella asked, clearly over the moon with herself for that one.

Max laughed. "Are you sure you don't want to come home with me tonight?" It was playful, yet sincere.

"I do want to come home with you. But slow, remember? We screwed things up royally by racing ahead last time."

"Right, right. Vaguely remember that."

"At least ... for a little while."

"I'll follow your lead."

She sat up straight and rolled her shoulders. "My lead says I should probably get some sleep. With so much pop-up planning this week, I've fallen wildly behind. I have three big deadlines looming."

"Wow. So, business is still good?" Max handed her credit card to their server, who snatched it with a smile and a wink as she glided by.

"It's booming and I'm getting several new inquiries every day." She stared after the server. "She just winked at you. Why is the world obsessed with you?" She held up a hand with a laugh. "Never mind. I know exactly why." Then her brows pulled down.

"Where did your mind just go?"

"You're out of my league."

"The most ridiculous sentence you've ever uttered."

"People don't wink at me in martini bars. They forget to fire me."

"I have a feeling they do wink at you. Maybe you just miss it."

"Aww. Really nice save, but it's not true." Ella squeezed her hand. "I'll take comfort in the fact that perhaps someone will someday."

Max winked right on cue, and Ella laughed.

"Nailed it."

"You're totally in the club now."

They waited for Ella's car in front of the bar, hiding out beneath the awning when it started to pour. "Well, at least we have a memorable ending to our night," Max said, holding her hand out to feel the rain. A clap of thunder shook the sidewalk, and, instinctively, Max pulled Ella close as the two of them laughed. That is, until they realized they were now pressed up against each other.

"I'm not sure I mind at all," Ella said, voice low.

Her car pulled up, headlights cutting through the rain. It was time to say goodbye.

"Let me know you're home safe," Max said, reluctant to let go.

"You do the same," Ella replied, eyes lifting to meet hers. Then she rose onto her toes and tugged Max down by the collar of her coat, their mouths meeting in a kiss that tasted like passion fruit and possibility.

The rain continued to fall, but Max barely noticed. Ella's lips lingered just a beat longer, like she wasn't quite ready to let go either.

"Goodnight, Max," she whispered. "Tonight was good. Really good." Ella's eyes sparkled.

"I find that it just keeps getting better." They went in for one more searing kiss before Ella broke away and made a mad dash for the car, screaming the whole way in the rain as Max laughed.

Ella raised a hand to her through the window as the car pulled away, taking with it the woman who occupied most of her thoughts these days—smart, beautiful, and kind.

Max stood there under the awning long after the taillights disappeared. The night had taken a U-turn she hadn't at all expected, but, honestly, it felt like things were supposed to have happened this way. Her heart thudded like it had just agreed to something it didn't fully expect, but wanted so badly anyway.

She stood against the wall beneath that awning, waiting for the rain to subside while grinning like a fool in love. Wait. No. Scratch that. She wasn't in love. Not exactly. The rain had slowed to a sprinkle, and Max decided to brave the elements and head back to the museum.

Still, as she stepped into the soft drizzle, she couldn't deny one thing: she was definitely falling.

"You're dressed nice again," Ella said, taking in Rachel's maroon blouse with the tie around her neck.

"What do you think of this look? I'm going for 'I dress better than all of you, but I'm still very much a team player.'"

Ella frowned. "That's a complicated ask. I suppose I could get there."

"Good. Leighton Morrow is in town."

"I have no idea who that is. Should I?"

"If you ever want to work in corporate retail, it might be a good idea."

"Thank God I don't." Ella gave her head a shake. "That was close. Are you going to see Leighton-with-the-last-name about a job?"

"No. But I'm going to a networking event she's speaking at in hopes of connecting with someone who wants me as their next Someday Vice President." She shrugged as if it was totally going to happen. "She works for Carrington's corporate in their community relations department. A New York nepo baby, but she knows her stuff and she's bisexual. Plus, everyone important will be there eating small sandwiches and sticks of celery and pretending we love one another."

"That sounds awful," Ella said, frowning.

Rachel nodded around her PowerBar. "Oh, by design. If we aren't miserable, do we even work in fashion?" She placed her hands on the counter. "So ..."

"Hmm?" Ella asked around her yogurt. She was trying to branch out from Hoopties, expand her horizons. She was already dubious, however. Hoopties were the superior breakfast food.

"I'm guessing you saw Max last night after the event?"

"I did." A pause. Ella wasn't sure how to maneuver this conversation. New territory and all. She decided to fall on her sword and admit her uncertainty. "I'm sorry, but I don't know the rules just yet." She turned to Rachel, palms to the ceiling in question. "Do I tell you about this stuff or bury it?"

"New to me, too," she said and tossed in some uncomfortable laughter. Finally, she gave her hair a toss and refocused. "Let's try telling me. We can always pivot."

"Fair. So, we grabbed a drink at Dirty Little Secret and caught up."

"And it was good, I take it?" She didn't sound overly hyped for Ella or demand every little detail the way she would about any other woman, but she sounded generally support-ive, which was huge—bonus points for the new, very adult Rachel.

Ella kept her smile in check because it had been better than good. Sleep was a glorious thing, but she'd had trouble achieving much because she'd been thinking about Max's smile. The way she'd looked in that black dress and overcoat. The kiss that curled her toes and turned her the hell on for hours after they'd said their farewells. And when she'd woken up that morning and remembered that Rachel had given them her blessing, it felt like the world was welcoming her with open arms, bursting with possibility. But there was no need to show any of that off at this point. "Yeah, it was really good to spend time with her again."

"I feel like this was a good start. Let's leave it there. Love you. Impressed that you're eating yogurt," Rachel said, pointing at Ella with her small handbag.

"I'm about to trash it. Who am I with this in my hand?" She pushed it away.

"While you figure that out, I'm gonna get out of here and go network my ass off. You'd better design like your life depends on it. Don't you have a deadline this week?"

"Three. No idea how I'm gonna pull them off. Maybe I do need the yogurt." She picked it back up again.

Rachel blinked. "This is a battle I'm going to leave in your capable hands." She patted Ella's shoulder. "You got this. Maybe you can reward yourself with junk cereal right after."

"Thanks. Knock 'em dead with the celery."

Rachel gave her hips a shake as if dancing to an imagi-nary beat. Ella could never look that good on an imaginary dance break, another reason she appreciated the talents of others.

Once alone, Ella checked in on Doug, who had been on the phone with the insurance company all morning, trying to wade through red tape, but was making progress. They would start work on transforming the shop as soon as they received the sign-off from the agents handling the claim.

With four bites of yogurt still in the carton, Ella decided she could afford a simultaneous doom scroll while she ate, delaying the start of her work session. A cute talking dog. Her friend Cassandra's birthday party. Oh—her parents had stumbled onto an impromptu parade in Brussels.

Then she froze.

Her heart spiked into overdrive.

There, in vivid color, was a series of wedding photos. Britney—the very woman she'd fallen for and been broken by —had gotten married. To Katelyn, the woman she'd been seeing for the past eight months, the one she'd met shortly before ending things with Ella forever. They looked ridiculously happy, gazing into each other's eyes as they exchanged vows, laughing as they fed each other cake, wrapped in a slow dance that screamed, *We're so incredibly in love.*

The photos offered a near-cinematic glimpse into the day Ella had once imagined for herself. And even though she didn't long for Britney anymore, she still found herself clutching the counter, breath caught, as a life she'd once pictured played out without her.

The day took on a different tone after that little discovery. Ella wasn't exactly unhappy as she added color to her sketch of a big-shouldered soccer player with his foot on the ball, as a sassy redhead stood to his right with a flirty gaze. Instead, she just felt low. The photos were a blatant reminder of a time when she hadn't felt like enough. It honestly wasn't so long ago, either, and residual waves of self-doubt rolled over her incrementally throughout the morning into the afternoon.

As the sun set, she still felt low and angry with herself. Britney shouldn't have the power to affect her mood or diminish her self-worth. And yet she did. That was on Ella. She closed her tablet and rubbed the back of her neck, sore from staring at the screen, just as an incoming call hit her phone. She checked the readout and saw it was Max, who was likely just getting off work. She slid onto the call, already feeling lighter. "Who is this?" she demanded.

"Your attorney."

That did it. She went warm and smiled easily. "It's dangerous to tell you this, but when you say things like that, I'm pretty much at your mercy."

Max laughed quietly. "Well, now you've done it. I can woo you with formal closing arguments in my kitchen if you want."

"Um, I want very badly."

"Done. Are you ready for this week's book club?"

Ella deflated. She had exactly one day to read the book she hadn't had time to get to.

"I'm not gonna make it."

"Let's have a reading night. Come to my place. Are you free?" A pause. "I should have led with that. My mom says I was a bossy child, just assuming the other kids would do what I said. I'm working on it."

"For how long now?" Ella asked with a grin. She was walking circles around the kitchen like a fourteen-year-old missing her girlfriend whom she had just seen the day before.

"About thirty years."

"So any minute now."

Max laughed. "What's the verdict?"

"You're still doing it!"

"I told you. I'm nothing if not an opportunist, especially when it comes to luring you over here."

"You mean about tonight? Reading books together? I love the idea. What can I bring? How about popcorn? It's my first love."

"Competition from popcorn was a subplot I wasn't expecting, but now I think I'd very much like popcorn. How would you feel about me whipping up a couple of Cuban sandwiches?"

"Perfect, and I'm an excellent assistant. I can slice those puppies in half like a James Beard-nominated chef. But that's all I can do. Don't ask me to actually cook or assemble. I live on cereal."

"Get over here already."

"Give me twenty minutes."

TWENTY-ONE

Read Me Like One of Your Romance Novels

R eading quietly on a couch with Ella, a bowl of buttery popcorn with parmesan between them, and the wind gently rattling the windows was one of the better ways to spend an evening. The romance novel about a grumpy librarian and the sunshiny reader who pulls her out of her shell was good, but, honestly, the chemistry between the characters had nothing on them. Especially tonight. The slight touches throughout the evening, like when Ella had passed behind Max in the kitchen and placed a hand on the small of her back, or when Max rested her hand in Ella's lap for the first thirty minutes of their read, were both domestically satisfying but also torturous at the same time. Max's skin tingled around Ella. She became hyper-aware of her body and even more so of Ella's, and the touching seemed more frequent the more they shared the same space. Eventually, Ella moved the silver popcorn bowl and slid her body up against Max, who wrapped an arm around her as they read. That little move changed everything, slowly dismantling Max's ability to focus. The scent of Ella's hair, the press of her skin, the way she slowly turned every page, as if she couldn't bear to say goodbye to it, had Max losing interest in her book fast.

"What page are you on?" she asked at one point.

"A hundred and eighty-one," Ella said, not looking up. "What about you?"

"Two ten. You're catching up."

Eight minutes later, she peered over at Ella's book again. "What's been your favorite part of the book?" She was a kid seeking attention, but couldn't help it.

"I like the way Avery can't concentrate on her work when Emma's in the library. The tension is really trickling in. My favorite part." She went back to reading, clearly lost in the story.

"Yeah. Tension is rough."

Another five minutes passed, and Max realized that she'd read the same paragraph eight times without comprehending any of it. She was, however, able to fixate on the way Ella's hair rested on her shoulder. The smooth column of her neck. She remembered tracing it with her tongue.

"You're trying to distract me," Ella said, noticing Max's gaze. "Because you're distracted." She pulled her focus from the page and regarded Max with those big blue Disney eyes.

"No. I'm not. My attention is 100 percent on this novel and everything that's happening in it. Stop talking to me."

Ella gasped in exaggerated fashion, but Max was too busy rereading the paragraph for the ninth time and making sure to look riveted while she did it. Ella didn't seem to care and calmly took the book from Max, placed it on the table, and slid onto her lap. Oh. This was so much better than she'd planned. What had she done to deserve this, because she'd write it down.

"What if I want to talk to you?" Ella asked.

She met Ella's dancing eyes and eased into a lazy grin. "Then maybe that could be arranged."

Ella's gaze dropped to her lips, and a ripple of anticipation tiptoed through Max's midsection. "What if I wanted to kiss you?"

"I would probably be at your mercy."

"Say less."

Praise every star in heaven because Max was seeing them now with Ella straddling her lap. Someone up there had answered her prayer. Ella cradled Max's face and brushed her lips once and then back again. That was all it took. The dam broke with that little taste, and no one cared about librarians anymore. The ever-present fire between them leapt to life with a roar. Ella went back in, this time with her lips parted and hunger driving the kiss. Their lips pressed and clung as if savoring every heated second. Encouraged, Max pushed her tongue into Ella's mouth, tentative, and then again without hesitation. Ella mirrored the move, sending heat licking its way from Max's toes to her fingertips. This was the kind of make-out session that threatened to burn the place down. Urgency enveloped every kiss and caress until nothing was slow anymore. Every part of them that could touch was touching, and Max's head went dizzy with lust and determination. She wanted her hands on Ella's breasts, her lips pressed to Ella's skin. She wanted, wanted, wanted, until she couldn't hold back another second. Holding Ella to her, she lifted up, shifted to the right, promptly deposited Ella onto her back, and lowered herself on top, ready to take what she needed.

"Okay, that was impressive," Ella said, eyes wide. "This might be better than reading."

Max laughed quietly. "I'm putting that on my business card."

"I want one." Ella's hands landed on her waist and then promptly slid down to cup her ass. Max's hair fell forward, framing them as they kissed with wonderful abandon. They were free in so many ways these days. No more sneaking around or wondering what this thing was between them. They were real and true and unencumbered. Not to mention on fire. Ella raised the thigh between Max's legs and pressed upward, which had Max pulling her mouth away, sucking in air. Pinpricks of pleasure shot through her system, and every inch of her body sat at attention. Sliding a strand of hair behind her ear, she closed her eyes, sat up, and took a moment to steady herself.

"You okay?" Ella whispered, hand to Max's cheek. The tenderness of her voice brought Max back into the moment. She opened her eyes, and they connected.

"I'm driven wild, but surviving," she answered, her lips tugging to a partial grin.

"Good because I wasn't done with you," Ella said with a smile. She sat up, joining Max, a look of determination layering onto her features. Her gaze flicked to the hem of Max's shirt, and she lifted it, making her intentions known. Max had no problem helping and pulled the shirt over her head, leaving her in the red bra she'd purchased not too long ago, you know, just in case. "Are you fucking kidding me? Have you ever modeled lingerie?" Ella asked, kissing the underside of her jaw, before returning her focus to Max's chest.

"Can't say I have."

"Well, if you ever need a break from the law." Ella shook her head, and with one finger, she traced the top of the lacy cup. Max swallowed, wet and beginning to throb. That same finger began to trace her nipple through the fabric. The ache intensified. She felt the nipple pebble and press against her bra. She rolled her lips in, tortured and attempting not to beg. This was Ella's show. Ella, on a mission, pulled down the red cup, freeing Max's breast. With her lips parted, she dipped her head, lifted the breast to her mouth, and pulled the nipple inside.

"Fuck," Max said, closing her eyes, and sliding her hand into Ella's hair, an anchor and a request for more. Ella sucked, licked, and skated her teeth over that nipple until Max found herself lifting her hips, searching for purchase, anything. Ella pulled back and looked down at Max's hips.

"Oh, do you want to be touched?" Ella asked innocently, easing her onto her back. Max nodded and watched as Ella undid her pants and shimmied them down to her ankles. Her underwear was next.

Ella touched her lightly. "You're so wet. I bet I could help with that." It was only seconds before Max felt Ella's hot mouth between her legs. The open-mouth kiss nearly sent her over the edge. She closed her eyes to revel in how amazing she felt. Ella's tongue traced intricate patterns that drove her absolutely wild. She rocked her hips softly to the rhythm until it became quick little pumps that had her climbing and climbing. Ella pulled her mouth away and kissed the inside of each thigh, Max's stomach, before looking up at her.

"Sit up for me."

She liked the look in Ella's eyes and wondered what she had in mind. She did as she was told, realizing that Ella wanted Max in her lap, which she could definitely accommodate. As soon as she settled there, Ella's fingers slid inside, pulling a whimper from her throat because it was so damn satisfying.

"There ya go. Ride my hand." Ella's eyes were cobalt, which meant she was every bit as turned on as Max was.

It also meant that Max was happy to accommodate. She slowly began to move, taking in the way Ella's gaze shifted to her breasts and how they bounced with each hop or thrust. Every time Max came in contact with Ella's hand, her now swollen clit brushed Ella's thumb, sending her tiny rewards. But she needed more. Chasing the sensations, she rocked faster and faster against Ella, pushing her desire higher and higher as the pressure climbed to a dizzying level. At long last, with one firm press of Ella's thumb, Max careened and broke in a bright spark of bliss that had her crying out and digging her nails into Ella's shoulders. The unrelenting rush scattered her to pieces. It was the payout that just kept giving, as did the small brushes of Ella's thumb.

"That was fucking intense," Max said, pressing her forehead to Ella's.

"Wow. Can I just say that I enjoyed that so very much?"

"*You* enjoyed it? *You?*"

Ella chuckled. "Max. You have no idea." With her fingers still curled inside, Ella shook her head in awe. "I had no idea reading books with you could be so satisfying."

"Speaking of satisfying, we're not done. I'm gonna need you on your back."

It was only a few moments before Max was following her down with big plans for the rest of their evening that involved Ella and not a stitch of clothing.

SATURDAYS WITH NOTHING pressing on the calendar had become Ella's favorite kind, especially when they included Max. That morning, they'd joined a painting party at Doug's, tackling the freshly restored walls with rollers, laughter, and a rotating playlist. Doug's sister came, the rest of the Weepers showed up, and even Beverly made an appearance, tie-dye scarf keeping her gray hair out of her face. She spent most of her time getting more paint on her clothes than the walls and needling Doug every chance she got, purely for her own amusement. "You know, Doug, you might get the wall done by Tuesday if you go just a little slower."

"You worry about yourself," he told her amid a measured stroke. He'd opted for a sage color this time, moving away from basic white.

Ella had a sneaking suspicion he liked the back-and-forth. Or maybe it was simply the romantic in her, pairing everyone up. Before leaving the house that morning, she'd even suggested Rachel might consider pursuing a romance with her former supervisor, who'd reached out about helping her find a new position somewhere. Rachel hadn't been able to let go of the grudge, which seemed like excellent fodder for a tension-filled romance. Sign her up.

"Just because you're giddy over Max-fucking-Wyler doesn't mean I should date Millicent, who is so uptight that I don't think I've ever seen her hair out of a French twist. She's the reason my position was eliminated," Rachel huffed. "She's also twelve years older than me."

"This just gets better and better." Ella chewed the inside of her cheek. She felt the urge to design the cover for this story. "She's gay, right?"

"From what I'm told. But it's hard to imagine Millicent dating."

Ella's brain raced ahead. "And with the layoffs, she was probably just doing what the company's bottom line told her to do. I have a feeling she was conflicted about it, Rach. That's why she reached out. And maybe she misses you. Have you considered that angle?"

"No, because it's weird. You're reading too many romance novels. And now you work on them, too. We're going to need an intervention."

Ella examined this thing from all angles. "She's also beautiful. I saw her photos on Instagram."

"Millicent? It doesn't matter. She has ice in her veins." She waved a hand, over it. "I can't with you. It's never gonna happen," Rachel said, scoffing. "You must have birds and butterflies chasing each other around your head and blinding your vision. The most logical explanation. I'm off to shower."

"Big Saturday plans?" she called after her.

"Getting my nails done this morning and headed to Lisa's tonight for her informal engagement party. Remember her from my holiday party two years ago? Wanna come?"

Ella closed one eye. "Max and I kinda made plans to not make plans."

"Ah. Well, I'd say bring her, but I'm not there yet." She held up a hand. "Not that I won't ever be. I'm working on the evolution of Rachel, but it's gonna happen one step at a time." She turned for her shower.

"Hey," Ella called again, a softness coming over her.

Rachel turned, and the lighthearted smile fell away when she saw the look on Ella's face. She shifted her weight. Vulnerability flashed. "What? Why are you looking at me like that?" She'd never been one for interpersonal moments, which was why their relationship rarely dipped out of the playful realm.

"I wanted to say thank you for the effort you've been putting forth. I know none of this has been easy."

"No. It hasn't. Thank you for seeing that." She pulled in air as if gathering her courage. "But you're my person, and I want the world for you, so there's that. And now we're done with the sentimental display. Thank God." The words came out as one long run-on sentence that made Ella grin.

"We're done," Ella said. "Go. Find the shower you seek." But she understood the sentiment of that blurt. After all, they were all works in progress attempting to take shaky steps forward in the world. It wasn't all that easy. Extending each other a little grace went a long way.

"Where did you drift off to?" Max asked as they strolled the outdoor nighttime market Everly Springs hosted every third Saturday.

"Just wondering why I haven't hit every one of these things. It's so quaint out here."

The cobblestone street was lit with string lights zigzagging overhead, casting a golden glow on vendor tents and perusing locals. The scent of kettle corn, spiced cider, and something smoky—maybe brisket or grilled peaches—hung in the air. The day had been long, but Ella refused to give in to her fatigue, very much enjoying the night with Max, warm at her side. They held hands as they browsed the various tents and booths, looking for the next great find.

"My mother would love this." Max picked up a white and blue tea kettle with a very intricate floral pattern. "Honestly, she could probably use a nice gesture about now. She's starting to feel the effects of the treatment."

"Oh no," Ella said, frowning. "Is she just feeling weaker overall or nauseous?"

"I don't actually know. She says she's fine."

Ella paused. "I'm not following."

"Because you were raised by a mother who probably admitted when things were hard. That wasn't my mom, still isn't. You have to be the best, work harder than everyone else, and show superhuman strength and resilience."

Ella blinked. "That's a lot."

"I don't think I realized how much until I moved out and started life on my own." She shrugged. "But I know her well enough to see that she's much more tired than usual. She's not staying at the office as late. All of the signs are there that the medication is beginning to take its toll."

"So, if she won't admit anything is wrong, how do you help?"

Max handed the man behind the table with kind eyes her credit card. "You bring her a beautiful tea kettle and hope it cheers her up and lets her know you care."

"What about a simple hug?"

"Um, that's tricky. Under the right circumstances, sure. But it's something I generally feel out first."

Ella frowned, trying to understand. "Because it might show weakness?" she said slowly.

"Now you're with me." Max touched her arm. "Is that Olive?"

"It is. Olive!" Ella yelled. Their friend turned at the sound of her voice. She offered a shy wave, but made no point to come over. That was weird. She was standing with a man of about her age, who leaned into her ear and whispered something, making her laugh.

"We might be intruding," Max said quietly.

"Are they on a date?" Ella asked.

"The mystery of Olive and her personal life continues," Max said with a perplexed grin.

They walked on. A busker strummed an acoustic guitar near the fountain, his open case scattered with singles and change. Max dropped a five as they passed, and they all exchanged a smile. As they rounded the corner to the new row of vendors, Ella let what she learned about Max and her upbringing sink in. It explained why she was so driven, so put together, and unflappable. Because those things had been required of her. Ella touched her heart where it tugged for the little girl who just wanted to be good enough. She wasn't quite sure what to say, but at the same time, felt it should be something. She turned, her lips parted, grasping for words, but the beauty before Ella stole the air from her lungs. Max's profile, lit by the amber market glow, was all sharp cheekbones and soft curves. A breeze caught her dark hair and let it fall again, and Ella knew—without question—that she'd remember this moment for the rest of her life.

"Your hair's a little tousled."

Max lifted her hand to smooth it.

"No. Don't." Ella caught her wrist and slid her hand back into Max's, lacing their fingers slowly. "You're stunning."

Max seemed struck. Her features relaxed into a small smile, and if Ella wasn't mistaken, Max Wyler's cheeks colored the slightest shade of pink. Was that even possible?

"And I'm sorry if you've ever felt that you weren't good enough."

Max squeezed her hand, but didn't say anything. Instead, she leaned in and brushed Ella's lips with her own. She pulled back slightly, but didn't go anywhere. Instead, she lingered in Ella's space and met her eyes. The scent of her raspberry shampoo wrapped around Ella, sun-warmed and sweet. For a second, the world went still. Max's eyes searched hers, steady, open, like she was asking a question without words. And that's when Ella understood. Max was letting her see all the way in.

Ella's breath caught, not from nerves, but from recognition.

This wasn't just attraction—it was safety. It was history and hope layered together in one moment of connection.

She reached up and tucked a strand of Max's hair behind her ear, letting her fingers linger.

"I see you," Ella whispered.

Max smiled, something soft and unguarded breaking across her face. "I know."

For Ella, the day had felt like an important one for several reasons. They'd helped Doug piece back together his store. She'd shared a few key moments with Rachel. But the most significant part of her day was the step forward she and Max had taken in their relationship; their emotional bond was stronger for the honest moment they'd shared. Max was opening up to her, and it felt like the curtains were being lifted.

She'd stayed at Max's place that night, and they'd come together in a clash of heat, this time more familiar with each other, more comfortable. Ella took her time with Max's body, watching the way her soft touches affected Max, how her firmer ones changed the sounds she made. She wanted to memorize all the little ways to make Max scream her name and how to prolong her orgasm for as long as humanly possible. Where had that tiny scar on the back of her shoulder come from? And where was her favorite place on her body to be kissed? Ella's very important study would take time, but she was more than willing to be patient and put in the hard work. She smothered a grin, looking forward to all that information gathering.

Hours later, as the warm rays slanted through the blinds, brushing their skin and wrapping them in the morning light, Ella stirred. She sighed happily at what she saw: a mass of dark hair splayed across her pillow and the soft skin of Max's arm and shoulders visible above the sheets. She couldn't help but imagine waking up like this every morning, as overeager as that may have been. The concept was almost too much to envision. She'd heard the phrase afraid to hope and fully realized its meaning now.

"It's Sunday. Why are you awake?"

She looked down and grinned because she loved Max's raspy, quiet, and adorable sleepy voice.

Ella slid back down beneath the sheets and pressed her body to Max's. Neither of them had felt the need to put on clothes to sleep in, well, *after*. Max's arm immediately went around Ella's waist and pulled her in even closer. Her eyes were closed, but a small smile played on her lips.

"You're so warm," Ella said, savoring the skin-on-skin contact. She could get used to this. She slipped her leg between Max's, intermingling them. That did it. Max's eyes opened.

"This might be one of my favorite wake-ups in the history of wake-ups." She kissed the underside of Ella's jaw softly, slowly. "Never leave this bed."

"Could be a nice existence," Ella said, looking skyward. Max's lips were on her neck, and her eyes fluttered closed. She was in awe of how quickly her body was responding to the attention. The subtle ache had already started, and she squirmed ever so slightly in response. Max, who missed nothing, read the cue and began a soft caress of the inside of her thigh. She heard her own exhale. "What are you doing?" she asked. Max's answer was to move to her other thigh, lightly tracing, softly tickling, pulling so many sensations. So close. Yet so far. If there was ever a case of yearning to be touched, this was it. Ella lifted her hips, asking. Max answered, touching her softly. She pulled her mouth from Ella's neck and watched her face instead.

"How's that?" she asked quietly, administering the featherlight touches between her legs.

"More," Ella managed, pushing against Max's hand, feeling control slipping away.

Her fingers moved into Ella's folds. She stroked her slowly. First one pass, then another, carefully avoiding the one spot where Ella so desperately needed her because she knew exactly what she was doing. Ella sucked in more air as the pressure between her legs climbed steadily, her need causing her to slam her eyes shut and hold on, uncomfortable and needing release quickly. She rocked her hips, hoping to increase the friction. Heat licked its way up her body, a small flame spreading rapidly until she felt it everywhere. Her face heated, and her skin prickled with sensitivity. Max slipped two fingers inside and began to move. A moan tore from her lips, raw and unrestrained, before she could stop it. She lifted her hips, granting Max better access, and moved with the steady, devastating rhythm of Max's hand, a hypnotic beat all their own. The need was visceral, a delicious, unbearable kind of torment.

"You're fucking sexy," Max murmured. "And you're getting closer, aren't you?"

Ella nodded, but words were too hard. She focused on one thing —a singular, very primal goal. She rode Max's hand, increasing their pace and moving herself closer and closer to the finish line. She was nearing the edge of the cliff, desperate now and working for it. Max's thumb brushed her clit and she cried out, the sensations overpowering her. So very close. Another light touch. A third. Ella broke in a shocking burst of pleasure that tore through her, leaving her trembling, her thighs tightening instinctively around Max as she gasped her name. Waves of bliss crashed over her, relentless and over-whelming, until she had no choice but to surrender entirely to the force of it.

"Dead. I'm dead. You killed me," Ella murmured as she slowly returned to earth. She lay there, limp and in heaven.

"You are the most gorgeous dead person I've ever seen."

Max slid down the bed and kissed Ella's breast, pulling the nipple into her mouth.

"Don't do sexy things right now. Your sexy limit has been reached."

"Can't help it," Max said, undeterred. She skated her teeth across the nipple, sending pinpricks of pleasure and pain. Dear God, it was good. How Ella was still aroused by not just the sensation, but the image of her breast in Max's mouth was beyond her. It seemed impossible. Yet, here she was, turned on again, just moments later. She felt the subtle stirring between her legs and squirmed.

"Max," she said.

Max moved to Ella's other breast, sucking a nipple, while still kneading the first. "I'm obsessed with your body," she said, going back in. She kissed Ella's stomach, her thighs. "Oh, I think we're going again." She nodded up at Ella.

"I don't think I'll be able to—" But the second Max's tongue touched her center, the sentiment died on her lips. She was already so sensitive that it was only another couple of seconds until she was tumbling again, lost in an oblivion so powerful she saw white lights on Max's ceiling. Her hips rocked of their own accord as she rode the remaining shock-waves of her second fucking orgasm. It wasn't even 9 a.m.

Max climbed up the bed and stared down at her, topless and beautiful. "Did I say good morning yet?" she asked with a smile.

TWENTY-TWO

To Working and Wine

E lla got to book club extra early that week. Could it have been because she hadn't seen Max in thirty-six hours and wanted to lay eyes on her gorgeous face, hear her thoughts on the book, and drink wine with their friends on a day that felt so ridiculously good that she couldn't quite stand it? Yeah, that was entirely it.

She climbed the steps quickly and smiled at the new pillows Stevie had placed on the swing. Brighter colors, signaling a turning of the page, maybe? She knocked once and opened the door, letting herself in.

"You didn't have to bring anything," Stevie said, meeting her in the hallway and happily accepting the spinach arti-choke dip Ella had learned to make on Pinterest. "But I'm gonna eat the hell out of this."

"As well you should. I was in the mood. Even the crostini are homemade," Ella reported with a proud smile. She was incredibly domestic now that she was in a relationship. And given that she was working pretty steadily, she felt a little safer spending more money at the grocery store. "Am I first?"

"Nope. Ari's in the kitchen, scoping out the wine choices.

She can't decide if it's a white night or a red, and dammit, I feel like it's both."

"I've always liked your approach." She followed Stevie down the short hallway that would deposit them between the kitchen and the living room. "And how are you? Any hot dates lately?"

"Very funny," Stevie said, with a sideways grin, and then looked away. "Just me living my boring life. Did you know they moved trash day to Friday? That's about the extent of my excitement." But there was just something about her demeanor that told Ella there was more to that story. Maybe she was still talking to that woman from the club and wasn't ready to share the details just yet. Ella could certainly understand and would honor her privacy until Stevie was ready to talk about it.

They found Ariana in the kitchen pouring a glass of pinot grigio, which meant white had won the day. "Max isn't here yet. Tell me everything."

"Well, hello to you, too."

"There's no time for hello," Ariana said with excited intensity. "How hot and heavy are the two of you exactly on a scale of one to ten?" She held up a hand. "Stop. I already know it's a ten simply from observing you from feet away. It was a flawed question. What I should have asked is: Are you official?"

Ella smiled and nodded. "We're giving things a try and so far, it's been going really well."

Stevie swatted Ella on the ass with a magazine from the counter. "You should have said that the second you walked in."

"It's been about seventy-five seconds, so I think we got to it pretty quickly. And damn, you have an impressive swing." She rubbed her ass cheek and sent Stevie an impressed stare.

"I used to pitch for the girls' softball team in college."

Ella stared at her. "And you didn't know you were a lesbian?"

That earned her another swat. Gentler this time.

"Best part?" Ariana asked.

Ella collapsed against the counter in surrender. "The way she looks at me. I'm not someone who's always felt … special, you know? And with Max, I don't know how to express it other than to say I really do."

"Then you should see the way she looks at you from our POV," Ariana fanned herself with her hand.

Stevie nodded. "She sometimes chews on the inside of her cheek when she's studying your profile."

"It's so off-brand for Max that I just love it. She's gone on you." Ariana lifted her shoulders to her ears as if she couldn't stand the cute. Ella soaked up every second. She didn't need validation that what they had was real, but somehow hearing it out loud from others made it all the more vivid and exciting. Ella blinked, trying to remember that this was real life, as happiness moved through her like sunlight warming a long, shadowed room.

"Are we dishing on Max before she gets here?" Morgan joined them at the kitchen party. "I put a fresh batch of walnut brownies on the coffee table," she said to Stevie.

"That's exactly what we're doing," Ariana said matter-of-factly.

"Bless you," Stevie said regarding the brownies.

Morgan nodded as if reporting for duty. She had her long, blond hair in a ponytail and wore a denim jacket, like an ad for a department store or a Girl-Next-Door-Barbie. "What I would like to say about you and Max is that it's ridiculous how well you fit together. Especially the little book debates you have. It's like watching a real-life rom-com play out in Stevie's living room." She shrugged. "I'm glad you've finally worked out the kinks."

Stevie raised an eyebrow.

"Not those kind," Ella said, though she wasn't opposed to exploring if they were being honest. "Well, at least ..." Her voice trailed off to the sound of laughter and clapping from her friends.

"I'm missing something," Olive said, clutching two bottles of wine with her lips pursed. "And I brought the expensive wine we like. Catch me up."

Stevie pointed at Ella, her eyes dancing. "This one might be a tiger in bed."

"Oh," Olive said. A pause. "I guess that tracks." More laughter hit.

"I don't know what's happening in there, but it sounds a little raucous."

The sound of Max's voice made Ella grin. "They're having a little fun with the subject of you and me."

"Hell," Ariana said. "I think you're both having more fun than the rest of us."

"I will agree with that," Max said, arriving in the entry-way. Ella's mouth went dry. *Fucking look at her.* She wore black pants, black booties, and a black sleeveless shell. She knew Max well enough to know she'd likely had a colored suit jacket over it all for a pop of contrast, probably left in the car after work, but this look made her appear very "Cool Rider" on top of a ladder, and Ella was here for it. Max met her gaze and widened her eyes, the amused grin tugging at her lips. Yep, they were both in fantasy land. Max knew Ella's stares well enough and had decoded this one in no time. Ella shrugged at her innocently, as if to say, *Can't help it.*

"I dropped some stuffed olives on the coffee table."

Stevie blinked. "Since when did you all start bringing all this food? I thought I supplied the food. You occasionally buy me dinner." She turned to Olive, who had her dark hair in a knot at her neck tonight. She'd definitely upped her game lately, looking downright sexy herself. "And you, going all in on the expensive labels."

Olive deposited the wines on the counter. "Just felt like splurging."

Ella surveyed the group, feeling like everyone was on their own personal high. She looked around the faces of her new friends and wondered about the trajectories of all of their intersecting lives. What had prompted each one of them to go out of their way that night and up the enthusiasm of their food game?

Ariana raised her hand. "I brought nothing. I'm the loser who mooches off of her book club buddies because they had a shit week. I don't deserve you all."

"Yes, you do. And because of your week, you get an extra brownie," Morgan said, her brow furrowed in empathy. After the comment, they shared a sweet smile, and Ella was beginning to really appreciate the friendship they had.

"Shall we head to the living room and bring this meeting to order?" Stevie asked with one clap of her hand, the glamorous cougar football coach.

"Okay, but I'm going to warn you, I have some feelings about this one," Ella said.

Max laughed. "You? Feelings? Whatever are you talking about?" They'd already debated their differing opinions on the book in short form, but Ella was ready to get into it now. Once again, Max thought the author went on for too long after the happily ever after, and Ella relished the epilogue, hoping for many more pages. She was the more forgiving romance reader, the unwavering champion of the genre. Max would come around, though. Ella could already see the cynicism begin to fall away, a parallel for their own burgeoning relationship.

As the others filed into the living room, chatting about how the blurb gave too much away, Ella hung back and met Max's gaze. "Don't be jealous just because you're not as in touch with your sappy side, Wyler."

"Is that what we're calling it?" Max asked, giving her hand

a tug so she could hold her a minute in the kitchen. "Also, can I just say hi?" Her lips captured Ella's, who immediately went up on her toes for better access, pressing their bodies together for a stolen moment, a promise of more to come. There was no way they weren't going home together tonight after being apart for two days. She'd missed those lips more than she would have ever imagined.

"Are you two joining us, or do you need a little laundry room time?" Stevie called out to the sound of laughter from the rest of the room.

MAX COULD LISTEN to Ella talk for days. Tonight, as Ella animatedly discussed *Follow You Home*, the romance novel they'd all just finished. Max found herself completely trans-fixed. It wasn't just what Ella was saying, though Max loved the way she picked up on themes no one else had mentioned, but how she noticed the quiet moments between characters and treated them like revelations. It was how she said it, too. She lost herself in the rhythm of Ella's voice, the way her hands moved when she got excited, her mouth curving around certain words like they meant something more. There was also a slight rasp to her laugh and this softness when she said some-thing vulnerable. Max felt each note like a tug at something deep inside her. She wasn't just hearing Ella—she was absorbing her, imprinting every expression, every nuance, every blink-and-you-miss-it smile.

"You've been quiet, Max. What are your thoughts on the All is Lost moment?" Morgan asked as she popped the last piece of brownie into her mouth.

Oh, right, the participation part of this meeting. She closed her eyes for a moment as if internalizing her very complicated thoughts. Actually, she'd been pulling herself out of the fantasy she'd dipped into, which started with her pulling Ella into her lap. She rolled her lips in, buying more time. "I'm going to be honest and say that I understood why Marissa put up her hand when she found out about Laurelai making all of those career plans without including her. I wish she hadn't run away, though. I'm not a big fan of the author using miscommunication as a source of conflict."

Olive nodded. "Wouldn't you say that many real-life conflicts are born from humans' inability to have a simple conversation, though?"

Max grinned at the challenge. Olive was always thoughtful. "True. I see it every day at work. But can't I escape real life every once in a while?"

Ella shrugged. "The drama kept me turning the pages. I don't know how to argue with that."

Ariana, who was on her stomach on the floor with her chin propped up on her hands, shifted onto her forearms. "Speaking of turning pages, I think we should read your first cover design next," she said to Ella.

"You should know it's a straight book. Are you all up for it?" Ella asked. "A brooding male MC. A hockey stick. Who knows what he does with it?"

"Gird your loins," Stevie said with a smirk.

Ariana nodded solemnly. "I don't know what that phrase means, but it sounds sexy. Is the book?"

Ella shrugged. "If you like rugged hockey players."

"Hmm. That's trickier. I want to support your first professional cover, though, so my vote is a hearty yes."

"Bring on the straight drama." But Max then remembered the night at the market when they'd spotted Olive with her possible male date and decided to ease up on the joking. Instead, she decided to throw her an opening, just in case she wanted to grab it and dish a little. "Olive, you're quiet tonight. How are things?"

"With me?" Her eyes went wide.

"Yeah, I noticed you texting a lot, and it made me wonder

if you had a hot little situationship you'd like to share with the class. No pressure if you'd rather not."

Ella passed her a look, but Max couldn't help herself. She'd had a glass of wine.

Olive narrowed her gaze. "You seem like you know more than you're letting on, Maxine."

Max grinned and took a sip of wine. They were onto something.

"Well, is there something to know?" Ariana asked, taking the reins.

Olive smothered a smile and took a deep breath. Oh, damn. She was giddy about this person. "I suppose you want me to confirm if the rumors are true." She looked over at Stevie, who seemed to give her a nod of encouragement. Apparently, she knew all. Max sat taller, ready to be supportive and excited for Olive, whether she was expanding her sexuality to include cis men or maybe dating a nonbinary person. Whoever it was, they had certainly made Olive happy, and that was huge. "Stevie and I are in love."

The room went silent. "Stevie," Ariana repeated, pointing. "Which Stevie?"

"Do you know a lot of them?" Stevie asked with a laugh. She reached over and took Olive's hand, lacing their fingers. Right then and there, four jaws dropped.

"So, all that texting you do with the sexy smile on your face?" Morgan asked, attempting to keep up. They all were.

"Was to this one," Olive affirmed. Her cheeks colored pink, and she looked around at the faces of her friends with such pride that Max felt a sentimental lump rise in her throat.

Stevie smiled. "I guess you didn't catch the sexy smile on my face when I peeked at what she wrote."

"This is downright scandalous," Max said, slapping the arm of her chair.

Ella shook her head. "It's downright romantic, too. Wait a

minute. So, the guy we saw you with at the market was just a red herring?"

"At the night market? That was my cousin, Geoff," Olive said with a laugh. "We get together a couple of times a year, and the market is a favorite of his. You thought we were on a *date*? That's hysterical."

Ella turned to Max. "We were so far off base."

"We're going to have to turn our amateur detective badges in because we completely missed this," Max told her.

"Gonna have to resign from the Scooby-Doo gang," Ella said solemnly.

Max stared straight ahead. "Pretty sure they blocked our number already."

"Okay, stop being so in sync with each other," Stevie said, pointing at them one after the other. "It's freaking me out how adorable you are."

"Not as much as this new pairing is freaking us out," Max shot back. "Stevie, when did all this crop up?" she practically shouted.

Stevie sent Olive a smile and turned back to Max with a lifted shoulder. She looked absolutely demure, which was new and amazing on Stevie. "Truth time. We'd been flirting for a few months before I realized that I felt more for Olive than I ever felt for Dom. That's when I decided to come out officially and end my marriage."

Max nodded. "I know that wasn't easy."

"No. But it was easier than it should have been, and that was telling." She raised her shoulders in sadness. "It took another month before I admitted that all I wanted to do was be alone in a room with this one."

Ella fanned herself. "I love this story more and more."

"Our own personal romance novel," Morgan murmured with a dreamy gaze. "And you!" she said, whirling on Olive. "You're sneaky. I thought you had some secret life, but it was right here in front of our eyes. When did you know Stevie was endgame?"

"When she opened the door for the first time and invited me in for book club. I thought she was the most beautiful woman I'd ever laid eyes on."

In that moment, Stevie blossomed like someone finally seen—her eyes shining, her whole body stilling as if she didn't want to miss a single word. It was the kind of softness that comes when a heart hears exactly what it's been waiting for.

The room went quiet as they took it all in.

"I'm so happy for you both," Ella said, her voice laced with reverence. "That you were lucky enough in this great big world to find each other."

One at a time, they each chimed in with their own words of sincere congratulations, and the evening shifted into more of a celebration, the book forgotten, at least for now. They used the time to catch up, lounge, eat, and get to know each other even better than they had before. It felt like they were stepping into a deeper level of friendship.

"Hey," Stevie said, cradling her wineglass. "I'm just really excited about this group."

Ariana slid a brown strand of hair behind her ear. "We're an unlikely gang, aren't we? But dammit, we work."

"To working!" Max said, hopping up and extending her glass to the middle of the room. The others followed suit and clinked their glasses together, laughter bubbling up as Morgan nearly spilled her drink.

"To working and wine!" Stevie added, grinning. She cranked up the music that had played quietly in the background until now, and, just like that, the room burst back to life, full of voices, movement, and the easy joy of people exactly where they were meant to be.

TWENTY-THREE

Romantic Headquarters

D oug's Books had been through a lot, but was slowly beginning to show signs of rising from the literal ashes. The building had undergone quite the overhaul, including debris removal, water damage mitigation, specialized cleaning for the removal of smoke and soot, and electrical rewiring to ensure future safety. While they awaited the building inspection, they worked toward transitioning the interior back into a bookstore.

Ella pitched in as much as she possibly could, whether that meant helping Doug in his quest to choose new bookshelves or unpacking new inventory, which was actually her favorite task ever. Slicing open a brand-new box of books and seeing the covers revealed in all their glory was her own personal form of worship. Who would have imagined that when she lost her job at a marketing firm, it would be *books* that not only saved her but also transformed her life in every way possible? As she held a copy of Casey McQuiston's newest release, she inhaled the wonderful scent of a fresh, new book ready for someone special to creep off to a corner and devour. People would host book club discussions about this book, hold it in the highest regard on their favorites shelf, or conversely, throw it across the room in frustration. She smiled at the impact it would have on so many.

That's when she heard a noise she distinctly recognized, sniffling. She stood and turned, looking for Doug, the only other human in the closed shop at 9 a.m. on a Thursday. He had to be the source.

"Doug?"

More sniffling, but no answer. She heard a higher-pitched sound akin to a whimper.

"Are you okay?" she called, frowning, peering around the corner to see Doug in his maroon cardigan, sleeves too long, sitting in a chair with his head in his hands.

Hearing her approach, he lifted his face, tear-stained and twisted with sorrow.

Her breath caught. "Doug," Ella whispered, her heart shattered at the image.

"I just want it back the way it was," he choked out. "I want to go back. I won't plug that coffee pot in again. I promise." A sob shook him. "I miss my store."

Ella took a deep breath and nodded. It made perfect sense. Doug had spent so much of his time working to restore the shop and thanking everyone for all they'd done that he likely hadn't taken time to grieve for what was. Instinctively, she moved to him. He wasn't a touchy-feely person, but she wrapped her arms around him anyway, and he leaned into the hug. For several moments, they sat just like that as she allowed him to cry. "I'm so sorry," she said finally. "I don't know why things like this happen, but maybe Doug's 2.0 will be every bit as amazing. Maybe it will even surpass your expectations."

"Yes. Maybe." She could feel him nod and straighten. "I'm crying like an old fool."

"You're well within your rights as a human being. I think you have to let yourself feel, grieve."

He sighed and sat back. "Sometimes I just can't imagine starting over. I'm a creature of habit and like things just so."

"I definitely identify." She gave her head a shake. Her path hadn't been as catastrophic, but it had been daunting. "I upended my life, took on a whole new job and relationship. But you know what? I'm happier than I've ever been." She was, too. For the first time in a very long while, she felt in the foreground of her own life. She wasn't the faceless woman behind a laptop, turning in projects that no one even recognized as hers. She had a girlfriend who appreciated the little things about her. Her quirks. And that made all the difference. "And maybe in the end, you'll be happier than ever before, too. But I think it's okay to let yourself mourn for the old store."

He stared into her eyes. "You've been a nice friend to me," he stated. His gaze was coated in gratitude and warmth, two emotions that weren't common for Doug, at least on the exterior.

She nodded. "You've been a good friend right back."

"We're a couple of book weirdos, aren't we?" He sniffled.

"Yeah, but the best variety." He gave her hand a squeeze, stood, and brushed off his pants as if he'd been sitting in dirt. She knew it was the emotional equivalent, and he was wiping away the excess, gearing up to go back to work with a level head. And he would. This store would be amazing once again with incremental work and a little bit of tender care. The books demanded it.

She stayed at the shop through the afternoon until the sun began its descent in the sky, opting to work on her latest cover right there, knowing her presence, even as she huddled quietly in the corner with her tablet, was a form of support for Doug on what had been a hard day.

Afterward, she swung by her place to grab some clothes, give Rachel a squeeze as she moved through the kitchen, and head to Max's, where she spent most of her nights these days. She didn't knock because she was expected. Breezing into the kitchen and expecting to see Max prepping a meal or pouring a couple of glasses of wine proved unsuccessful. "Ms. Wyler? Where might I find thee?" She strolled through the living room, smiled at Max's leather attaché on the floor near the square coffee table that doubled as a seat. She heard the water the closer she walked to the bedroom. They'd just texted a few minutes earlier. Max must have decided to hop in the shower for a quick revive and relax. While she wanted to waltz into the room and join her beneath the stream, Ella took a seat on the bed instead, just in case Max was angling for a few moments on her own to decompress. It was only a few minutes before she emerged in nothing but her towel. Ella's mouth went dry.

"Well, hello," Max said, her lips easing into a smile.

"Hello," Ella said, blinking in amazement. Max's long legs and the round tops of her breasts peeking out of that towel were the very things she needed in her life at this moment. "Early evening shower?"

Max nodded, a stray strand of dark hair falling just shy of her right eye. "I had an angry couple this afternoon. Lots of shouting. Very little listening to reason or logic, which made for a frustrating afternoon. I wanted to wash all of that away so it didn't touch our evening. Also, hi. I missed you."

"I missed you, too." Ella met her brown eyes. "I want you to know that I very much appreciate the shower, only because it brought me to this moment."

"Is that right?" Max's eyes danced. "What moment would that be?"

"The one with you in this towel. Looking like that." The expanse of smooth skin had Ella's mouth watering and her fingertips itching to trace every curve.

Max let go of the two ends of the towel she had clasped in front of her, and the whole thing dropped to the floor. "What towel was that?" she asked with innocent eyes.

With a sweet smile, she moved past Ella to the dresser and began to look for a T-shirt, leaving Ella standing there, still like a video buffering, to take in the show. And she did. She watched from behind as Max perused her clothing options. Her long, dark hair rested on the olive skin on her back. Ella followed the lines of Max's ridiculous body from the trim waist that flared into the curve of her hips to the perfectly round ass and ridiculously sexy thighs. Ella wanted to touch her so badly it hurt. She also couldn't help but notice Max taking her sweet time, which was too much encouragement to ignore. She approached her from behind and placed her hands on Max's waist, and smiled when she went still. "Oh, hello." Max turned her head to the side and met Ella's gaze over her shoulder. Her eyes were hooded, the desire more than evident behind them. She seemed to like the objectification.

"What is it you're working on over here?" Ella asked.

"Oh." She swallowed. "I was just organizing the drawer a little. It's out of control."

"Well, don't let me interrupt you. Organize away."

Max relaxed her arms and then continued to explore the contents of her T-shirt drawer, rearranging items and straightening what needed to be straightened. In the meantime, Ella did some exploring of her own. She eased lower on Max's waist until her hands landed on the curve of her ass, which definitely needed a full caress. She closed her eyes, losing herself in the feel of the warm, soft skin. But it was merely a means to get to where she really wanted her hands. On a mission, she slipped one between Max's legs and stroked her ever so softly from behind, closing her eyes at the warm, wet heat that she found there. Max exhaled audibly.

"Don't mind me," Ella said. "Keep going. That drawer needs you."

"Right. The drawer."

With her foot, Ella nudged one of Max's legs to the side, widening her stance just enough. Then, with deliberate softness, she ran her fingers through the gentle folds between Max's thighs, her touch barely there—just a whisper at first, then another. She lingered in that teasing rhythm until she felt Max shift, angling herself into Ella's hand, silently pleading for more. But Ella held back, never quite letting her touch reach Max's clit, on purpose, of course.

Instead, she stroked in a steady, coaxing rhythm, up and down, just enough to let Max grind into the motion. The friction built quickly, the slick heat of it coating Ella's fingers. She loved Max this way. The sound of her soft gasps, the way her fingers gripped the edge of the dresser, the subtle whimper that told Ella exactly where she was in her climb. The louder one that said she was closing in.

That was her cue.

Ella adjusted her hand and slid two fingers inside, pumping steadily and slowly. With her other hand, she reached around and circled Max's clit with the pad of her thumb—once, twice, then a few purposeful strokes. Max cried out, her body jerking as the orgasm broke over her. She kept moving, hips rocking against Ella's hand, drawing out the aftershocks of pleasure.

Ella leaned in and kissed the back of Max's shoulder, her lips catching a slight tremble. Wet hair clung to her cheek, and she smiled at the scent, clean and sweet, like fresh peaches. She closed her eyes and let herself breathe it in, anchoring the moment before either of them said a word.

"Good day at work?" Ella asked finally, which prompted laughter from both of them.

Max turned in Ella's arms, her chest flushed from the orgasm, water droplets still beaded on her breasts. "God, I love being fucked by you," Max said, just before claiming Ella's lips in an open-mouthed kiss that rocketed heat from Ella's head to her toes. Her center began to ache with anticipation. Her body knew Max now and prepared itself for her. Their chemistry was as automatic as the sun rising on the horizon each morning. Max pulled back and met Ella's eyes. "But as for my day, I still have a little work ahead of me." She walked Ella toward the bed. "Luckily, it's my absolute favorite kind." She glanced down. "Now let's get you out of these clothes."

~

"Sonya, are you free?"

"For about three minutes. I'm working on getting the financial affidavits submitted for the Dawsons. They were slow in getting everything to me, and now they want me to jump through hoops."

"Well, you do it better than anyone I've ever met."

"After that, I need to start translating the Morales mediation into the formal settlement agreement, and then I'm going to smoke a cigarette and put my feet up on my desk."

"You don't smoke."

"Well, sweet cakes, I'm starting today." Sonya arrived in the doorway of Max's office and paused. "Why don't you look stressed? I feel like I'm ready to pull my hair out using a spork and no anesthesia while you're fresh as a daisy." Her dry delivery was, as always, spot-on.

Max grinned. "First of all, stand down. Don't do that because you're having a killer hair day. Second of all, I don't know what it is, but I have more energy lately." She shrugged. "Not as many things bother me."

Sonya nodded. "You have a girlfriend you like."

"I've had that before."

"No. You've had girlfriends you're *into*. This is different. You actually want to talk to her on the phone. In the middle of witching hour, which is so off-brand for you, it's shocking." Around their office, all of the clients seemed to want something around 3:30 p.m. That's when one spouse violates a custody agreement, or the other changes their mind about everything and wants to head to court, abandoning mediation. It's when all the fires had to be put out. Max had always had

Sonya hold all personal calls during witching hour, but she'd changed that rule for Ella.

"Yes, I do like her. I like everything about her." She turned sideways in her chair and found herself drifting back to their quick breakfast on the go this morning in her kitchen. Ella'd had that kid's cereal she loved, and Max had toasted an everything bagel. They'd eaten standing up and swapping details about their days ahead while Max packed her attaché. Ella had walked her to the door, and they'd shared a lingering kiss in the hallway. It had been so ridiculously domestic and mundane that Max couldn't stop thinking about it. Without realizing it had happened, Max was now imagining house shopping, figuring out who was covering dinner that night, and heading to their favorite restaurant on the weekend. That could be their life. "I'm doing things I never thought I'd do, Sonya, and I can't decide if I should be concerned or not. I might need an intervention. Head and heart are not recognizing each other."

Sonya narrowed her gaze. "I admit that I like the more relaxed version. You smile for no particular reason. You eat yogurt. Love looks good on you."

"There's been no declarations."

"But you're thinking it." Sonya held up a hand. "No need to respond. Just sit with it for a little bit. And you need to get back to your mother."

Max sat up straight. She'd forgotten that she'd called during a session. "The Johnstones were so agreeable today, I was thrown off and my morning was weird." Sonya stepped out, giving her privacy, and Max waited for her mom to pick up. But she didn't.

"Heyo."

She frowned. "Dad? You're picking up Mom's phone."

"Yeah. She's here in the hospital, so I took the call."

"Why are you at the hospital?"

"They admitted her this morning. We're at Crescent Hill

in the back. She has a nice room. What's that? Oh, she said to tell you why we're here. She fainted, and they had trouble getting her blood pressure to stabilize."

"It's standard procedure to admit," her mother called. "We do it all the time."

Panic flared anyway. "Dad. Why didn't you call me?"

"Your mother called you. We were waiting for you to call back."

She pinched the bridge of her nose. Her father hadn't seen the gravity of the situation, as always, and her mother was still in everything-will-be-fine-even-if-I-die mode. Neither was helpful.

"I'll be there in twenty minutes."

Sonya shot around the doorjamb, eyes raised. Max hung up, explained the situation as she grabbed what she needed from the office. At the very least, she could get some work done from there. "This does mean you'll have to reschedule my Zoom with the Normans. I can stay late on Monday if necessary."

"Don't give it another thought," Sonya said with a wave of her hand. "I have everything under control here."

"Don't know what I would do without you, Sone."

Max hurried to her car, put one AirPod in her ear, and called Ella as she pulled out of the parking lot. As always, they were planning to spend the evening at Max's place. Ella had stayed with her fairly consistently for a couple of weeks now. Not *every* night, but close enough. Rachel had joked that it was her romantic headquarters, which wasn't off-base.

"Hi. I know you're working, but I wanted to let you know that I won't be around tonight."

"Oh, that's okay," Ella said. "I'm guessing you need to work late. I can stay at Rachel's."

Max appreciated the understanding tone. "Actually, I just found out my mother was admitted to the hospital. I'm heading there now."

"Oh, God. Max. That's not good news at all."

"I know," she flipped her signal for a right-hand turn, "and I'm guilt-ridden because I should have kept a better eye on her."

"Hey, slow down. You do a lot for your parents."

Max shook her head because it didn't feel like enough. "My mom casually mentioned feeling tired, but as a physician, she downplays her symptoms. Doctors aren't the best patients."

"So the stereotype is accurate."

"Incredibly." She sighed, the sound of Ella's voice making her yearn for more time. "How was your day? I hate not seeing you."

"You will. Soon." A pause. "And maybe I can come up to the hospital tomorrow and keep you all company, maybe put together a little gift basket of some essentials."

Max squinted at the road, imagining her mom's reaction. "Yeah. Maybe so," she said, knowing that it might not be the best idea for Ella to make an appearance. "I'd better say good-bye. Traffic ahead."

"Hey, be safe, okay? And make sure you eat something. Are your clothes warm enough?"

Max smiled, touched at the way Ella cared for her. She was a thoughtful and nurturing human. "Thank you. I have my suit jacket."

"Even better," Ella said in her playfully sexy voice. She did love Max in her work clothes. "Keep me updated, okay? I'll be thinking about you all. Oh, and call if you need anything, and I can drive it over."

"You're awesome, you know that?"

"No. Say it daily."

Max laughed and opened her mouth to say more. It was the moment in a call when two people might say *I love you* before saying goodbye. The truly startling part was how natural it would have felt for Max to take that risk.

She could almost hear herself saying it. No panic, no rehearsal. Just the truth.

And that was the part that caught her off guard. Not the feeling itself, but how easy it suddenly seemed. How *right*. It was shocking to realize she was here, reaching for something that she'd just months ago sworn she didn't want or believe in. She honestly didn't think it was possible. Not after everything. Not after the way things had unraveled before. And yet, here she was. Wanting to say it. Knowing she could.

She needed a minute. A little more time to get used to the idea that she could want this. That she *did*.

So instead, she steadied her voice. "I will," she said. "Thank you."

A breath.

"Goodnight, Ella."

"Goodnight, Max."

She ended the call and left the AirPod in her ear, the urge to speak still humming through her like static. She hadn't said it. Not yet.

But the words were there now, waiting. And so was she.

TWENTY-FOUR

The Who Chef

M ax hadn't made it to book club that Tuesday night. Her family had still needed her, and with them, she was 100 percent where she should be. Didn't mean that Ella didn't miss her. The discussion that week had been relatively tame. The Weepers rarely agreed, but this week was an exception. The book of the week, *Hot Girl, Cold Brew*, left them collectively underwhelmed. Without a debate or Max, the book club felt a little tepid. Stevie and Olive spent much of it making eyes at each other, no longer hiding their feelings in front of the others, which made Ella miss Max all the more. She missed their private exchanges, how one would shoot the other a smile when something funny was said, or wide eyes when something surprising was revealed. Those little check-ins had begun to matter to Ella, and she would never take them for granted again.

"So, how is Max's mom doing?" Ariana asked, as they stood at the sink, rinsing out their glasses so Stevie wasn't left with all the work.

"Oh. Much better. She's scheduled to come home later this week." She placed her glass on the drying rack and frowned, remembering the gift basket she'd meticulously assembled with handpicked items she'd found at a variety of stores on the main drag. The soft hand towels. The hand-carved bars of soap from a lavender farm in Kansas. The cooling eye mask. Lip balms and much more. She'd hoped very much that Dr. Wyler would find comfort in the array and had been happy to put in the time. But every time she'd tried to bring the basket by the hospital to say a quick hello, Max had a reason it wasn't the best time. And that was fine. It was normal to monitor visitors. She was getting in her own head about it and wondered if seeking a second opinion might snap her out of it. She paused and turned, hesitating.

"What's up?" Ariana asked, likely sensing her unease.

"Um. It's probably nothing, but is it odd that Max doesn't want me to bring a gift basket to the hospital?"

"No." Ariana shifted her lips to the side as if pondering further. "Not entirely. Some people prefer their privacy when they are not feeling well. Max's mom is someone who likes things to a high standard, and Max has always been the little kid wanting to please her."

Ella nodded, latching onto the logic. It made total sense when she heard Ariana express the sentiment out loud. "You're right. I'm overthinking all of this, probably because I have a little relationship PTSD. I need to work on my confidence and trusting what we have going." She leaned her back against the counter. "I think I'll just drop the basket at the front desk or send it with Max. There's no reason I need to deliver it personally."

"I think she'll love the gesture," Ariana said, lowering her head to find Ella's gaze, which had been on the swirly pattern of Stevie's aqua countertop. "You did a nice thing, and she knows that."

She met Ariana's gaze and forced a smile, reminding herself that none of this was about her. "You're completely right." The Wyler family was going through something difficult and likely needed space. She could easily provide that for

Max and would be ready when she needed something. Not that standing on the outside looking in was easy. She swallowed, hands sliding into the back pockets of her faded blue jeans.

"Everything okay?" Morgan asked, joining them. Her soft demeanor made Ella melt.

"I think I'm just missing Max tonight."

Morgan immediately opened her arms, and Ella walked into them, very much appreciating the show of friendship these women offered without a single moment of hesitation. They'd welcomed her into their group from the start, and she was beginning to fully absorb how lucky she was. "It's gonna be okay, E."

She offered Morgan a squeeze and straightened. "It is. And your support, all of you," she said, realizing that Stevie and Olive were off to the side looking on with genuine sincerity. "Since the moment I arrived at that first meeting, it has meant the world to me."

Ariana shrugged. "We'll always be here for each other. That's what we do."

"I've never said this before, but you all are my escape," Olive said, stepping forward. "The one night a week when all the stress can just stay the hell outside while I come in and spend time with my friends and my books. I treasure each of you."

"Well, now I'm all choked up," Morgan said, hugging Olive this time.

"We have a definite lovefest on our hands," Ariana remarked.

"I have an idea," Stevie said. "Let's do it all again next week." She looked at Ella. "And maybe Max will be back to join us."

"I think she will," Ella told her, reaching out to squeeze her hand.

She went home that night and, instead of sketching on her

tablet or checking her email, as she usually did, she picked up another book and cracked its spine. A romance, of course. The kind with a slow burn, a stubborn main character, and an ending that would make it all worthwhile. She wanted to lose herself in something positive, in the promise of happily ever after, a reminder that it could be hers, too. Not just on the page, but in real life. Did she think of Max as she read the professions of love three hours later? She absolutely did. And when she drifted off to sleep early that morning, it was with a hopeful smile on her lips and a nagging feeling in her chest that she chose to ignore.

THE PRIVATE HOSPITAL room was quiet but not hushed, dimly lit by a single wall sconce that cast a soft, amber glow across the pale linoleum floor. Max had grown accustomed to the sounds over the past few days. The machines near the bed hummed steadily, broken only by the gentle hiss of oxygen and the faint, rhythmic beep of the heart monitor. All precautionary. Her mother was making significant progress, and her vitals had stabilized, pleasing the doctors. Tonight, Max sat in the corner, curled into the half-broken recliner like she was trying to take up less space than needed, her eyes fixed on the slow rise and fall of her mother's chest. The air smelled faintly of antiseptic and something sweet, maybe the flowers her father had left on the windowsill, already beginning to wilt.

She checked her phone to find a goodnight message from Ella. She placed the screen against her chest, a makeshift embrace and the only way to hold Ella close in this moment. She'd tested the waters with her mother, who'd sucked her teeth and frowned when she mentioned Ella swinging by with her gift basket.

"No, no, no," she'd said automatically. "Tell her thank you, but we're okay."

"Is this because she's a woman I'm dating?"

"Let's not do this right now, Maxine. I'm tired."

"I know. But can you just tell me why?" Max asked. She knew why, and it was because Max and Ella weren't her ideal Christmas card.

"I know she's a nice enough woman," her mother had said, "but why do we need her here with us when things are hard? This is family time. If it's too hard for you to be here with me, I understand."

The guilt was out in full force, which, of course, was by design. With a deep breath, Max closed her eyes and wished for better days ahead—her mother working on her laptop at the kitchen table, the sun setting on the horizon as she drove Ella to that cute little lakeside restaurant they'd talked about trying out, or even something as simple as Ella's arms around her as she fell asleep that night.

Maybe she'd manifested it, but letting herself into her apartment and seeing Ella standing in her kitchen later that night felt like an answered prayer.

"Hi," Ella said. "I know you weren't expecting me, but I just did a little tidying up, and thought I'd linger since you said you were on your way home soon. I can just say hi and get out of your hair. You must be tired."

Max didn't hesitate. She dropped her bag and walked straight to Ella, hauling her in and kissing her with determination, a glass of crisp, cool water for the thirsty. She knew she'd missed her for these handful of days, but seeing her face, smelling her hair, put in perspective how *much*. "You don't have to go anywhere," Max said, smoothing her hair. "I'm exhausted and my brain is mush, but it would be nice to just ... be."

Ella reached up and stroked her hair, searching her gaze, probably trying to assess how she was. "I would love to stay. What can I get for you? A drink? A snack? Wanna just lights out and crash?"

"I am kind of hungry." Max looked around the kitchen, trying to recall what she had on hand.

"Why don't I make you one of my favorite breakfast tacos? Don't get too excited. It's the only thing I make."

"I'm listening."

"We're talking eggs, bacon, and so much cheese you won't believe it all packed in a warm tortilla."

"I'm about to cry that sounds so amazing, but I don't have half of those ingredients."

"You're in luck. I brought some groceries by in case you hadn't had a chance."

Max covered her face in disbelief. "I'm in awe right now."

Ella held up a hand. "If that seems too forward, please just say so. I wanted to make this week easier on you, but I'm also well aware that you might not want me slipping in and out of your apartment."

"But that's exactly what I want."

It felt like air was sucked out of the room. They each went still and stared at each other until a small smile crept onto Ella's face and grew. "It is?" Her voice was tiny and cute.

"Yeah," Max said, the stress of the day falling right off of her with that utterance. This right here was everything she needed.

"Good," Ella nodded as if allowing it to sink in as she gathered the ingredients from Max's fridge. "Sit down. I got this."

"It doesn't feel right to just sit and watch you cook. Here." She moved around the kitchen, grabbing a pan, a spatula, and anything else she could think of that Ella might need. "I'm the chef's assistant."

"My sous chef," Ella said.

"Your who chef?"

They shared a laugh, which came way too easily for such a simple quip. But it was late, they were punchy, and so damn happy to see each other.

Perched on the bar stool that sat up against the tall portion of her counter, Max kept Ella company while she moved through the kitchen like it was a dance she'd choreographed in her sleep. She had bacon sizzling and cooling on a paper towel-lined plate. She'd warmed the tortillas one by one on the skillet. And Ella was now whisking eggs in Max's chipped green bowl with impressive focus. "So," Ella said, not looking up as she poured the eggs into the pan, "want to know exactly what you missed at book club?"

Max placed her palms flat on the cool, granite surface. "Tell me. What did I miss?"

"Not much. I promise. We mainly just all agreed that the book was meh and talked about our lives a bunch."

Max relaxed. "I'm still sort of jealous."

Ella nursed the eggs into a fluffy scramble and began to plate the tacos, adding a healthy amount of shredded cheddar. "This is the best part," she told Max with serious eyes. "You don't skimp on the cheese."

Max nodded. "I'm learning so much about you tonight. I'm gonna be the best who chef in Everly Springs." She accepted the plate with the amazing-smelling taco. "How's Rachel?"

Ella covered her mouth after the bite she'd just taken. "Amazing, now that she has a job. She's been floating around the house for 48 hours now. I saw her doing ballet in the living room, which has always been a sign she's happy."

"Good for her. Get that ballet on. Where was she hired?"

"Get this. Carrington's." Ella's blue eyes went wide while she waited for Max to react.

Max paused, taco halfway to her mouth. "She hates Carrington's. They're the enemy. According to her, they're everything that's wrong with department stores."

"They were until Montclair's laid her off and Leighton Morrow, executive at Carrington's, came to town and wowed Rachel with her ideology at some event. They've exchanged cards and have been in contact. And now it's led to a job."

"Well, well. That's honestly good news. I can't believe I'm genuinely happy for her, but here I am. I'm apparently a maturing adult."

"And the universe applauded."

Max basked in the imaginary ovation. "Tell her I said that's awesome."

"You two are gonna be thick as thieves one day."

It didn't sound half bad to be close with the people who mattered to Ella, and maybe reimagine her relationship with Rachel. Max took a bite and sank into the savory wonder that was the breakfast taco, slamming her hand onto the counter to emphasize her immense feelings. Was there a better late-night dinner in existence? She challenged the notion. "You are a witch sent to win favor through bacon."

Ella placed a hand on her hip. "I've been called many things, but that's a new one."

"Can't hear you." Max drew a circle near the side of her head. "The hum of happiness is too loud in my ears."

Ella laughed. "You were hungry. I've never seen you eat so fast in my life."

"Well." Max raised a cheeky eyebrow and waited.

Ella's eyes widened, and her cheeks slowly glowed pink. "You're in a mood tonight. It's fun."

Max set down the last two bites of her taco. "Honestly, it's because this was such a wonderful surprise." She held eye contact with Ella so she understood she was speaking from the heart, her voice laced with sincerity. "Every moment with you is."

Ella offered a wobbly smile. Was she misting up? A lump arrived in Max's throat, uncomfortable and stubborn. "Don't get emotional or I will, too. And I'm not a sap."

"Well, stop saying nice things," she squeaked. Uh-oh. Ella's eyes welled.

Max's traitorous tears arrived right on cue. "Dammit." She slid her plate away and slumped back in her chair, letting out a laugh that turned into a sigh halfway through. "Why does everything carry so much weight when you're tired?"

"I think that's called losing your filter." Ella smiled over her last bite, watching her with a warmth that didn't need words. "You're just a little raw, and that's okay."

"Truth. I think I almost cried because the tortilla was warm."

"You did cry," Ella said gently. "A little."

Max let out another short laugh, embarrassed and too tired to care. "Right. Cool. Love that for me."

Ella stood and held out her hand. "Come to bed, Maxine Wyler."

She didn't argue. The exhaustion had reached that bone-deep, not-funny-anymore stage. She followed Ella down the hallway, flicking off lights as they went. By the time she slipped into bed, the sheets cool and familiar, she was already halfway gone.

Ella slid in behind her, and Max instinctively curled in close. The contact was nothing more than shared quiet, but Max felt her whole body begin to exhale.

"You okay?" Ella whispered, easing closer. Her arm circled Max and rested lightly on her stomach.

Max didn't answer right away. She let her eyes close and let the quiet settle.

"Yeah," she murmured. "Now I am."

She hadn't realized how much she'd needed this, Ella's presence, steady and sure. Not to fix anything. Just to be here. Just to make the night feel less heavy.

Her breathing slowed, tension seeping out of her one heartbeat at a time.

And for the first time in what had been days but felt like weeks, Max fell asleep right away.

TWENTY-FIVE

Have Yourself a Messy Little Christmas

The holidays were sitting in Max's lap way before she was ready. Businesses were decked out in green and red, and fully decorated twelve-foot Christmas trees lined the streets of downtown. Max always marveled at how fast the town transformed from generically charming to Santa's own personal village. The stores piped in carols from Burl Ives to Kelly Clarkson, organizations sent out invitations to their annual holiday gatherings, and Max moved through space and time with a tentative smile on her face. Her world felt entirely different this year. She had a girlfriend she was wild about on one hand, an event that caught her completely by surprise. Who even was she these days, tossing aside her cynical notions about romance and moving through the world like a grinning fool?

On the other hand, she was still dealing with the repercussions of a family who'd been through a stressful time. Her mother had been out of the hospital for a couple of weeks now, and though she still had treatment ahead of her, her numbers were moving in the right direction. The chemo was working, but it was too soon to claim victory. Though patience had never been Max's strong suit, she noticed her ability blossom as she spent more and more time at her mother's side. Appointments, infusions, or just hanging out at the house. Unfortunately, that meant time away from Ella. This wasn't the time to force a new relationship on her mother, who showed no interest in hearing about the two of them. She wasn't sure what to do about that, and continued to shelve the issue. There'd be time to sort it all out down the road.

"I don't think you should go to Oklahoma for Christmas," Max said as they lay in bed one morning. "It's too warm there. Stay in the frigid temperatures with me. We can wait for Santa."

"I don't know," Ella murmured, pulling Max's arms around her tighter. "It's like nineteen degrees out there."

"Then we can take our clothes off and keep each other warm."

"Don't tempt me with your body."

"I have to. It seems to be your weakness."

Ella shook her head. "You know me too well."

With Ella traveling west to Tulsa to spend Christmas with her family, it would mean being apart for a little over a week, which seemed brutal, given that they already weren't getting enough time together. "Will you at least FaceTime me each day? Send all sorts of nudes?"

She felt Ella's stomach contract with laughter. "Oh, sure. In between Christmas gifts and eggnog, I'll snap a few. My mom won't mind."

Max snuggled close, spooning Ella, who wore Max's Jingle All the Way T-shirt and her own adorably cute pink bikinis. She wanted to slide her hand inside them, but it was 6:30 in the morning, and Max needed to be in the shower in fifteen minutes if she wanted to make her first client meeting of the day. She planned to enjoy every one of those minutes, staying close to Ella for as long as possible until the cruel work world ripped her away.

"Are you looking forward to seeing everyone?" She slipped a hand under Ella's shirt and caressed her breast.

"Yes. It's been a while since we've all been together. I hear my brother is bringing a girl he's been seeing."

"That should be interesting." She gently traced Ella's nipple with the tip of her finger. She heard her inhale quietly.

"Mhmm. They make a cute couple. He posted a couple of shots on Insta, and he had this very genuine smile that tells me he's happy. I look forward to you meeting them all soon. But I know you need to stay close to your mom for the holidays."

"Yes, but one day I want to see where you grew up. I want to know everything about what makes you you." She placed a slow kiss on the back of Ella's jaw just as her alarm sounded. "Unfortunately, I have to take a shower." She pushed herself up and headed to the bathroom.

"Did you really just get me all hot and bothered and sneak away?"

"I would love nothing more on earth than to spend thirty minutes making you claw those sheets, but I have the Dickinsons at 8 a.m."

"Not the Dickinsons," Ella said with mock reverence. She propped herself on a forearm and grinned.

Max laughed, too, liking it when Ella teased. That playful glint was too adorable. "And they like to show up early and insult each other in the waiting room. The longer they sit there, the angrier they get, and the more work it is for me to convince them to compromise." She sighed and melted for a moment. "But you have amazing breasts. Have I ever told you that?"

"They miss you," she said, shaking them in Max's direction. "Come play with them some more."

Max swallowed, arousal flooding her system. This woman looked too good lying in that bed, blond hair on her bare shoulders. Max wanted to do decadent things to her, and she didn't want to wait until tonight to do it. She checked the clock. There was no time left. Didn't matter. "Come in with me?" she asked, walking backward, tipping her head in the direction of the walk-in shower. She greatly appreciated the remodel that made it extra spacious. There was even a quartz bench she could imagine putting to use.

"Oh, yeah?" With a twinkle in her eye, Ella was up and moving. "Good morning to me."

"To us," Max said, sliding her hand in Ella's hair to her neck and crushing her mouth to Ella's.

ELLA's favorite Christmas carol was "Have Yourself a Merry Little Christmas." The quiet, almost internally spoken lyrics made her thoughtful and soft. She had it on while she worked at her desk, adding detail to the jacket of one of the characters on her cover. Francesca was her name, and, apparently, she was about to be blindsided by a visit from a past girlfriend who broke her heart years ago. "Gear up, Frankie," she said as she gently drew a fold in the fabric. "Hold onto that jacket."

Her phone, which had been playing her music, buzzed on the nightstand across the room. She hurried over and grinned when she saw her father's face on the screen. She took a seat on her bed next to the open suitcase. "Is this Santa?" she asked after sliding onto the call.

"You have to admit. I'm a damn good one." Her father offered his famous "ho ho ho," cultivated after years of playing Santa at the local elementary school holiday parties. His *The Night Before Christmas* was not to be missed. "How are you, Penny?"

She grinned at the childhood nickname, sprung from when she was seven and found his car keys after he'd torn the house apart looking for them. He'd told her she was his lucky penny, and it stuck. "I'm having a great day and just finishing up some work before I move on to trip plans. I want to go shopping for some road trip snacks. Is it even a road trip without good food?"

"I taught you well." He took a deep breath. "Hey, I want to run something by you and see how you feel."

She tracked the hesitation in his voice and frowned. "Okay, sure. What's up?"

"Everyone here is thinking of hanging on a bit longer and maybe celebrating the holidays here in Bavaria. Nuremberg has an amazing Christmas market. They do a whole big thing."

"Wow. I bet it's beautiful." Her heart sank like a stone in a lake.

"Yes! The city goes nuts for Christmas, and your mom and I thought, 'You know what? We're getting older now, and how many more chances will we have to experience Christmas in Germany?'"

"Right. I hear you." Her mind was working quickly to understand the implications. They wouldn't be back in Tulsa this week. They were bailing on her again. And didn't once think, *We're getting older now. How many more chances will we have to celebrate Christmas with our daughter?* She felt like she needed to sit down, like she'd been punched in the stomach. But because she was already sitting down, there was nothing left to do but absorb the pain. There would be no Christmas at home.

"We were wondering what you would think about cele-brating New Year's at the house instead? We could do a whole spread. Noisemakers, firecrackers. All of it. Your brother and Heather are both in."

Silence. She blinked back hot tears. Her throat ached with a combination of sadness and humiliation. Unwanted, that's exactly how she felt. Again.

"But, listen," he said, perhaps sensing the gut punch, "if

this gets in the way of your plans, we can skip it and come home. You say the word."

"I'm not going to tell you that you should want to spend Christmas with me."

"Oh, hon," he said. "That's not it at all. Of course we want to spend Christmas with you. We love and miss you."

"I know." Just not enough, she finished in her head. "Have a good time in Germany. I'll see if I can change my ticket and come for New Year's."

"I honestly can't wait. We're going to have the best time." A pause. "Ella's in! She's all about New Year's," he called some distance from the phone.

"Best news ever," she heard her mother yell. "I can't wait to be with my kids. We love you, Ella!"

"Love you, too," she said with maybe a little less exuberance. "Have a great Christmas."

Her dad paused. "Well, don't say it like we're not going to talk to you five times between then and now."

"We need to FaceTime so I can show you around the town," her mother said, taking the phone. "With you designing book covers now, you will appreciate the storybook aesthetic over here."

"I'm sure I will. Oh, you know what?" She brushed away a stray tear before it had a chance to feel like reality. "Someone's at the door," she lied. "I'll talk to you soon, okay?"

After a quick goodbye and a promise to regroup later, they ended the call. In silence, Ella stared at the wall, dejected and not sure what to do with herself. She looked at her tablet, still on its stand, but had lost her motivation to work. She turned to the open suitcase on the bed next to her and spotted the white sweater she'd packed for Christmas Eve. The little spice packets she found in town that she planned to put in everyone's stockings. With a sad shake of her head, she closed the suitcase, unable to stomach the sight of its contents.

So, she'd stay in Everly Springs for the holiday. Nodding,

she worked on talking herself into all the ways she could turn this around, shove her feelings to the side. She wasn't worthless. She mattered to a lot of people. Remembering Max's sweet words that morning in bed, urging her to stay, helped. They had been playful but based in truth. She had people here who cared about her, and it was important for Ella to remember that.

Hell, if she let it, this might be the most memorable Christmas ever.

"It's going to be okay," she told herself. Sadness chased her the rest of the day, but she pulled herself out of it each time it swarmed. By the time Max swung by to pick her up for their dinner date, she teetered right on the edge. She must have seen it the second Ella met her at the door.

"What happened?" Max asked, her face falling when her eyes met Ella's. She didn't hesitate, instantly opening her arms. "Come here." Ella moved right into them, her face crumpling. There was something about a soft place to fall that made letting go feel not only okay but necessary.

With Max's arms around her, the weight Ella had been carrying all day finally found a place to land. She pressed her face into Max's shoulder, clung to the familiar fabric of her coat, and let the tears come.

"They're staying in Germany," she said into the quiet space between them. "For Christmas. They're not coming back."

Max's hand moved in slow, calming circles on her back. "Oh, no. Ella, I'm so sorry."

"I was so stupid to get excited," she whispered. "I should've known better."

"You're not stupid," Max said gently, pulling back just enough to look her in the eyes. "You wanted to go home and see your family. That's not stupid."

Ella gave a watery laugh. "I don't even know where that is anymore. Germany?"

Max tucked a strand of hair behind her ear. "Right now, it's here. With me. Okay?"

Something in Ella cracked further, but it hurt less this time. She nodded, her throat tight. "I just wanted to matter."

"You do," Max said. "You matter so much."

And for the first time all day, Ella almost believed it.

TWENTY-SIX

The Ghost of Christmas Present

E lla scrunched open one eye and checked the clock. It was almost eight in the morning, the news ushering in a bolt of holiday excitement. Go time. Christmas morning was here, and she couldn't wait for Max to see the new briefcase she'd splurged on. The two of them had different ideas about the right time to rise on this special day, with Ella arguing vehemently for 7 a.m. and Max, the sleepyhead who didn't often get to lounge in bed, asking for somewhere closer to ten. They'd compromised and agreed on eight. But it was finally here, and she couldn't wait to celebrate with Max, who was curled into her side like a sunbeam of warmth.

"Merry Christmas," Ella whispered, turning her body toward Max and kissing her cheek softly. "Do you think Santa came?"

"I know he did. He brought you." Max smiled, though she'd yet to open her eyes.

"You're being cute in the morning again," Ella said. She kissed Max's nose this time. "You're also indescribably warm, which makes staying in this bed entirely tempting."

"See?" Max mumbled. "I know what I'm doing."

"Not so fast, though," Ella said, giving Max a squeeze. "There are presents to open. There's hot chocolate with marshmallows to sip. We need to absorb every Christmassy detail of every tinsel-lined minute." She stared at the door and called out, "Alexa, play my Holiday Crunk It List."

"You are on Christmas crack," Max said with a laugh. She peered at the clock over Ella's shoulder just as the living room erupted in a club mix of "Deck the Halls." "And you're five minutes early."

"I couldn't wait," Ella said with a triumphant grin over the music. "And it's close enough. Come on. Let's go."

"I have to kiss you first. Christmas rules."

Ella looked skyward and slid on top. It was becoming her favorite good morning spot. "I never argue with Christmas rules," she said solemnly and let Max pull her down for a wake-me-up kiss that did its job, sending tingles to her toes and making her yearn for things definitely on her Christmas list. "We're not going there right now," Ella said as Max's hands began to wander. "Uh-uh."

"Are you sure, though?" Max asked. "Because the level of cute also makes me want to do sexy things to you, and the way you're looking at me isn't helping."

"And trust me, I want to do all the things back." She sat up, straddling Max's stomach, and hooked a strand of hair behind Max's ear. "And I plan to. Just not before Christmas cheer."

"Then I'm accepting a rain check. Take me to the predescribed cheer."

"You got it," Ella said, erupting into her biggest grin.

After grabbing robes and brushing their teeth and fluffing their hair and kissing up against the bathroom door like damn professionals, Ella tugged Max's arm and got her seated on the gray and white couch in her living room. She assembled a tray of breakfast pastries she'd shopped for specially, and once they each had a piping mug of decadent hot chocolate, they opened presents.

Max beamed at her new black leather attaché, her cheeks coloring rosy pink. "Stop!" she said, holding it up. "I'm so particular about my work bags, but you nailed it." She clutched it to her. "It's like you know me or something."

Ella held her thumb and forefinger close. "Little bit."

Max leaned in for a kiss and then went right back to ogling the bag that had stretched Ella's new income. "This is honestly the best and so generous. It's also very much my style."

"I have another one for you." Max bounded to the tree and back with a small square box wrapped in a big silver bow. She'd already given Ella a box of romance novels from past book clubs she'd missed before arriving in Everly Springs and an adorable new white cardigan with navy piping, knowing they were what she liked to wear when she worked.

"You didn't have to get me anything else!" Ella said, accepting the gift with a colossal grin probably extending off her face. It was a perfect morning, and it made her wonder if missing Christmas with her family this year was how it was meant to be. Perhaps today was an arrow sign to nudge her further along the path with Max. Sure, they'd had their hiccups, but the love between them seemed palpable—even if they'd yet to voice it to each other.

"Well, I wanted to. It's nothing big, but it makes me smile, and I'm hoping it does the same for you."

Ella unwrapped the box and opened the lid. Inside, nestled in a white mat and silver frame, was a 5x7 photograph of the two of them grinning at the camera with Max's arms around Ella. It was the night Max was all wound up from a tough afternoon at work, and Ella suggested they get ice cream at the cute place with the twinkly lights and picnic table seating. Just the simple outing had made all the difference in

Max's demeanor. Her shoulders had relaxed, and she'd breathed a little deeper. The two of them had laughed together and stolen bites from each other's dishes, even swapping again when it became clear they'd ordered all wrong. Max had snapped the shot just before they'd left the little shop and sang along to Lady Gaga's newest on the drive back to Max's. It was a beautiful gift, and Ella's immediate reaction was to stare at it in awe before moving into Max's arms. "It's perfect." She kissed her softly. "I love it. It's going on the right side of my workstation, so I can stare at it throughout the day when you're at work and I miss you."

"That's fitting because I already have its twin on my desk at work."

Ella's chest burst with warmth. "I didn't know that."

"Well, of course not. It would have ruined the surprise."

They filled the rest of the morning with a leisurely breakfast and a thorough dive into the stockings they'd filled for each other. When it got close to lunch, Ella turned to Max. "What are you wearing to your parents' house? I want to make sure I'm not out of place."

Max went still, and she frowned. "Um, I'm not sure." She started to say more and paused, seemingly unsure what to do with herself.

What had Ella just missed? "Everything okay? You got weird."

She took a moment. "No. Everything is—I didn't realize you planned to come."

"With you on Christmas?" Ella quirked her head, not exactly following. They'd planned to spend the day together. It was Christmas, and Max's family was important. "Why wouldn't I go?"

Max sighed. "With my mom's illness, the day is already going to be incredibly stressful. If I bring you with me, I think it may add a certain amount of stress to the day."

Ella blinked at Max, letting the meaning of the words wash over her. "You don't want me at your family's Christmas."

"Of course I want you there. I always want you everywhere. I'm obsessed with you."

"So, your mother is the one who said she doesn't want to meet me?"

"No." Max held her eyes closed, struggling. "She hasn't said that she doesn't want to meet you. I think I just figured—"

"That it was more important to keep everyone happy." She swallowed, taking a significant beat. Control was important in this moment because she wanted to be heard. "At the expense of my feelings," she said calmly. Max's eyes widened, but she must have been at an impasse because she hadn't said anything. This would have been the moment to regroup, backpedal, tell Ella that it had just been a misunderstanding, and of course she wanted her there with the family.

"I'm sorry. I can tell that I'm screwing this all up. Just give me a minute."

"It's okay," Ella said simply. She gathered her things, shifting into autopilot, hoping to get out of there before any true emotion spilled out. Her head ached, and her cheeks flamed. The embarrassment trickled in more and more as the seconds ticked by. It was happening all over again.

Max's eyes were on her, tracking. She reached for Ella, but Ella stepped aside to avoid the contact. "What are you doing? You're leaving?"

"I am. I'll let you get ready, and, honestly, I don't think I have the fortitude to argue, play the victim, or sit by and watch with my hands folded in my lap while another person who is supposed to care about me puts me in the back seat of their life."

"Please don't think that's what I'm doing. My relationship

with my mother is this unique house of cards, and my family has been through a lot recently."

"I get it. They're lucky to have you." She walked to Max and met her gaze with intention. "But I want someone who feels lucky to have me."

"I do. God, Ella, please. Don't walk away." Max pinched the bridge of her nose in frustration. "What can I do here?"

"I'm not walking away. But you have somewhere to be, and I need a little bit of space. I think we have conflicting goals and that's a problem."

Max didn't argue, likely because what Ella said was true. It meant they had a very big problem on their hands, and Ella didn't have the solution at the moment.

She moved silently around the room, picking up stray ribbon and wrapping paper and placing her possessions into a neat pile. The remnants of a beautiful morning now looked like rubble, debris reminiscent of her feelings in this moment. She hadn't expected Max to bulldoze her heart, especially on Christmas, but she was flattened all the same.

Max was sitting on the arm of the couch when Ella made her way out of the bedroom, dressed for the day. "I hope you have a Merry Christmas, Max." She kissed her cheek. "Hug your loved ones. Keep them close."

"Ella," Max said quietly.

But Ella didn't stop. She couldn't.

THE SMELL of cinnamon and pine hit Max the second she stepped through the front door. It was thick with nostalgia and, in this moment, utterly unwelcome. It was Christmas, a season she adored. It was the kind of afternoon she looked forward to. Yet, somehow, she resented its presence now as something critical threatened to boil over from within, something brewing for far too long.

From further in the house, Bing Crosby was crooning about a white Christmas, and the hum of holiday cheer buzzed like static under Max's skin. She wanted to scratch it away.

The foyer looked precisely the same as it had since she was a kid, with pine garland draped over the staircase banister, a plate on the entry table with peanut brittle no one ever got around to eating, and her mother's porcelain nativity scene arranged with obsessive precision just next to it. The baby Jesus, she noticed, had been turned ever so slightly to face the door, like he was sizing her up. "Stop it, Jesus."

"Max! There you are. Merry, merry Christmas, sweet-heart." Her mother's voice floated in from the kitchen, sweet-ened with performative delight. "You're late."

Max shrugged out of her coat and tried to shrug off the ache in her chest with it. Her stomach was still knotted, her thoughts stuck on the conversation she couldn't stop replaying. The pain in Ella's eyes caused by Max's own stubborn habits haunted her. The protective fence she'd erected around her life and herself wasn't retired after all. Who knew?

She hadn't meant for the holiday to start with hurt feel-ings. But here she was. Life without Ella made no sense, and now there was a definite possibility she'd lost her for good. Her own damn fault. No more. Something had to give.

"Merry Christmas," she called out flatly, her voice swal-lowed by the crackle of the fireplace and the distant sound of her dad cursing, probably tangled in twinkly party lights.

"Be right there," he yelled. "Ho, ho, ho!"

Her mother appeared around the corner, clad in a festive sweater featuring a sequined reindeer. Her lipstick was already perfect, and her hair, slightly thinner from treatment, was smoothed into place. "Just you?" she asked, eyebrows lifting with nonchalance.

Max forced a tight smile. "Yeah. Just me."

A pause. Her mother's smile didn't shift, but Max could

feel the satisfaction radiating off her like heat from the oven. She'd won without having to lift a finger.

"Of course," she said. "We'll have a great morning with the rest of the family. They'll be here any minute. Do you want to fix up? Freshen your lips?"

"I don't. No."

"Very well." Her mother kissed her cheek and fluttered away to one of her many last-minute tasks. She'd regained her strength in spades since her hospitalization, on a new protocol that seemed much more targeted to her body. They'd be sharing a late lunch in the formal dining room, which meant there were many finishing touches to attend to, and Max, as always, would be expected to assist.

She exhaled slowly. She was here. She was home. And she already wanted to leave.

With a deep breath, she headed into the kitchen, encountering her father in the entryway. He pulled her in for a hug and placed a kiss on top of her head. "Merry Christmas, M."

"Merry Christmas, Daddy." She tried to brighten for him. The success was debatable.

"How's Ellen doing?"

She followed him into the kitchen. "It's Ella. She's not having the best time. Her family stood her up for Christmas." She accepted the basket her mother handed her and automatically began to fill it with the warm rolls cooling on the sheet. They had a silent shorthand in the kitchen after so many of these family events.

"Well, that's unfortunate," her mother said. "Their family must not be as close as ours."

"I don't think that's necessarily true. Every family is different."

"Why are you defensive? I don't understand. It's a happy day. Be happy."

That was her father's cue to grab a cookie and escape. Coward.

She squinted, annoyed. "Can you just order someone to be happy, though?"

"I don't know. You tell me." She shrugged and moved to the refrigerator as the song shifted to "Winter Wonderland."

"I'm not having the best day." She'd not felt so dejected in a long time.

"Why are you sad?" her mother asked. "I don't understand. Pull yourself together before the others get here." Max swallowed. Once the extended family arrived—her father's sister, her mother's cousins—the flurry of activity would whisk them away for the rest of the day, caught up in a charade of polite smiles and tired rituals. No one would notice if she stayed quiet. In fact, that was preferred. But the words were clawing at her throat now, bitter and hot, and if she didn't let them out soon, she'd spend the rest of the day simmering in silence while everyone else decked the halls and tossed back her father's spiced wine.

"I don't think I can just play along anymore."

"Don't be dramatic. Do you want to try the dessert? I think you'll like the bibingka. I made it extra sweet for your father. Extra sticky, too."

Her muscles tensed. She saw every tactic in vivid color now. The diminishing of her feelings. The redirection to something less flammable. "I don't want to taste the dessert. I want to have this argument."

Her mother sighed, set down the stack of plates in her hand, and turned fully to Max. "Go ahead then if you must. Tell me why you're upset, and we can move forward!" Her voice was commanding. Her brown eyes were hard, challenging. Max knew the look all too well. It meant she didn't appreciate the emotional detour when she had a one-woman show ahead of her. The stagehand was out of line. Her blood ran cold, and she braced herself. This was usually the moment Max backed down. Not today.

"Because Ella should be here with me right now." She

pinched the bridge of her nose. "And it's my own fault that she's not because I run around like a windup toy who only knows how to chase your approval."

"And why is my approval so awful? I'm your mother."

"I'm a grown woman, Mom."

"Well, you're not acting like one. You'll have your whole life to spend with this woman, if that's what you want. This could be your last one with me."

"Please. You're too domineering to die, and everyone knows it." She straightened, just as shocked that the words came out of her mouth as her mother seemed to be. Her mother gripped the kitchen counter behind her, as if she needed it for support. Max didn't buy it. She reined in her anger and turned to her mother calmly. "You can let go of the counter. I don't think the truth is going to knock you over."

"If that's really how you feel, then go."

"She doesn't want to see me."

Her mother's features softened. Maybe she sensed the enormity of Max's emotions, her feelings for Ella. Perhaps she realized the part she'd played in all of this. Who knew? She wasn't the kind of woman who would actively share. "She'll come around. It's the holidays. Take her some of my cookies."

Max closed her eyes and leaned against the counter. "It's going to take more than that."

"You're a smart woman. You'll figure it out."

The front door opened, and the sound of excited voices floated in. The guests were arriving.

"That's your Aunt Betty." Her mother dried her hands. "I'd better go say hello. She's bringing that creamy green bean dish your father loves." She looked back. "Maxine. Smile. You will fix everything." A hesitation hit. "I'll help if you want."

Max didn't answer right away. She just looked at her mother, truly looked at her—and saw the pride, the fear, the love, all tangled up in practiced control. What was it like to be her? Trying, but unable to get out of your own way?

Alone, without a word, Max pulled out her phone and turned it over in her hand.

Ella's name stared back at her.

She tapped out a message. Short. Honest. A start.

As the front door shut again behind another round of guests, Max took a breath and hit send.

TWENTY-SEVEN

Retired Inner Warriors

W ell, at least it had been a memorable Christmas. That's what Ella told herself, anyway—a flimsy consolation prize to keep her from slipping into the familiar abyss. It had been two days. Max had reached out multiple times, always with soft, apologetic messages full of concern and uncertainty. But they hadn't seen each other.

> I think we could use a little space.

Ella paused and typed some more.

> Can we take some time to get our heads together?

A day? A week?

Ella went quiet. She hadn't known. She still didn't. After some back and forth inside her own head, she canceled her New Year's trip home. She needed some distance between her and the rest of the world, and that included Max. She wasn't sure space would help, or if anything would. The common denominator in every single scenario seemed to be her. She couldn't suddenly make herself more special or deserving of a spot in the lives of those she loved. She closed her eyes and lay back on the couch under the pile of blankets that had served as her fortress. She was behind on all of her projects for Cover Crush, but couldn't quite bring herself to focus on romance when hers was on the brink of ending. She'd never felt the intensity of feelings she experienced for Max, and she knew exactly what that meant. The level of heartbreak she was experiencing only confirmed it. She was in love. And how do you walk away from that? Also, how do you stay when the flag is waving red? Her head and her heart were in a vicious war.

"You're still on the couch," Rachel said, coming to sit at her feet. She'd just come from a New Year's lunch date with some of her friends, meaning she looked terrific with those lazy beach curls and a pale pink sweater that said soft yet in charge. She'd likely even talked to other humans like a civilized person. She lifted Ella's legs into her lap and plopped her arms on top of the blankets. "Hey, kid. Gotta tell you something. This is not the inner warrior energy we need."

Ella didn't so much as lift her head from the couch pillow. "I checked, and my inner warrior had to retire. She sells insurance online now."

"Then we need to rescue her ASAP. Nothing that's happened here is irreparable."

"You only say that because you don't have my brand of baggage."

"No. I have my own. We all do. And if mine were hanging me up, you'd talk me through how to maneuver around it. Make it my bitch. You have an unworthiness complex."

Ella held up a finger. "We prefer the term chronic invisibility. Or maybe conditional relevance. Background character syndrome? Wallflowers R Us?"

"Whatever you want to call it, it's not going to get in the way of what you want in this life. I didn't want you to be with

Max. You and I both know that. That was me letting my baggage get in the way."

"Jealousy?"

"More like a member of the selfish bitch society."

"Ah," Ella smothered a smile. Rachel said it. She hadn't.

"But once I resigned membership, I can safely report that Max makes you smile like I've never seen in the years I've known you." In response, Ella tossed a blanket over her head, unsure she was prepared to hear all this. "Doesn't hold a candle to Britney or even the ridiculous Hoopties."

Ella peeked out from the blanket. "You think Max tops Hoopties?"

"As far as you go, all signs point to yes. And I'm not saying that your feelings aren't valid. I'm just hoping you'll at least hear her out. If she blows it again, you can kick her to the curb. She's definitely not a perfect person. But who is?"

Ella sobered, ready to go there. "You had a much harsher characterization of Max a few months ago."

Rachel nodded and swept a strand of hair behind her shoulder. "It's possible I'd blown a few things out of proportion to soothe my ego after we split." She shrugged. "I don't like that I did that. I can also acknowledge that I wasn't the best version of myself when we dated." She patted Ella's blanket. "She probably put up with a lot of less-than-mature behavior."

Ella nodded, taking the new information in stride. Given what she knew about Max and what she'd suspected for a while now, it made sense. It was nice to hear the words from Rachel's mouth, however. Cards were now entirely on the table, even if they should have been from the beginning. She could get angry at Rachel for not being forthcoming and lecture her on friendship, trust, and honesty. But did she have any right?

"I appreciate you clearing that up," she said. She would offer Rachel as much grace as she'd shown Ella not long ago, because they'd all made many mistakes on this journey. "I know breakups are hard." She nearly cried saying the word, wondering if she'd be dealing with one of her own in the not-so-distant future. The reality made nausea bubble up in her stomach. She didn't want to ever return to life without Max, but everything felt particularly bleak. "But hearing Max is a great person isn't exactly shocking. I know she's great. But is she great for me?"

"In other words, does her baggage match yours?"

Ella smiled, imagining them trying to cram a million suitcases in a tiny car. "Good question." She looked behind her meekly. "Do we have popcorn? I would die if there was hot popcorn with butter."

Rachel laughed. "Coming right up. And after that? We're getting you off the couch and touching some grass."

"Grass is overrated."

Rachel stood, adjusting her sweater and brushing imaginary lint from her jeans. "You don't have to make every decision today. But you *do* have to put on pants."

Ella gave a half-hearted groan. "That's asking a lot."

"Popcorn first. Pants later."

She left the room, humming something from the *Encanto* soundtrack under her breath. Ella stared at the ceiling for a long beat, the weight of the blanket oddly comforting. She wasn't sure what she was going to do about Max—about any of it. But maybe, for today, popcorn and honesty with a friend were enough.

She wasn't ready to move on. But maybe, *maybe*, she was ready to stop hiding.

THE HOUSE WAS dark and quiet when Max arrived for a short visit with her parents after work. That was strange. Her mother's car was in the driveway, and she had no appointments that

Max knew of. It was uncharacteristic. "Anybody home?" she called, letting herself in through the garage door that fed into the kitchen. She looked around the dormant space. Had they even had dinner? The customary aromas that generally greeted her were also absent.

"In here," she heard a meek voice call.

She followed the sound into the living room, which was also dark except for the glow of the television. She turned to her right, and tucked beneath a patchwork quilt on the couch sat her mother. "I was just watching a few of the old videos." Her voice sounded wobbly.

Max wanted to see her face. "Can I turn on a lamp?"

"Of course," her mother said, immediately sitting taller, in what seemed to be an attempt to pull herself together.

She chose the small lamp on the opposite end table, the one she knew would cast the least amount of light. With a click, the room was cast in a soft glow. Max turned and saw her mother, red-faced and tearstained. "Are you okay?" she asked, sitting next to her. "Do we need to go to the hospital?"

She was greeted with a laugh. "It's ironic to realize my child thinks it's an emergency when I cry. That shows me the precedent I've set."

Max relaxed. "So, you're okay. You're just emotional?"

"For the past three hours, I've been watching my life literally pass before my eyes. Your father's watching a football game at the bar with Chuck, and I decided to take a trip down memory lane." She gestured to the screen. "Do you know I put you back on that bicycle four more times after you fell off and asked me if you could go inside?"

Max followed her gaze to the television where the home video she'd been watching had been placed on pause. She saw herself with a dark ponytail and purple shorts on top of a brand-new two-wheeler. She remembered the details of that afternoon as if it were yesterday, and it had been stressful. Lots of crying, falling, and getting back on the bike. But eventually she'd done it, skinned knees and all. She'd ridden all the way down their street without assistance.

She turned to her mother. "You wouldn't let me give up."

She closed her eyes from wariness or regret. It was hard to know which. "But I also wasn't listening to you. You told me what you needed, and I continued to push." She lay her head back on the couch, her cheek pressed to the cushion, as she gazed at Max thoughtfully. "All this recent time to myself has me seeing things quite differently."

"Why do you think that is?"

She shook her head in awe. "I've told my patients for years that serious illness can change them in many ways, including up here." She tapped her temple. "And now I know it's true. I'm them. And I'm not sure how to be right now." She folded her hands in her lap.

Vulnerability was not in her mother's repertoire. Max blinked, not quite believing the conversation they seemed to be having. She decided to listen instead of saying too much, sensing somehow that it was for the best and what her mother needed.

They were both quiet, letting the moment exhale and have itself. Emotions swirled, the room thick with them like clouds before a downpour. Max understood, unequivocally, that this was an important conversation in their relationship and that the words spoken would shape the future in front of them.

"I was too hard on you," her mother said finally, meeting Max's eyes with sorrowful ones. "It was all I knew. My mother was hard on me, and hers was the same." She reached for a tissue and dabbed beneath her nose. "We weren't permitted to make mistakes, and I saw the benefit in that through achievement. But there's a price to pay, too."

Max nodded, knowing all too well. For the first time, however, she saw herself in her mother. She saw the daughter who watched her own hopes and dreams get pushed to the side, extinguished. Maybe she hadn't wanted to be a doctor.

Maybe Max's mother dreamt of one day being a zoologist. Who knew? Max realized that she'd never really asked. A mistake that now ushered in a swarm of regret.

It would be simple to correct her mother and let her off the hook. Tell her she'd given Max a fully loving childhood, and they had nothing to talk through. Max couldn't do that. She'd lost too much. Something had to change, and she had to make it happen.

"I'm sorry you had a difficult time when you were young," Max said. "And I'm also sorry that you carried it with you into motherhood. You did a lot of things right with me, but your expectations were a difficult hurdle to leap." She turned her palms upward and studied them as if they contained the perfect set of words to communicate her feelings. "But I can't leap any more hurdles."

"You fell in love," her mother said softly.

"I did." Max shook her head, finding power in sharing that information out loud. A painful lump lodged itself in her throat. "She's afraid of me now. I made her feel small, and I hate every second of that knowledge. She shines brighter than any person I've ever met."

Her mother nodded, thoughtful. "Then you make sure she knows that." She pressed down on the couch cushion with one finger. "You correct the mistake. If she matters to you as much as you say, you run toward her with all you have, not away. You lead with honesty and you make yourself vulnerable."

It was the first piece of usable romantic advice her mother had ever offered her. It was also the first time she'd ever encouraged her to find love with a woman. Max sat with the understanding, reeling from the unexpected twist. Today, the milestones were raining down like sprinkles on a cupcake. Max wanted to be sure she didn't miss any.

"Vulnerable has never been my strong suit," Max admitted.

"That might also be my doing," she said. Her eyes held

apology, which released a heavy dose of truth right in the center of Max's already swirling emotions.

"I just wanted you to love me," Max said, her voice a strangled whisper. "I used to lie in bed at night and pray for it."

Instantly, the tears in Max's eyes were mirrored in her mother's. She sat forward and met Max's gaze. "I loved you so much," she said emphatically. "Maybe too much. I thought pushing you to be your best self would help you in life. Make you strong."

"All I needed was for you to believe I was. Once I had that, I would have had everything. I could have moved mountains."

Her mother exhaled slowly as she reached for a tissue. "I failed you in that," she said quietly. "And it's painful to know I can't go back and fix it. But let me say it now before another minute goes by. I believe in you, Maxine. I always have."

Max nodded and absorbed the words, or at least attempted to. It would take her time to believe them, but she was willing to try if her mother was. Because they couldn't go on the way they had. There was too much at stake.

"But, it's not too late, you know." She sent Max a wobbly smile, the lines around her eyes more prominent. She appeared older today, smaller. Maybe it was the toll the treatment had taken on her body, or maybe it was because she wasn't dressed like Dr. Mayumi Wyler, wearing navy lounge pants and a gray T-shirt without a stitch of makeup to be seen. It crafted an individual who seemed a little less daunting, just a woman across the couch offering what help she could cobble together.

"I hope you're right," Max said, her gaze falling to the tan woven rug. Her heart hung heavy, and every part of her held recriminations for how things had gone with Ella on Christmas morning. Correction: how she'd treated Ella that morning. This was all on her.

Her mother reached down the couch and covered Max's

hand with her own, squeezing it tightly. "I have an idea. If you have the time to stay, why don't I make some hot cocoa? We can watch a few of these family videos and talk about what went wrong between you and Ella."

Max sat back, struck. "You said her name."

"Why wouldn't I say her name?" her mother asked, her brows pulling together.

"You've always referred to her as my girlfriend or that woman you're seeing."

"I have?"

Max nodded.

"Hmm. Well, it seems I have a few things to work on."

"Okay, this is too weird," Max said, holding out her hand like a stop sign. "Now you're actively admitting you're not perfect. Is an asteroid about to take us all out?" She feigned looking skyward.

Her mother picked up the remote. "Shhh, and watch the home movies. And after that, I have some ideas about Ella. You have to work in some big moves."

"Big moves, huh?"

"Absolutely."

Max smiled, a soft, surprised thing that crept up before she could stop it. Maybe this was what growth looked like. Not grand gestures or perfect endings, but two people in tough spots, sitting on a couch, watching the past flicker across a screen while figuring out how to show up for an uncertain future.

She settled deeper into the cushions as the tape resumed, the sound of a small voice on the screen calling for her mom. It echoed through the room like a benediction.

They sat on the couch, one cushion between them, letting the story of who they'd been remind them of who they might still become. The ground felt shaky, but for the first time, Max looked over at her mother and wondered if there just might be hope for them.

TWENTY-EIGHT

Books, Blushes, and Whooshes

E lla marveled at the newly installed shelving, slightly less haphazard than the last arrangement, but every bit as packed in as the old store had been. Doug's Books had come a long way in a short time. The progress was a true testament to the power of the community. It turned out that when people care enough, they can move mountains.

Doug beamed, clearly proud of his new space. "What do you think?"

"You are looking so good, my friend." She turned in a circle, absorbing the beautiful new touches like the small clock on the wall with numbers made to look like typewriter keys. Due to her unfortunate couch time and self-imposed isolation, she hadn't been in the store in nearly a week.

"That woman you like is here."

Ella quirked her head. "The woman I like?"

"With the hair," he said, swishing his imaginary locks in a sincere method of communication. "She came in a few times to see if you were working on your book covers behind the tablet thingy. You haven't been here, so she'd buy a book and leave. Sold three so far. Maybe you should stay away." He offered a wink and hefted a box from the floor onto a stepladder. More inventory was beginning to arrive from the distributors, which is one of the reasons she'd forced herself to come in. She'd apparently hired herself as his unpaid employee.

"Max," she said, peering around a shelf she wasn't quite familiar with yet. Max knew Ella often opted to work at Doug's a couple of days a week around this time. Though Ella had no idea she'd been stopping by to see her. A familiar whoosh of excitement hit because she missed Max with every fiber of her being. A second whoosh of nervous energy was right behind it because she didn't know how to be herself anymore, given her new understanding of how things worked.

"That's the one. She's over there next to my new hot titles shelf. I think I'm gonna put a wall of flames around that section, as if the whole thing just ignited from pure heat."

"I like the plan," Ella said, following Doug's general gesturing toward the far wall of the store. "I'm gonna go talk to Max and then I'll be back over to help with the blaze of books."

"They're so hot you can't handle it," he called after her.

"I believe it."

He was in much better spirits today, which was heartening to see. Even his humor was back in full force. She followed the curve of the new shelving until she came to an opening where two beautiful new tables sat alongside each other like old friends. Max approached, carrying a cup of coffee.

"I took the liberty when I heard your voice," she said. Her smile was guarded but laced with hope.

"Thank you," Ella said as she accepted the coffee swirled with just the right amount of cream. Max knew her ratio: not too dark, not too light. It wasn't just the coffee, either. It was Max remembering the details, always. That had to count for something.

Max exhaled. "So, I'm here." She was dressed for work in

a slim-fit maroon blazer and black pants, which meant the stop at Doug's was a late morning detour in her day. She'd made the time.

"You are."

"I was afraid if I texted again, you'd be polite, but distant."

"I would have been," Ella said. She let her bag slide off her shoulder. "Doesn't mean I don't still like you." *Love.* She knew the word was love, but this wasn't the time or place to go there. That information would stay tucked safely behind her heart.

Max seemed relieved. Her features relaxed. "That's a start." They shared a tentative smile. The ground felt shaky, and the future seemed dubious. But they were still *them.* She felt it all over just being in Max's presence. How could both dynamics exist? "I like you, too. And I want us to figure this out."

Ella shrugged. "And how do we do that, Max? I can't go down a path I've already explored. I know how the story ends. If there's another way, I'm all ears." She tried not to hold her breath, but this felt like a crucial moment.

Max took a seat and gestured for Ella to do the same. She slid into the chair across from Max and, unsure what to do with her hands, folded them like a student waiting for class to begin.

Max took the cue. "I think about what happened at Christmas a lot. I know I was in the wrong, but acknowledging my mistake and moving forward wouldn't get to the crux of the actual problem."

"I think you're right." The words were helpful and promising, but she couldn't quite let herself get her hopes up when she was still very hurt.

"I think you deserve more than an apology. So, I'm going to say this and then I'm going to get out of your hair and let you work."

"Okay."

"My mission to keep my family happy has become an invisible habit, so second nature to me that I didn't register its effect. I crashed and burned because life isn't about doing what appeases others. My mother has always been a prominent figure in my life, and my need for approval would become a never-ending quest if I let it."

Ella nodded, remembering their very candid conversation at the night market.

"I'm not going to. I've had those conversations, and if you allow me to show you, you will never find yourself without light on your face again. You'd be my priority because I love you, Ella." She held up a finger. "You don't have to say anything. Just think about these words, and we can talk more later. Because I'm committed to keep showing up and letting you know how important you are." She touched the table. "Have a good workday, okay?"

Ella nodded again, struck. "I will. You, too." She stared in surprise as Max stood and left the shop. When the bell above the door dinged, she turned to the empty chair next to her and back again. Had Max just told Ella that she loved her and was planning to make changes in herself so they could have a future? It was a lot to digest. Her emotions warred and circled to the point that she didn't hear Doug approach, but all of a sudden, there he was.

"It's like one of those books you folks are always reading—right at the part where the heroine has to decide if she's brave enough to want something big." He gestured toward the door Max had just pushed through. "Here you sit, on the precipice." He held his hands up. "Do you take the big leap, shove all your chips to the center of the table, or run away forever?"

She snapped her focus from the door to Doug. "I don't know that I'd classify it as running away."

"No? Just me then? Hmm." He puttered away, mumbling something about too many boxes.

Was he right? Was she running from her fears before they had a chance to manifest fully? She'd been all about her and Max when it had been low-risk, but the stakes were higher the more she felt for this woman, who was as maddening as she was gorgeous.

"Let's find you some flames, D-Man."

Tuesday evening approached, and Max stood in front of the mirror for the third time, trying to decide whether confidence looked better with her hair down or pulled back. Her mother hovered nearby, equal parts nervous energy and fierce support, fussing with Max's collar like they were preparing for a wedding instead of a book club. But maybe it was both, in a someday kind of way. Max had never worn nerves like this before—this wasn't court, and it wasn't work. This was personal. Deeply personal. And it mattered.

"Do you want to rehearse what you're going to say?" her mother asked, smoothing down Max's hair, after she'd decided to keep it down and free. "You look fantastic. Any woman can see that."

"Thank you, Mom. No, I think I'm just gonna improvise."

"I didn't know attorneys did that. Don't you all meticu-lously prepare for court engagements?"

"It's not exactly an engagement," Max said with a wink. "Not that I wouldn't marry her. I would. Just so you know."

"These jeans are very sexy."

Max smiled and placed a hand on her mother's shoulder. "You're trying so very hard, but you don't have to call me sexy. I relieve you of any obligation."

"Oh, good," she said, relaxing. "I'm learning still. I rented *The L Word* DVD from the library."

"People still have DVDs? The library has *The L Word*?"

"We do," her mother said. "And they do. Your father's favorite is Alice."

Max winced, imagining them watching some of those spicier scenes, now wondering if it was better when they pretended she was straight. Nope. Wasn't. She tried to lean in. "Alice does have a lot of great lines."

Her mother patted her arm. "You're more of a Bette."

"Is this happening right now?" Max asked, tilting her head and slamming her eyes closed.

"Yes." Her mother grabbed her purse and stalked out of the house to the Range Rover. "And I'm the wingwoman. Dr. Wingwoman." She paused on the sidewalk. "Did I tell you I'm seeing patients again next week? Dr. Rivera cleared me to return to work, provided I monitor my energy levels. I'm going to begin with half days."

"That's fantastic," Max said, trailing her mom to the car. "Are you sure you're up for it?"

"I'm more than ready. I'm at my best when I'm with patients who need me. I can't think of a faster way to heal."

Max paused. It was the first time since her initial diagnosis that her mother had alluded to getting better. It was more than wonderful to hear that she was on board and ready to tackle this illness fully, punch it in the face, and get back to life as originally scheduled. "Now that's more like it. I like the fire in your eyes. Let's keep it."

"I'm using it for you today. Let's go see a book club about a girl. You drive."

"You sure you want to do this?"

"Does Bette Porter look good in a business suit?" She offered a playful wink and looked straight ahead, waiting for the car to whisk them away.

Max blinked, harnessing her newfound respect for her mom, who was trying hard to make up for lost time. "I could get used to this version of you."

325

"I know. Maybe I'll lead a group."

"I recognize project mode when I see it."

"But less about me, more about our mission." She rubbed her hands together. "I'm ready."

Max put the car in reverse and took a deep breath. "Then let's do this."

TWENTY-NINE

The Rewrite

The book club selection that week had been exceptionally hard-hitting. The couple had reminded Ella so much of her and Max. Not just in the broad strokes, but in the quiet ache between them. That instant attraction, but the delay in fully admitting what they were feeling. The stubborn main character who refused to be knocked off their ways, paired with someone who saw themself as an underdog. Was the universe trying to tell her something? Even the pivotal fight, where it all came crashing down, landed a little too close for comfort.

"What did you think of the book?" Stevie asked Ella. "You've been uncharacteristically quiet through all of our debating."

"I didn't like it." Ella looked around the room at raised eyebrows and understanding nods.

"Rare for you," Ariana said, squinting. "Does this new, more critical gaze have anything to do with Max, who is suspiciously not in attendance?" She stared straight at the chair Max usually occupied.

Stevie took a bite of a cracker. "She said she'd be late tonight and not to wait."

"Maybe. Probably. I don't know," Ella said. She was on edge. Max wasn't here, which meant everything felt less shiny. They were in limbo, and she couldn't take it anymore. She was on the precipice of taking the official leap and giving them that chance Max was asking for, but she needed one more tiny shove. She thought that maybe seeing her again, talking to her, and looking into those beautiful brown eyes might give her the reassurance she needed. And now … she was just mad at the world.

Just then, a car horn sounded.

"Was there anything about the book you liked?" Morgan asked, attempting to get them back on track.

Ella sighed. "I thought the dinner date—" Another long sound of the horn, this time, followed up by several short ones.

"Someone is really laying on that thing," Stevie said, turning in the direction of the street. "Do you think there was an accident?" She stood and swept her blond hair to the side.

"Attention, Weepers!" a voice called from outside. A familiar one.

Ariana swiveled her gaze to Ella, her eyes wide. "Is that who I think it is?"

"Is it? What's going on?" Ella asked, following Stevie to the door, the rest of the group not far behind her. When they arrived on Stevie's front lawn, there was Max, sitting on the edge of her open window, the Range Rover door closed, and the glass rolled down.

"M, is everything okay?" Stevie called.

"I'm sorry to interrupt, but I needed you all to hear something very important."

"We're listening," Olive yelled back with uncharacteristic volume. She was here for this and intertwined her fingers with Stevie's.

"What is happening?" Ella murmured, her heart hammering. Once again, she didn't know what to do with her hands. Why were they always so confusing?

"Sorry to interrupt book club," Max called, "but I figured if I wanted to rewrite the ending of our story, I needed to start by showing up in the middle of yours."

"I see what she did there," Morgan said quietly to Ariana.

"A good opener," Ariana said back.

"Ella, I've been trying to figure out the right words, the right moment, the right everything. And then I realized—I don't need perfect. I just need honest. That's all we'll ever need, and the honest truth is I love you."

"She's in love with you!" Mayumi called, hanging her head out of the passenger window. "Isn't that great?"

Ella's eyes went wide. Max's mom shouting from the rooftops, or a car window, had not been on her bingo card.

"And if there's still a chance, I want to be the person you choose," Max said. "Not quietly. Not someday. Now."

"Choose her! She's a good one. Do you know Bette Porter?" Mayumi shouted. Ella laughed because what was happening? "She loves you, Ella. And she's not the only one who thinks you're worth the leap."

"Hi, everyone," Max said, turning to the group. "I have to confess that I didn't believe in the kinds of romances we read about. In fact, I was positive they were downright fiction, borderline ludicrous, and a sham. They're not. I have proof, and it's in this woman standing here right now, and everything I've experienced since she first sat in Stevie's living room and gushed about Parker Bristow's last book. Ella Baker, listen to me when I tell you that romance novels have nothing on us."

"She has a point," Ariana said. "Do you remember any of the grand gestures involving the mom?"

"Can't say I do," Morgan said. "Bonus points for creativity."

"I'm gonna have to step it up," Stevie said, putting her

arm around Olive, who reciprocated with a soft kiss. Apparently, romance was in the air all around.

"If you'll let me, I will spend every day showing you that you're the most wonderful and important person I've ever met. When you walk into a room, the temperature changes, and people smile. That's the kind of power you carry." All eyes were on her. The Weepers were nodding along. Morgan dabbed at her eyes. "Can we please pick up our story and keep going?" Max said, her voice steady but thick with emotion. "No more limbo. No more wondering. Just … us. I love you, Ella. And I want to build something real with you. I want to be the person you come home to, even on the messy days. Especially on the messy days."

The silence that followed wasn't empty—it was full of memory, of hope, of all the words they hadn't said but had felt pressing between them for weeks.

Ella stepped forward slowly, the damp grass crisp beneath her shoes. Her chest ached, but in that kind of way that meant something was shifting. Finally.

She didn't shout. She didn't make a speech. She just said, quietly, "You showed up."

"I did. And I always will."

Their connection locked into place. Ella could breathe again. "And you brought your mom. Hi, Dr. Wyler. It's nice to finally meet you."

"Hi, Ella. You, too." She came around the front of the car and leaned in. "I'm the wingwoman today. How'd I do?"

Ella held her hands up, still in awe and touched that she was a part of this. "No notes. You were fabulous."

Mayumi seemed pleased with the review.

Max gave a small nod. "She insisted on being here."

Ella grinned. "And I'm happy you did."

"So, what do you think? Can we make up and move forward together?"

"Say yes," Morgan said in an exaggerated whisper.

"Hurry," Stevie added.

Another beat. The group fell silent as a blanket of anticipation covered everything. Ella exhaled. "Come here," she said finally.

Max pushed away from the car, walking across the lawn slowly like she was afraid the moment might vanish if she moved too fast.

When they met in the middle, Ella reached for her hand first. Just that. A quiet promise. Max's eyes filled with tears that threatened to spill at any moment. "You're my everything, and there's no mistaking that. I love you, too," Ella said, her own emotion strangling her voice. The kiss that followed wasn't a grand finale, it was a soft beginning.

And somewhere behind them, Mayumi exhaled in relief like she'd been holding her breath for weeks. "Well," she said, "that's more like it. I can head home and rest easy."

"Five stars!" Ariana yelled. "A definite reread."

Still holding onto Max, Ella turned and regarded her friends, who looked on with such affection. Every single one of them had been a positive force in her life, and she was happy they were able to share this moment with them.

Mayumi stepped forward and gave Ella a quick hug. "Enjoy book club and we'll have dinner soon, okay? All four of us."

"Yes, ma'am. You have no idea how much I would love that."

Mayumi accepted the keys from Max, slid into the driver's seat, and pulled away to enthusiastic waves and applause from all the Weepers, who understood the value of what they'd just watched.

"Are you sure you have a complicated relationship with your mother?" Stevie asked Max, leading them all inside. "She seems like a darling."

Max laughed. "Trust me. There are layers involved."

Ella watched Max's car as it disappeared down the street, which Ella imagined meant they'd be driving home together, which honestly sounded nothing short of perfect. As the other four Weepers filed inside, Ella tugged on Max's hand, pausing her there on the porch. Once they were alone, she went up on her toes, wrapped her arms around Max's neck, and stared deeply into her expressive brown eyes.

"I'm really happy to see you."

Max opened her mouth to respond, but Ella captured it in a kiss that communicated everything she wanted to say privately, including that Max looked so ridiculously hot that Ella didn't know what to do with herself. She wanted to run her hand through that gorgeous hair and press her skin to Max's, absolutely nothing between them. In fact, she might stay there forever.

"Well, that kiss was worth waiting for," Max said, eyes still closed when they came up for air. "Let's skip this meeting, go back to my place, and never leave." She picked up a strand of Ella's hair and placed it behind her shoulder.

"We absolutely cannot," Ella said. "It's once a week, and we made a promise to the book when we read it."

"To the *book*?" Max laughed. "If I didn't love this side of you, I might be offended."

"What's an hour?" Ella asked.

"Fine. But after that, I have plans."

"What kind?" Ella asked, her stomach muscles tightening.

"The kind that starts with me stripping you out of those jeans. And ends with you forgetting your own name."

"You two joining us?" Stevie called.

"We'll be right in," Ella yelled back, her hands beneath the back of Max's shirt. "One hour."

For the next sixty minutes, Ella did her best to listen intently to the back-and-forth, picking up where they left off before Max's momentous arrival. Olive thought the sex scenes were too tepid. Morgan loved the wallflower who came into herself by the end of the book and learned how to stand up for what she wanted. Stevie liked the wine that Ariana brought. All the while, Ella felt Max's gaze on her and could barely string two coherent thoughts together. Every time Max shifted in her seat, whether stretching her legs out, propping an ankle casually on her knee, or running her thumb slowly around the rim of her wineglass, Ella's body reacted like she'd been touched. She tried to nod at Morgan's point about too many characters, offer something intelligent about secondary arcs, maybe even agree with Olive's hatred of food descriptions just to get the conversation moving. But Max kept watching her with that look, like she already knew exactly what Ella wanted, and was in absolutely no rush to give it to her. She knew what she was doing, and it was torture.

At one point, Ella caught Max briefly touch her tongue to her bottom lip. It was completely silent. Devastating. Thirty-two minutes. She could survive thirty-two minutes.

Ella gripped the stem of her wineglass like it might anchor her to the earth. She offered a vague comment about pacing, suggesting that it could have been more varied. She pretended not to notice the deliberate way Max's hair fell in haphazard waves after she ran her fingers through it.

Eighteen minutes, she informed herself.

Now seventeen.

But by the time Ariana stood to stretch and suggest they all call it a night, Ella was already halfway out of her chair, carrying a handful of empty glasses into the kitchen. After helping to tidy up, she said a quick goodbye and stalked to the door with intention. She didn't wait to see if Max followed.

She already knew she would.

She hadn't even touched Ella yet, not really, and already Max felt like every inch of restraint she'd practiced tonight was unraveling now that they were alone. The lights were still off when they'd fallen into the condo, keys fumbling in her shaky hands. That is, except for one lonely lamp in the living room that cast a quiet glow into the entryway where Max had Ella pressed up against the wall.

She wanted to go fast. Everything in her longed to tear away the fabric separating their bodies, but she refused to rush this much-anticipated moment. She brought her mouth to Ella's, who kissed her back like she was starving. Her tongue was in Ella's mouth, which was so goddamned satisfying it made every part of her curl into itself. The sound Ella made when Max's fingers slid under her shirt was going to live in Max's bloodstream forever. With every murmur and moan, Max reveled. The heated skin beneath Max's fingertips, smooth and sensitive, begged to be explored. Kissed. Worshipped. She pulled her lips away from Ella's, but only so she could kiss the side of her neck, intoxicated by the familiar scent of her orange blossom shampoo. *Home.* Because how many times had she buried her face in Ella's hair?

"Touch me," Ella said quietly, cradling the back of Max's neck, her fingers threaded through her hair. "Right against this wall."

She was already unbuttoning Ella's jeans. When her fingers slid into the wet warmth of her underwear, she closed her eyes and moaned. This was everything. Ella began to roll her hips, her head tossed back, hair tickling Max's arms as she held Ella around the waist.

"You feel so fucking good," Ella managed.

Max let her set the pace, matching her rhythm, sliding through slick folds, grazing her clit again and again until it was clear Ella hovered just near the edge, desperation swarming her. She bucked her hips, pressing into Max more and more with each thrust until finally she cried out loudly, the dam having broken. Her features relaxed as she rode the waves of pleasure in a display that caused warmth to spread in Max's chest.

"That was inspired," Ella said. "I needed that from you and that damned wall for over an hour now."

"I'm not exactly done yet," Max said, reclaiming her hand and finding Ella's lips for another searing kiss. It took three-point-four seconds to usher Ella into her bedroom around the corner and another two to press her back to the mattress. Knowing how turned on Ella got when Max undressed for her, she took her time and showed off the new lingerie set she'd purchased in case such an occasion presented itself.

"Your breasts should be in history books," Ella said once they were out, going up on her forearms to take in the view. "But that would mean I'd have to share them, and there's no chance of that."

Wearing only the matching red underwear, she crawled onto the bed and on top of Ella, who needed no encouragement. As Max leaned over her, Ella pulled a nipple into her mouth, holding her breast in place from beneath. Ella moved to the other breast, paying equal attention. She was nothing if not fair.

"I want you out of these clothes," Max said.

"Okay, Counselor," Ella teased, a slow grin spreading as she sat up and pulled her shirt over her head.

Max's breath caught at the sight of her. She loved the confidence, the comfort, the way the light skimmed the tops of her breasts. They made quick work of the rest of Ella's clothes, each movement efficient but reverent, like unwrapping something cherished.

Just as she began to lower herself, Ella's hand pressed gently to her shoulder, stopping her.

"Hey. I love you," she said softly, brushing her thumb across Max's cheek.

Max leaned into the touch. "I love you, too. So damn

much." Her voice cracked at the edges of it, truth slipping through all her defenses. She wouldn't hold back her emotions from Ella anymore. All cards on the table. She loved this woman and would spend every second showing her.

They kissed, slow and sure. Max cradled Ella's face for a moment, memorizing it—then deepened the kiss as Ella's body arched toward hers. Her hand found Ella's breast, thumb brushing across soft skin, and she pressed her thigh between Ella's legs, feeling the shift as tenderness gave way to need.

"Ahem." Ella tilted her head in the direction of Max's red, lacy underwear, the last of the clothing between them.

"Oh, you want these off?"

Her eyes were dark. "How am I supposed to properly fuck you with them on?"

Max sucked in air. "I love it when you talk like that. It does intense things to me."

"Yeah?" Ella pulled Max into a scorching kiss that left her dizzy. "Well, there's a lot more where that came from. I have definite plans."

"Not until I make you whimper. It's my favorite sound of yours." She leaned her mouth very close to Ella's ear. "Turn around."

Ella's breath hitched, but she did as she was told, her movements fluid, trusting. Max's hands slid down the curve of her back, slow and deliberate, until they rested at her hips.

"God, look at you," Max murmured, more reverence than command now. "You have no idea what you do to me." The sight of Ella like that—on all fours, bare, waiting, already trembling with want—nearly unraveled her.

Ella glanced over her shoulder, flushed. "Then show me."

Max pressed a kiss to the base of her spine. "Tell me if anything's too much," she murmured. Another soft kiss, as she caressed Ella's very smooth ass.

Ella looked back over her shoulder, eyes heavy with heat. "The only thing too much is not having you inside me."

That sent a jolt straight through Max's core. She reached between Ella's thighs, teasing her with fingers, building the pressure until Ella's hips rolled against her, seeking more. When Max finally entered her, Ella let out a sound that landed somewhere between a gasp and a moan.

Max placed one hand on Ella's hip and, with the other, moved with slow, controlled thrusts, watching the way Ella's body responded to every shift and grind. She was so expressive, so open, it undid Max completely.

Max kept her rhythm steady, each thrust angled with intention, her free hand sliding around to stroke Ella exactly the way she liked. The combination made Ella arch back into her, a litany of soft, breathy moans falling from her lips.

"Just like that," Ella gasped. "Don't stop."

Max pressed a kiss between her shoulder blades, her own breathing ragged. "I've got you."

Ella's hands fisted the sheets. Her whole body trembled, so close, so ready. Max could feel the shift in her, the way tension coiled tight in her core.

"Let go," Max whispered. "Come for me."

And Ella did, her body clenching around Max's fingers as a cry tore from her throat, high and broken and beautiful. Max held her through it, slowing her movements but never letting go, her own heart thundering.

"That was so good," Ella said, breathless and falling onto her side.

Max met her there so they were lying face-to-face. She touched Ella's cheek with her fingertips. "Do you know how much I've missed this? How much I've missed you?"

"I'm starting to understand," Ella said, brushing a strand of hair off of Max's forehead. "Come here," Ella said, pulling Max to her. "I want you close."

"You'll always have me close, Ella."

Ella wrapped her arms around Max and held on, savoring the overflowing emotion, the well of feelings, the love. "I'm so in love with you, Max. There's nothing that compares."

"I love you, too," Max said, kissing her softly, thoroughly, like they had all the time in the world, and they did.

THIRTY

Fries, Mayonnaise, and Us

I t was almost as if the universe knew that things had fallen into place. A week went by. And then six. Each moment Ella spent with Max was better than the last. They were so very different, which kept life interesting and full of silly debates and discoveries.

"I don't understand how fries dipped in mayonnaise are allowed by law when ketchup is sitting *right* there," Ella once told Max as she watched her across the table at Maple and Main, the little diner near the center of town.

"I have a feeling you've never tried it."

"Oh, and I think we're gonna have to leave it that way. Pass the ketchup, weirdo," she'd said with a challenging grin. It earned her a kiss first.

"Did you taste the mayonnaise?" Max asked, nodding with authority.

"Gasp and glare. You tricked me with your mayonnaise lips, and know it."

Max had sat back in the red vinyl booth looking like the winner of the third-grade spelling bee. "Worth it."

But at the same time, the two of them were in sync in the ways that mattered. They took care of each other when one had a hard day, instinctively knowing to take up more of the slack. They were tolerant of conflicts in their schedules and took turns compromising when necessary. Ella had even had dinner with Max's parents at their home. Twice. Mayumi told her all about her treatment plan and how encouraged the doctors were feeling about her progress. Max's father, Glenn, promised to show her how to box just like he'd taught Max. She was looking forward to it, and enjoyed shopping for her own gloves with Max.

That morning, Ella woke to a gorgeous March offering that made her want to lift her shoulders to her ears. Crisp and only mildly chilly, with sunshine streaming in through Max's kitchen window, as if it were painting the walls with warmth.

Max was dressed for work in gray pants and a white dress shirt with oversized cuffs as she stood, sipping her coffee near the pot, when Ella padded in, still happily wearing Max's oversized Commanders T-shirt, her newfound favorite.

"Good morning, babe."

Ella rubbed her eyes and grinned. "Hey, you. I didn't even hear the shower." She took a moment to stretch before finishing her walk around the island.

"You were sleeping hard. Here. I made you a cup," Max said, handing the oversized blue mug to Ella. They grinned at each other and shared a kiss before Max continued on her way, packing her bag, assembling her lunch, and generally looking fantastic while she did it. Ella cradled the warm ceramic mug in both hands and used the time to wake up while Max moved around the kitchen, accomplishing her morning tasks. Ella loved these quiet moments. Somehow, Max seemed lighter this morning as if she might float away, which made sense. It was precisely the way Ella felt these days, too, like a missing puzzle piece had clicked into place, making everything as it should be.

"What are your plans today?" Max asked.

"Hmm. Let's see. Doug is looking at a soft reopening in a

week, so I'll swing by and see what kind of intense muscle I can lend his way." She offered a quick flex of her nonexistent biceps. "I don't know if you know this, but I'm freakishly strong." She'd woken up feeling playful and leaned into it.

"I didn't." Max's eyes went wide. "Just look at you, you hulk. Want to meet me at the gym after work? I was gonna get in a few punches on the bag. You can meet Amanda."

"The gym friend? I'm starting to think she's a unicorn who exists only within those walls." Ella sighed. "I'd love to, but I'm grabbing dinner with Rach."

"Give her a hug for me."

Ella placed a hand on her hip and shook her head. "You two have come a long way."

"She sent me a text, you know, while we were apart."

Ella widened her eyes. "I did not. Say more words."

"Something to the effect of: get your shit together, Wyler, and fix this. She's worth it."

Ella relaxed against the counter and grinned. "I owe her a drink, then. Rach doesn't mince words."

"Never," Max said appreciatively. "And what else today?"

"Well, I have an appointment with a realtor to take a look at some spaces. Rachel deserves her guest room back, and my finances are doing so much better since I've picked up some big covers. Did I mention that I've raised my prices? I'm still getting bookings like crazy."

"Because you're a ridiculously good digital artist. When you wave that electronic pencil around, I'm immediately wet." She sipped her coffee and placed the mug on the granite countertop.

Ella laughed and approached. "I mean, we could put that to the test."

"Or we could just do this." She pulled Ella in and kissed her slowly. "Same effect."

"I forget how good our mornings are."

"And how good they will continue to be. That's why you should cancel that appointment and move in with me."

Ella smiled and then went still. "I can't tell if you're joking or serious."

"Attorneys rarely joke, Ella." She washed out her mug in the sink. "I'm entirely serious. We both know you'll barely sleep at that new place. Move in with me. We're in love."

"We are, and I love saying it out loud. I love you. I just said it again."

Max relaxed into a lazy grin. "I love you, too, and you need to know how deeply I'm in this thing." She raised a shoulder. "I want you here all the time. My life is yours, and I want my home to be. What do you say to that?"

What did one say to that? Those were big words and they sucked up all the air. Ella tried to wrap her mind around the offer. This was a big step. One she didn't take lightly. "I say yes. I want to move in. I want to live together." Her eyes went wide and she covered her mouth. It was out there now, voiced for Max and the cosmos to hear. It didn't matter. She embraced the vulnerability, laughing when Max scooped her up, feet not quite touching the floor. "Okay, now who's freakishly strong?"

"Best compliment ever. I kill myself at the gym. Do you understand my pain?" she said, looking up at Ella. "There should be some reward, and it's this moment."

"I'm very impressed with you. I want to show you later." Ella kissed her as she slid back down Max's body, which she loved every inch of. How did she get so lucky?

"At our place."

Ella closed her eyes, overwhelmed by how happy this giant step forward made her. They weren't just a couple. They were moving forward with their lives intertwined. There would be dinners together, lazy nights on the couch, snowball fights, and cozy book club meetings with stolen glances while Ariana and Stevie argued over pacing. Ella pressed her cheek to Max's shoulder and let herself imagine all of it. A real life. Theirs. One they were building, day by day, together.

Ella clung to Max a little tighter, the weight of the moment settling in beneath her ribs. There had been a time not so long ago when she'd believed she wasn't enough. Not steady enough, not successful enough, not lovable in any lasting way. She'd spent a long time waiting for someone to see her fully and stay anyway, and now here Max was.

It undid her a little, in the best possible way.

Maybe the best love stories weren't the ones where someone came to the rescue, but the ones where someone held your hand and said, *You're already everything*. Max had done that, over and over, in ways both loud and quiet. In ways Ella could finally believe.

She smiled through the tears that suddenly sprang up, pressing her forehead to Max's. "Okay," she whispered. "Let's write the next chapter."

And she meant it. Because she knew now that she wasn't just part of a love story, she was someone's favorite one.

Max grinned and swept a strand of hair from Ella's forehead. "And the one after that, and the one after that until the pile is unending." They shared another kiss against the kitchen counter before Max grabbed her lunch. "Sonya's husband is hosting a happy hour at Dirty Little Secret on Friday for her birthday. What's your late afternoon look like?" She slid the strap of her attaché onto her shoulder.

"Totally free. I can make it. Oh, I want to try their pear martini."

"Perfect. Martinis, it is. I gotta hurry because I have an eight-thirty, but I'll grab your dry cleaning on my way home. I love you. Text me and tell me all about Doug's."

"You got it, and I love you, too." Ella watched, coffee in hand, as the love of her life headed for the door. She had the whole day stretched in front of her, and her heart overflowed.

Maybe it wasn't fate or magic or even perfect timing that

brought her here to Max. Maybe it was something better—two people who chose each other again and again, when one obstacle after another was tossed onto their path.

They never gave up. They understood that love wasn't perfect.

It wasn't just the swoonworthy moments, but the quiet ones, too. The morning coffees and shared routines, the learning, the laughter, the softness of being truly known. If this were a romance novel, Ella thought, this would be the part where the reader closes the book with a smile, knowing that the best love stories don't end on the last page. They just keep going.

Epilogue

One Year Later

THE HOUSE LOOKED GORGEOUS. After a year of hard work, Max honestly couldn't believe they'd made it to the finish line in advance of the housewarming party. The property, with its colorful garden and quiet, open stretch of land in the back, felt like something out of a dream. The house itself was two stories of rustic charm. Weathered wood siding, deep front porch, and wide windows that let the light pour in. It made sleeping in on weekends an exercise in joy. Those gorgeous windows had been at the top of Max's must-have list when searching for a house that would be their first purchase together. Inside, it was all clean lines and high-end finishes: warm oak floors, a chef's kitchen with tall green cabinets and gold hardware, picked out by Ella, and a fireplace framed in stone they'd chosen together. Every room felt intentional, like it knew it was meant to be loved.

Max's condo had been wonderful to her during the years she spent there, meeting her every need. But it wasn't just her anymore, and now she knew with certainty that it never would be again. That meant they'd need a space that was for both of them, that reflected both of their needs and style. Ella now had her own office for design that looked out over the expansive yard that backed up to a greenbelt full of towering trees, winding trails, and the kind of quiet that made space for creativity to bloom.

"I'm here," her mom's voice said, floating in from the entryway. "I let myself in because it's a party. Your father will follow me later." The guests weren't set to arrive for another half hour, but her mother would want to play deputy hostess, so, of course, she'd arrived early.

"Come on in!" She heard Ella say cheerfully from the other room. In the past year, the two of them had inched closer and closer until they'd become tighter than peas and carrots. Max was 100 percent confident that her mother preferred Ella to most any other human, a good balance of sunshine to her no-nonsense outlook, which she had to admit had softened considerably since her bout with cancer.

"I brought homemade sweet rolls. They're in the warming basket you got me."

"I love mine," Ella said. "Isn't it the best?"

"Science is my passion, and when you combine it with cooking, I'm a happy woman," Mayumi said. "Is my daughter being good?"

"She's been wonderful. She just installed the cutest little wishing well in the back. Running water and all. She can pretty much do anything around the house."

Max smiled as she strolled into the room. "Hear that, Mom? I'm handy." She kissed her mother on the cheek and accepted the bread. "You didn't have to bring anything."

"No, no. You always bring something. Always," she said emphatically, as if Max needed to memorize the directive for the future. Okay, some things hadn't changed. She relaxed into a smile. "But you always do, because you are smart and kind."

"Nice save," she told her mom.

An hour later, the house was christened by the arrival of friends and loved ones. Sonya shared anonymous stories from the mediation trenches in the open kitchen as she poured and served the batch cocktail she had brought with her, her gift to the party. Stevie and Olive arrived looking like an adorably happy couple. Max caught them stealing a kiss near the hors d'oeuvres table. Wasn't it interesting how it had all worked out? Olive had recently moved into Stevie's place and was now their second host each week. The four of them had each found their person at the Read It and Weep Book Club, the place you apparently went for singles matches.

"Everyone came," Ella said with a grin, pressing her shoulder against Max's. "And I think this counts as Rachel's third date with Amanda." Max followed Ella's gaze to the two strolling through the living space hand in hand.

"The cheeseball with the cranberries is outta this world," Doug said, puttering by with a rare grin on his face.

"Glad you like it," Max told him, though he hadn't waited for a response.

According to Ella, the shop had been overrun with customers this week when a slew of new romances were released. Doug's Books was better than ever.

Ella exhaled. "They all seem happy and talkative and have food and drinks. I think that means we can relax and take it all in."

Though Max had helped in any way she could, Ella had emerged as the event planner of their couplehood and had put together the heart and soul of the gathering. Like every-thing she touched, the evening was planned to perfection.

"Should we say a few words?" Max asked, threading their fingers, knowing she had more than a few already assembled.

"Oh, I'm going to leave that to you," Ella said. She'd

never been a fan of the spotlight, and that was okay. "But I will smile and stand next to you in solidarity as your cohost. I might even nod a couple of times. Prepare yourself."

Max squeezed Ella's hand. "I love the plan. Let's get everyone's attention."

As they moved to the center of the room, Max made sure the ring she'd been meticulously designing with the jeweler for months was secure in her pocket. She nodded in her mom's direction, which prompted her to take out her phone and begin recording. Sonya, also catching the agreed-upon cue, dinged her glass three times with a spoon, which brought the room to a gradual hush. Their guests turned to her with expectant smiles, waiting.

"Wow, it's so quiet in here," Max said, feeling her nerves swim to the surface, an unusual feeling. She swallowed them back, wanting to do this thing right. "Ella and I are so happy that you're here to celebrate with us tonight. Our new home is everything we hoped for, and we wanted to share it with you. In many ways, this place is a culmination of our journey together. That journey wasn't always easy, but it was ours, and it brought me to this very moment, when I couldn't be happier." She turned to Ella and smiled. "This woman on my left changed my entire outlook on life when she stepped into mine."

A collective "aww" rippled through the room. Ella beamed, and her cheeks bloomed.

"I was a cynic when it came to love stories and finding forever. But it turns out, I was just frozen in place, waiting for Ella Baker to get here already and show me the way." Rachel, who stood in the corner smiling, offered her an encouraging nod. "Because of Ella, I now see the good in the most mundane. I look forward to lazy Saturdays and strolling the night market in town. Everyone, I *garden* sometimes." That pulled a laugh. "I don't exactly recognize myself, and it's the best feeling ever." She lifted both shoulders. "I'm head over heels in love and know without a doubt that's not going to change."

"Wow. I love you, too," Ella said.

"But let's talk about the house a minute, because it's nice. I like it. But let's face it, it's not complete."

Ella frowned and quirked her head, clearly wondering what Max meant. They'd had several conversations about the house being perfect.

"Nope. This house is very much looking for a commitment from us. It wants to know we're in this forever, and I am. I plan to be by this woman's side until we're watching the sunset in rocking chairs on that porch with hot toddies and fuzzy socks."

"We'll need a photo of that," Ariana called, cupping her hands around her mouth.

"Deal," Max said with a laugh. "But one thing first." Max pulled the small velvet box from her pocket just as an uncomfortable lump rose in her throat. Ella looked at the box in shock as Max knelt before her on one knee and opened it. When their eyes met, Max couldn't hold back the tears any longer. The love she felt for Ella was so all-encompassing that it permeated every piece of her. There was a quiet gasp in the crowd. Ella covered her mouth with one hand, but not before Max saw it tremble.

"Is this real?" she asked.

Max nodded. They'd talked about forever, about wanting to get married when life quieted down, but never an explicit timeline. And if Ella wanted a long engagement, she'd give it to her. She'd give her anything she wanted. But for Max, on her end of things, she didn't want to wait another minute to marry the woman she loved.

"Ella." That's when the well of emotion engulfed her, stealing her voice. Their friends waited in silence. Max brushed away a happy tear. "Ella," she said again. "I love you beyond words. You dazzle me every day with your kindness, beauty, talent, and the way you make the world a happier, more exciting place. No room is the same when you walk into it. No human being is unaffected. I would very much like to marry you and ensure you're in all of my rooms from now on. Would you do me the honor, Ella Baker? Will you marry me?"

Ella exhaled and shook her head slowly. "Yes. I'd marry you right now." She sank to her knees, meeting Max right where she knelt, cupped her face, and kissed her deeply to the swell of applause and a couple of whistles, surely one from her dad. Everything in Max leapt for joy.

Their friends clapped and whooped, some with hands over their hearts, as Ella pulled Max into a second kiss that was soft at first, then deepened with a kind of quiet urgency, like she needed Max to feel the yes in every part of her.

When they finally pulled apart, Ella rested her forehead against Max's. "Look. You knocked me off my feet," she whispered.

"Well, you rewired my whole world." Max's breath caught. She reached up to cradle Ella's face, her thumb brushing the damp edge of her cheek.

After photos, lots of champagne, and multiple tours of the house, they settled in for a night of laughs and storytelling with the group, which became smaller and smaller as the night progressed. Her parents kissed them both and took their leave, a roster of patients to see in the morning. The Weepers shared a group hug and previews of what each thought of next week's book so far. Rachel and Amanda exchanged a sultry look that said their evening might have only just begun.

Later, after the last glass had been washed and the house had gone still, Max found Ella upstairs in their bedroom, standing by the open window in one of Max's worn T-shirts, moonlight spilling across her bare legs. She looked over her shoulder with that slow, familiar smile—the one that always felt like the moment was meant just for her.

Max came up behind her, sliding her arms around Ella's

waist and pressing her lips to the curve of her neck. "You know what I was thinking?" she murmured.

"Mmm?"

"That this house might have good bones, but you're what makes it home."

Ella turned in her arms, eyes soft, fingertips tracing the line of Max's jaw. "Then let's fill it. With books and coffee and morning kisses and years."

"And you," Max said, brushing her mouth against Ella's. "Always you."

The ring sparkled on Ella's hand as it curled around the back of Max's neck, pulling her in. They kissed again, slow and unhurried, right there in the quiet dark, wrapped in warmth and promise, and the unshakable sense that this was only the beginning of their very own HEA.

Acknowledgments

This book has been an adventure in every positive sense of the word. Thank you so much for reading what I call my love letter to the romance genre. I've been devoted to it ever since I was a kid, sneaking copies of my older sister's romance novels and locking myself in the bathroom to read them, completely enthralled. Those stories lit a spark that has never gone out, and I love getting to add my own to the shelves.

I owe endless gratitude to the people who helped bring this particular book to life. To my editor, Lynda Sandoval—a thoughtful story partner with the most hilarious and brilliant ways of leaving notes in the margins. You make me laugh, you make me think, and you make me better. To Avery Brooks, my meticulous copy editor, whose remarkable attention to detail and gentle guidance are unmatched. Thank you for catching what I miss and keeping me on track.

Quinn Riley, thank you for providing your immense talent and voice to bring these characters and their story to life on the audio version. I feel so lucky to work with you.

A big thank you to Ink and Laurel for creating a gorgeous, bookish cover that perfectly captures the spirit of the story. And to the proofreaders, your dedication and eagle eyes mean a great deal.

To Alan, Everett, and Camryn—thank you for letting me drift off into daydreams, for tolerating the scattered notebooks and late-night typing, and for always pulling me back with laughter and love. You are my *greatest* adventure and my home.

And finally, thank you to the readers. You've stuck with me, read my stories, and cheered me on, and I can't begin to express what that means to me. You are why I write, and why I'll keep writing, always.

About the Author

Melissa Brayden is the multi-award-winning author of twenty-nine contemporary sapphic romance novels and loves her job. She's a dedicated fan of all kissing scenes, enjoys gallivanting on TikTok, and spends most of her time chasing two short humans around her home. Though writing romance is her full-time job, much of it is spent on donuts, wine, coffee, and staring off into space.

Also by Melissa Brayden

www.ingramcontent.com/pod-product-compliance
Lightning Source LLC
Chambersburg PA
CBHW030234120726
47903CB00005B/1477